Possessed by a Dark Warrior

Felicity Heaton

First printed April 2016

First Edition

Layout and design by Felicity Heaton

ETERNAL MATES SERIES

Kissed by a Dark Prince
Claimed by a Demon King
Tempted by a Rogue Prince
Hunted by a Jaguar
Craved by an Alpha
Bitten by a Hellcat
Taken by a Dragon
Marked by an Assassin
Possessed by a Dark Warrior

Find out more at: www.felicityheaton.co.uk

CHAPTER 1

Bleu landed without a sound in the middle of the dense crowd, the vapours from the short teleport shimmering around him for a second before he kicked off, leaving them in his wake as he broke through the throng. His steady gaze locked on his target, focused there even as he felt his six men appear a short distance behind him and begin to pursue him. Two came to flank him, the remaining four spreading out through the disgusting gathering of creatures like black tendrils, taking down any who dared to stand in their way.

He would have killed them all if he had the choice, but his mission was clear—retrieve the two elf females with minimal fuss.

Gods, he would give anything to sink his fangs and his blade into many of the wretched bastards present at the black market auction, a suitable punishment for their despicable behaviour, trading in flesh and lives.

He snarled, baring his fangs at a fool who rushed into his path in his blind panic, and swept his hand over the length of his black sword, commanding it to transform into his preferred double-ended spear. He swept the curved blade at the end before him upwards, slicing across the side of the male as he turned red eyes on him. Vampire.

Bleu bit out a nasty curse and gave himself a split-second off the mission that had been his sole focus for the past three weeks, all the time it took to spin on his heel, bringing his spear around in a deadly black arc to relieve the vampire of his head. The male toppled onto the black ground, some members of the crowd shrieking as they leaped away from the pool of blood cascading from his neck. Bleu would have paused to spit on the foul abomination, a disgusting shadow of his own noble species, had his second in command not taken the lead at that moment, shouting orders at the other elves and propelling him back into action.

Darkness dropped like a veil, and the panic in the arena increased, the crowd growing frenzied as they tried to make off with their sick prizes, scurrying away from the scene of their crimes. A chill swept through the oval canyon and Bleu sensed magic, a powerful enchantment that warned he wasn't alone in desiring to rescue one of the poor souls being thrown onto the slab and sold as meat by the ringmaster of this terrible circus.

He threw a glance off to his right, to the black stage, easily able to see it using his heightened vision. A male. Bleu paid him no heed as he raced onto the stage, to a shifter female. A Hellcat. No wonder there was such a large crowd.

The other female on the stage moved so swiftly he couldn't make out anything about her, leaping onto the back of the fallen angel who was responsible for the auction. His heart gave a painful beat as she roared and attacked, a sharp sensation that went through him and gave him pause, causing his step to falter and his breath to still.

He swallowed hard and frowned at the odd sensation, hazily aware that he should recognise it but unable to comprehend why.

A male swung into his path, stealing his focus away from the stage, and Bleu cut him down with his spear, shoved him aside and sprinted harder, catching up with the rest of his team.

The damned bastards who had purchased the elf females as if they were animals had backed them into a corner, tucked against the black rock and the dark wooden stage.

If they thought that would stop him from slicing them open from balls to brains, they were fucking wrong.

His mood degenerated as he reached them, a darkness as thick as the one that had veiled the world in black descending over him, and he slowed his step until he was stalking towards them, the crowd parting to allow him through, as if all present could sense the dark intent rolling off him.

The hunger to deal justice with his blade.

Light from the torches around the canyon and on the stage flickered back into life, the sensation of magic weakening as the darkness lifted.

His vision responded in an instant, adjusting to the bright light and dulling.

He flexed his fingers around the black engraved shaft of his spear and sent a mental command to his skin-tight armour, ordering the small obsidian metal scales to flow over his hands and form his claws over his fingers.

His violet eyes locked on the male stood slightly forward from the other two. The elf females huddled naked behind them, clinging to each other, their fear a palpable thing that drummed in Bleu's blood, blackening his mood.

Bleu signalled with his free hand, slowly raising it, and his six elf warriors spread out, encircling the men, giving them nowhere to go.

He snarled at them, flashing his fangs. He would deal with them first and then he would deal with the fallen angel who had orchestrated this market, daring to take two of his kind from their kingdom.

The leader foolishly lashed out at one of the warriors on his left, brandishing a sword made of steel. *Steel.* A pathetic mortal made weapon for a weak creature.

Bleu drew down a deep breath, catching the scent of their blood, and wasn't surprised that it matched their weapon. Mortal made. These three were from that realm, but in their blood was a hint of fae, an ancestor that had given them access to this realm.

Hell.

He curled his lip at the three men and dropped his hand.

Six elf warriors launched at the men, easily overpowering them, and Bleu wished he had orders to kill not contain the fiends.

"Thank you, but I have to go." A soft female voice rose above the din and Bleu stilled. "I have to fly."

A chill skated over his skin beneath his armour, his eyes slowly widening as he finally comprehended why he had felt such a strange yet familiar sensation on seeing the female on stage attacking the fallen angel.

Fly.

He spun on his heel to face the stage.

A heartbeat of time passed, a split-second that felt like an eternity as he stared up at the female on the stage, taking in the striking violet-to-white eyes that he would never forget as they locked on him. Her lips parted, long lashes falling to shutter those incredible eyes, and his pulse hammered into overdrive as the three long scars on the left side of his neck tingled. He slowly raised his hand to rest his fingers on his armour over them.

He inched his right foot forwards.

Towards her.

She turned in an instant and he could only watch as she transformed into an enormous violet dragon, tearing stunned gasps from the remaining few people in the arena. She reared onto her hind legs, flashing the white stripe that ran from beneath her jaw, down her throat, and under her ribs, and beat her wings, the white membrane between her purple wing bones stark against the dark sky of Hell.

His breath left him in a rush as she threw her head back, her long white horns almost touching her neck, and roared, the sound deafening as it echoed across the land.

"Wait!" He launched onto the stage in a single leap, unwilling to let her escape him again.

She snarled through gleaming white fangs each as long as his arm and swept her left paw downwards, delivering a devastating backhand that hit him square in the chest, knocking the air from his lungs and sending him flying across the arena so fast that he didn't have a chance to teleport.

His back slammed into the rough black rock, fire searing his bones as his mind scrambled, the pain so intense that he couldn't breathe, couldn't think or feel anything for a second.

All the time it took for the dragon to launch into the air, her enormous wings sending gusts of wind at those remaining on the stage, almost knocking them over.

He couldn't let her escape him again.

He wheezed as he pushed onto his feet and staggered towards her, his ears ringing and vision wobbling.

He growled as she took flight and used the last of his strength to call a portal. Green-purple light shimmered over his black armour and he dropped into the darkness. It dissipated a second later as he landed on the stage where the dragon had been.

Bleu bit out every curse available to him in his native tongue, his legs wobbling beneath him, barely strong enough to support his weight as pain wracked him.

He stared at the dragon as she flew into the distance, unable to pursue her in his current condition, forced to watch her as she disappeared into the gloom.

Slipping through his grasp once more.

The world around him dulled and then light pierced the darkness, colourful and bright, twinkling.

Bleu let his breath out slowly and inched his eyes open, his vision slowly coming into focus, sharpening the beautiful display of light above him. The delicate small flowers on the tree sparkled like starlight and he lost himself in watching them. A warm breeze blew across him, causing the long grasses and colourful flowers that surrounded him to bend and dance, and their scent to fill the air with sweetness that sank deep into his soul.

Whenever a stronger breeze blew, the blooms on the trees would flutter closed in a wave before opening again, shining brighter than ever.

Beautiful.

He rested in the grass, encompassed by nature, bathed in her warm and comforting light.

His muscles felt liquid beneath his skin, his bones loose, his body filled with a floating sensation, one that he couldn't remember feeling in a long time but he still knew the name of it. Peace.

He lifted a heavy arm and managed to run his fingers through the longer lengths of his blue-black hair, preening it back as he tried to remember the last time he had felt this sedated and relaxed. Long enough that it felt foreign to him now. Centuries perhaps.

Millennia.

Gods, maybe he hadn't experienced it since he had left his home village to join the ranks of the soldiers, swearing to protect his kingdom and his princes.

He had been serving one of those princes for forty-two centuries, almost his entire life. It had become his whole life. It was his purpose.

Had been his purpose.

He threw his arm across his eyes and heaved a sigh as he pushed away from that thought and crushed it out of existence by focusing on the nature surrounding him, soothing his weary soul and bringing him a moment of peace that he knew would be all too brief.

He switched his focus from the nature around him to the dream once he began to relax again, picking out every detail of what was actually a memory, a moment that had occurred only months ago.

He pushed deeper into his memories of the female, running back to another time three centuries ago when their paths had crossed in a dragon clan's village. The scars on his neck tingled, luring him into drawing his arm away from his eyes to run his fingers over them. Scars she had given to him.

He focused on them and turned the clock back another four centuries, to when he had first set eyes on her.

She had been in her dragon form, her violet scales dark in contrast to the white of her breast, an invader in the elf kingdom and one he had been dispatched to pursue and capture, and bring to justice for her crimes.

She had stolen something precious from Prince Loren, a powerful sword of elven making that had belonged to his father and had been protected in the palace, locked safely away from the world where it could do no harm.

In her reckless hunger for the sword, she had rampaged across the elf kingdom, laying waste to many villages, slaying thousands of his kin.

He had fought her near the border with the First Realm of the demons, where mountains rose high into the darkening sky beyond the elf kingdom, beyond the sphere of the light they brought into their realm to make it verdant and give it life. She had escaped them but then she had returned a short time later. That time, he had led the charge against her, but she had been stronger than he had anticipated, had injured several of his warriors and himself too. They had lost her, and he had hunted for her for decades before he'd had to move his focus to matters regarding his prince's safety.

Four hundred years later, when Prince Loren had sensed the presence of the sword again, linked to it through the blood of his father, Bleu had led the three finest elf warriors in the army to the dragon realm to seek her out and regain the ancient blade.

He squeezed his eyes shut as he recalled crossing paths with a slender female in one of the villages and she shimmered into being in his mind, as if it had been only yesterday. Her tightly pulled back hair accentuated her striking sculpted features, her face bathed in the shadows of the small thatched stone building she had exited. He had questioned her, so entranced by her beauty and how she kept her head bowed, a touch of shyness to her behaviour, that he had allowed his men to leave his side to question others.

A foolish mistake.

He had dropped his guard and she had lunged at him when he had pressed her about the violet and white dragon, her talons raking down his throat and her incredible eyes flashing dangerously at him as she came into the light.

It had taken him a moment to realise she was the dragon he hunted, long enough that she had fled before he could stop her, transforming and flying away from him just as she had in the arena only a few months ago.

Bleu stroked the scars on his neck. The proof of her sin and a constant reminder of his unfulfilled mission. She had slaughtered thousands of his kin, had stolen something precious to his prince, and extremely dangerous. With such a weapon, she could slay an entire legion of elves with one swing. Now that she had surfaced again, he wasn't going to let her escape him.

This time, he would capture her and bring her to justice.

The flowers above him in the trees twinkled, their warm light flowing over him, soothing the fatigue from his body. He had been tracking her for what felt like forever, but he wasn't sure how long he had been gone from the elf kingdom. Not more than seven days, perhaps ten at most. Time had lost meaning in his pursuit of her, his mind so focused on his mission and following all the leads he had to their conclusion, or to the next lead that drove him ever onwards, inching closer to her.

He would complete this mission.

He had never failed one, wasn't the sort of male who could leave things unfinished. He always had to see them through to the end, even when that end was one that hurt him. He couldn't leave a fight, could never surrender, not even when his life was at stake.

He would finish this.

Bleu rose fluidly onto his feet and stretched, clasping his hands together above his head. His fingers brushed the flowers on the trees, causing the blooms to briefly close and the light to dip, before they reopened and glowed brighter. The grass tickled his calves as it sprang back and wavered in the warm breeze. Nature cocooned him in a brief sweet embrace that he savoured, aware that it would be a while before he could visit this place again. He tipped his head back and brushed his fingertips across the deep green leaves of the tree that had given him shelter, silently thanking nature for her comfort and for restoring his body, driving the weariness from it enough that he could continue.

He stalked forwards, his bare feet lightly compressing the grasses as he walked through them, heading towards the edge of the forest. With a simple mental command, his armour flowed from the black and silver bands around his wrists, the scales rippling over his body to cover his nudity.

Boots formed over his feet first and then the scales raced upwards, over his calves and thighs, cupping his backside and groin, before encasing his stomach and chest, and running down his arms. He kept his hands unprotected and ran his fingers over the scars on the left side of his throat again, his thoughts locked on the dragon female as he strode out of the forest.

The warm light of nature gave way to the darkness of the Fifth Realm of the demons, the calming soft touch slipping from him and leaving him cold inside. Black gravel crunched beneath his boots as he marched up the incline, heading into the gloom, his eyes rapidly adjusting to the grim realm, sharpening to pick out the subtle difference between the bare obsidian lands and the deep grey sky of Hell.

Bleu halted at the brow of the slope, standing at the precipice where the black land plummeted into a deep canyon. He scoured the lands beyond the canyon. The Third Realm of demons.

Beyond that was the mountainous home of her kind.

Dragons.

If his information was correct, he would find his next lead there.

He called his black blade to his left hand and narrowed his eyes on the deep distance, all of his focus on it.

He was closing in on her.

Seven hundred years of hunting were finally going to end.

CHAPTER 2

Taryn skirted the border of the village, remaining as far from it as possible as she hurried across the hilly terrain. She kept her head down, a tattered swath of black cloth she had picked up gods only knew where or how long ago covering it to conceal her hair and her face. Her heart drummed a sickening rhythm behind her breast and the thick roll of cloth she carried on her back, the leather strap attached to it tight across her left shoulder and breasts and around her right ribs, felt heavy today.

Heavier than yesterday, which had felt heavier than the day before.

The closer she drew to the edge of the dragon realm, the heavier her burden grew.

She tensed as a dragon flew overhead, going still and hoping her black leather trousers, boots and top, and the cloth over her head would camouflage her against the obsidian land. The drumming of her heart grew fiercer and she struggled to breathe as she waited for the dragon to move on, reaching the edge of her senses.

Her gaze flicked in that direction and she watched the great green beast land in the village in the distance.

Gods, she needed to fly.

That need surged through her and she was close to shifting when she caught herself, and the cold reminder of what would happen if she took on her dragon form slithered through her.

The dragons would see her, her cover would be blown and she would probably come under attack from her own kin.

Not only that, but this close to the edge of the realm, near the mountains that bordered it, there was a chance that he would sense her from where he waited beyond the cragged peaks. On the other side of the treacherous black range was a valley, a realm that few dragons dared to cross into and that many whispered dark and gruesome tales about.

The Valley of the Dark Edge.

Her final destination.

He waited there.

For her.

For her cargo.

Taryn trudged onwards, her feet sore from walking and heart aching with a need to shift and take flight, to shed the tethers of her mortal form and fly free.

She needed to fly.

Instead of surrendering to that powerful urge, she wrapped her arms around herself and marched forwards, her eyes locked on the peaks that stood between her and her destination.

Between her and her twin brother.

Tenak was waiting for her.

She had kept him waiting long enough.

The road was little more than a winding narrow path that soon gave way to only rock as it led her upwards, into the foothills of the mountains. She moved her focus to her feet, picking a route over the treacherous and steep terrain. Rocks shifted underfoot, bouncing down the side of the mountain, tumbling into the valley. She lost track of time as she walked, weary and sore, the ache to fly growing stronger as her instincts roared that she could reach the other side of the mountain range in no more than a few beats of her wings if she shifted.

The temptation was great, but the instinct that warned Tenak would sense her if she shifted kept it tempered, stopping her from giving in to it. She removed the cloth from her head when the nearest village was nothing more than a speck on the horizon and the dragons remained at a distance.

Afraid of the mountains because of the male who lurked beyond them.

She blew out her breath and combed her fingers through her shoulder-length hair, untangling it from the violet roots to its white tips. They were dirty, dull with grit from the journey, and she couldn't remember the last time she had bathed. The fantasy of a warm bath kept her mind occupied as she soldiered onwards, clambering over boulders and edging around rocks that blocked her path.

She pressed her back to one as she shuffled around it, her eyes on her feet on the narrow ledge and the several hundred foot drop below. If she fell, she would have to shift to save herself. Her pulse pounded at the thought and she breathed deep to steady it, reassuring herself that she wouldn't fall. She reached the edge of the ledge and safety, and scrambled up over another rock.

As she hit the top of it, she paused, the black rock biting into her knees through her trousers and her palms, and looked back in the direction she had come. The whole world stretched before her, endless peaks that were home to her kin, harbouring almost a hundred clan villages within their valleys.

Home.

It had been her home once, centuries ago, before her brother had stolen it from her.

She turned her head in the other direction, seeing down into the valley beyond the mountain she climbed and to the ones that surrounded it, larger and more formidable than any range in the dragon realm. A red haze clung to the bases of many of the mountains in the distance, as if flames filled their valleys, and fiery veins streaked the ones off to her right, ominous cracks and booms echoing from them.

The Devil's domain.

Taryn lowered her violet-to-white gaze to the valley below her. Nestled between the Devil's domain and the dragon realm, it belonged to neither, a no man's land that had once been the realm of the Hell beasts and other fell creatures.

It was now Tenak's kingdom.

He had claimed it through blood and fire, slaughtering all who dared to stray into it.

Her blood chilled and she shifted onto her backside, shimmied to the edge of the rock and carefully started down the other side of the mountain, ignoring the instinct that whispered at her to turn back.

She couldn't.

She knew what she was doing might be the end of her, but she would accept that, as long as it was the end of her brother too. She had neglected her duty for too long and she had to finish it now, before Tenak turned his wicked gaze back on the dragon realm and the other kingdoms of Hell, bent on bringing them all to their knees so he might rule them.

The rock was sharp underfoot, slicing into the soles of her boots, as if the valley had teeth and wanted to take a bite out of her.

She lifted her right foot to rub it and give it some relief, and her left one slipped. She bit down on her tongue to stop herself from shrieking as she skidded down the side of the mountain, afraid that she would draw attention to herself. The scent of blood surrounded her, the hot stab of each rock burning in her palms as she groped for a hold, and her teeth cut into her tongue when her fingers caught on a crack in the mountain and she jerked to a halt.

She lay there for some time, breathing hard, struggling to steady her heart. Her entire body shook, teeth clattering as adrenaline and fear refused to ebb away, combining to strip her strength.

When she finally calmed, she pulled herself up onto her knees, found a small ledge where she could rest and scanned the mountainside. She had pushed herself too hard, had walked too far and had almost paid the price. If she had shifted to save herself, or cried out, there was every chance her brother would have sensed her presence and come to her, and she wasn't ready to face him yet.

The quiet voice at the back of her mind asked whether she would ever be ready?

She had been putting this off for two lunar cycles already, coming up with excuses to avoid making the journey to the valley and facing her brother.

Her gaze stopped on a ledge with a dark recess just a hundred feet below to her left. She would rest there, gather her strength, and then she would continue her journey. She wouldn't turn back. She wouldn't give up. She would keep marching forwards and stick to her plan.

Taryn edged down the steep slope on her backside, slipping at times, slowly making her way towards the ledge. She breathed a sigh as she crawled onto it and saw that the recess was larger than she had expected, forming a small cave. The rock wrapped around her as she entered it, comforting her as it spoke to her dragon instincts. Many of her kind lived in caves, preferring their ancient habitat to the newer ideal of living in villages.

She was old enough to appreciate a cave, to feel soothed by cool rock surrounding her.

She stopped near the entrance and looked down into the valley, scanning it for any signs of life. Nothing. She scoured the mountains that surrounded the valley and frowned at the far end of it, squinting as she tried to make out the range there. She swore there was a structure built against the mountain, rising out of it. A castle?

Was her brother there?

She moved to the wall of the cave, sat on her backside with her legs crossed, and unfastened the leather strap that cut diagonally across her chest. She removed the thick roll of black cloth from her back and settled it beside her, placing her hand on it and feeling the power vibrating through her palm.

Her cargo resembled nothing more than a rolled blanket for sleeping on, fastened with two leather straps at either end, but it was something precious.

Extremely precious to Tenak.

To others too.

She lifted her hand and touched the thick leather straps that circled her wrists too, feeling the power in those, the same as was in the straps on her cargo. She rubbed her thumb over the Hell beast hide, feeling the symbols carved into the dark brown leather.

Magic.

It concealed the contents of the blanket, and her presence too.

If she removed either the straps on the blanket or the cuffs around her wrist, her brother would sense their presence and come, wild with a need to reclaim what he viewed as his property—both the sword and her.

Taryn closed her eyes and leaned back into the wall, seeking the peace of sleep. It refused to come, her mind throwing images of her journey at her, of battling Hell beasts and avoiding her dragon kin. She had wanted to speak with them so many times, but fear they would blame her for her brother's crimes had forced her to keep her distance.

Perhaps she should have remained with Loke, a dragon male who was like another brother to her, but she had feared she would bring their kin's wrath down upon him too and she loved him too dearly to place him in such danger.

Danger.

She shuddered, a sudden cold sweeping through her when she thought about the danger she might be in. Was in. Loke had witnessed a vision of her, a gift born of his more powerful dragon blood, and it had been on her mind since she had collected the sword from him and had left his cave.

She couldn't help feeling that she was marching towards her death, just as he had seen.

It was part of the reason she had taken so long to finally set out on her journey to face her brother.

She was afraid.

Bone-deep afraid.

She had been through hell the past three centuries, passed between owners as if she was nothing more than a beast, a piece of meat they could attempt to break and drag down into a depraved world where she would think only of pleasing her master. Even though she had endured a life that would have caused many to take their own, she didn't want to die.

Taryn lowered her gaze to the wrapped sword beside her and rested her hand on the blanket that covered it again, feeling its power resonate through her palm. The sword was all her brother thought about. It was all he desired.

She was risking her life by bringing it here, and by returning to Tenak. If he didn't kill her on the spot when she revealed herself to him, he might only be luring her into a trap to kill later.

And what if she failed?

What if he took the sword and she couldn't stop him?

She would have delivered the whole of Hell into his hands.

Gods, she was a fool.

She knew she should take the sword and turn back before he could sense her, but she couldn't bring herself to do it.

She had sworn to stop her brother seven centuries ago, when she had discovered his plan to steal the sword from the elf kingdom because he viewed the sword as belonging to him, not the elves. It was forged of the blood of their grandfather, one of the strongest dragons to have lived, in ancient times when an elven king had ruled in the mortal realm and her ancestors had been free to fly there. That elven king had captured her grandfather and bled him, pouring his life force into the metal of the blade, and mixing it with a single drop of his own blood.

The blade was power.

The strongest of the elven metals and the strongest blood forged into a single weapon that gave the wielder control over ancient magic contained in the blade. It could cut through any armour or weapon, but its true power was the ability to condense the magic it contained into an arc of pure light that could cut through an enemy horde with one swing.

Taryn had tried to stop him from stealing the sword, but she had failed.

He had taken the blade but she hadn't given up, and in the end she had managed to steal the blade from him before he could use it.

Now, it was her bait. It was her way of regaining her brother's trust and stopping him from killing her as payment for her betrayal. She was determined to end everything and she had little time to carry out her plan. She had delayed too long, afraid of facing her brother.

Afraid of facing a world without him.

This was her responsibility though, her duty, and she had to be the one to carry it out.

Because a life in slavery had more appeal, had been better, than a life lived in fear of her brother.

If she didn't go to him, he would eventually come to her, would leave a path of destruction in his wake as he scoured the realms for her. She had heard the stories. Every few years he ventured out from his valley, razing lands and slaughtering thousands as he hunted for her and the sword.

She had that blood on her hands, but she wouldn't bear any more. She would end it.

She would use her life in slavery, the one she was trying to leave behind, the memories she wanted to purge, to win Tenak's trust, pretending that the three centuries of torture she had endured had driven her mad with a need for vengeance, filling her with a thirst to rain dark terror down on all the realms.

Taryn shuddered and curled up, pulling her knees to her chest. She rocked slowly, her eyes locked on the wall across from her, not seeing it as she battled the memories that surged to the surface. She focused on Loke, picturing his face, his bright aquamarine eyes that had shown a wealth of concern when he had handed over the sword and told her of the vision.

Told her of the terrible things her brother had done.

Tenak had grown mad with a hunger for violence, bloodshed and death.

It was that madness that had gripped him that she was going to use to her advantage, making him believe they were infected with the same terrible disease of the mind and they were kindred spirits once more.

Her plan was flawless, but she still couldn't stop the doubts from creeping in and taking hold of her. She had tried to shake them, but in the end she had realised that nothing she did would silence them, and she had set off on her journey with them echoing in her mind.

Maybe she should have left the sword with Loke.

Her brother was stronger than she was, both in dragon and mortal form. He had killed anyone who had strayed into his kingdom. What made her think that she wouldn't suffer the same fate?

She was his blood.

His twin.

His other half.

She knew she could make him recognise her, because she had done so in the past. He'd had spells of madness before, back in the days before he had grown obsessed with setting himself up as the ruler of Hell and stealing the sword from the elves to make that happen. She had brought him back to her then, and she could do it again.

She had to be strong and believe in what he had once told her—that he would never hurt her.

He never had.

Even in his darkest rages, he had never raised a claw against her.

If anyone could get close enough to him to end him, it was her. She had to try. If she failed, she wouldn't be alive to see the horror he would unleash on Hell anyway. He would surely kill her.

Taryn shoved away from that grim thought and refocused on the wall, breathing steadily to centre her mind and steady her heart, and her nerves. She steered her mind towards calmer waters, to thoughts that would soothe her so she could sleep well and gain the rest she needed.

Her head and heart filled with images from better days long past, of her brother and Loke. It had felt good to see Loke again after their centuries apart. He was the only person in Hell she was close to now, the only one she trusted. He meant the world to her, was the brother that Tenak had once been, a very long time ago. Loke had taken care of her for thousands of years, over half of her life, after Tenak had grown distant and obsessed with power.

It was still difficult to think of the things her brother had done in her absence and believe they were true. The male she had grown up with had been gentle, tender and affectionate. How had he grown into one who would lead a legion of dragons to their deaths, promising them power and wealth, and then using them as shields on the battlefield, sending them out first so he could weaken the enemy before claiming victory himself.

Her dearest brother.

She loved him, but since escaping the slavers and learning of the things he had done, she was beginning to wonder whether she only felt that emotion because it was what she should feel for him as her twin. Was she blinded by their bond?

She had truly loved him once, with all of her heart, but she couldn't condone his plans or the things he had done in their centuries apart, slaughtering masses of demons and fae, and even his own beloved kin.

Taryn closed her eyes and settled her chin on her knees, hugging her legs closer to her chest. Her heart felt heavy behind her breast, weighted with the sins of her brother and her responsibility as his sister, and the black future that awaited her if she succeeded in her mission.

A world without him.

A life alone.

Tears burned hot behind her eyes but she refused them, drawing a deep breath to hold them at bay and blowing it out as she sought calm. She pushed away from her sombre thoughts, not wanting to think about it any more tonight. She just wanted to close her eyes, leave her worries behind for a few short hours, and hopefully, she would feel stronger come the morning.

The comforting arms of sleep drifted around her and he was there waiting for her.

Sinful. Wicked. Beautiful.

The elf.

His sinful smile was in place, those violet eyes shimmering with wicked allure as he gazed at her, casting black magic on her that had her falling ever deeper under his spell.

Taryn shoved away from sleep, forcing herself awake again, afraid of dreaming of the male she knew pursued her. Hunted her. He was always one step behind her in this waking world, but forever one step ahead in the dream one, waiting for her to succumb to the lure of sleep and fall back into his arms. Those strong arms would wrap around her, filling her mind with ridiculous hopes as he drew her against him.

Each dream only strengthened her dragon instincts, making her ache with a need to possess him, to sink her claws into the beautiful male and make him belong to her.

Her finest treasure.

Taryn fought the lure of sleep, the lure of the elf male, but he was too powerful, casting an enchantment over her and drawing her back to him. She was too tired to push him away this time and fell easily into the dream, right into his arms, craving the comfort of him even when she feared he would be the one to kill her.

Just as Loke had seen in his vision.

The dark elf male feathered his fingers across her cheek, the touch so light she shivered from it, and slipped them beneath her chin. He tilted her head up, his violet gaze turning hooded as it dropped to her mouth, filled with delicious intent. She didn't resist him, didn't have the strength to deny him this time.

She welcomed the kiss, the tantalising brush of his firm lips across hers that stirred the heat in her veins into an inferno and made her burn for him in her dream, and ache for him in reality.

Hungry for a taste of him.

Her dark warrior.

CHAPTER 3

The mountains seemed endless, stretching as far as his eyes could see across one hundred and eighty degrees of his field of vision. Bleu stood high on a cragged ledge, his back to a black mountain that many in Hell would find forbidding, because it marked the border of the dragon realm. He could see a few flying into the realm, their jewel colours bright against the dull grey sky. He hadn't lived in the time when dragons had been free to fly in the mortal realm, but he could easily imagine how majestic they would have appeared against a dazzling blue backdrop spotted with pale clouds.

Dragons had been allies of the elves once, so many millennia ago that the only proof they had of their friendship were tattered pieces of the ancient records of the elven kings and queens, scratched onto thick leather now so brittle they would break if someone dared to remove them from the delicate glass case that contained them in the castle.

The castle.

Bleu turned his gaze towards it, instinctively aware of which direction his home lay in, feeling the familiar tug in his gut that told him to return to it. He had business there, and he had never been one to ignore his instincts. They were rarely wrong, and right now they were blaring a warning at him to step back from the dragon realm and seek a safer course of action.

He needed a team if he was going to venture into the realm of dragons and dare to question them about one of their own kind.

It was too dangerous to head in alone.

Dragons were fiercely protective of their own kind, even those they knew had committed a crime that had given their species a black name in the language of the elves.

He didn't fancy ending up as roasted elf, so he would return to the castle and form his team—the same trio of warriors that had been with him the last time he had hunted the female dragon.

He focused on his body, calling his portal, and green-purple light shimmered over the scales of his black armour. Darkness swallowed him and when it receded, he was standing in the bright sun-filled verdant courtyard of the castle.

It towered above him, a beautiful mixture of pale and dark stone quarried from the mountains, shaped to form tall towers topped with conical tiled roofs set on a series of large square buildings with balconies that ran across their length. The main building stood five storeys tall, and the thick towers rose to spear the darkening sky and added another six levels.

A warm breeze chased over the high walls surrounding the castle and rustled the leaves of the trees in the orchard around him, carrying the scent of their blooms. Nature embraced him again, a tender touch that soothed him after being surrounded by the darkness of the demon and dragon realms.

He began to relax and then tensed again when Prince Loren appeared right in front of him, his handsome face dark and his violet eyes flashing as he shoved his fingers through his neat blue-black hair and began to pace. His formal knee-length jacket flapped around his legs with each agitated stride across the pale gravel path that spread outwards from the portal, intersecting the lush grass that grew beneath the trees.

Something was wrong.

Wrong enough that his prince had left a council meeting to come straight to him.

Before he could ask his prince what was bothering him, Loren turned on him.

The dark crescents beneath his prince's eyes concerned him and he took a step forwards, growing determined to find out what was worrying him and find a way to relieve his prince of whatever burden his shoulders held.

"Where have you been?" Loren said, a slight sombre edge to his voice as he halted before Bleu, his bright violet eyes searching Bleu's. "You have failed to return to the castle since Vail came."

There was a tone in those last three words that conveyed a wealth of hurt but relief too. Loren always sounded that way when speaking of his younger brother, but Bleu held no love for the mad prince himself, not since he had gone to war with Loren and the elf kingdom, and had decimated an entire legion of the army.

The legion Bleu had served in under Vail.

He had been one of only a handful of survivors.

He wasn't sure he would ever be able to think well of Vail, not even after everything they had learned about the reasons he had attacked his own kind. The things he had seen Vail do were branded on his mind, seared on his soul, together with the deep pain he had caused Loren. Bleu couldn't forgive him.

"It has been a lunar cycle… so I will ask again… where have you been, Bleu?"

A month?

He could only stare at Loren as that sank in. He had thought it had been a week at most since he had left the castle, intent on returning to the last place he had seen the dragon female and seeing if he could uncover any clues that might lead him to her.

A month.

"Did your disappearance and subsequent avoidance of your home have anything to do with Vail… because he has left with Rosalind." There was a softer note to his prince's voice now, a soothing one that had no effect on Bleu as it dawned on him that his leaving had in part been because of Vail's sudden appearance.

But not because he despised Loren's brother.

He rolled his shoulder in a casual shrug, trying to let the epiphany roll off him just as easily, but failing dismally. His mood blackened again, just as it had that night a month ago when he had learned another fool had fallen under the spell of a bond.

A male no one in their right mind could love had found someone who loved him, and fuck had it stung.

"Good for him," Bleu muttered and turned to walk away.

"Answer me, Bleu," Loren barked and he halted, freezing to the spot and aware of the danger he was in.

Loren rarely raised his voice, especially to him. When he did, he meant business, and right now his prince was throwing off vibes that warned he was liable to break with convention and throw him in the cells if he was disobedient. It would be a first. Bleu had mouthed off to him, had behaved with little respect at times, and never had his prince punished him.

Bleu slowly turned back to face him.

"Did you stay away because of Vail?" Loren whispered, a heartfelt plea for an answer that told Bleu his prince didn't want to punish him this time either, but people were watching them closely, and they would expect Loren to do just that if Bleu showed an ounce of disrespect.

He shook his head. "No… Vail isn't the reason I have been away from the castle."

It was the truth.

Well, mostly the truth. Vail wasn't the whole reason he had left or the reason why he had been away.

He had just been the last straw.

Seeing Vail bonded to his fated female on a day that had been Loren's wedding day to his own mate Olivia, and had brought the happily mated couples of Sable and Thorne, and Bleu's sister Iolanthe and her mate Kyter to the elf kingdom had hit Bleu hard.

He hadn't really thought about his actions at the time. He hadn't really considered why he had left or what he had been feeling. He'd had a pressing need to investigate the dragon and he had left to do just that.

But an entire month had passed, and the look in Loren's eyes told him that he had worried him, that the tone Bleu had heard in his voice and the sombre edge to his eyes had nothing to do with Vail, and everything to do with him, and that Loren wanted answers now.

Bleu had none to give to him, at least none that answered the questions in Loren's eyes, because he didn't want to look too closely at his reasons for leaving.

Instead, he would give his prince a safer explanation for his behaviour.

"I tracked the dragon," he said and Loren's expression gained a curious edge and he stepped closer to Bleu. Bleu sighed and raked his fingers over his longer hair, preening it back from his face as he tried to figure out where to begin. He knew how important the sword was to Loren, and he had sworn to retrieve it, and now he felt he was on the verge of fulfilling that promise. "I believe she has returned to her own realm for some reason. Perhaps the dragons there are hiding her, or she has gone to see someone, or she believes she will be able to conceal herself again among her own kind. I only returned to assemble a team so I might track the dragon into her own realm."

Loren began pacing again, his head bent and the thumb of his left hand playing on his lip. His prince had never been able to keep still when thinking. It drove the council of elders mad when he silently paced back and forth in front of his throne, and that often amused Bleu no end. Anything that pissed off the council was fantastic in his opinion. They were antiquated idiots who stuck firmly to the rules and had given his prince nothing but pain and heartache for the forty-two centuries he had been at war with Vail, constantly badgering him to kill his brother.

Bleu had been all for killing Vail, but he never had been able to bring himself to do it whenever they fought. He had always faltered when dealing the killing blow, aware of the devastating pain it would cause Loren if he took Vail's life.

Now the council were probably giving Loren hell as he attempted to convince them to allow Vail back into the elf kingdom now that he had proven he had been nothing but a pawn, a puppet controlled by a dark witch, and was maddened by the terrible things he had done.

Bleu couldn't see them agreeing to that, and he couldn't see his prince giving up this time either. Loren was a stubborn bastard at times, especially where those he loved were concerned.

"I have experienced fleeting sensations." Loren glanced across at him but didn't slow his pacing, taking long strides across the path, only needing three to reach the grass before he had to turn back around.

His prince needed a bigger space to work off some of his tension. Bleu would have offered to spar with him, but the urge to pull his team together and head into the dragon realm was growing stronger, and the thought of delaying his departure was near painful. He had to get back to the dragon realm.

He had to find her.

"They are familiar… and it took me some time, but I have realised what they are. It is the sword." Loren huffed and his lips twisted into a grim, self-reproaching smile. "I admit that it has taken me some time to decipher the sensation… because my connection to it is not as strong as Vail's… but it has surfaced again. Perhaps the dragon has retrieved it from wherever she hid it?"

Bleu didn't like the sound of that. They still didn't know why the dragon had stolen it or whether she had any ill intentions. She could easily decimate an entire demon army with it. But if that had been her agenda, why would she have waited so long to carry it out?

Why had she hidden the sword?

He wanted to believe that she viewed the sword as treasure and only treasure, but there was still a part of him that feared she meant to use it, that she had been waiting for some reason. Dragons could see the future if they were born of a strong bloodline. Had she seen something in her future and had stolen the sword because of it, and had been waiting all this time for that future to come to pass?

Loren's hand clapped down on Bleu's shoulder, jerking him away from thoughts of the dragon and what might lie ahead.

"Hunt the dragon. Eliminate her. Retrieve that sword for me, Bleu."

Bleu had the feeling his prince was more aware of his innermost feelings, the ones he had tried to bury deep and ignore, than he would like and was giving him a mission to focus on in order to take his mind off things.

To give him a purpose again.

"The dragon we met in the mortal realm, Loke, had no information for me when I spoke with him." Loren's expression turned troubled again and he worried his lip with his thumb, the black slashes of his eyebrows drawing down.

Bleu suspected the dragon knew more than he had admitted to Loren. He wanted to speak with the one called Loke, but Loren had agreed to leave him alone if he gave them whatever information he had. That only deepened Bleu's suspicion of him. If the male knew nothing, why had he pressed Loren to promise to never approach him again?

Loren sighed, and Bleu caught the wary edge to his eyes as they slid his way, sensed the tension in him increase before he opened his mouth to speak.

"It might be best we speak with Vail," his prince said and Bleu could see why his mood had shifted. Loren wanted to be the one to go, but he couldn't, so he was going to dump the task on Bleu's shoulders, even though he knew how little Bleu liked his brother.

He was entrusting him with the task though and Bleu wouldn't fail him. No matter how little he liked his new mission, he would carry it out to the best of his abilities for his prince. He could set aside his personal feelings about Vail for long enough to speak with him about the sword. If Loren was right, and Vail had a stronger connection to it, the elf male might be able to help him locate it, cutting down the amount of time it would take him to find it.

Loren tilted his head back, another sigh escaping him as he stared up at the sky.

Bleu could sense his desire to leave the elf kingdom and speak with his brother, but it would be a dangerous move. Loren had clashed with the council too many times since they had discovered Vail had been placed under a spell, controlled by a witch and forced to do her bidding. He couldn't push them right now.

It was bad enough that he had obviously ditched a meeting with them to speak with Bleu the second he had returned to the castle.

It didn't exactly make him feel great either. His gut squirmed, churning from the thought that he had worried his prince enough that he had risked angering the council in order to see him. Loren needed to restore some of the peace between him and the council, not upset them further. He needed to remain at the castle with them, attending to his business as the ruler of the kingdom, placating the council.

If it would help Loren achieve that peace with the council, Bleu would stomach visiting Vail in his stead.

"I will go," Bleu said, a bitter taste coating his tongue as he thought about seeing Vail again. Not only Vail. Rosalind would be there too.

Happily mated.

He shoved those two words away, ignoring them and the sting they caused behind his breast, and focused on Loren.

His prince still looked troubled, his crystal violet eyes locked with his and flooded with concern.

He squeezed Bleu's shoulder and the corners of his lips tilted in a half smile. "Be gentle with Vail."

Bleu huffed, his mood souring again. He was perfectly capable of playing nice with Vail long enough to get whatever information the mad bastard could give to him.

Loren's smile grew. "I know that look, Bleu. Give me your word."

It was degrading to have to do it, but he had long ago decided he would do anything for Loren. Even talk with Vail.

"I swear I will be nice to him." Bleu shrugged free of Loren's grip, his mood darkening further as he spotted a slender brunette female hurrying towards them from the castle, her pale blue skirts drawn up and away from her feet. Fantastic. It was time he left. He bowed his head to Loren. "I will report what I discover."

Before he could turn away, Olivia reached Loren. Her arm immediately looped around his right one and Loren looked down at her. Her smile for her mate was dazzling, near blinding, and Bleu looked away as she tried to turn that happiness in his direction.

"I'm so glad you're back. Loren was worried sick." Olivia's words struck hard, each one driving a spike deeper into his heart.

He didn't need her adding to the guilt he already felt and he certainly didn't have time to stand around and watch as Loren gazed at her, an altogether too soft look on his face, as if his mate was a damned angel descended from Heaven straight into Hell.

But he couldn't pull himself away or stop himself from looking at them as they smiled at each other, sickeningly in love.

He couldn't stop himself from thinking about the others. Iolanthe had Kyter. Sable had chosen Thorne. Someone had even been insane enough to fall in love with Vail.

He growled under his breath before he could think the next thought, the one he could feel coming.

One he didn't want to acknowledge.

He didn't need a mate.

He didn't need anyone.

He just needed to keep hunting the dragon.

He stiffly bowed his head, turned on his heel and stalked away from them, his focus locking onto his mission once more. He ignored the words of hurt Olivia spoke to Loren and just kept walking, heading towards the grand archway in the wall, his pace gaining speed.

The garrison came into view as he passed under the archway, an imposing pale three storey square building off to his right. Horses whinnied in the stable as they were groomed, tended to by the youngest soldiers. He bowed his head to the ranking officers that he passed, exchanging silent greetings with them. As commander of the legion directly under Loren's control, he held a rank above all of the males present, but he had never elevated himself to such a position. He didn't demand respect from his subordinates, or treat them as inferior as some of the commanders of the other legions did. He preferred to work alongside his men, as an equal.

Bleu halted and backtracked as one of the males he had come to see walked out of the stable block, dusting down his black trousers, the wood-and-leather soles of his boots a steady click on the cobbles.

Leif.

The bastard looked more like Loren every day. Sometimes, Bleu swore he emulated their prince. Other times, he decided it was just genetics. Leif was born of noble blood, had an irritating regal bearing and aloof tone of voice bred into him.

Leif's step slowed and his purple eyes drifted towards Bleu, his fine black eyebrows dipping as his lips compressed.

Leif was rarely pleased to see him too.

He blamed Bleu for losing the female dragon three centuries ago, believed Bleu should have been less concerned with bleeding to death from the brutal claw marks she had placed on his throat and more concerned about grabbing hold of her before she could run.

Bleu couldn't hold it against him. He would have felt the same had Leif been the one in his shoes, placing his life above the mission. They shared a compulsion to complete missions, and he was banking on that drive still being there, making Leif want to take up the hunt for the dragon again.

"There is only one possible reason you have shown your face now and if it has anything to do with the rumours going around the garrison about a shady black market arena and our dearest commander being launched across it by a female dragon, then you can count me in," Leif snarled each word as he stalked towards Bleu, darkness rolling off him, hunger to continue their mission. "You took your damned time returning though. Dacian has been putting poor foolish soldiers into sickbay for the past three lunar cycles."

That was a nice way of saying that Dacian was taking out his frustration and impatience on the soldiers he was meant to be training in the ring. Bleu sighed. The big elf warrior had never learned to express his emotions in other ways, always preferring to unleash them in the ring in the form of fighting.

"I suppose he is there now?" Bleu was already heading in the direction of the open stretch of sand behind the stables before Leif could answer.

The male fell into step with him, and Bleu almost felt as if it was Loren there. Same six-five height and slender build, same neatly clipped blue-black hair and ridiculously noble profile. Leif lacked something though.

A sense of humour.

Even Loren had one of those.

But where Leif lacked it, the fourth member of their troupe had it in spades.

Fynn's raucous laughter reached Bleu's ears long before he had finished traversing the narrow cobbled alley between the stable block and garrison. He rounded the corner and found the young elf male sitting on top of the low dark stone wall that enclosed the training area, rocking back on it but somehow maintaining his balance as he laughed his backside off at something. His long ponytail swayed with his movements, brushing across his bare back, reaching the small of it.

Bleu peered into the sand-filled ring and grimaced.

Dacian lay on his back, sand pushed up around his bare broad shoulders, his naked feet resting in a groove in the amber dirt. Bleu followed that track to the one who had laid one of their biggest, most brutal, warriors out cold.

No wonder Fynn had been laughing.

The young female elf breathed hard, one hand still tucked defensively against her chest and the other still outstretched, her palm facing Dacian.

Bleu clapped slowly.

Fynn stopped laughing and snapped his head towards Bleu. The female blushed a deep shade of red. She was pretty. As vicious as Bleu remembered too.

He bet that the sparring match had been Fynn's idea. Dacian hadn't been there the time Fynn's sister had come to visit, so he hadn't witnessed that she had some of the strongest telekinesis Bleu had ever seen, her gift a natural one from the gods. She had begged Bleu and Leif to train her, but females weren't allowed in the ranks, a tradition still firmly in place today.

Bleu had trained his own sister in secret, passing on everything he had learned so she could fight and defend herself. That knowledge had probably saved her life countless times.

By the looks of things, Fynn had done the same with his sister.

If Bleu had his way, the council would listen to him and allow females to enlist. Elf females were only marginally weaker than elf males. There was no reason for them not to have a place in the army if they desired it.

The young female elf brushed her jaw-length black hair from her face, blew a rogue strand upwards, and bowed.

Fynn grinned. "She's a cocky little runt, don't you think?"

His sister glared at him, but held her tongue. Bleu could see she wanted to retaliate, but his presence was silencing her.

"No more cocky than her brother," Bleu said and sighed again as he looked from Fynn to Dacian. "Although, I would prefer you didn't damage my men when I need them."

The female bowed her head again and Bleu smiled inwardly at the same time as Fynn's grin widened. It was cruel to tease her, but amusing too. It reminded him of when Iolanthe had been younger, and life had been easier.

Dacian groaned, his face contorted, and he rolled onto his side. He slowly pushed himself up and shook his head, dislodging the sand that clung to his shorn hair and revealing the long scar that cut diagonally across his scalp. It had been a close call the day he had received it. An axe in the back of the head was the sort of injury most elves didn't walk away from, but Dacian had incredible senses and had felt the blade before it had reached him, swiftly calling his helmet to shield his head.

The big elf huffed and pushed up onto his knees, sat back on his heels and dusted himself off.

When he swung his icy violet gaze towards the female, she squeaked and curled up, squeezing her hands together in front of her chest. Dacian lumbered onto his feet and heaved another sigh, shifting his thickly-muscled shoulders with it and causing his honed chest and stomach to tense. He had at least two hundred pounds on the poor female and she wisely backed towards her brother when Dacian advanced on her.

"Weapons, you said. A fight with weapons," Dacian growled through bloodstained fangs and pinned his violet gaze on the female first and then Fynn.

Fynn tensed, his smile fleeing his face. He shrugged, but it came off stiff. "Telekinesis could be considered a weapon."

Not by a warrior like Dacian. The psychic powers available to elves were only used in defence by those of the warrior class, viewed as a last resort when traditional weapons, and even claws and fangs, failed and they were close to losing their lives.

Dacian snarled, flashing his fangs.

The little elf female teleported, reappearing behind her brother, using him as a shield. Not the wisest move. Dacian wasn't the sort of male who cared if he had to go through a friend to get to a foe.

His steady hard gaze shifted back to her and then he did something that left Bleu wondering what the hell had happened to change the male.

Dacian backed down, huffing as he strode away from her and her brother, muttering things beneath his breath.

Bleu eyed him. Maybe he hadn't changed. Maybe Dacian had always been lenient on females.

He looked back at the female in question.

Or maybe Dacian had a reason to be lenient on this one.

She whispered something to Fynn, who nodded, and then she teleported. Dacian looked back in Fynn's direction, a brief glance before he swiped a grey cloth from the wall near Bleu and rubbed himself down with it.

"I take it from your appearance that we have a mission again?" Fynn dropped to his feet from the wall and strode across the sand, all humour gone from his face.

Bleu nodded. "The rumours running around the garrison are true. I encountered the female dragon again, and Prince Loren has ordered us to complete our mission."

All three males nodded in unison, and Bleu nodded too, a sense that their mission was finally coming to a close running through him, a familiar feeling that was comforting and made him feel at home.

Loren had given him a purpose, and he was going to fulfil it.

"We will not fail this time."

CHAPTER 4

The valley seemed larger from the floor of it, the mountains taller and more forbidding as they loomed over her. She felt small and vulnerable, her step uneasy as she walked forwards despite the voice in her heart that told her to turn back.

To leave before he realised she was here.

Taryn pulled down a deep breath, wishing it would steady her even though she knew it wouldn't. The last thirty breaths she had sucked in to calm herself had had no effect, so it was ridiculous to expect the thirty first to succeed where they had failed. There would be no settling of her fears, not until she had faced them.

Her eyes locked on the distant citadel where it rose from the black rock of the mountains at the opposite end of the valley as if they had birthed it, the sheer spires as pointed and cragged as the peaks beyond it, causing it to blend into the range. It sent a chill through her just to look at it, a place fit for a king but also for a killer.

Distant howls of Hell beasts mingled with the thunderous boom of rock splitting open in the valleys beyond the one she traversed, but down in the basin of the Valley of the Dark Edge, it was quiet.

Ominously quiet.

No sign of life stirred in the black land, but the shadows that crawled outwards from the gnarled black trees still made her jittery, causing her to jump at times when a flash of amber light shot up from one of the jagged fault lines she had seen in the other valleys and made them dance across the obsidian earth, reaching towards her like smoky claws.

There was only death in this valley.

It surrounded her, always there wherever her gaze fell.

The evidence that her brother killed anything that roamed into his domain.

Taryn slowed as she passed another set of bones, picked clean and startlingly bright in the dim light that passed for day. This one was the skeleton of a Hell beast, enormous and canine-like, with broken horns that protruded from its broad skull. She had fought enough of its kind to recognise one without its flesh.

She pulled her gaze away from it and continued walking on a direct path to the castle. It was closer now, but she had been walking for hours and had crossed only a tiny fraction of the valley floor.

Another flash of light leaped across the land as lava spewed high in a valley beyond the mountains to her right, and she stopped dead, her heart lodged in her throat and her eyes fixed on the empty pits in the skull just metres ahead of her.

Dragon.

Tears filled her eyes as she walked towards it, shaking her head as her heart ached. Her eyebrows furrowed as she neared it and she reached a hand out. It trembled in the air and her instincts told her to turn away, to not look at the skull of one of her kind, the damning evidence that her brother had truly lost his mind.

He had killed a dragon.

Taryn swallowed hard and laid her shaking hand on the beaked snout. The bone was cool beneath her palm and her senses stretched along it, mapping the shape of the skull, from its enormous teeth to the ridged bone above the eye sockets, to the four horns that flared back from the top of the skull.

Still gold in colour.

She dashed away the tears in her eyes with her free hand as she tried not to picture the dragon as it would have been, a beautiful and majestic gold, its scales shimmering and reflecting what little light pierced the dragon realm.

Tenak had killed it.

He had destroyed its beauty.

Gods, she felt sick.

She covered her mouth and looked beyond the skull, to the shattered bones of its spine and ribs, and the scattered wing bones that lay around it. It had been big. A male. Ancient.

She turned away, screwed her eyes shut and fought for air. Her fingers clasped the leather strap across her chest, the power of the magic humming beneath her fierce grip, drawing her focus to the weapon she carried.

A sword capable of ending her brother with one blow.

She swore to the dragon gods that she would avenge her kin. She would stop her brother.

Taryn marched forwards, pinning her gaze on the citadel again, her steps steadier and stronger than they had been in centuries. She knew her purpose, and she wouldn't falter. Her brother had gone mad, and she would stop him before he turned that madness on anyone else.

She closed her eyes briefly as she passed the barbed tip of the dragon's tail and prayed to the gods and her ancestors that she didn't end up like the poor soul. Her step faltered but she forced herself to keep marching, refused to slow her pace or allow her fear to get the better of her. She had a plan, and she believed in it.

Her brother had lost his mind, and to win his trust, she would act as if she had lost hers.

She lost herself in going over her plan as she walked, her feet growing sore again in her boots as the miles stacked up. The light in the valley began to fade. Night was falling. The dragon realm was so far from the elf kingdom that the light the fae brought into their world from the mortal one was weak when it reached it, barely able to drive the darkness back in the day, and leaving the world pitch black at night.

Her mind filled with images of what that fae kingdom had looked like and her bones warmed with the memory of how the light had felt on her skin. It had been so bright that her eyes had hurt and the land so colourful that it had been like a fantasy. A dream.

Did the mortal world look like the elf kingdom?

Was it lush and green, threaded with blue rivers, spotted with all the colours possible?

Gods, she could imagine that it was, and it made her ache to see it, to fly there as her ancestors had, long ago before they had been banished to Hell.

Her shoulders itched, her wings aching for freedom, the urge to shift rushing through her once more and pushing at her control.

A roar shattered the silence and robbed her of her breath.

Taryn stiffened.

He was coming.

A black shadow loomed above the castle, wrapped around it for a heartbeat before it spread enormous wings and took flight.

Her fingers shook so hard she struggled to tear the leather cuffs off her wrists, her breath trembling across her lips as she tore at the thick material.

"Hurry, hurry, hurry," she chanted as she ripped at the leather and one finally gave way, falling to the earth at her feet. She began to work on the other, her eyes darting between it and the shadowy dragon racing towards her. She had to get the cuffs off to break the spell. It was her only chance of getting him to recognise her.

Or at least, she hoped he would recognise her.

She ripped the second cuff off just as he landed hard only metres from her, causing the ground to shake and sending a blast of grit at her on a gust of wind that knocked her onto her backside. Pain bolted up her spine from the impact and she ground her teeth.

Out of the gloom, a rich deep violet head emerged, gigantic compared with her in her mortal form.

Bright violet eyes focused on her and the short spines that followed the ridge of bone above them rippled as he snorted, blowing hot air at her and the scent of ash. He growled, a strange disjointed sound that undulated around her, and bared his fangs. They gleamed in the low light, each as long as her arm, as sharp as a blade.

Taryn didn't dare move.

He snorted again. Scenting her.

She waited, stilled right down to her breathing, willing him to recognise her. She held his gaze, searching it for that glimmer that would tell her that she had succeeded and he knew her. Those enormous violet eyes remained focused and deadly, narrowed on her, showing no sign that he recognised her as his kin.

His blood.

He shifted back a step, his broad wings folding against his back, so the white membrane was barely visible, and shook his head as he clawed at the ground, long talons raking at the black earth.

He was conflicted, unsure of her, but that didn't mean she was safe. He could eat her in one snap of his jaws.

Taryn risked it and raised her right hand, holding it out to him.

His focus darted to it and his elliptical pupils narrowed into nothing more than vertical slits.

But then they widened again and she swore she saw a glimmer of recognition in them.

He lunged at her and she swiftly rolled out of the path of his strike, narrowly avoiding his bite, and launched onto her feet. So she had been wrong and he didn't recognise her. She was quick to run with plan B, slashing a claw across her palm and spilling her blood as she turned back towards him.

Tenak went to lunge at her again but stopped dead, snorted and then inhaled deeply, his white chest expanding as he took a full breath down into his lungs. He exhaled hard, the hot fierce blast almost knocking her on her backside again, and then growled, the low rumbling sound encompassing her.

Her cut hand shook so badly it jumped around all over the place. She caught her wrist with her free hand to steady it and raised both towards him, so he could smell her clearly.

This had to work.

She had his attention, and this time she was sure he was beginning to recognise her. It was taking him longer than she had expected, but then she had been gone a while and he was lost to the darkness. It had often taken him some time to recognise her during his fits of madness.

He breathed in again, the nostrils in his beak flaring, and then lowered his head.

Relief swept through her and she bit out a sob, her adrenaline leaving her in an energy-draining rush as Tenak began to shift into his mortal form.

The relief was short-lived as the weight of the sword concealed in the blanket on her back reminded her that she wasn't out of the woods yet. She still had to convince her brother to spare her life and forgive her, and if he sensed the sword she carried, he would do neither of those things. He would kill her.

She felt sure of that now.

The misguided beliefs that had plagued her during her journey, the lies she had told herself to keep her feet moving forwards, had fallen away now and she could see clearly.

Taryn looked at her twin where he stood before her, deep purple leathers encasing his powerful legs and his bare chest ridged with the honed muscles of a formidable warrior, his face as she remembered it but eyes foreign to her. They resembled hers, violet around the outside of his irises and white around his pupils, but while hers were only tinged with madness, his were wild and crazed.

He had truly lost his mind.

He stalked towards her, standing at least seven inches taller, radiating danger and deadliness that made her want to back away. It was a struggle to hold her ground, but she managed it.

She didn't manage to hold back the flinch and the gasp when he shot a hand out, grasped the back of her neck and hauled her up to him though, forcing her head back and her eyes up to his.

He snarled through teeth that were still all sharp. "Why have you returned to me… after you left me… left me… alone in this dark world… without you?"

Taryn breathed hard, heart hammering and blood pounding as she shook from head to toe. His claws pressed into the sides of her throat, his grip on her nape fierce and unyielding, and she feared he would break her neck.

Her eyes darted between his, so familiar but so foreign, as if there was something else living inside her brother's body, a sick beast that had driven the good male out and taken residence within him.

The pressure of his grip increased.

Memories surged.

Cold steel pressing on the back of her neck. Heavy on her wrists. Her ankles.

Tenak blurred in her vision as she went limp, her strength giving out, and she felt his arms around her, supporting her as she collapsed under the weight of her past.

He came back into focus, sharper than ever as her mind crumbled, and gods she hated acting like him, acting mad with a hunger for revenge against the kingdoms, because it came too easy for her and she feared it would swallow her whole and she would truly become like him.

She clawed at his chest, tried to break free of his hold. She needed to fly. He refused to release her and she curled her hands into fists and beat them against his shoulders. She wriggled and his grip on her tightened, sending her deeper under the tide of her memories. Hands on her. Hands.

Touching.

Taryn roared and gave one mighty shove, catching him in the face with her bloodied right palm and his chest with her left. His grip gave out and she stumbled free of his arms, twisting and staggering away from him. She couldn't breathe.

Cold steel. Heavy. She had to fly.

She clawed at her hair and collapsed to her knees as the black mountains closed in around her like the walls of a cage.

"Sister." Tenak's deep voice wobbled in her mind, distorting into that of others.

The males who had purchased her.

Who had tried to break her.

She shook her head and curled over, breathing hard against her knees, fighting back as she tried to claw her way towards the light and shed the grip of the darkness.

"I did not leave you," she snarled as tears streamed down her cheeks and dripped onto her knees to roll down the black leather. "I was taken."

"Taken?" he snarled and the darkness in that single word frightened her.

She shrieked as hands caught her and pulled her onto her feet, twisted her to face their owner, and lashed out, clawing at the male. The scent of blood hit her and her fight fled her body, her muscles turning liquid again beneath her flesh. Her brother.

Taryn hurled herself at his chest, buried her face against his neck and shuddered as she sobbed.

He was still for a moment and then his arms carefully closed around her, the touch meant to comfort, but all it did was terrify her.

She broke free again and paced away from him, clawing her hair back from her face as she breathed hard and fast, chanted in her head that it was over. She was safe now. Free.

Free.

She was free.

She needed to fly.

"Who took you from me?"

Who indeed?

She looked back over her shoulder at her brother, recognising him this time. Her precious brother, his face bloodied and chest streaked with crimson that dripped from dark slashes. The darkness in his eyes pleased her now, the hunger to maim and kill—the same darkness and hunger that beat in her heart.

"Slavers," she whispered, filled with a ridiculous fear they might hear her and come for her again, might find her here.

That fear turned to hope a moment later. She snarled and willed them to try and take her, to come and see what her brother would do to them. He would make them pay. The increasing darkness in his eyes warned that she was speaking her thoughts aloud and they pleased him.

He already wanted to kill those who had hurt her, and she would give him more cause to want their blood on his hands, would weave a lie to draw him to her side.

"They took the sword… I only stole it because I wanted power like you… I was going to use the sword to get it," she muttered and his face darkened at the mention of the blade she had taken from him. "I wanted to be powerful too. I was going to give it back. I wanted to be like you."

She fell to her knees again and scratched at the earth, feeling that maybe she was already like him.

Mad.

"I kept track of it… but I lost it… the second male who bought me hid it."

"Second?" Tenak snarled and came to tower over her again, a formidable sight as his eyes glowed with violet fire. "How many…?"

She was glad he couldn't finish that sentence, because she was finding it hard to keep the memories at bay enough to spin her web and catch him in it as it was. It wouldn't take much to push her back over the edge.

"Six," she whispered and fought the faces of her owners as they came to her, pushing them back down inside her, refusing to look at them or those of the people who had traded her. "There were six before I escaped."

Escaped.

When the elf was there.

The elf.

She looked down at her dirtied bloodied hands. At claws that had marked him. He would be coming for her. She was sure of that. She was sure that he had been hunting for her since their paths had crossed again three lunar cycles ago.

Taryn lifted her eyes to Tenak's face and he hunkered down in front of her, his steady violet-to-white gaze so warm and soft, so beautifully familiar and comforting now that she wanted to cry.

She tensed when he reached for her, but then she was in his arms, held gently against his bare chest, his warmth seeping into her, and all she could do was rest there and let him be strong for her.

He growled low in her ear. "I swear… together we shall make all of Hell pay for what they have done to you."

Gods, that sounded dangerously appealing.

Taryn sat with her head against his shoulder, her eyes fixed on the black mountains in the direction she had come, her bones vibrating with awareness that urged her to move faster, to accelerate her plan.

The elf was coming.

He believed her responsible for stealing the blade and attacking the elf kingdom seven long centuries ago, killing thousands of his kind. He could never feel anything for her other than hatred, and she had been fine with that, because it had meant he would never end up at the mercy of her brother.

But now she had delayed too long and her dragon instincts warned that he was closing in on her, and when that happened, the future would grow clouded and uncertain.

Both for her.

And for the elf.

Her fated male.

CHAPTER 5

His mouth caressed sweet fire across the top of her breasts, breathed it up the line of her throat and seared her lips with it as he claimed them again, his fierce inhale stirring the embers that burned in her blood too, setting it aflame.

Taryn arched up against him, desperate with a need to feel his body against hers. Cold scales greeted her bare flesh, but couldn't cool the fire burning inside her, a flame he had lit seven centuries ago. She moaned into his mouth as he plundered hers, the dominance of his kiss driving her deeper into her desire and stirring it to staggering new heights. She mewled, clawed at his arms, craved the feel of his warm skin beneath her fingers and his lips on her throat.

Fangs in her neck.

He drew back, breaking away from her lips and denying her. His wicked smile drew a growl from her that caused it to only grow wider, more amused as he tortured her with his distance.

She caught him around the nape of his neck and pulled him back down to her, tore a sweet gasp from his lips as she hooked her right leg around his backside and rolled him over, landing on top of him. It was her turn. She had been a slave to him for long enough, letting him master her.

It was time she mastered him.

She pressed her hands into his chest, her belly fluttering at the hard feel of it beneath her palms, all power and strength. It spoke to her dragon instincts, fanned her desire until it burned hotter and all she could think about was fulfilling her need of him.

Her male.

He gazed up at her, his wild blue-black hair tousled and blending into the black rock that was his bed as she sat astride him. Those bright violet eyes challenged hers, held her still with a steadiness and confidence that made her tremble. He knew she was afraid to take charge, had lived her life in the shadow of her brother, held under his yoke, and he wanted to see if she could rise to the task of taking command.

She could.

Taryn threw off her fears and palmed his chest through the small black scales of his armour, skimming them down to feel his pebbled nipples beneath them. He moaned, the strangled sound delighting her together with the way he tipped his head back, his eyelids dropping to steal those dazzling jewels from her gaze. Pleasure. She could feel it rolling through him, already building towards a crescendo.

A powerful peak of desire that she knew would leave her quivering from head to toe, trembling and boneless, and would do the same to him.

With little more than a thought, she peeled back his armour, watched it as the scales swept over his pale skin and revealed it to her.

His violet eyes darkened as his armour cleared his legs in its race towards the twin metal bands around his wrists and she groaned as the hot steel length at the juncture of his thighs kicked against her, brushing between her legs.

His hands clamped down on her hips and he held her in place as he lifted his, grinding his rigid shaft against her core, each undulation of his hips making the head caress her aroused nub. She trembled, breath stuttering as bliss rolled through her in time with his movements, ebbing and flowing, pushing her higher. His deep male growl of satisfaction and the feel of his eyes on her, the hot shivery ache that coursed through her whenever he gazed at her, combined to tear an answering moan from her lips.

Gods, she needed him.

She couldn't remember a time when she hadn't dreamed of him.

Yearned for him.

Even when she knew this was all she could have of him.

Taryn tipped her head back, felt the heat of his gaze on her throat before it drifted lower, settling on her breasts. She held back her smile as she lifted her hands and teased her nipples, rolling them between her fingers and teasing him at the same time. His hips thrust harder between hers, sliding the entire length of his cock along her slick core. His guttural groan sent a thrill through her, shot fire to her belly that pooled lower. His next thrust spread the new flood of desire that flowed from her along his hard length, making it slide easily to the pert bead that craved his touch.

She bit her lip and trailed her hands down from her breasts, aching for more. He beat her there, his hands skimming over her thighs and dipping down. His thumbs brushed the edges of her groin and she moaned, the sound ripped from her throat before she could contain it. She could almost feel his satisfied smile as he edged closer to where she needed him. Her nub pulsed, body flexing against her will in eagerness, hungry for his touch.

His thumb brushed her and she shuddered, a wildfire burning up her blood, rushing through every inch of her. He pressed the pad of it against her, holding it there and tormenting her.

Taryn dropped her chin and growled at him, flashing her teeth.

His eyes darkened further, the hunger in them arousing her to the point of pain, and she couldn't keep still. She lowered her hips and rocked on him, rubbing herself up and down his length, causing his thumb to shift against her and tease the aching bead.

Her breathing came quicker, falling into a rhythm with his as he swirled that thumb around her and she fell forwards, bracing herself on her palms against his bare chest. His flesh was warm beneath them, muscles hard and corded, his entire body tensed and on delicious display as she ground against him.

When she moved further forwards, causing the blunt head of his cock to brush her entrance, he bared his fangs at her and his ears flattened against the sides of his head, growing more pointed and luring her gaze to them.

She ran her hands up his chest and his neck, leaning over him, stealing her body away from his. He growled, the sound one of irritation now, frustration that she had removed herself from him. The anger dissipated the moment her fingertips brushed his ear, trailed upwards to the pointed tip, and teased it.

He groaned low in his throat, wrapped his arms around her and pressed down on her bottom, bringing her back into contact with him, in line with the wild jerks of his hips as she stroked his pointed ears.

His nails dug into her backside as she leaned closer to him, his hips lifting to keep their bodies together. She brushed her lips across his, a brief sweep that had him moaning, and then shifted her head to one side, stealing her mouth away from him and earning another reprimanding growl.

She killed that one too, transforming it into a moan as she tongued his ear, licking from the lobe up to the tip.

"Gods," he breathed in her ear and clung to her, pinning her against him as he thrust between her legs.

She moaned and shuddered, embraced the fire burning through her whenever the head of his cock rubbed her sweet spot, ached to feel him buried deep inside her, claiming her.

She flicked the pointed tip of his ear with her tongue and he trembled, barked out a moan that had her smiling wickedly, her confidence shooting into the stratosphere. She owned him now. He was under her command. A slave to her.

Taryn squeaked as he was suddenly on top of her, his hands braced on either side of her ribs and his hips nestled between hers, his cock pressing delightfully along the length of her with the tip resting against her nub.

His wicked smile beat hers hands down.

His violet eyes dropped from hers to her lips and she silently pleaded him to take her mouth.

Take her body.

He seized her lips in another demanding kiss and she arched against him, unable to stop herself. She moaned as his tongue stroked the seam of her lips and opened to him. He thrust past her teeth and she met him, tangled with him and fought him back. He groaned and settled his weight on her, dropping to his elbows as he began to thrust, rocking between her thighs, teasing her ever higher.

He shook when she stroked his right fang with her tongue, teasing it as she had his ear.

It was sharp, reminding her of her own fangs when she was in dragon form. She pressed the tip of her tongue to the point and the coppery tang of blood flooded her mouth. He groaned, thrust harder against her, kissed her deeper.

Hungry for a taste of her. She could feel it in him—the need, the yearning, the craving to taste her.

It ran as deep in his blood as it did in hers.

He broke away from her lips and kissed along her jaw, shifting his body down hers at the same time, stealing his cock away from her. She still couldn't stop her hips from rocking, thrusting to meet only air, her mind frazzled by the feel of his lips on her throat. He sucked and licked, teased with nips of his teeth that didn't break her skin. Driving her wild.

She couldn't take it.

She clawed at his shoulders and he stilled, going tense above her.

The scent of blood grew thick in the air.

She gasped as she saw what she had done, scoring her talons across his flesh and leaving vicious grooves in his skin that swelled with crimson.

Her eyes leaped to his, meeting their darkening depths, and she swallowed hard.

"Blood for blood," he whispered in a husky deep voice, thick with desire.

She didn't have a chance to respond.

Stars exploded across the black ceiling above him as his fangs sank deep into her throat and her body jacked off the ground as he pulled on her blood, sending it all rushing towards him and causing an inferno to sweep through her in its wake.

She moaned with each pull, grasped his shoulders and stayed locked in position, her backside lifted off the black earth and pressed against his.

He drank deeper, his noisy suckling filling the thick air together with her panted breaths.

His left hand skimmed down her spine, across her bottom and over her thigh. A moan quivered on her lips as his thumb pressed into her pert bead and two fingers speared her core, sliding easily into her slick flesh. He pumped her steadily, in time with his drinking, lifting her ever closer to release that still felt painfully beyond her reach. His thumb swirled around her nub as he thrust his fingers, and she flexed around them, her body beyond her control as she sought a climax she knew would scatter her in pieces.

His fangs sank deeper into her throat and she balanced on the edge, trembling there.

He denied her, slipped his fingers free of her flesh and left her bereft.

She opened her mouth to plead him to return to her but he denied her again, removing his fangs from her as he drew back, rising above her.

Blood coated his lips and dripped down his chin, and gods help her, but she wanted to kiss him, found the sight of him fresh from tasting her the most erotic thing she had ever seen.

His eyes held hers, fierce amethyst that stole her voice and commanded stillness from her, pulling her firmly under his spell.

His hand brushed her inner thigh and then the blunt head of his length nudged against her slick channel and she moaned, unable to contain the sound as pleasure rippled through her, hunger so fierce it was hard to keep still as he slowly pressed forwards, on the verge of filling her at last.

His fangs flashed between his lips as he growled down at her.

"Mine now."

A distant roar shattered him into a million pieces that rained down on her and she gasped as darkness engulfed her and then a single flickering golden light broke through it.

She stared across the large sparsely furnished room at the candle burning on the mantelpiece, her heart hammering against her chest and breath coming so quickly she felt dizzy. An echo of pleasure still rippled through her, a shadow of what she had felt in her dream.

She raised trembling fingers to her throat, to the place where he had marked her.

Her fated male.

Fated.

She snarled.

She had decided long ago that fate was cruel.

It had been cruel to show him to her seven centuries ago and make her recognise him for what he was. It had been cruel to choose him as the one who hunted for her, believing her a murderer and a thief, making him bent on killing her.

It was cruel to tease her with him in her dreams each night, the only place where they could be together.

Taryn drew her knees up to her chest and breathed out slowly, the candle becoming a hazy blur of light as her body tingled with unfulfilled need, an endless hunger for her mate.

He was coming.

She could feel it in her bones and her blood.

He was coming and she wasn't sure she was strong enough to face him again, to see the darkness in his stunning eyes that was directed at her, the hatred and the venom, the desire to end her. She closed her eyes but all she saw was the vision Loke had witnessed, one she now felt sure would come to pass and nothing she could do would stop it from happening.

Fate was cruel indeed.

Because it had made her mate her executioner.

CHAPTER 6

Bleu was three hundred percent certain that this was a bad idea. He had left Leif, Fynn and Dacian at the stronghold they had used during their previous hunt for the female dragon and the sword, a stone fortress long abandoned by the elf legions, left to rot because it now stood on a peaceful border between the elf kingdom and the First Realm of the demons.

Prince Loren had negotiated a treaty with the First and Second Realms centuries ago, the only two that bordered the elf kingdom. That treaty had created a barrier between the elf kingdom and the other five demon realms, stopping them from marching into elven lands and bringing war to Loren's doorstep.

War born of fury over the heinous acts committed in their lands by an elf.

Bleu eyed the quaint thatched cottage nestled on the fringe of a quiet village and surrounded by a vibrant walled garden and lush English countryside. The noon sunlight warmed the old sandstone of the small one-and-a-half storey cottage and glinted off the small windows on the ground floor and those in the roof. The reeds used to create the roof arched over each window in a sweeping curve that made Bleu feel as if nature herself had built the home. Such a peaceful place, it was almost impossible to picture the elf male he had come to visit living in it.

The elf who had been responsible for the atrocities in the demon realms and many more.

Vail.

Bleu had been standing here on the narrow silent road just a few hundred feet from the cottage for the gods only knew how long, debating whether to proceed with his prince's plan to speak with his tainted brother about the sword. His gut said it was a terrible idea, and it was difficult to ignore that, or the voice that whispered he should have brought backup with him.

Bleu shook his head.

He had been right to order his men to remain at their temporary headquarters, getting it back into order and ready for their hunt, resupplying it with weapons and anything else they needed from the castle. It was important that they were prepared, and that any elves who had moved into the vicinity of the garrison were removed to a safe distance. The lands around it had been empty on both sides three hundred years ago, making it the ideal place to set up base, because if the dragon attacked them it would only be him and his men in the firing line.

Bleu hoped that was still the case. He had no desire to drag innocents into this war.

It was also important that he didn't anger the elf he was about to visit, and he knew the male well enough, had fought him enough times over the past forty-two centuries, that he knew Vail would view a band of four warriors as a threat.

Both to him and his mate.

As the sun crept lower, leaving its zenith, and a warm breeze teased the bright red roses that clung to the rough creamy walls of the cottage, and the colourful rosebushes that lined the path to the front door, Bleu blew out a breath and marched forwards.

To his doom, probably.

This was not going to go well.

He approached the low wall enclosing the garden and cottage, his steps silent on the road. A bird sang in the distance, the beautiful song offering him comfort as his heart pounded hard against his breast. He reached his senses out, digging them deep into the nature that surrounded him, drawing strength from it as all elves did.

His hand shook as he reached for the low wooden gate and he tensed to steady it, a brief flex of muscle that did the trick. He pushed the bleached arched gate open and strode down the path, the hem of the long black coat he wore over his armour swirling around his ankles.

A soft female voice rang out from the rear of the cottage and Bleu diverted course, following the narrow golden gravel path that cut through lavender and rosemary bushes and curved towards the right side of the house.

He rounded the building and spotted Rosalind hanging washing on a line supported between two apple trees, her long black dress reaching her knees and a grim contrast against her wavy ash blonde hair. The breeze blew again and she muttered a ripe curse not suited to her delicate appearance as she wrestled with her hair, tugging it out of her face.

"Hand me those pegs." She pointed to a small bag hanging at the end of the line furthest from Bleu.

"Rosalind," Bleu said.

Her head snapped around, blue eyes enormous and rosy lips parted.

An unholy snarl sounded and then Vail was right in front of him, standing between him and Rosalind, his skin-tight armour in place and fangs enormous as he flashed them at Bleu. He backed towards his mate, his right hand stretched behind him, snarling the whole time. He reached Rosalind and caught hold of her waist, his black clawed fingers blending into her dress as he guided her behind him.

"Leave… keep away from my ki'ara. She is *mine*," Vail snarled in the elf tongue, his tone as black as midnight in the demon realms. His ears grew pointier, flaring back against the wild strands of his blue-black hair, and every instinct Bleu possessed fired in response to the threat.

It took all of his will to stop himself from hissing back at the wretched male.

It was only Rosalind's soft apologetic look when she leaned to one side, peering past her mate, that stopped him.

"I am not interested in your mate," Bleu muttered in his native language. "What is it with you and Loren and your females?"

A frown flickered on Vail's face at the mention of his brother, and then his eyes darkened dangerously, black encroaching to swallow the violet.

Bleu held his ground, body vibrating with awareness of what was about to happen. He had seen that look in Vail's eyes enough times to know to brace himself and prepare for a fight.

Rosalind gently laid her hand on Vail's right shoulder and Bleu couldn't believe his eyes as the vicious male transformed before them, that delicate hand taming the beast. The dark hunger for violence disappeared from Vail's eyes in an instant, becoming a soft but pleading look as he turned them on his mate. She stepped up beside him, her left hand still on his shoulder, and stroked his arm with her right, all the way down to the sharp tips of his claws.

Vail's gaze followed the path of her fingers and his shoulders relaxed as she worked whatever magic she was casting on him.

Not magic involving spells and potions. Nature's magic. A magic he didn't want to think about because it was already souring his mood, and that had been rather sour to begin with.

Love.

It was there in that touch, in that stupid soft look on Vail's face, and the smile on Rosalind's lips.

Bleu wanted to retch.

He cleared his throat instead, gaining a far more palatable snarl and black look from Vail.

Rosalind petted Vail's hand. "Let him speak. He's here for our help."

Vail turned that scowl on his mate. "He is not to be trusted. You vowed he would never come here."

She had? That stung. Bleu had thought them something akin to acquaintances, if not close to friends, after everything they had been through.

The darkness in Vail's eyes shifted again, lightening as his eyebrows furrowed and he stooped to catch Rosalind's hand. He brought it up to his armoured chest and stared down into her eyes, his violet ones pleading. As mercurial as ever. Vail's mood always had been dangerously unpredictable.

"He is dangerous. Make him go away. He will seek to harm me through you and I cannot bear it."

Now Bleu was just offended. "I will not… and besides, I knew Rosalind first."

Vail hissed at him, his eyes almost jet black and pointed ears flattening against the sides of his head.

The elf male released Rosalind's hand and turned on him, the black slashes of his eyebrows dropping so low that his eyes were nothing more than slits as he glared at Bleu.

"What do you mean?" Vail bit out and then snapped back to Rosalind, his eyes wild and filled with hurt. "Did you lie? Did the foul creature truly admire you in the Third Realm… did he desire you? Did you—"

Rosalind pressed a finger to his lips. "Nothing happened between us. I only said those things to make you jealous so I would know your feelings for me."

Bleu arched his left eyebrow at that, and being termed a 'foul creature'. It seemed Vail's opinion of him was as low as Bleu's opinion of Vail. And what the hell had Rosalind been thinking using him as a method of making Vail jealous? No wonder the male hated him and didn't trust him.

"I love you, and only you," Rosalind whispered, her head tipped back and blue eyes fixed on her mate's violet ones.

Vail's expression softened but it didn't last long. Storm clouds descended again, darker than ever as he slid his gaze towards Bleu.

"I still desire the male to leave." His eyes dropped back to Rosalind and emotions danced across his face as his eyebrows furrowed. "I do not wish to be reminded of the things I have done… not today… please?"

Rosalind offered her mate a sympathetic smile and opened her arms to him. Vail stepped into them, stooped and clasped her to him as he buried his face in her fall of golden hair. She held him, cupping the back of his neck, stroking the shorter lengths of his blue-black hair. When she blinked, her eyes darted from the trees behind Vail straight to Bleu, and starlight flickered in their blue depths as they darkened, the sense of power he felt flowing from her growing stronger.

Bleu shifted back a step and that was when it hit him.

The reason why Vail was troubled today, more so than usual.

His stomach dropped to his feet, the space in his chest going cold as he cursed himself for not realising it earlier. He could have avoided disturbing Vail, upsetting him, if he had chosen any day other than today to visit him.

Any day other than the anniversary of the one on which, all those thousands of years ago, Vail had fallen under Kordula's spell and attacked his own men, slaughtering most of his legion. A battle Bleu had barely escaped with his life.

Rosalind murmured softly to Vail and his fingers tightened against her waist, black claws pressing in to clutch her, as if she was the only anchor in the storm of the emotions battering him. Bleu could sense the turmoil and pain in him, hurt that he had caused.

He backed off another step, an apology balanced on his lips, but then he remembered why he had come. He couldn't leave without asking for their help. The fate of thousands, no, millions of lives depended on him now.

And on Vail.

He looked at the male, feeling deep in his gut and his heart that this was Vail's chance, his shot at taking a giant leap towards redeeming himself. The elf had taken thousands of lives over the last forty-two centuries, but he could save millions in the next few minutes.

"I didn't know," Bleu said. "I am not here because of that. I am here because I require your help… I need to find the sword."

Confusion crinkled Rosalind's fair eyebrows.

Her mate instantly lifted his head, turning sharp violet eyes on Bleu. "The sword?"

Bleu nodded. While his mate didn't know what they were talking about, Vail knew exactly what sword he was looking for and was aware of what had happened to it seven centuries ago, and the determination steadily growing in his eyes said that he was willing to help.

Vail opened his mouth to speak.

The air off to his left shimmered and another elf appeared on bended knee, breathing hard, black stilted ribbons like smoke twisting around him.

Bleu stilled right down to his breathing, tensing in perfect unison with Vail, unable to believe what he was seeing.

Fuery.

The tainted elf raised his head, black eyes locking on Vail's face for a split second before they dropped to his boots and he bent his head lower. The tangled strands of his shoulder-length black hair swept forwards to conceal his face, but Bleu could feel the agony as it rolled off him. His bare fingers dug into the earth, bunching the grass into shaking fists.

Bleu couldn't take his eyes off the male as he was hurled through time. A night barely a few months ago rose around him, reconstructing itself as if he truly had leaped through time. He saw Fuery standing across from him in Kyter's nightclub, a black and terrible shadow in the dimly lit expansive room, his eyes filled with darkness and lust for bloodshed, claws itching to destroy and take the lives of all he viewed as an enemy.

A shadow of the noble male Bleu had known as a youth.

That Fuery whirled back in time with him, to a battlefield where he loomed over him, his hand outstretched. Bleu saw himself take it, swore he felt the breeze as he was pulled onto his feet, and saw Fuery's lips move in silent words that he felt warming his soul and boosting his courage before the elf turned away from him. He raised his black blade, his head held high, violet eyes bright and focused on the enemy as he commanded the legion to move forwards. Bleu could only stare as he kicked off and swept through the enemy, cutting them down with ease and leading the charge.

A male Bleu had adored, admired and aspired to be, and had mourned, grieved for while flooded with pain so fierce it had felt as if his soul had been tearing apart.

The present Fuery moved, causing the past to swirl into a maelstrom of colourful smoke and dissipate.

"Commander Fuery," Bleu whispered, lost all over again, as rattled by his presence as he had been back in Kyter's nightclub.

He had lived four thousand years believing him dead, murdered by the male who was looking down at him through astonished violet eyes that seemed to reflect all of Bleu's feelings.

He couldn't breathe.

Bleu stumbled back a step as the past rushed back, sweeping him along in a torrent too strong for him to fight, impossible for him to break free of and find solid ground again.

Rosalind shifted her gaze to him and it filled with concern, her fingers twisting in front of her as she bit her lower lip. He knew she wanted to come and aid him, but it would be a dangerous move, one liable to cause her mate to turn on him, Fuery and possibly even her.

Bleu shook his head, silently telling her that he would find his balance again. He just needed a moment. Gods, he needed a moment to breathe.

An image of the silent forest in the Fifth Realm filled his mind, called to him to return to it as he had so many times, finding peace in the solitude and beauty of the place. He fought for the strength to push away from that urge, aware that it had served a purpose far different from the one he had believed.

It had become his place to hide whenever things had become too intense for him, too painful to handle.

He had buried himself in nature, craving the soothing touch of her, to rid himself of the cold emptiness that had invaded his very soul.

The loneliness.

Vail canted his head, causing strands of his wild blue-black hair to drop and brush his brow, his violet eyes pinned on Fuery.

His second in command.

His chest heaved with each deep breath he drew, stretching the scales of his armour, and his fingers curled into claws at his sides.

His eyes darkened dangerously.

Bleu waited for him to explode. If seeing Fuery again had caused Bleu shock, even when he had crossed paths with the male just months ago, then he couldn't imagine what it was doing to Vail, and on today of all days.

They both had awful timing.

Fuery lifted his head again, his face twisted in pain, a broken male that Bleu wasn't sure was quite with the world. The darkness was strong in him, his tainted soul showing in his black eyes, barely a sliver of violet remaining in them.

Vail stepped towards him.

Bleu held his breath, convinced that Vail was about to turn violent because of the day they had all chosen to invade his life.

Fuery clawed at the ground. Even Bleu could see how shattered he was, only a fragment of the male he had once been, and that he was adrift, a lost little thing floating on an endless sea of pain.

Suffering.

Gods, he was about to suffer a lot more.

Vail stopped right in front of Fuery, slowly crouched and raised his right hand.

Not in a vicious strike, but in a soft touch, a gentle cupping of Fuery's ashen cheek in his palm.

Bleu's breath rushed from him and he could only stare at Vail and Fuery, marvelling at how different Vail was as the corners of his lips pulled into a very strained and forced smile. He was trying to master the darkness inside him, the hunger that Bleu knew had to be filling him, urging him to lash out at those who might hurt him and his mate. Bleu could see it all in his eyes as the black fought the violet, the darkness pushing for control.

He was trying to be a better male.

Rosalind's smile said it all as she watched him interacting with Fuery.

"I am glad you are alive," Vail whispered in a low voice, one filled with a tone meant to be calming and soothing. "But you are not well."

Fuery closed his eyes, hiding his black irises, and lowered his head. Bleu had been shocked by the extent of the darkness in him, the hold it had on him, when he had met Fuery again in the nightclub. He had seen it control Fuery, driving him into a rage, and had seen another elf, Hartt, bring him back from the abyss.

Not the damned edge, but the black abyss itself.

Fuery was more than tainted.

He was lost.

They had squads who hunted his kind and dealt with them in the only way the kingdom condoned.

Killing them.

The tainted were viewed as black marks on the name of the elves, spoken about in fearful whispers among the population and used as a constant reminder to do good and hold back the seed of darkness that lived within the souls of all elves.

No one spoke of the lost.

No one was brave enough.

"This garden seems to work miracles," Vail continued and lifted Fuery's head, silently commanding the male to look at him. Fuery's near-black eyes darted between his and he swallowed hard, a look on his face that was somewhere between imploring and astonished, as if Fuery craved Vail's attention and affection but couldn't believe he was being given it or deserved it. "It has given me back much of my light… it holds back the darkness for me. Perhaps it might do the same for you?"

Fuery looked as if he might pass out.

Bleu willed the poor bastard to breathe, to just open himself up and believe that Vail wanted to help him, accepting it as real.

Vail looked over his shoulder at Rosalind, seeking her permission.

Bleu wanted to bite out a warning to her.

Fuery was dangerous and Bleu didn't think there was any way of bringing him back to the light. He was too far gone. Vail was tainted by darkness, but not to this degree. Bleu could see the hope in Vail's eyes though, the need to believe that it was possible to completely erase the black stains from an elf's soul. He needed to help Fuery, and not only because he probably felt responsible for what had happened to him. He needed it because it would help him too. It would strengthen his belief that he could be saved.

"We have room for a guest," Rosalind said with a steady soft smile. "But we really must speak with Bleu first. Remember?"

Vail looked lost, as if he had forgotten all about Bleu, which went down about as well as a mug of hydra toxin. He schooled his expression when the elf male looked his way, hiding his irritation from him.

The male nodded and rose to his feet.

Fuery immediately grasped hold of his left leg, clinging to it.

Vail reached down and stroked his fingers through Fuery's long hair, and Bleu couldn't help but wonder how it was all going to end. Fuery was insane, madder than Vail had ever been. If Vail managed to redeem him, to bring him back from the darkness even only enough to bring just a touch more violet back to his eyes, it would be a miracle.

"Don't linger too long, Vail." Rosalind gestured towards the house after her mate acknowledged her with a brief glance in her direction and started towards it.

Bleu was swift to follow her and caught her before she reached the arched wooden door at the rear of the property.

"It is unwise to have a tainted elf in your home," he said.

She smiled gently at him, warmth in her bright blue eyes as she pushed the door open. "I know that, but Vail needs him here. He needs company he trusts and he does get horribly bored when I have to work. It'll be good for him."

She made Fuery sound like a damned pet, not the violent assassin Bleu had seen hungering to kill both friend and foe.

"I do not think it will be good for you at all. Fuery is dangerous," Bleu muttered, stooped and followed her into the small kitchen of her home, careful to avoid banging his head on the dark wooden beams that ran across the low pale ceiling.

Rosalind gazed out of the leaded window at her mate, her smile growing wider. "You don't have to worry about me. I can handle the elf, if I have to… but I don't think I will. Vail won't let anyone hurt me."

He had to concede that point. Vail would probably kill Fuery if he tried to harm Rosalind. It didn't mean she was safe though. Fuery was as old as Vail, and just as powerful. Plus, he had spent the past gods knew how long as an assassin. There was a chance that Fuery might win if they fought.

Bleu rolled his right shoulder in a shrug that felt anything but casual and those damned feelings he tried to let run off his back refused to do just that.

He looked away from her. "Be careful anyway."

He felt her gaze on him, piercing and powerful, as if she could look right down to his soul with just a glance, and ignored her as he tried to tamp down his unruly emotions. He wasn't in the habit of showing anyone he cared, not anymore, but everything was piling up on his shoulders and it was getting more difficult to let it all just roll off him as he usually did, not letting it sink below the surface of his skin.

It all became too much, his feelings colliding within him, mingled with the knowing looks that both Loren and Rosalind had given him, ones that drew him close to admitting things that were best kept unspoken and unacknowledged.

He turned his thoughts to the female dragon and the turbulent flow of emotions quickly calmed, becoming as still as a millpond within him and restoring his focus.

On the only thing that mattered to him.

His mission.

CHAPTER 7

The back door to Bleu's left opened and Vail stalked in, swiftly placing himself between him and Rosalind. Was Vail always going to treat him with mistrust now? It wasn't their chequered past that had the elf male wary around him, firmly on the edge, either. It was Rosalind's fault. She had stamped an image of them together on Vail's mind during their courtship, branding Bleu as a rival during a time when Vail had been ruled by his instincts as her fated male. Vail was never going to trust him again.

"Tea?" Rosalind said, her voice light and airy in the thick heavy silence.

He shook his head at the same time as Vail. She muttered something under her breath and stomped off, heading towards the centre of the cottage. Bleu waited for Vail to follow her before daring to move. He had been to the cottage before so he knew the way to her drawing room but decided it was best he followed close on Vail's heels so the male knew where he was.

Vail ducked under the doorframe in the left wall of the narrow hallway that ended at the front door. Bleu followed him inside, his gaze immediately running over the familiar room. It was as messy as ever, with books stacked everywhere and on everything besides the green velvet armchairs that nestled around the inglenook fireplace to his left.

Rosalind arranged her black dress and sat on the one with its back to the leaded window. The colourful roses continued to sway in the breeze, the dazzling sunlight bathing them in life, and he itched to be outside again, immersed in nature. An unsettling sensation slithered over his skin beneath his armour and he looked across at Vail to find the male glaring at him again, his eyes narrowed and verging on black.

"Sit," Vail snapped and Rosalind chastised him with a frown of her own.

He glanced at her and his face lost all darkness, and Bleu could only marvel at the extent of her effect on him. But then, that seemed to be a problem among mated males.

All the ones Bleu knew acted as if they'd had their balls cut off when their female was upset with them.

All the more reason to remain free of a bond.

He liked his balls the way they were.

"Take a seat," Rosalind said without taking her eyes off her mate and Bleu guessed the offer was aimed at him, not Vail.

Vail remained standing and folded his arms across his chest as Bleu took the armchair opposite Rosalind and knocked a small bundle of books over with his boot, scattering them across the grey slate floor. Vail's expression darkened again.

"Never mind." Rosalind got off her chair, crouched and stacked the books. She looked back at Vail. "See. No harm done."

Vail didn't look convinced.

Why hadn't she used her magic? When Bleu had been here before, she had moved furniture with it. It would have been easy for her to wave a hand and restack the books.

It dawned on him that Vail was the reason. He had a penchant for killing witches, and Bleu had seen magic send him off the deep end and into a black rage before, unleashing the darkness within him. He recalled what Rosalind had said about Vail getting bored when she had to work.

Bored because he stayed away from her when she was using magic, occupying himself elsewhere, beyond the sphere her power would taint.

Rosalind walked over to a worn leather chaise longue below the window and started dragging it towards the fireplace. Vail went to her, gently removed her hands from it, and pulled it for her, effortlessly moving it into place with the curved armrest closest to her chair. He sat down on it and glared at Bleu again.

Bleu took it as a cue to speak. "I need your help tracking the sword. I need to use your connection to it to locate it."

Vail looked troubled and shifted his gaze to Rosalind. She sat beside him and placed her hand on his right knee, and the slender male dropped his focus to it, his expression turning lost again.

No, not lost.

Afraid.

He feared what Bleu was asking him to do.

Why?

Vail swallowed hard and closed his violet eyes, turning his noble profile to Bleu and reminding him just how alike he and Loren looked. "My bond with the sword is strong because of my blood, but it is weak in this realm."

There was an edge to those words, a tremor that spoke of the fear Bleu had noticed.

"Perhaps it would be better to ask—" Vail cut himself off and turned his face completely towards Rosalind, and she squeezed his knee.

"Loren sent Bleu here, and that means he needs your help. No one is forcing you to do this, Vail. If you're not comfortable, you can say so." Rosalind smiled at her mate as he opened his eyes, leaned back against the couch with a weary sigh and looked into hers, a soft edge to his that spoke of love so deep that Bleu wanted to retch again. Mates. He suppressed a shudder. Gods forbid he ever found his.

The tiny voice in the pit of his soul whispered that he wanted to find her.

Hadn't he been searching for her for millennia?

Waiting for her for centuries?

Hunting for her?

He frowned at that and shoved the thought aside, refocusing his attention on Vail and willing the male to agree to help him.

"I have tracked the one who stole the sword back to her realm of dragons but I need a location, somewhere to look. The realms are vast." Bleu leaned forwards, resting his elbows on his knees, feeling the rippled surface of his armour pressing into them as it gave beneath the pressure. "If I could uncover her location, I am certain I will be able to retrieve the sword for your brother."

Vail's expression grew softer, warmer still, and Bleu felt like a bastard for playing on his love of Loren to convince him to agree to help him. Loren would throw him in the cells, or worse, if Vail hurt himself trying to sense the sword's location, but Vail was their best shot, as Loren knew, and Bleu couldn't head into the dragon realm without a clue about where to search for the sword.

Not only would it take him months to scour the land, but he would probably end up as roasted elf, together with the rest of his team. That much questioning of dragons was bound to stir some rage somewhere along the line. He wanted to keep the risk to a minimum, and that meant having a good starting point, or better still, Vail being able to tell him a location within a short distance of the blade.

"Will you help me?" Bleu searched Vail's rich violet eyes as they swung his way and waited with bated breath.

The darkness in them pushed, a black tide that surged from the edges of his irises towards his pupils, driving the purple back. He was playing with fire, and the part of him that would always hate Vail enjoyed seeing the male suffering, having to battle the darkness his vicious acts had awoken in him.

Bleu eased back in his chair, disgust at himself swift to rush through him on the heels of that feeling, and tried to look at Vail in a better light, the same golden shiny one that Loren used to wash away the black shadows cast by Vail's sins.

He wasn't surprised when it didn't work for him.

Vail slowly nodded, and, holy fuck, Bleu actually witnessed a little glow of shiny light fall on the male, enough that he actually thought good of him for the first time in what felt like forever.

"I'll help." Rosalind tucked into the corner of the chaise longue, the leather creaking under her slender weight as she positioned herself near the armrest and patted her knee.

Vail obediently swung his legs up and laid back, resting his head on her thighs and folding his arms across his stomach. His booted feet hung off the end of the seat, soles resting on the floor. At six-feet-six, an inch taller than Bleu, his feet probably would have fallen off the end even if he'd had his head resting on the arm of the chaise longue.

The male looked up at Rosalind, who gazed down at him, her blue eyes soft and filled with tenderness. She gently brushed the blue-black strands of her mate's hair from his forehead, the action seeming to soothe him as if she had the touch of nature herself, and for a flicker of time, a split-second in which his guard fell, Bleu envied the bastard.

He quickly shut down that feeling and any associated with it, stopping them before they could surface and wreak havoc on him. He wasn't interested in a mate. He had a mission, a purpose, and he was going to fulfil it.

Vail closed his eyes, exhaled slowly and sank against the seat, his entire body visibly relaxing into it.

"Just focus," Rosalind whispered and continued to stroke his brow, his hair, and even teased the pointed tips of his ears.

Bleu wasn't sure how that was going to help him relax and focus. Just the thought of a female teasing his ears was enough to have his blood pounding and all rushing south.

Vail didn't seem to have that problem as his mate fussed over him, speaking in a low gentle voice, coaxing him into a sedated state.

Was it magic she was weaving with her voice and touch? A form of a spell that went undetected by her mate?

It seemed as if it was as emotions flickered across Vail's face, turning it soft one moment and twisting it into darkness the next. Whenever it turned vicious, Rosalind soothed him and he relaxed again.

Sank deeper under her spell.

Bleu was beginning to feel sedated himself when Vail finally broke the silence, speaking in their native tongue.

"The dragon realm," he murmured and then his voice grew louder and clearer, as if affected by his connection with the sword as it strengthened. "Beyond its borders… I feel it. Waiting. Calling to me. *Screaming* for me."

Vail's breathing deepened and his hands twitched against his stomach, claws scraping over his armour. Rosalind's free hand came down on them, clasping them and stopping them before they could slice through the black scales. Elf armour was only weak against the same material. It was wise of Rosalind to stop her mate, not only because he could hurt himself, but because in the act of cutting himself with his own claws he would spill blood and tainted elves were deeply affected by the scent of blood.

Bleu didn't want to have to go back to Loren and report that he had driven Vail into a fit of bloodlust.

Loren would probably see red himself on hearing it.

"It needs me," Vail whispered in a broken voice in English and a tear slipped down his temple, soaking into his dark hair above his ear. "Gods… it calls for me."

"I know." Rosalind brushed her thumb across the back of his hand and his armour peeled away from it, leaving it bare for her to caress. She smiled and kept with her stroking, soothing her mate as best she could. "Where is it waiting, Vail?"

His breaths came quicker and he shuddered. Her eyes widened as he raked his fingernails over his stomach and then his chest, and struggled against her, his entire body lurching off the seat. She pressed her right hand against his forehead, pinning his head to her knees, and trapped his arms against his chest with her left. Strange words fell from her lips, a soft chanting that filled the air with the tinny scent of magic. The hairs on the back of Bleu's neck stood on end, an odd sensation skittering over his skin beneath his armour.

His every instinct warned him to remain where he was, even when a part of him wanted to aid her.

Vail's eyes snapped open.

Edged down towards him.

Froze his backside in place on the seat.

Black.

They were as black as midnight.

"Vail," Rosalind snapped and slapped her mate across his right cheek.

The darkness instantly evaporated, disappearing literally in a blink of the eye as Vail blinked and looked up at her, his violet gaze confused for a heartbeat before he groaned and screwed his eyes shut.

"It's okay," she murmured softly and resumed petting him, her grip on him loosening as he relaxed again. "You just had a little moment. Nothing to worry about. Happens to us all."

Bleu eyed her. It did?

Rosalind was quirky, her mood flitting from serious to bubbly so quickly it sometimes left him dizzy, but he had never seen her having a 'moment'. Did the witch have a dark side too?

It would explain why she could love a male like Vail.

"You don't have to go back in." She smiled down at Vail as he opened his eyes and looked up at her again, weariness in his.

He really did need to go back in. Bleu needed to know where the sword was and beyond the border of the dragon realm meant nothing. There were countless realms beyond its borders.

"I am fine," Vail gritted out, sounding for all the three realms as if he really wasn't. Stubbornness evidently ran in the family bloodline. How many times had Bleu heard Loren tell him that he was fine when he was falling apart?

Vail closed his eyes again, heaved a sigh, and started to relax. Rosalind began murmuring the same soft encouraging words she had used before, and again the sensation that they were magic ran through Bleu. She was so small and slight, but she held such power over her brute of a mate. It was incredible.

For four thousand years, Bleu had been convinced that Vail was a beast with no conscience, a monster made flesh and bone, unable to feel anything or be tamed by anyone.

But a tiny female had tamed him.

Had made him love, and even live again.

It all seemed so impossible.

Was this the power of a bond? Was it magical enough that it could save even the blackest soul?

"I feel it," Vail whispered in the elf tongue. "Beyond the dragon realm."

Bleu wanted to point out that he had already told him that but held his tongue instead. He leaned forwards as the air thickened, the sense that Vail was forging a stronger connection with the sword through sheer will alone running through him as he watched the male's expression shifting. Vail gritted his teeth and bared his fangs on a pained snarl, the black slashes of his eyebrows meeting hard as he grimaced.

Rosalind shot Bleu a black look that blamed him for her mate's suffering.

Holy fuck, something was wrong with him, because he wanted to tell Vail to stop. He didn't want to see the poor bastard suffer any more.

He was on the verge of stopping Vail when the elf exhaled a string of words in a torrent that took Bleu a moment to rewind and unravel.

"It waits near the Devil's domain, in a valley at the border of the dragons."

It was a start, but he needed better information than that. The border between the dragon and Devil's realms was long and treacherous, and it could take months or years to scour it.

"It is all I can give you from here." Vail's deep voice filled the tense silence and Rosalind stroked his chest and his hair.

Bleu looked at Vail, at the sweat dotting his brow, and listened to his ragged breathing as he twitched under Rosalind's tender touch, and didn't have the heart to ask him to try harder or mention the possibility of him travelling to Hell with Bleu's team where he could get a clearer picture of the sword's location.

Vail wasn't ready for that.

He was struggling, hurting himself by helping him, and Bleu actually felt sorry for him. He had never thought he would take pity on Vail, that his opinion of the elf could change for the better, but seeing him suffering in order to help another was enough to have him feeling that way.

He also suddenly had the impression that keeping the peace with the council of elders wasn't the only reason Loren hadn't been able to come to his brother and had tasked Bleu with the mission instead.

In fact, he had the distinct impression that his prince had known that his feelings towards Vail would soften, his anger lessen, if he saw the male with his mate and saw how traumatised he still was by the things he had done, but that he was fighting to better himself and make amends.

And, gods help him, but Bleu felt enough for the male to offer a few words that were both born of gratitude and a desire to help him on that path.

"Loren constantly thinks of you, and he is trying to get the council to allow you to return home."

Vail looked across at him, the black receding from his violet irises, and the corners of his lips quirked into a smile that wasn't forced this time. It was odd seeing Vail smile again, really smile, as he had so many millennia ago before everything between them had changed. Seeing it left Bleu wondering something that he didn't like, because it made him cold inside.

When was the last time he had really smiled?

Not a forced one, designed to placate others or because it had seemed the right response.

Really smiled.

He recalled laughing with Kyter and Iolanthe when he had been helping them a few months ago, and how it had warmed him but it had felt so foreign to him too.

He wasn't sure he had smiled or laughed with meaning for millennia before that day, and he hadn't since.

Iolanthe had told him once that he had been a changed male, one grim and sombre, since he had stopped talking of his dreams to her, of his one true desire.

The one he had set aside in favour of serving his prince.

The one he was beginning to yearn for again, despite all his protests and attempts to pretend otherwise, as he watched Vail with Rosalind, saw the love and devotion they shared in the life they lived together in the small cottage.

The dream of finding his mate.

CHAPTER 8

Taryn left her bleak quarters in the castle behind, obeying her urge to escape the confines of the room her brother had given to her. It was enormous, like all the rooms in the black citadel, but the walls had still closed in on her as she had paced, planning her next move.

She hurried down the stone steps to the next level, fearing she would run into Tenak. She had left him hours ago in his large empty library, pawing over a crudely drawn map of the kingdoms of Hell and muttering about his plans for them all. Being around him the past few days had been harder than she had expected.

It had made her realise the depth of his madness, the hold the sickness that infested him had on him. He thought only of killing and subjugating, ruling all those he viewed as beneath him.

Today, when he had started talking about her role in his righteous plan to bring Hell to its knees before him, she'd had to make her excuses, stating that she was tired from her journey and needed rest. Tenak had turned concerned eyes on her, had touched her hand and had bidden her a good sleep.

Her hand still felt chilled from that touch.

She rubbed it and quickly crossed the large entrance hall, heading towards the open arched door.

Tenak never bothered to close it.

That chilled her most of all, that certainty that he could slay any fool who dared to enter his home.

He had been kind once. Protective and fierce, but kind. He had flinched like any youth when dealing a blow in the training ring, had apologised countless times to those he hurt by accident or whenever he won a match. Now the cold eyes of a warrior looked back at her, tinged with madness, corrupted by a hunger for power. She doubted he would flinch if he had to fight the Devil himself.

He certainly wouldn't apologise.

She broke out into the sloping area of smooth rock that she supposed was the courtyard of the castle. It had been carved deep into the mountain, with jagged sections left standing in a ring around it, natural walls at least twenty feet tall.

There was no gate in the wall that enclosed the castle, no weak point. Any attacking forces without the ability to teleport or fly would have to use ladders to come over the walls or risk scaling the mountain to reach the rear of the castle.

The lower section of the castle was heavily fortified too, with only narrow arrow slits for windows. She looked back at the arched doorway. If an enemy tried to enter that way, there was a thick steel portcullis ready to drop on them and seal the door.

It was a grand castle, a perfect example of one, but she couldn't imagine who had built it.

Here in the Valley of the Dark Edge, so close to the Devil's domain.

Had it been his men who had created the building that loomed above her, cragged towers reaching towards the dark grey sky?

It suited her image of the male who had once ruled all of Hell, and still ruled half of it. He was dangerous and mysterious, little more than a myth or perhaps a legend. She only had stories to go on, and those stories had been told to her as a child four thousand years ago. None had seen him in long millennia.

Or if they had, they hadn't lived to tell the tale of the beautiful fallen angel who had given birth to this land and the demons who filled it.

Taryn stared beyond the high mountains that formed the valley, her gaze on the amber glowing sky to her left where the Devil's domain stood.

She wanted to see it.

As a child, she had been warned to stay away from the valleys close to the Devil's realm, for wandering baby dragons were the food of the beasts his kingdom contained.

She had met a fallen angel once.

He had tried to sell her at the black market, the one where she had crossed paths with the elf again.

Her gaze grew hazy as she thought about that elf male, her senses instinctively reaching out across the land, drifting over it like smoke as she searched for him, part of her fearing she would sense him near and the rest of her aching to find him there.

Taryn whipped her focus away from the elf and pinned it back on the mountains. She wanted to see the Devil's lands. Today, she would scout that section of the valley.

She closed her eyes and willed the shift, but forced it to come slowly, embracing the pain as her bones grew and distorted, broke apart to form new shapes beneath her skin. Scales rippled over her and she used what magic she had to cast her leather trousers, boots and corset away, baring herself to the elements.

The warm breeze caressed her naked skin a split-second before the scales covered it, and she fell onto all fours as she allowed the shift to accelerate. She opened her eyes as her vision sharpened and the ground dropped away from her as she grew, transforming swiftly into her dragon form.

She threw her head back and roared as she beat her wings, the feel of them battering the air flooding her with joy she couldn't contain, not even when she still feared her brother would hear and follow her.

Taryn spread her wings, stretching them wide, so the white membrane between her violet wing bones pulled taut. There was something deeply satisfying about stretching her wings in such a manner, feeling them from where they joined her shoulders to the very tips of the bones that intersected the membranes.

She carefully placed her front paws down on the black wall, towering above it now, and beat her wings. Her back paws lifted off the ground and she stopped her wings, let her paws touch the ground again, and then sank low and kicked off, launching into the air. The valley fell away in an instant, becoming nothing more than a black streak before it blended into the rest of the lands, a blur of shadow.

A sea of darkness.

She beat her wings, holding herself suspended above Hell, her sharp eyes picking out clusters of light in the swath of black. Whenever she focused on one, her vision zoomed in, revealing the village. She scanned each one in the dragon realm, something that was becoming habit, an urge that she found as difficult to deny as the need to fly.

She pretended she wasn't looking for anything in particular, even when she knew in her heart that she was.

The elf male.

When her scan of the dragon realm was complete, she spread her wings and soared lower, letting the wind buffet her as she swept back down towards the valley. She twisted her body, lazily spiralling downwards, the black lands nothing more than a whirling blur that rushed past her eyes, punctuated by a brief flash of light.

She flapped her wings to slow her descent and skirted the valley, denying the urge to fly higher again and look towards the source of that light.

The elf kingdom.

She had realised two days ago that she could see it when she flew high, able to pick out the golden light that filtered down on it and part of the lands that surrounded it. It had been so green, filled with colour and warmth. Life.

It had tainted her view of the rest of Hell, painting it in a dull light that left it wanting.

Even the dragon realm, her beloved home, now appeared black, cold and grim to her.

She turned her gaze towards it as she neared the end of the valley, looking back in the direction she had travelled to reach her brother, and then pulled her eyes away as she banked left. She followed the mountain ridge, heading towards the Devil's domain, and started her work, charting all the escape routes she could take if necessary.

Her tension faded as she flew, her mind occupied with small tasks, thoughts pulled away from the castle that often felt too cramped and her brother's plans. She focused on flying, feeling the warm air on her face and wings, flowing over her scales and curling around her tail.

As she circled back around, passing the castle, she gazed down at it.

A bolt of fear ran through her, scattering her calm.

That fear had steadily been growing since her brother had taken her in, keeping her awake at night and setting her on edge around him. He hadn't mentioned the sword since she had said it was gone, but she knew he hadn't forgotten about it. It was his ultimate treasure, and that was the reason she had hidden it deep in the bowels of the castle, in a place far from the ones he frequented in his daily routine.

Taryn breathed deep, her nostrils flaring as she took a massive gulp of air down into her lungs. She opened her jaws and exhaled, and the taste of ashes coated her tongue. Her ancestors would have breathed fire but all she could do was breathe ashes, her power diminished by the roof of Hell that stole sunlight from her scales and magic from her bones.

Her kind had been losing powers that were rightfully theirs since they had been cruelly banished from their home, cast into Hell and cursed.

It was just another cell, larger and grander than ones she had occupied during the last three centuries, but a cell nonetheless.

It held her, trapped her away from the light, stole her power from her and made her weak, leaving her at the mercy of others.

Fire blazed through her blood, impotent flames that licked at her skin and wanted to burst from her, desperate to mix with the fetid air of Hell and burn her grim cage to ashes.

Taryn flew harder, needing to feel the air in her lungs and rushing over her scales. She needed to fly. Her wing bones ached but she refused to slow. She couldn't. She had to keep flying. She had to be free.

Had to fly.

It was a compulsion, one she feared would drive her mad if she denied it.

Pain burst along her entire left side and she barrelled right, an agonised roar escaping her as she dropped through the air. Sharp claws pierced her scales, savagely raking over her ribs and back, close to tearing into her delicate white wing membranes. She turned wild eyes on her foe, her heart pounding hard and blood thundering as she instinctively lashed out with her barbed tail. It struck hard.

On the shoulder of the violet and white dragon who was driving her down towards the mountains.

Tenak.

Taryn cried out again as she crashed into the ground at the base of the mountain, jagged rocks punching hard into her right side and boulders and gravel spraying ahead of her as she slid across the uneven terrain.

He rose above her when they came to a halt, his front paws on her hip and shoulder, pressing her down into the black ground. He bared huge sharp teeth at her, his violet-to-white eyes wild and filled with fury that she could now sense in him. Anger at her.

She hurled her head back and shrieked as he raked claws over her left flank, scoring long gashes in her scales. The pained sound echoed off the mountains, mocking her with its feebleness.

Tenak snapped at her wings and neck with his jaws and she tried to scramble away from him, kicking at him with her back legs. She caught him in the belly with her talons and he snarled at her, his elliptical pupils narrowing into thin deadly slits.

The pounding of her heart grew frenzied as fear seized her, her eyes locking on his fangs as he launched at her again, aiming for the base of her left wing.

He was going to kill her.

Taryn kicked hard with both back paws, slamming them into his belly and knocking him back just as his jaws closed. His fangs clacked together bare inches from her wing bone and he growled at her. She kicked again, frantic with a need to escape him.

Only one thing could have caused him to turn on her.

He had found the sword.

He must have used her scent on the cloth, tracking it through the castle.

As he reared back, looming above her, bloodlust shining in his narrowed eyes, she did the only thing she could to save herself.

Taryn shifted back into her mortal form. Her weaker form.

Fear was clouding her judgement and she had to see through it to the truth, trusting that he didn't want to kill her. He just wanted to punish her for taking what belonged to him.

His greatest treasure. His prized possession.

She had to trust that his dragon instincts and his instincts as her twin brother were still strong enough to prevent him from attacking her when she was weak and he could easily kill her.

He remained staring down at her, cold merciless eyes pinned on her as she huddled on her side, naked and trembling. Blood coated her, seeping from the gashes he had inflicted, the wounds burning even as the red liquid cooled her skin around them, catching the steady breeze that blew across the valley.

Taryn prayed to the ancient gods and closed her eyes, bracing herself for his killing blow.

May the gods have mercy on Hell. She had failed everyone. Tenak would kill them all now he had the sword.

The expected blow didn't come and she managed to convince her lungs to work and her eyes to open.

They did so slowly, fear still flowing through her, poisonous whispered words that said he would strike her down the moment she set eyes on him.

Tenak stood before her in his mortal form, dark purple leathers encasing his legs. His handsome face was dark as midnight, grim and forbidding, filled with the anger she could feel flowing from him and over her. His cold eyes held hers, sending a deeper tremor through her, one that wracked her right down to her soul.

She had looked into the eyes of hundreds of males, all of them wretched and dark in some way, foul and twisted, but she had never looked into their eyes and witnessed what she could see in Tenak's.

He wanted to kill her.

She had never feared those males, her masters, as she feared her own brother.

"You had the sword," Tenak growled and advanced on her. She shifted onto her bottom and scooted away from him, until her back hit a boulder and she had nowhere to run to escape his fury. He bared sharp teeth at her and his eyes flashed like fire. "You kept it from me. You *lied* to me."

Taryn shook her head, shifting her violet-to-white hair across her bare shoulders. "No. No, Brother."

He snarled. "Liar. You deceived me. You stole the sword and you kept it from me. It is mine, Sister. *Mine.*"

"I know," she said and he stilled, some of the tension leaving his muscular body as he eased back a step and eyed her, silently commanding her to continue. "I was bringing it back to you."

He didn't look as if he believed her. She had to convince him that she had been returning the sword to him or her quest to free Hell of her brother's demented plans was going to end here, with her back against a rock, caged between it and him.

Caged.

She wrapped her arms around herself and fought that word, that feeling it awoke in her, sinking the sensation deep into her bones until she felt trapped in her own skin.

The trembling worsened as she began to lose the fight and she started to rock, stared at his knees and desperately tried to hold the pieces of herself together so she didn't fall apart. Not now. She needed to convince her brother to believe her. She couldn't slip into the madness. She fought it, but no matter how fiercely she pushed back against it, it was gaining ground, pulling her down into the darkness.

"I am to believe you meant to return the sword?" Tenak hunkered down in front of her, his deep voice little more than a thick growl as he glared at her.

His lips twisted in a vicious smile that faltered when he reached out to touch her and she flinched away. A frown flickered on his brow, a brief flare of anger in his eyes that she felt was directed at someone else and not her.

At the males who had shattered her in a way, even when she had believed herself unbroken.

"I escaped," she whispered, not strong enough to put more force behind her words. They shook from her lips, trembled as fiercely as her body. "I spent months tracking the sword… and I stole it back… I was bringing it to you."

His face darkened again and he curled his outstretched hand into a fist and drew it back to him. He unfurled it and pressed it against his bent knee, mirroring his other hand. The position caused his bare chest and arms to tense.

A display of power. A tactic many male dragons employed where females were concerned. He was making sure that she knew he was stronger than she was, both in this form and his dragon one, silently keeping her in line and under his rule by eliminating any thought about attacking him.

"If you were bringing it to me," he murmured in a low voice that was so calm it set her on edge, screamed at her that he was close to lashing out at her again, "why did you not give it to me that day I found you here in the valley?"

Taryn swallowed hard and managed to force her eyes up to meet his. "Because you were angry with me… as you are now. I was afraid. I feared you would kill me. I fear you will—"

"I would never kill you," he interjected, and brushed the backs of his fingers across her cheek. The next second his hand wrapped around her throat and he snarled, "But if you are lying to me… I will butcher you."

Taryn's heart skipped several beats before slamming hard against her ribs, and she quickly shook her head. Her eyebrows furrowed as the fear that had already been flowing through her shot up to a level where it was hard to breathe, and almost impossible to find her voice to speak and convince him otherwise.

His hand tightened around her throat, sending her careening beyond the reach of fear as fury rose up to overwhelm her.

Cold steel. Heavy. Tight. Choking her.

She hissed at him, grasped his wrist and yanked it away from her throat, twisting it hard at the same time and tearing a pained yelped from him.

"I was bringing the sword to you," she snarled, the darkness in her voice shocking her, but not enough that she could escape the grip of it.

She tightened her grip on Tenak's arm, digging her emerging talons into his flesh and spilling his blood. His eyes darkened but they no longer frightened her. If he wanted to fight her, she would fight him back, and he would learn that she was no longer the meek little female he had always protected.

She was a fierce dragoness.

"I brought it to you because I need you to help me make them pay." She bared her fangs and spat on the floor between them, aiming it at those who had caged her, who had somehow broken her despite her attempts to stop them. "I want to make them all pay."

Tenak's grimace became a dark smile that pleased her too much, promising her retribution.

Vengeance.

"You are the only one who can help me!" she hissed and held his gaze, knowing that his only reflected the madness, the hunger for bloodshed and violence, that filled hers. "You are strong… more powerful than I… and with the sword… you will be *invincible*."

Tenak grinned and rose onto his feet, easily shaking her grip. He held his hand out to her, his eyes filled with a bloody promise, one she wanted to accept even when she knew she shouldn't.

"This valley is *our* kingdom now… but soon all of Hell will cower at *our* feet."

Taryn placed her trembling hand into his and allowed him to pull her onto those feet he spoke of, and the image his words evoked terrified her.

Because she had made it possible.

As she stared up into her brother's eyes, she could only feel one thing.

She had made a terrible mistake.

And all of Hell was going to pay for it.

CHAPTER 9

Bleu sipped the dark bitter liquid, the cream mug warming his left hand, and stared at the bustling mortals. Their idle chatter blended into one stream of sound that filled the silence in his mind as he relaxed in a corner of the large warmly-lit room, surveying them and picking out the differences between each individual. He took another sip, enjoying the buzz that chased through his entire body each time the liquid hit his tongue. He had become accustomed to the brew the mortals called coffee, slowly introducing himself to it, aware that it held the same risks as alcohol. Too much, too quickly and he would be hit with the full effects in a heartbeat, and the thought of bouncing around like a maniac, jacked up on caffeine, was not appealing.

It also tended to make it hard to hold his mortal guise. His black apparel of t-shirt, jeans and a long coat was only part of his disguise, and the easiest one to control since they were clothes he owned and had teleported to him before entering the establishment. The one he was in danger of losing control over was the more important part of his disguise, an elven trick that allowed him to blend into his environment by changing two key areas of his appearance—his eyes and his ears.

Right now, his eyes were a more human shade of green and the tips of his ears were rounded, but if he lost control, they would change back to violet and to pointed.

And gods help him if he really lost control and his fangs descended.

So, small sips were required, caffeine in moderation.

He sank into the armchair, green gaze idly following a male as he crossed the room to a group of waiting friends who greeted him with warm smiles and affectionate embraces. Losing interest, he switched his focus to another patron of the shop devoted to the dark brew, a younger male, one so awkward in his own skin that Bleu wanted to shake his head and give the boy a few pointers in how to hold himself with confidence, commanding the respect of those around him.

The teen shuffled from foot to foot in the queue, bright gaze leaping between his red scuffed shoes and the female serving behind the counter.

A crush, perhaps?

He had been young once, but he had certainly never been so unsure of himself, so embarrassed around females.

What in the gods' names did mortal society do to young males to turn them into such pathetic limp creatures, afraid of their own shadow in the presence of a pretty female?

He snorted and took another sip, diverted his attention elsewhere and settled it on a slightly older male, this one looking as if he had indulged in far too much feasting. His shorn hair was visibly receding as he removed a cap and then replaced it, neatening it as he moved through the occupied tables. The male stopped at one where a lonely female sat and Bleu canted his head. The female was pretty enough. Not beautiful, but she had kind eyes and a warm smile for the male as she stood and embraced him.

Bleu huffed and shut them out as they began to kiss, no longer interested in watching them.

He swirled his cooling coffee in his mug, his eyes on it, the gentle buzz in his veins quietening as his body purged the caffeine and the silence in his mind dissipating, whispered thoughts surfacing as his focus turned inwards.

He had come to this place to fill some time, but perhaps he had only thought that. Perhaps he had subconsciously had an ulterior motive for venturing to a place where mortals were known to pass idle time, thinking about things in their life or meeting with friends to talk.

Perhaps he had come here to think too.

That realisation seemed to open the floodgates, filling his mind with too many thoughts, all of which clashed, crashing against each other until the comfortable silence he had been enjoying became a cacophony he could no longer ignore.

The coffee cup shimmered out of focus, replaced by Loren in the courtyard, looking at him in a way that had spoken to him, telling him something without his prince having to use words, answering the question Bleu had done his best to ignore.

Why had he left the elf kingdom a month ago?

He could easily lie to himself, keeping the one he had been living rolling and pretending the truth was the lie instead, but he was tired and everything over the past few days had mounted up on his shoulders and they felt heavy now.

Pressing down on his heart.

His prince was right.

He had left because he had no longer had a purpose or a place where he felt he belonged.

For four thousand two hundred years, he'd had the purpose and that place, but now things were changing.

No.

Now everything had changed, and it felt as if it had happened in the blink of an eye.

Forty-two centuries, most of his life, lived in the same way. A routine that had been ingrained so deeply in him that now that it was gone, he wasn't sure what the hell he was doing anymore.

His prince no longer needed him as a personal advisor, or to take care of him. He no longer had to attend to Loren's morning ritual, entering his rooms at the castle before he woke to open the curtains and the double doors to allow light and air into the space. He no longer had to ensure Loren had the blood he needed to heal whenever he was injured, or that he didn't overwork himself and had the rest he required to remain strong.

He had been reduced to a glorified bodyguard, his primary responsibilities taken away from him.

By Olivia.

Loren's mate and the kingdom's new princess.

Olivia had replaced him, and Loren no longer needed him.

It was the same with Iolanthe, his sister. She had Kyter now, her mate who travelled with her on her adventures when she was hunting for an artefact, there to get her out of whatever trouble she landed herself in. It had been Bleu's job once.

For his entire life, since Iolanthe had been brought into it, he had watched over her, had protected her and taken care of her.

Now she had another male to do that for her.

His fingers tightened around the mug, threatening to shatter the delicate clay.

He no longer had a purpose when once his purpose with those two people, the two he was closest to, had meant everything to him. Serving as Loren's aide and commander, and protecting his sister, had been his life and he had loved it.

Bleu closed his eyes, his eyebrows dipping low as he tried to shut out the noise of the coffee shop and the roar of his heart as it ached, throbbing madly behind his ribs. He rubbed the spot over it with his free hand, shifting the black t-shirt he wore. It was just the caffeine making it pound and hurt. Nothing else.

He set the coffee cup down and focused on something else.

The dragon.

His thoughts were quick to shift to her whenever he felt lost and adrift, uncertain. He mulled over everything he had learned in the last month, every shred of information, even the small titbits that had seemed like nothing at first glance. He lost himself in his hunt instead, systematically shutting down the parts of him that were shaken by the changes in his life.

Changes that were jarring and unsettling, difficult for him to process.

Gods, he wasn't processing them at all.

Loren knew it. Bleu had seen it in his eyes and knew what the male had wanted to say to him, what he would have said if they had been in private.

He had responded to the upheaval in his life in the only way he knew—by distancing himself.

Loren had pointed it out countless times during their centuries together, always with a smile, a laugh in his voice even though he was deadly serious, as if he thought delivering it in such a manner would stop Bleu from glaring at him.

It never did.

But he didn't know how else to react. He hadn't received the lessons that Loren had during his upbringing, given training in handling delicate situations often involving the feelings of others, ones that had enabled him to process his own emotions too.

Bleu had been trained as a soldier from his youth, taught how to respond to situations in a more tactical way, and that was exactly what he was doing now in order to protect his heart from taking more damage.

He had withdrawn in order to regroup.

He sipped the coffee and grimaced as the cold liquid hit his tongue, set the cup down and pushed it away from him, sliding it across the dark wooden surface of the round table. He kept his hand outstretched, fingers resting on the table top, his green eyes fixed on them, his mind wandering a course that was unfamiliar to him.

One that had it connecting to the heart he had locked behind walls of elven metal so impenetrable he had thought it safe, when in reality it had been exposed all this time, allowing Loren and Iolanthe to steal a piece of it and leave him bereft as they had left him behind.

He growled under his breath and fought to push his thoughts onto a more stable path, one free of the tangled web of emotions slowly snaring him and pulling him deeper into his feelings.

Rosalind flashed into his mind, a fleeting image of her looking down at Vail, her blue eyes filled with adoration and tenderness, and Vail gazing back up at her, the corners of his lips tilted into a satisfied and peaceful smile.

Bleu curled his fingers into fists and the sound of wood creaking hurled him out of his memories and back to the present. He stared at his serrated claws where they were still pressed deep into the table top and the long ragged grooves he had cut into the wood with them without even realising it.

He hadn't issued a command to his armour.

Hell, he hadn't even had it out under his mortal clothing of black jeans, boots, t-shirt and long coat.

It was out now though, covering him from toe to neck, forming his claws.

A response to the darkness that had surged through him on remembering how tender Rosalind had been with Vail?

He drew down a deep breath and focused on his armour, willing it to return to the black and silver bands around his wrists. It obeyed, but not instantly, taking more than a second before it responded to the command. Not good.

If he wasn't fully in control of his armour, it was because he wasn't fully in control of his emotions.

His eyes widened.

He swiftly raised his bare hands to his ears and grimaced as he found them pointed, their tips long and thankfully covered by his hair. He willed them to change, felt them become rounded again and knew his eyes had switched to green too, concealing what he was.

Holy fuck, the council would have him in the cells in a heartbeat if he exposed their kind to mortals.

Perhaps thinking in a room filled with them hadn't been his wisest move after all, but it wasn't as if he had known his jealousy would darken his mood to the extent that he lost control over his emotions.

Jealousy.

Bleu blew out a hard breath.

Gods, some fucked up part of him was jealous.

It was envious of Olivia for being closest to Loren now. It was resentful towards Kyter for taking his role as Iolanthe's protector. It was jealous of Vail for being able to find someone to love him.

When Bleu couldn't find someone who could love him.

He almost laughed out loud when it hit him that Iolanthe would have been proud of him for actually working through his feelings and admitting the things he had—that Sable had wounded him, and seeing his friends and sister finding their mates, getting caught up in bonds and love, had tipped his world off balance.

So he had run away, seeking solitude, space away from everyone who had hurt him and time to come to terms with everything that had happened. It was still too much. His life had been the same for four millennia and now everything was different and it felt as if it had happened in the blink of an eye to him.

He couldn't deal with it.

His focus immediately leaped back to the dragon, pulling her to the front of his mind. The riot in his head dulled, his emotions settling as he worked through everything he had uncovered about her.

Only this time it struck him that there was a deeper reason he always thought of her whenever things became too much for him.

She was the only constant, the one thing he could depend upon to be the same as before as his world crumbled around him.

She was his anchor in this storm and his reason for swimming forwards, pushing onwards when there was a part of him that wanted to stop and just let the waves crash over him and suck him down into the darkness.

He felt eyes on him but he didn't seek out their owner. Females had been studying him constantly from the moment he had entered the coffee shop. Watching him closely. Many of them did it secretly, but others did it openly. Boldly. They courted his attention, but only one female could hold it right now, had seized it in her talons with a grip so fierce he couldn't shake it.

The dragon.

His fingers idly caressed the scars on his neck and he cursed under his breath in the elf tongue as they tingled in response.

She could have cleaved his head off with the blow that had given him this permanent reminder of her. If he hadn't come to his senses and ducked to his right at the last second, she might have done just that. He had been a fool, underestimating her strength and how dangerous she was, but he had learned his lesson.

This time, when they crossed paths, he would succeed.

He caught the handle of his cup and brought it back to him. He turned it in his hand, tipped it towards him, stared down at his reflection on the surface of the black liquid. He would find her. It was only a matter of time now that he had assembled his team. When he returned to their stronghold, he would issue the order to head out. They would scour the dragon realm and not stop until the female was within his grasp.

The sensation of eyes on him grew stronger and harder to ignore. He could understand their reasons for studying him—elves had beauty and grace that attracted mortal eyes.

He looked up through his lashes at the females dotted around the room, the ones whose eyes were on him. It would be easy to bed any one of them. Hell, he could bed more than one at a time and they wouldn't complain. Had done it plenty of times in the past. He leaned back and openly eyed them, gaining pretty blushes from some and bold smiles from others as he leisurely perused them.

He could lose himself in any one of them for a short time.

His green gaze settled on the blonde behind the counter.

The one who had been giving him come-fuck-me smiles all night.

He was tired of being alone. He needed some female company, even if it was only for a short time.

Even if it couldn't be forever.

CHAPTER 10

Bleu shuddered as nails raked over his shoulders, clawed at his hair and tugged on it. He groaned and kissed lower, trailing his lips over the flat of her stomach, blood heated to a thousand degrees as his mind raced forwards, towards his destination. The female moaned and wriggled, bucked up against him in a way that spoke of frustration.

Desperation.

He would give her the release she craved soon enough. She just needed a little patience, because he needed a little time to get her to the point where that release would blow her mind.

He licked her warm skin just above her hip and she spread her thighs, inviting him lower. He growled in his throat and kissed downwards, open mouthed wet ones that had her trembling beneath his touch, moaning with each brush of his lips across her flesh. She wriggled again and he pulled back, silently admonishing her by withdrawing from her.

She pouted, a pretty little one that had him aching to forget what he had been doing, rise over her and take her lower lip between his teeth to nibble on it.

Bleu raked his eyes over her bare body, traversing firm rounded breasts peaked with dusky nipples begging for his mouth, and the flat plane of her stomach, downwards to the place where he wanted to be.

She brought her legs together, stealing it from view.

He frowned at her, earning a wicked smile, and held her gaze as he skimmed his hands up her thighs to her knees and edged them apart, forcing her to open to him again. Her little breathless moan almost did him in and he groaned right back at her, his eyes dropping to the apex of her thighs. She glistened with arousal in the candlelight, making his mouth water and fangs itch, and his hard cock jump in anticipation.

Gods, she would be warm and welcoming, tight around him.

He dipped his left hand between her thighs and felt just how wet she was as she bucked against his fingers, rubbing herself along them. He took hold of his cock in his right hand, unable to deny the urge to fist it as he touched her, running his hand up and down its length as he kneeled between her legs and edged his fingers lower.

Her eyes widened as he pressed one inside her, her body quivering as she tipped her head back and moaned, the low sound filled with pleasure that he could almost feel in her. He increased his grip on his length, matching how tight she was around his finger, and breathed hard, struggling to tamp down the surge of desire as he imagined being inside her.

She rocked against him, riding his finger, and he withdrew it and released his cock before he made a fool of himself. Her glare chastised him but it faded when he leaned over her, his eyes on hers, and lowered himself. Her gaze turned hooded as he swept his tongue over her aroused nub, flicking the pert bead with the tip, eliciting a gasp from her. One of her hands shot to the top of his head, fingers tangling in his hair, gripping tightly, as the other one clutched the pillow above her head.

Her teeth sank into her lower lip and her eyebrows furrowed as he laved her, long slow strokes from core to nub, tasting every delicious inch of her.

When her moans grew in volume, her body tense and flexing, seeking release, he slipped two fingers back inside her. Her heat scalded him, her moisture coating his fingers and allowing them to easily slide in and out. He groaned against her and lightly bit her pert nub, and couldn't stop himself from rubbing against the mattress to find some relief of his own.

Fuck, he needed to be inside her hot little body, claiming her and spilling himself, feeling her quake around him as she climaxed.

He needed to lose himself in her.

He reared up and over her, caging her between his arms as he supported himself on his fists between her arms and her ribs. She gazed up at him, eyes hazy with desire, dark with need. He growled and kissed her, hard and deep, possessing her mouth in the way he wanted to possess her body. She moaned into his mouth and wrapped herself around him, pulling him down into contact with her. Her moist core pressed against his cock, and his eyes rolled back in his head as he groaned and barely stopped himself from rocking against her, dimly aware that if he did it would be game over and he wanted to find release inside her.

The warmly-lit room spun past him in a blur and he sank into the mattress as she landed on top of him, her smile wicked and eyes hungry. He didn't resist her as she claimed his wrists and pinned them above his head, shoving them hard against the pillows and then pushing them higher. He obeyed as she made him hold the wooden bars of the headboard, clutching them and surrendering to her.

She lowered her dark gaze to his lips and then his chest, and briefly dipped her body to press into his, caging his erection between them and scalding him with her wet heat. He closed his eyes and tipped his head back, and rocked his hips, easily sliding between her thighs, tearing delicious moans from her.

Her breath was hot on his right cheek as she kissed across it, teased him with a brief brush of her mouth across his and continued down the other side of his face. He shuddered as she swept her lips down the line of his throat and kissed the scars on it, mouth following each long ridged line that darted from behind his ear to his collarbone. When she reached the end of the last mark, she kept moving lower, kissing across his chest.

She raked fingernails over his pectorals and he groaned as she caught his nipples, sending a spark of pain-pleasure skittering across his skin. The moan became a growl as she moved lower, stealing her body away from his and leaving his cock exposed to the cooler air. He wanted to haul her back up to him, roll her over and plunge deep into her, but he forced his hands to remain where they were, locked around the headboard, and focused on her as she moved lower, her lips trailing fire across his abdomen.

Anticipation swirled and built inside him, cranking him tighter. His cock kicked, balls tightening as they waited, eager for her attention.

She held herself away from him, only her lips touching his skin together with the satin brush of her hair. Torture. He rolled his hips, every muscle flexing as he tried to reach her, and she clucked her tongue at him. Her hands caught his hips and she pinned them, holding him in place, tearing a groan from his lips that shocked him.

Gods, he had never sounded so lost before, so desperate and wild, but he couldn't stop himself. He needed her, ached for her touch and for release. She had to feel that. She had to know what she was doing to him, driving him to the edge and over it.

Bleu ground his teeth and frowned as she breathed on his cock, bathing the sensitive head in moist heat.

Too much.

He shuddered and moaned, and began to uncurl his hands.

The first brush of her lips over the head of his length had them clamping so tight around the wooden poles that he heard them snap beneath his grip. He couldn't feel them give though. He couldn't feel anything but the intense rush of pleasure that blasted through him as she kissed down his cock and licked back up it, flicking her tongue over the head before tonguing the slit, driving him so far over the edge that he was freefalling with no way of saving himself.

It was game over when she wrapped her lips around him, taking him into her hot mouth, shattering his control.

Everything blurred into one stream of pleasure, bliss so fierce that he lost himself entirely, becoming nothing more than sensation. He rolled his hips in time with her movements, driving back into her mouth as she sucked him.

Gods, this was what he had needed and he revelled in it, gave himself over to it and let it seize control of him, driving everything else out of his mind.

Losing himself in her.

Her gaze was hot on him as her hand joined her mouth, stroking down as she took him back inside and up as she sucked, each one harder than the last. He swallowed and tried to convince his eyes to open, to seek her and watch her as she worked magic on his cock, but it was impossible as he spiralled higher, burned hotter. Her free hand cupped his balls, tugging and teasing, stroking and pushing him higher still.

Hotter still.

He couldn't take it.

He growled and tensed, every inch of him going taut as his lips peeled back off his teeth. His fangs punched long and his ears flared back, the pointed tips extending as fire and lightning rushed through him.

His hips jerked up, thrusting his cock deep into her mouth as it pulsed, throbbing hard and shooting jets of his seed into her. She swallowed around him, caressed his shaft and his balls, teased him down as he fought for air, her touch gentle now as if she sensed she might break him.

He was on the verge of shattering completely, numbed by his powerful release, blinded by pleasure that was more intense than anything he had experienced before.

When his breathing slowed, his heart settling at last, and he had control over his body again, he slowly opened his eyes and looked down at the female.

Soft striking eyes met his.

Violet-to-white.

The most beautiful eyes he had ever seen.

Gods, a male could lose himself in those eyes and never want to come back.

Bleu reached for her and brushed his fingers across her cheek. Her eyes darkened, lips parted, and his heart gave a hard kick as she took his thumb into her mouth and sucked it, holding his gaze.

His cock stirred, hungry for more of the beautiful female who reacted so sweetly to him, passionate and ardent, fierce and possessive.

A little bit wicked.

His perfect match.

Darkness encroached, snuffing out the candles, throwing her into shadow, and he frowned as it swallowed him.

Bleu breathed hard, trembling all over, flushed with heat as his heart pounded. He frowned, confused for a moment, and then groaned and screwed his eyes shut as he threw a mental command to the bedside lamp.

He didn't want to look.

He convinced his eyes to open.

Shame swept through him as he stared down at his bare legs tangled in the dark blue sheets of the double bed and his cock where it still pulsed against his stomach, and then he grimaced all over again when he spotted the warm liquid pooled in his navel and running down his right side.

Fantastic.

He bit out a sigh and sank into the bed, his body still trembling with the release running through it, turning his bones to rubber beneath his liquid muscles.

Gods, he hadn't felt a release like that, that intense and powerful, in… he wasn't sure how long. He didn't remember it ever feeling that good in reality, and it had only been a dream.

How good would it feel in reality with her?

Bleu shoved that question away before he could supply an answer to it, scrubbed a hand over his face and shook his head.

It was never going to happen. She was an enemy of his kingdom, his princes.

Holy fuck, his day had just gotten a lot worse if he was thinking about Vail as one of his princes again.

He groaned.

That groan only worsened as a soft knock sounded on the door of his room and a familiar female voice travelled through it.

"Are you well, Brother?" Iolanthe said. "You were screaming… or something like it."

A blush blazed up his cheeks. Yes, his day had just gotten so much worse. The last thing he needed was his little sister hearing him climax from a damned dream. He shouldn't have stopped to rest at Underworld, the nightclub in London owned by her mate. He should have gone straight back to the stronghold.

"I was having a nightmare," Bleu snapped, because it seemed true the more he looked at it.

Dreaming of the female dragon was a fucking nightmare.

His whole life felt like one right now.

He recalled the coffee shop, and how he had been on the brink of flirting his way between the pretty blonde's thighs when the damned dragon had hijacked his mind and his body, and any enthusiasm he had felt for the mortal had deflated. Suddenly, every female in the café had looked unappealing, and all he had been able to think about was the beautiful female who had haunted him for centuries.

The bedroom door opened a crack and Bleu teleported in an instant, appearing before it and slamming the flat of his palm against it, forcing it shut.

Iolanthe squeaked.

"I'm naked." A reasonable excuse since he was naked and the evidence of his depraved hunger for the female dragon was now running down his thigh. He growled. "Give me a minute. I need a shower."

"I will wait in the break room. Come along when you feel ready to talk, Bleu." She moved away but he remained standing at the door, his hand pressed against it and not to keep it shut anymore.

It trembled as it supported his weight.

Talk.

Bleu cursed his little sister for being so damned astute, so attuned to him. He didn't do talking and she knew that, so he wasn't sure why she thought he would this time.

Or why he ended up taking a quick shower, throwing his jeans and t-shirt on, and padding barefoot down the narrow corridor to the break room.

To talk.

CHAPTER 11

Iolanthe looked up as Bleu entered the break room of the nightclub, a basic kitchen tucked into the corner of the room behind her. Her long black hair spilled around her shoulders, blending into her dark satin robe, and her violet eyes greeted him with a tender warmth that only served to pull a sigh from his lips.

Her slender fingers toyed with a red mug filled with coffee, and there was another cup on the round white plastic table top opposite her.

He shoved his damp hair out of his face and slumped into the chair in front of the mug she had evidently poured for him.

He lifted the hideously decorated white cup to his lips, ignoring the spritely unicorn on it. She had chosen it on purpose, secretly amusing herself with how he would react to being given such a childish, feminine drinking vessel. He wasn't going to give her the pleasure of seeing the reaction she had envisioned. He wasn't in the mood.

"What is wrong, Brother?" Iolanthe set her red mug down and her face filled with tenderness and concern that warmed him, lifting his mood and chasing away the black storm clouds, leaving him on the verge of sighing into his coffee like some damned female as he contemplated an answer to her question. "When you came to us tonight looking for a place to rest, you did not look tired… you looked weary. Something is troubling you."

It was, and there was little point in denying it. Iolanthe had been born stubborn, a determined little thing from the moment she had been brought into his world like a ray of purest sunshine, a gift from the gods themselves. She had quickly learned to bend him to her will and the ways of getting whatever she wanted from him, and he had always had difficulty denying her.

"I am hunting the dragon again," he said and the look she gave him warned that he wasn't giving her what she wanted—he was giving her excuses.

She folded her arms across her chest.

He sighed into his coffee and couldn't believe he was about to do this. He was going to talk to her. Hell, his world had already changed beyond recognition. He might as well keep rolling with it and change some other things too.

Or roll them back to how they had been centuries ago, when he had shared everything with Iolanthe, before he had closed himself off.

He needed to do that now, getting it all off his chest, or he would probably go mad.

"Why were you in the mortal realm?" she said before he could speak and he knew she wasn't going to like the answer.

"I came to see Vail about tracking the sword." He frowned at the table. "Fuery was there."

He didn't need to look at his sister to see the black scowl she was giving him, or reach with his senses to detect the anger that rose in her.

It wasn't anger towards him.

She was angry about what Vail and Fuery had done to him, and had been all her life.

"If I ever see that male again, I will not be held responsible for my actions," she bit out and he almost smiled.

Fuery had always borne the brunt of her anger, and part of Bleu cherished how fiercely she reacted whenever his name was mentioned, turning into a vicious little thing on his behalf, filled with a hunger to act out some sort of vengeance on the elf male.

Her violet eyes landed on him and he looked up at her, his amusement falling away as their gazes locked and she stripped away the barriers around his feelings. He cursed her and the way she had always been able to do that, tearing down his carefully constructed defences. He had tried so hard to hold her at a distance as he did with others, not allowing her to see how deeply things affected him.

"You have that look again," she whispered with a knowing half smile. "You hate it, but we are siblings, bound by blood."

He huffed. "I do not hate it."

Iolanthe leaned forwards, reaching across the white plastic table top to place her hand over his. She squeezed it and he looked down at their joined hands and then up into her eyes.

They were soft and warm, filled with affection. "You always were easy for me to read… but perhaps that is only because you showed yourself to me… before you shut that male away behind a wall of false smiles and easy laughter that never reached your eyes. I know you, Bleu. I know you because I know me. We are cut from the same cloth."

He wanted to look away from her, to bring up that barrier she spoke of, but he didn't have the strength.

Her smile turned sympathetic. "You are passionate… emotional… and though you try not to be… you are. You love deeply and that only makes you easier to wound without people realising it, especially when you refuse to show those feelings. You ache for your fated one, and so you foolishly fall for any female who bestows smiles and affection on you."

He pulled his hand away from hers and glared into her eyes. She didn't repent.

With a smile, she said, "Do not pretend you do not want your ki'ara."

He never had and he saw little point in attempting such a farce with his sister, since she had been the one he had subjected to his ridiculous prattling about finding his mate all those centuries ago.

A sigh escaped her and she leaned back. "I wish people did not hurt you. I wish Vail had not darkened your heart and Fuery not slammed the barriers around it shut."

Bleu set his jaw and kept glaring at her. Suddenly, talking didn't sound so appealing, not when she was determined to drag his heart through the darkest reaches of Hell.

He stared into her eyes, silently challenging her to dare to say more on the subject. He knew his past. He knew the pain Vail and Fuery had caused, the scars he still bore inside. He could never forgive them for what they had done to him, and he could never forgive himself for allowing such a weakness to gain a hold inside him.

He had been weak. Young and foolish. He had admired and respected Fuery. He had admired and respected Vail too.

He had damn near adored them.

That adoration, that devotion, had only got him wounded.

The story of his fucking life.

Iolanthe's knowing sigh grated on his last nerve and he bared his fangs at her.

She scowled at him. "Do not blame me for the actions of others."

Why not? Hadn't she hurt him too?

Hadn't Loren and Sable?

She talked of him holding himself at a distance and closing himself off in order to avoid being wounded, but such tactics didn't work. The evidence of that was right in front of him. He had built walls around his heart, determined to never allow anyone into it again. He had refused to feel deeply for anyone, so he wouldn't be hurt again. He had fought to purge that weakness and never allow it to infest him. He had decided to be strong.

Invulnerable.

Yet, Iolanthe and Loren had somehow breached that barrier, and even Sable had broken it.

Gods, was there no way to protect himself?

"Speak to me, Bleu," Iolanthe whispered and he realised he had stopped again.

He had withdrawn into himself, something that was habit now, difficult to break even when he wanted to talk with his sister in the way he had long ago, telling her everything that was on his mind and in his heart.

She moved to the seat on his left, placed her hand over his on the table, and stared at it, her expression shifting towards sombreness.

"You are not alone." She kept her gaze on their hands but he felt as if she had pierced his soul with the awareness in those four words, had looked right down into it and had seen the truth he tried so hard to hide. "You are not unloved. I am sorry that she hurt you… that I hurt you."

She lifted her bright violet gaze to his.

"One day you will hurt me back. One day you will find that ki'ara you dreamed of and she will steal every drop of your love."

Bleu couldn't ignore that, or the ripple of hurt that went through his sister. He turned his hand beneath hers and clasped it as he looked deep into her eyes.

"Ridiculous. I will always love you. Forever, Iolanthe. No one can take my love away from you." He wasn't sure anyone even wanted to try, that he would ever find his fated one, but he was sure that if he found his mate, his love for her wouldn't diminish his love for Iolanthe.

She toyed with his fingers, her eyes on them, and smiled mischievously.

"Since you know that in your heart, and our hearts were created the same, you must also know that mine is as constant in its affection as yours." She slid him a sideways glance. "Do you not?"

Bleu nodded and then frowned as he realised she had tricked him into admitting that he did know that, had made him realise that he knew it to the very depth of his soul.

"My love for Kyter does not take any of my love away from you." She swept her fingers across his cheek and frowned back at him. "I am sorry it has troubled you though. I never wish to hurt you… although I do seem good at it."

He managed a smile at her attempt to lighten the mood. "I have lost count of the number of bones I have broken because of you… or the number of assassins and mercenaries who count me among the list of foes they wish dead the most."

She shrugged and smiled, an innocent little one that might still work on her mate when she got herself into trouble and needed help but had long ago lost its effect on him.

"So what was your nightmare about?" That question hit him hard in the gut and he could only stare at her as he considered his answer.

As seconds ticked past, her gaze grew more curious, venturing deeper into his eyes as if she could find the answer there.

"It was just a nightmare." He hadn't told her details about his dreams in the past and there was no damned way he was going to start now.

"Do you often have nightmares about the dragon?"

His breath left him in a rush and his eyes darted between hers, and he might as well have just tossed all his cards onto the table because her little smile was victorious. Damn, she had played him again and he had fallen right into her trap. He had to be more careful around her. She was clever, used to winkling information out of people who didn't want to talk, a trick that was useful in her line of work.

His eyebrows knit in a tight frown and she huffed.

"Do not give me that look. It was not difficult to put two and two together to come up with four, Brother. You came here looking weary, and you spoke of hunting the dragon again. I know that it plays on your mind now as it did in the past, and it was easy to guess that the dragon was the focus of your nightmare." She always had been able to see right through him, and perhaps talking a little about his mission would prove helpful.

Iolanthe had travelled across Hell during her adventures, into areas most didn't dare traverse, including lands bordering the Devil's domain. There was a chance she would be able to give him information that could lead to him finding the dragon.

But he had to be careful, gathering the cards he had scattered in front of her and holding them close to his chest this time, because if he talked too much about the female dragon, his sister would probably see through him again.

He needed to keep her thinking this conversation was all business, that the dragon was just a mission to him.

He paused.

Was she something more?

He really wasn't sure, and he was too tired, too fresh from the dream, to consider an honest answer to that question.

"The dragon surfaced again a few months ago, and since I had free time, I decided to track it across Hell and see if I could uncover where it had gone." He leaned back in the chair and Iolanthe rose from hers, took their two coffee mugs and walked to the opposite side of the room, to the kitchen there. She lifted the jug from the machine, refilled their mugs, and brought them back to him. He looked down into his as she set it on the white table in front of him and took the seat across from him, gaze growing unfocused as he stared at the dark surface. "When I returned to Prince Loren, he tasked me with hunting the dragon and allowed me to pull together my old team."

Iolanthe laughed. "And is Leif still in love with Prince Loren?"

Bleu smiled, couldn't really contain it as he caught the mischief shining in his sister's eyes, and the way her lips curved said that she liked seeing him smile again. It fell from his face as he considered how much he had changed from the male she had grown up with and faced the truth she had put out there—that he forced smiles and laughter when the situation called for it.

He hadn't really had much to smile or laugh about in the last few millennia. It felt as if he had slowly forgotten how to do such things, each false smile or laugh stealing more of his ability to allow real ones out.

"I believe Leif still holds a deep affection for our prince." Bleu couldn't hold that against the male though, because he had behaved in such a way once, desperately emulating a male he wanted to be more than anything in the world in the ridiculous hope that male would notice him.

The difference was, he had been a youth at the time and Leif was a grown male.

"You hold one too," Iolanthe said and he frowned before he realised that she wasn't talking about his feelings for Vail, ones that male had murdered together with most of his legion that night forty-two centuries ago. She was talking about his affection for Loren. "It is nice you have friends."

Bleu waved her away and sipped his coffee. Not hiding in it. He just needed the caffeine. His sudden thirst and interest in the drink had nothing to do with avoiding Iolanthe's knowing gaze.

"Ah… you are upset with Prince Loren too."

He scowled over the rim of his stupid unicorn mug at her.

Her victorious smile pulled a sharp huff from him. Played again. Fuck, he needed to stop falling into her traps. Hadn't he sworn to keep his cards closer to his chest? Yet here he was, tossing them all down in front of her again.

Iolanthe clasped her mug in both hands and held his gaze. "You will find your mate one day, Bleu… when you least expect it. You told me that only I could love you forever, that everyone only loved you for now or not at all…"

He was tempted to look away but he was damned if he was going to let himself go through with such a weak move, even when looking into his sister's eyes only made him feel the depth of what she was saying and it scoured his insides, hollowing his chest out and leaving it cold. He had told her those things when she had been on the verge of mating with Kyter, when his guard had been broken by Sable and his heart left exposed and vulnerable. He should have known she would remember them.

She released her mug and reached across the table, holding her hand out to him. He just stared at it and she sighed, a soft one that conveyed a wealth of hurt.

"You are wrong, Bleu," she whispered, her violet eyes round and filled with warmth as they held his. "The truth is, you will find your mate, and you will finally have the one female you have been waiting for and she will be worth that wait."

He hated to admit it, but it felt good to hear that. It hit him with the force of a Hell beast in a raging charge, but was as comforting as an angel's embrace.

He shook his head. "I am beginning to see why people dump their problems on others."

Iolanthe's laugh filled the room, a soft melody that almost made him smile again. "It is called sharing a burden and feelings, and you used to do it all the time…"

Her smile fell, sucking the light from the room, and she looked down at her coffee.

"Before I lost myself in the war with Vail," he said it for her and she lifted her eyes back to his, an apology shining in them. "I lost hope… but the war and protecting Loren became my life and my purpose, and I was fine with that."

"Was fine?" She frowned at him. "Past tense?"

"Am fine," he corrected but she already looked as if she didn't believe him.

"You were not fine, Brother. You merely thought you were. You gave up on something that had meant the world to you."

He shrugged that off. "I'm fine with it now."

The look she gave him called him a liar.

So it wasn't the truth, and there was little point in trying to pretend that it was since he had just spilled the bloody contents of his heart to her. It was ridiculous of him to attempt to deny that he wanted to find the mate he dreamed of now more than ever, when she had pieced together how seeing everyone important in his life happily mated made him feel, but it was habit and it was old, and those ones were the worst to break.

"Will you answer a question honestly for me, Bleu?"

He didn't like the sound of that, but he nodded, curious about what she wanted to know, even when he feared that it would hurt him.

"Actually… do not answer it… but think about it, as I have thought about it." That sounded even more ominous to him, and he leaned back in his chair again, not sure he liked where this was going at all. "Were your feelings for the huntress real or a product of your circumstances at the time?"

She toyed with her mug again as he tried to process what she was saying, his ears ringing as if she had just smacked him around the head with a mace, brain fuzzy as thoughts collided in it, unleashed by what had been such an innocent-sounding question.

Her lips moved and he had to focus hard to hear what she was saying above the riot in his skull.

"I saw at the time she had wounded you, and I believed you had loved her with all of your heart… but looking back now, knowing your feelings about seeing myself and Prince Loren find our mates… I am no longer sure."

Holy fuck, he wasn't either.

He had wanted Sable and that want had clouded his vision and his heart, but leaving the elf kingdom behind and focusing everything on pursuing the dragon female had cleared that vision and Iolanthe had just pierced the veil of shadows over his heart, allowing light to stream into it again.

That light washed over memories he had buried deep, feelings long forgotten, and he couldn't get enough air into his lungs as everything he had somehow suppressed came rushing back to the surface.

Leaving him reeling.

Gods.

He slumped into the chair, staring at his sister but not seeing her as it all fell into place and he felt like a fool.

Because of what had been happening at the time he had met Sable, he had somehow tangled together his pent up desire with the loneliness he had felt on seeing Loren wrapped up in Olivia, falling in love with her and torn yet excited about the prospect of having a mate.

The result had been him believing that he felt something more than mere lust for Sable.

When all along it had been impossible.

Because he had already met his fated female.

CHAPTER 12

Taryn paced her room, her legs trembling and body aching, but not from fear or her brother's attack. No. It was a dream that had left her weak and shaking, and in the most delicious way.

She shoved that thought out of her head. It had no place in her mind, or in her heart. Not when the dream she had experienced had felt more real than ever.

More dangerous than ever.

The elf male had slept in time with her and that vision had been a strange reality, shared between them as if they had been together, not countless leagues apart in separate beds. Each touch, sound, taste, sight and emotion had flowed through her, wrapped around her and left her lost in the male, in the passion and desire, and the sweet high of a coming together that had burned her to ashes.

She had often wondered how it would feel if they slept at the same time, sharing a vision, but she had never imagined that wild and frenzied need, that heat and hunger, and the sheer bliss she had experienced.

Bliss that had her quivering still, bone-deep satisfied.

Gods, *dear gods*, if the male could make being with him that intoxicating and powerful in her dreams, what could he do in reality?

It didn't bear thinking about.

She wasn't sure she would survive it.

She tried to divert the course of her thoughts away from the elf male and back to her brother, but the damned male refused to leave her and her mind kept conjuring images from her dream, visions of them naked and tangled together, lost in the throes of passion. She closed her eyes and gave herself over to those images, imagining him stroking his fingers over her bare skin, teasing her senses with the light caress. Her fingers trailed where his would, caressing over her right breast to catch her pebbled nipple before he dropped lower, sweeping his touch over the flare of her hip, torturing her with the anticipation of where he would head next.

Taryn bit her lip and skimmed her hand down the flat of her belly.

A feral growl rumbled through the castle and her hand stilled, her heart leaping into her throat as she swung her gaze towards the wooden door of her apartment.

Her brother had returned.

She swallowed hard, trying to get her heart back down into her chest, and used her limited magic to call her clothes, dressing in a pair of violet leathers and a cream corset. Fury flowed through the building, reaching under her door to caress around her ankles before swirling upwards to encompass her. Her brother was angry about something.

She rushed to the door, yanked it open and hurried barefoot down the corridor, the black stone cool beneath her bare feet. Her violet-to-white hair bounced across her bare shoulders with each stride and her eyes charted the course ahead of her as she increased her speed, concerned her brother was angry with her.

Or worse.

What if the elf male had been closer than she had thought?

Gods help him if he had been caught by Tenak.

When trying to hide the sword, Taryn had seen the cells in the dungeon of the castle, had scented the dried blood on the flagstones that had been old, but not old enough.

Her brother didn't only kill trespassers who entered his valley. Sometimes, he did far worse.

A female scream reached her ears and she skidded to a halt at the top of the grand staircase in the vestibule, legs trembling and heart racing as she smelled blood.

She shook her head, feet frozen to the spot even as a small courageous part of her said to intervene and stop whatever madness her brother was inflicting on the innocent female.

The greater part of herself was already too far gone, plunging deep into her memories, pulling up the darkness from the depth of her soul and throwing the black veil over her. Her knees struck the smooth stone, her breath leaving her in a rush as those memories swallowed her and the darkness held her in a grip so fierce she couldn't breathe.

Could only feel.

Cold hands on her skin. Hot breath on her neck.

Words whispered in her ear, a threat meant to stir fear that would weaken her, allowing the male to break her.

Taryn clawed at her hair and then at the male, shoving him away, fighting him as he tried to force himself on her. She raked talons over his flesh, scoring deep and spilling blood. Dug them into his skin until they hit bone and snarled through sharp teeth at him, snapping and growling, determined to take a chunk out of his neck and end him.

Strong hands clasped her upper arms, pinning them against her chest, and then she was on her back, those same hands pressing down hard on her shoulders.

Her dragon instincts roared to life and she lashed out, kicking and clawing, shrieking at the male as the transformation coursed through her. The collar around her neck didn't stop it this time. She roared as her form shifted, bones growing and scales rippling over her skin, and threw her head back as wings sprouted from her back, stretching wide to span the entrance hall. Her front paws hit the floor of the vestibule, one back leg remaining on the upper level and one on the staircase.

"Taryn."

That word was a blur in her ears, unfamiliar and strange, even when a dim part of her thought she should know it.

She knew nothing but fury, pain and rage, and a hunger to kill.

She reared back and lowered her gaze to the one who had spoken.

A male.

Her jowls peeled back off her fangs as she growled at him, her eyes narrowing and focus sharpening on the male. Blood pumped from deep gashes in his left side, coursing over his bare skin, seeping into the waist of his purple leathers. Blood that coated her claws too.

She raked her eyes over him, snarled when she saw the ties of his trousers were open.

He meant to break her.

She swept her paw down, slammed it into the male and sent him flying across the room. He grunted as he hit the wall, the sound satisfying but not enough, a mere hit of pleasure that birthed a hunger for another taste. She dropped to all four paws in the cramped space, twisted her body so she could reach the male, and lashed out at him again.

He leaped, springing high into the air, and she snarled as he landed on her paw as it struck the ground where he had been.

Infuriating male.

"Taryn!"

That word again. This time, it gave her pause, sparking a strange sensation within her.

She shook it away and lashed out again, sweeping her other paw around to catch the male. He growled as he twisted through the air, spinning, limbs flying in all directions, and barked out a delicious cry as he hit the wall above the arched entrance and then slammed into the floor.

She turned to strikc him again and fell to her right, the awkward angle of having her hind legs at the top of the staircase tipping her off balance. She crashed hard into the wall, whimpered as her right wing bent back, and flinched as her jaw cracked on the floor and the banister of the staircase jabbed into her ribs.

The male picked himself up and she snorted as he approached her, a soft look on his bloodied face.

He rubbed his right hand across his chest, smearing it with his blood, and held it out to her. "Taryn, stop this."

She snorted again and stilled as she caught the scent of his blood. Warmth flowed through her, a sensation that drove out the fear and left her sinking against the black wall and floor, her strength draining from her.

As it rushed out of her, she couldn't hold her dragon form and the world around her dulled as she shifted, her wings and tail disappearing and horns shrinking into her skin and scales sinking back into her flesh.

She breathed hard as she lay on her side, awareness slowly dawning, clearing the haze from her mind. Her eyes gradually widened and she looked at her brother, found him standing a short distance from her, holding his injured arm to his side.

The tender edge to his violet-to-white eyes didn't soothe her this time, couldn't steal away the pain and the anger.

He stooped to help her and she shoved him back and clothed herself before pushing onto her feet. She glared at him, fire burning through her blood, rage that she knew would blaze forever in her. Six masters. Three hundred years. A thousand lifetimes of pain and suffering. Nothing could erase that from her past.

No one could fix what had been broken.

"Taryn," Tenak started and she turned on him with a black snarl, flashing her sharp teeth at him and warning him to keep his distance. He backed off a step and lowered his hand to his side, but the hurt in his eyes wasn't enough to make her forgive him or desire to speak with him, not when he smelled of fae blood and sex.

"Never... *never* bring a female into this castle again," she snarled and advanced on him, her chest heaving against her leather corset as the fury in her veins reached boiling point. "I will kill you next time."

His eyes widened and then narrowed, darkness clouding them as his fingers curled into fists at his sides. If he tried to fight her, he would learn what three centuries of Hell had taught her.

How to kill without remorse.

How to survive.

He drew down a deep breath but she didn't relax, not even when his hands uncurled and his shoulders sagged, his stance shifting to a non-threatening one.

"I am sorry," he said but the apology wasn't enough.

Nothing he could say would be enough. All males like him deserved to die. Whatever doubts she had been having about her mission, he had snuffed them all out of existence, leaving her conscience clear and heart strong, determined to carry out her plan. He reached for her again and she glared at the hand he offered, one that had no doubt held the female in place or covered her mouth to stifle her screams.

Taryn snarled at it.

"Speak to me, Sister." He wisely withdrew his hand. "Tell me what happened to you."

She lifted her eyes to lock with his and growled the words she had long ago sworn to herself, when she had come close to surrendering, so tired from the constant fight against her captors, her spirit on the verge of breaking. A moment of weakness that she had to live with together with three hundred years of shame.

"Never… I will never speak of it to anyone."

Because no one would love her if they knew.

CHAPTER 13

In terms of epiphanies, this was a major fucking one.

Bleu stared at the white table top in the break room of the nightclub, heart banging around in his chest as everything crashed over him. He felt Iolanthe's gaze on him, questioning him, and sensed her concern, but he couldn't bring himself to look at her and couldn't find his voice to speak and tell her that he was fine.

Would be fine once his entire world stopped rocking and tilting anyway.

He had never been the sort to feel lonely and had long ago given up on his dream of finding his fated female. He had been fine with his life as a bachelor, married to his work with Loren and the kingdom.

He had been lying to himself.

He had been filling his life with work and shallow fleeting relationships because he had been covering the truth, unable to face it because he knew it would change his world and nothing he did would stop that from happening.

When he had seen his friends finding their fated ones and falling in love as they set out on a new path with their mate at their side, he had avoided them because he had been subconsciously trying to avoid the truth.

A truth he had been avoiding for the past seven centuries.

The dragon was his fated one.

He had known it the moment he had first tangled with her on the battlefield in the elf kingdom, shortly after she had stolen the sword, and the knowledge of what she was to him and to his kingdom, had torn him in two directions. She was both his ki'ara and the sworn enemy of his species.

In response to that knowledge, he had done what he did best. He had hurled himself into his position in the army and his work in order to avoid looking too closely at the recognition that had sparked to life inside him that day. He had shoved it to the back of his mind and had been so persistent in his desire to forget it, that he had somehow managed it.

Centuries later, he had forgotten he had even found his mate, had merely believed that he had decided to set aside that dream he had always told Iolanthe about.

Gods, it had been there in the back of his mind, locked deep in his heart all along though. A soul-deep awareness that he couldn't have his mate that had coloured everything in his life, making him view them as a nuisance and then making him jealous when he had seen others find theirs, able to start a life together with them.

One he could never have with his female.

He had buried himself in work because he couldn't have her. He had condemned himself to a life alone, one cold and devoid of love and light.

He hadn't even tried.

He had been a fucking idiot.

He groaned and tipped his head back, stared at the slightly grubby white tiled ceiling of the break room. Loren had told him once, several thousand years ago, that with age came wisdom. He wasn't sure that was the case for him. Seven centuries ago he had been old enough that he should have recognised the dragon female as his mate, his dream come true, and he should have done something.

He shouldn't have given up on her so easily.

His kingdom and his position meant something to him, but was it worthy of the sacrifice he had made?

He had changed himself, discarded the male who had always dreamed of finding his mate and had denied his true nature.

Seeing how fiercely Loren had fought for Olivia, and Kyter for Iolanthe, and even damned Thorne for Sable, had set him on edge for some reason, and at the time he hadn't been able to name it, but now he could.

It had made him angry.

With himself.

Every male he knew had fought to claim his mate, and he had fought to forget his.

He wasn't sure what kind of male that made him, but he didn't like it and it was time he changed.

Well, it was time he changed back.

He could no longer deny his true nature.

He couldn't bring himself to believe that there was a chance for him and the female, but he could finally see that it was a possibility. Nothing was impossible after all. He had proven that countless times and he should have tried to prove it with her too.

He had been wrong to believe that everyone but him was finding their mate.

His was out there. Waiting.

Running from him.

Gods, the thought of having her set his blood on fire but chilled him at the same time. He wasn't really sure of himself now or what the future held for him. Everything that had happened in the past few months had tipped him off balance, but he wasn't going to just give up and throw in the towel. He was going to figure everything out and come up with a strategy, one that would bring him and the female dragon together and give him a chance to speak with her.

It would be difficult now that he had brought Leif, Dacian and Fynn in on the hunt for her.

He cursed the gods. The trio would want to pursue the original plan of reclaiming the sword and they wouldn't care whether the culprit was caught or killed in the process. He couldn't even tell them that Loren had issued an order to capture the dragon, because their prince had issued the exact opposite.

In writing.

He cursed Loren this time. The male was only doing his duty, but Bleu wished he hadn't followed it to the letter this time. Normally, Loren allowed teams out on special missions without a written warrant. Maybe Bleu should have cursed the council. It was their constant bickering with Loren and pressuring him to stick firmly to the rules in order to placate them and restore some balance between him and the elders that had no doubt made Loren bother to issue his team mission orders in a formal manner.

Bleu groaned.

He wasn't even sure whether attempting to speak with the female was the right course of action. She had attacked his people, had killed thousands of his kin, and had stolen the most precious treasure of his prince. He knew that to be true, even when there was a piece of him that wanted to believe it wasn't. He had seen the sword on her person when he had first met her and there was no denying that, not even when it pained him to accept it.

His fated female was the enemy of his people.

His enemy.

"Brother," Iolanthe whispered softly and his groan deepened as he remembered that he wasn't alone.

He dragged a hand over his face and sat up, found her watching him closely with an edge of concern in her eyes.

"I'm just tired." Another lie. He really had to stop lying to his sister, but it was easier than spilling the truth—his fated female was a murderer and he had orders to kill her.

"It is the dragon, is it not? The mission plays on your mind and weighs on your heart for some reason."

Bleu gazed off to his right, to the door there, and sighed. "A little… but it is nothing for you to worry about."

Her eyes didn't leave him and he knew she wanted to say that she couldn't simply stop worrying about him. She didn't need to tell him. He shifted his gaze to her and held it, silently letting her know that. The bane of being a sibling, he supposed. One was always worried about the other for some reason.

"You could help me," he said and she perked up, sitting straighter in her chair, her violet eyes bright with enthusiasm that he scowled at because he knew the source of it. "I'm not asking you to come with me."

She huffed, her fine eyebrows knitting together and lips flattening into a mulish line as she folded her arms across her chest.

"Gods, you two look frighteningly alike sometimes." Kyter strolled into the break room, the overlong grey sweats he wore swishing around his bare feet, and yawned fiercely, his face screwing up as he flashed short fangs. He shuffled towards the counter in the kitchen area, scrubbing a hand over his mussed sandy hair. "I need coffee. Coffee… coffee… sweet coffee."

He opened the cupboard on the wall above the coffee pot and fumbled with a blue mug, barely catching it before it hit the dark counter, and set it down as he yawned again.

"Did we wake you?" Iolanthe said as she turned in her chair to look at Kyter, all sweetness and light now her mate was around.

The transformation was startling, but impressive. Bleu had never noticed the true depth of the effect Kyter had on her mood, but he couldn't fail to see it now. She had gone from irritated and grumpy to bright smiles in a heartbeat, her cheeks flushed with heat and eyes sparkling.

Bleu eyed the sandy-haired golden-skinned male in the kitchen and frowned.

He couldn't see the appeal himself.

Kyter was amusing at times, a good friend at others, but the rest of the time he was annoying as hell.

The jaguar shifter yawned so hard that his eyes closed and the coffee he was pouring into his mug hit the brim and flowed down the sides and all over the counter.

"Fuck," Kyter muttered and mopped up the mess. When he turned around, he scowled at Bleu. "That was your fault."

Bleu frowned right back at him. "My fault? I fail to see how you spilling coffee is my fault."

Kyter slumped into the chair to his left, between him and Iolanthe, kicked his bare feet up onto the white table, and sank lower, his coffee held in both hands above his naked torso.

The male slid a mischievous look his way. "It was your lusty screams waking me at this fucking ungodly hour."

Bleu growled at him, flashing fangs in warning.

The bastard just winked at him, the look in his eyes making it clear that he knew what had had Bleu crying out.

Iolanthe's gaze burned into him and he didn't dare look at her, didn't want to see how horrified she looked as she stared at him.

"I told you I was fighting," he said.

"No… you said you were having a nightmare."

"I was." Bleu shot her a look that demanded she let it go, one he'd had to use a thousand times on her in the past when she had been stubborn and acting like a Hell beast with a bone.

Kyter grinned. "So we're up in the middle of the fucking day because Bleu was having dirty dreams?"

Bleu hissed at him this time, his ears flaring back against the sides of his head, unable to contain the reaction or stop himself from threatening the male.

And confirming that he had been lost in a fantasy and not a nightmare judging by the wicked smiles Kyter and Iolanthe exchanged.

He crossed his arms over his chest and glared at both of them.

Kyter shuddered and muttered, "Far too alike."

Iolanthe petted her mate's leg and spoke to him. Bleu paid her no heed as he tried to figure out a way to convince both of them that he hadn't been having a dirty dream. It was only when she mentioned dragons and the sword that he dragged himself back to the room.

"Do you tell him everything now? Even things that were told to you in private?" Bleu frowned at her.

She shrugged. "We are mates. Mates tell each other everything."

Fantastic. He couldn't wait to come back to Underworld and have Kyter tease him about his desire to find his own fated female and everything else he had just confessed to his little sister.

"Since we are going to talk about my mission, perhaps you could help me. I need all the information you have about the dragon realm and the borders with the Devil's domain. Vail believes the sword is there, and you have travelled extensively in that area." He was about to tack on an order in the elf tongue to keep his private matters to herself when Kyter spoke.

"If you want information on the dragon realms and beyond, why don't you just ask Loke?"

"I would, if I knew the dragon's location. Prince Loren will not give it to me." He was also fairly certain that Loren would be angry with him for openly ignoring the promise he had made to the dragon, swearing he would leave him alone.

But Bleu hadn't made that promise, and he wouldn't be breaking it if he visited the dragon male and questioned him. The more he considered it, the more he wanted to do it. It would certainly stop him from wondering why Loke had pressed his prince to swear such a thing in the first place when Loke had given him no information on the female dragon or the sword.

Bleu had always obeyed his gut, and his gut was screaming that the dragon knew more than he had told Loren.

It was time he spoke with the male himself.

He looked across at Kyter. "You know where Loke lives?"

"No," Kyter said and Bleu was on the verge of snapping at him and asking why in the gods' names he had mentioned the male then when the jaguar shifter jerked his thumb towards Iolanthe. "But she does. She teleported Anais there once when Loke went radio silent and the huntress was worried."

He shifted his focus to his sister.

"I have a huge favour to ask you."

CHAPTER 14

Green swirled around Bleu as his feet hit the ground in the centre of the portal landing zone, the air surrounding him shimmering with the tell-tale trail of his teleport. He strode forwards, across the dewy grass, his back to the glowing portal suspended in the sky that acted as the sun in the elf kingdom. The warm light threw his shadow out long in front of him, stretching it towards the pale stone garrison a short distance away on a hill.

He focused on the squat two storey building that stood in the centre of a circular defensive wall and willed his portal. Power rippled over him and cool darkness followed it, a split second of infinite night that evaporated to reveal the arched wooden gate of the stronghold he and the others were to call home for the foreseeable future.

Bleu looked back in the direction of the landing zone, one of the few places in the kingdom where those teleporting into it could enter. It was closer than he remembered, and he would have been concerned if they had been tracking any species who could use the portal pathways into the elf realm, but they weren't. Dragons didn't have the ability to teleport.

He had never heard of them using the gates either, a method that allowed fae species such as shifters to enter Hell or travel around it.

No. If the female dragon attacked them, she would do so from the air, and that meant coming over the mountains to the rear of the old garrison. She would have to cross the First Realm.

Bleu looked towards it. He would send word to the demons, asking them to look out for dragons.

The sound of metal clashing pulled his focus away from the numerous smaller duties he needed to perform as part of his mission.

A grunt and growl followed it.

Bleu huffed and gritted his teeth, praying to the gods for patience.

Someone was sparring.

He banged his right fist on the huge arched door and waited. After a few seconds, it creaked open and Fynn appeared in view, grinning from ear to ear. It wobbled a little as he looked at Bleu, and Bleu pinned him with an ice-cold glare meant to freeze the damned thing off his face.

Dacian and Leif were the ones battling it out in the courtyard then. Bleu had seen them spar before and it had been less of a fight with weapons and more of a battle of wills.

A battle that had gone on far too long, neither willing to admit defeat.

Despite the difference in their builds, Dacian and Leif were too well matched, both skilled warriors with centuries of experience under their belts.

Both stubborn bastards too.

He couldn't afford to have this sparring match end as the last one he had witnessed had—with Leif sporting broken ribs and a fractured collarbone, and Dacian sitting on his backside with his tibia jutting out of his left leg.

Fynn drummed his fingers against the throwing knives strapped on both sides of his ribs over his black armour. The nervous twitch only grew in speed as Bleu slid him a black look meant to convey how annoyed he was that they had gone against one of his orders.

The one he thought he had hammered into their thick skulls with enough force to make it stick.

No one sparred, because heading into the dragon realm when injured was a death sentence and they couldn't delay the mission to wait for anyone to heal.

Bleu shot him another glare and then strode across the pale smooth flagstones towards the central building, and the two idiots going at it just outside it. He issued the command to his armour as he walked. The tiny scales rushed up his arms from the bands around his wrist and down his body, covering him just as his mortal clothes disappeared, sent away via his portal to his apartment in the main castle of the kingdom. Anything he owned, he could teleport.

Right now, he was debating teleporting his sword to his hand and beating some sense into Leif, Dacian and even Fynn.

"Funny… but I believe I gave an order," he barked in the elf tongue and both Leif and Dacian froze with their weapons held mid-swing.

They slowly turned to face him and he stopped a short distance from them, set his jaw and folded his arms across his chest, pressing the tips of his naked fingers into his biceps to stop himself from calling his blade.

"I could arrange for another team, perhaps one more willing to follow the orders I issue?" He shifted his gaze from Dacian, who rocked back on his heels into a relaxed position and lowered his black broadsword to his side, to Leif.

The slender male calmly sent his blade away and ran a hand over his short hair. He could act nonchalant all he wanted, but Bleu could see straight through it to the nerves he was trying to hide. If he sent them back to the castle, it would be in disgrace and with black marks against their names.

Leif's family would probably request punishment for him as recompense for him tarnishing their noble name with such insubordination.

Bleu wouldn't be surprised if Dacian's family went one further and asked for his execution.

While the two were matched in battle, they couldn't be further apart in standing. Dacian came from a long line of warriors. Leif came from a long line of pompous self-entitled nobles.

Bleu knew which side of elf society he preferred.

He looked back at Fynn where he still stood near the door, stroking his blades.

If he had to choose, Bleu would stand with Fynn. His family were farmers.

They might have that in common, but it wouldn't stop Bleu from setting him to rights when he confessed whatever misdeed it was that he was trying to hide. He wasn't nervous because Bleu had caught Leif and Dacian sparring.

Something else had happened.

He looked back at Dacian and Leif, and scrutinised them both, noticing now that there were no towels or refreshment waiting at the side lines, and no ring on the ground to mark the boundary of their battle. All things soldiers normally did when sparring.

Both males were wearing their armour too.

Because they hadn't been sparring.

They had been fighting.

He rolled his eyes and sighed. And he had thought it couldn't get worse. He was beginning to remember why he preferred to work alone.

Leif blurted, "Dacian and Fynn went to the dragon realm."

"Fucking wonderful," Bleu snarled and decided not to pray to the gods, because they certainly weren't listening and he wasn't even sure their counsel would be enough to stop him from spilling blood today.

He snapped his fingers.

The air shifted around him and Fynn was suddenly between Dacian and Leif. All three of them pressed their right hands to their armoured chests, directed their eyes straight forwards, and stood tall with their feet together.

It seemed he still had some authority.

"I would love an explanation." He looked around, spotted a stone bench near the side wall of the central building, and reached his hand out to it and focused on it. Using telekinesis on large heavy objects was taxing at the best of times, when an elf had a clear mind, so he wasn't surprised when it accidentally smacked Dacian in his right arm, knocking the male forward and tearing a pained grunt from his lips.

In Dacian's defence, he did regain his salute and perfect pose before the bench had even reached Bleu.

A warrior born and bred.

Bleu set the bench down in front of him, stepped over it and seated himself.

He eyed all three males. "I am waiting."

"When you failed to return as agreed, we thought it pertinent to assess the situation in the dragon realm as a team, venturing to a few of the villages that border the Third Realm to reconnoitre them from a safe distance." Dacian's deep voice was smooth and even, and Bleu raised an eyebrow.

He was nervous, fearful that Bleu would send him back to the castle.

It was always a dead giveaway when he scrounged together the fanciest words he knew in an attempt to sound more authoritative.

In a normal situation, Dacian would have said something more like 'You didn't come back and we were bored, so we went ahead and scouted the villages while we waited for your scrawny arse to return. You have a problem with that?'

Bleu appreciated that he had failed to return as agreed, but he didn't appreciate that his team had been so quick to disobey his orders.

The sparkle in Fynn's violet eyes was beginning to make him look as if he might explode if he didn't speak soon so Bleu turned his focus to the male.

Fynn rushed out, "One of the dragon clans were in an uproar when we tried to go there."

Nothing unusual about that since dragons often fought amongst themselves. The glimmer that remained in Fynn's eyes said that this particular uproar had been something other than the standard in-clan squabbling though, and that Fynn wanted him to ask before he would tell him whatever news had excited him.

"Go on." Bleu waved his left hand in the air, too tired to join in as required by the younger elf.

Fynn's expression lost some of its enthusiasm but enough remained that Bleu had to wonder where he got his energy. He couldn't remember ever being that filled with energy as a young male.

Maybe he had been before the war with Vail had erupted and changed him.

Fynn had never had to watch close to a thousand fellow soldiers being slain by their own commander.

Bleu schooled his features as he slowly snuffed out of existence every feeling that welled up on thinking about that day, not allowing any of his men to see the pain it still caused him. He was their commander now. The commander of the entire elf army. He owed it to them and every other soldier to stand strong and lead them to the best of his abilities.

Even when they were a challenge and disobeyed him, testing his patience.

"Of all things… there was an angel present," Fynn said with a wide smile. "An angel!"

That made Bleu's blood run cold.

An angel in Hell?

Sable had been hiding out in the Third Realm ever since an Echelon angel had made his presence known to her, demanding she come with him to Heaven. She had been convinced that she would be safe in Hell, and she should have been. Angels never entered this realm. It pained them to do so, weakened them and left them vulnerable.

But one was causing havoc in the dragon realm.

He didn't like it one bit and he wanted to investigate it, but he didn't have time. He would get word to Sable somehow, and maybe he could look into what the angel was doing.

"Since you and Dacian enjoy visiting the dragon realm so much, you will head back there." Bleu rose to his feet and all three males stiffened, their right hands pressing harder against their chests. At least they were beginning to behave in a more acceptable manner again. "I want you to scout the village we met the dragon in when she kindly left her mark on me. I have the feeling that it hadn't been chance that she had been there. It might be her clan… and that means you need to be on guard. Do not stray from each other. Understood?"

Fynn's left fingers twitched as if he wanted to stroke his blades and Bleu shot him a look that commanded him to speak.

"But the village… we thought the same thing. We went to scout it and that's where the angel was."

Interesting. He was even more curious about the angel now, and this was his golden opportunity to uncover what the creature was doing in Hell.

"All the better. You will question the clan members about both the female dragon and the angel. I have the feeling you'll be able to get some information out of the clan this time." He turned away from the trio and paced a short distance across the courtyard before turning back, using the automatic motion to clear his head. "They will believe she had something to do with bringing the angel to them and I'm sure if you press hard enough, they will talk. It isn't every day you see a violet and white dragon after all. Someone there must know her and they'll speak if you link the angel to her. If that fails, they will no doubt speak for the right price."

Leif arched an eyebrow at that and Bleu ignored him. Nobles were tetchy about the wealth of the kingdom. A few jewels out of the realm's coffers for those dragons who offered solid information was hardly going to bankrupt the kingdom, and if that information led to the capture of the dragon and the return of the sword, it would be worth the cost a thousand times over. That sword meant everything to Loren, and Vail, and in the wrong hands it was a death knell waiting to ring across all the lands of Hell.

"What are my orders?" Leif said, his tone holding a cold edge, one that Bleu was used to because he was sure he sounded the same when he was mulling over a mission, itching to get going.

"You will come with me." Bleu stopped in front of him and looked straight into his purple eyes. "I have a lead we will check out."

A very big lead.

A very big blue lead that would probably eat him if he went alone.

He held his hand out to Leif and looked in the direction of the dragon realm as he pictured the location Iolanthe had teleported him to just hours ago. He had considered going in alone, or with her at his side as his backup, but flying solo probably would have gotten him killed and he wouldn't risk Iolanthe, sure that the dragon would be upset when he showed up and started questioning him after Loren had promised to leave him alone.

Plus, he had already been late returning to his men and he really hadn't wanted to have to endure a marathon session of Leif giving him the gimlet glare whenever they were together. The male held grudges, especially where missions were concerned and when he felt he was being excluded. Leif's temperament had snagged him a spot on interrogation duty with him, and not only to spare Bleu his wrath.

The male had influence among the others. They looked up to him. He was also the biggest threat to the female, the one most likely to demand they obey the kill order that Loren had issued.

If Loke gave Bleu any information about the female dragon, any shred of something positive that might give him cause to order a stay of execution for her, then he wanted Leif to hear it first hand, straight from the dragon's mouth.

Leif placed his hand on Bleu's, his fingers closing around Bleu's wrist. Bleu gripped the male's arm and willed his portal to open. The green-purple light chased over both of them, darkness swallowing them whole, and then they were standing on the side of a black mountain, a valley stretching before them. Wind whipped up the side of the mountain, battering him and Leif.

The male released his arm and a blade appeared in it.

Bleu caught his wrist. "We are not here to fight. You will not need a weapon."

Leif didn't look convinced but he sent the sword away and nodded.

Bleu pointed to a ledge and the dark mouth of a cave, waited for Leif to nod again to show he had seen it, and then teleported solo to it. He walked forwards into the large cave, gaze scanning the meagre contents. A fire blazed in the centre, illuminating the black rough walls and a small stack of books and boxes beside the left wall. On the opposite side of the fire, a blanket covered the ground. Dragons had such basic tendencies.

He curled his lip at the thought of sleeping on the hard ground.

A feral roar blasted through the cave, piercing his ears and making them ring. He flinched back and quickly scanned the area ahead of him again. Not quick enough.

The bare-chested blue-haired male barrelled into him, taking him down onto the hard ground he had just been dissing, and so much for not being here to fight or needing a weapon.

Bleu grunted as his back hit the rock, the impact with it and the weight of the male landing on top of him pushing the air from his lungs.

He sensed Leif landing on the ledge before the dragon male whipped his head up and growled, bright blue eyes swirling like fire as he pinned them on his companion. Bleu used his momentary distraction against him, pressing his feet and shoulders into the ground and using all of his strength to lurch upwards in an attempt to dislodge the male.

An attempt that failed dismally.

And angered the dragon.

Strong hands closed around Bleu's throat and the male growled down at him, lips peeling back off teeth that were all as sharp as Bleu's own fangs.

The dragon bore down on him and Bleu wheezed as he fought for air.

"Unhand him, you wretched beast," Leif snarled and gods, could he sound any more lofty and noble?

Bleu refused to die with those ridiculous words ringing in his fuzzy mind.

He bucked up again and the dragon responded by pressing harder against his throat, squeezing it so tightly that Bleu lost the ability to breathe at all.

The male leaned closer and growled right in his face, a hank of his bright blue hair falling down across his brow. "Keep away from Taryn."

Taryn?

His heart gave a painful hard beat that had nothing to do with the fact he was about to suffocate.

Was that her name?

Gods, he could go to his death with that ringing in his mind.

Gladly.

"Loke!" A sharp female voice shattered the tense silence. "Get your bloody hands off him right this second."

A slender hand clutched the male's bare left shoulder and hauled him back. The dragon glared at it.

"It is him," Loke husked and then pinned Bleu with a black look that promised more pain than he was already experiencing, which was saying something since his vision was going dark now.

Him?

Bleu would have frowned at that but his body felt strangely unresponsive.

The dragon had told him to stay away from Taryn and now he was insinuating that he knew him somehow, but Bleu had never met him before.

The female appeared in his dim vision and began pulling at Loke's wrists, her blonde ponytail bouncing against her burgundy t-shirt with each attempt that only jerked Bleu's head off the black ground before making it smack painfully hard against it again, derailing his train of thought.

"Both of you, let him go or I will cut you down." Leif loomed over him, eyes bright violet and pointed ears flared back against the sides of his head as he aimed the tip of his sword at the dragon and then the female.

Big mistake.

Loke roared again, launched off Bleu and slammed into Leif. "You dare threaten my mate?"

"Oh, just fucking great." The mate in question threw her hands up in the air and got onto her feet. "Seriously… this testosterone bullshit has to stop."

She brushed her blue jeans down, taking her time about it considering that her mate had Leif in a chokehold and the elf was turning red as he struggled to break free.

Bleu slowly found his feet, swaying a little but determined to remain upright, and tried breathing. It hurt. Each breath he managed to pull down his battered throat scraped it raw. The blonde female's deep blue eyes issued a silent apology. He rubbed his throat, wincing as even the lightest touch hurt, and shrugged it off. She had no reason to feel bad. She wasn't the one who had attacked him.

Leif kicked the dragon in his blue-leather-clad shin, tearing a grunt from him but not shaking his hold.

Bleu frowned as an escape route hit him, but he was damned if he was going to mention it when Leif would think him an idiot since he hadn't thought about it when Loke had had him pinned.

Teleporting.

Leif seemed to possess some sort of telepathic link to him since he did it the second Bleu thought it, disappearing from the dragon's grasp and reappearing next to Bleu, his sword at the ready.

"I hear word of elves in the villages and now you appear," Loke growled low, his bright blue eyes fixed on Bleu as he advanced on him. "I will not speak with you."

Bleu stood his ground and would have responded, but he wasn't sure that speaking was an option right now. His healing ability was kicking in, but it would be a few minutes before he could use his voice again.

The dragon didn't even give him a second. The big male stormed off towards the back of the cave and disappeared into a tunnel, growling and snarling the entire time, detailing the ways he was going to kill Bleu.

None of them pleasant.

What the hell had he done to deserve such a reception?

He looked to the female. Anais. A hunter from Archangel. He had met her once, during the battle between the Third and Fifth Realms of the demons, when she had fought as part of Sable's team.

She seemed to recognise him too as she smiled and then sighed. "Sorry about that."

Bleu swallowed, testing his throat, and then squeaked out in English, "I do not mean the female dragon harm. I simply need to ask her about something."

Leif slid him a look, one that asked whether the lack of air supply to his brain had turned it to mush. He shut the male out and focused on Anais, because her smile was a little too knowing, as if she was privy to all the information he was concealing with his lie and knew why he was looking for the female dragon.

"Loke and Taryn are close, like brother and sister." She moved away to the fire and sighed again as the male dragon roared deep in the caves and the sound of rocks cracking apart reached them. Her blonde ponytail swayed across her back as she shook her head. "He's going to be in an awful mood for days."

She looked back over her shoulder at him.

Smiled again.

"You're lucky he didn't eat you." Anais turned back to face them. "Or squash you like a bug."

He knew that. He just didn't understand why the male had reacted so fiercely.

He grimaced, held his throat and forced the words out. "I've never met him before."

"No." She shook her head again. "But he has seen you… in a vision when Taryn was here. He saw you."

Bleu frowned and inched forwards, and was on the verge of asking what the male had seen when her blue eyes turned cold and dark.

"Loke saw you kill her."

It took all of his will to stop himself from staggering back a step when she delivered that blow. He stared at her, sure that he must have misheard, but the coldness in her eyes didn't lift and her expression remained sombre.

His blood dropped by ten degrees and he wanted to deny that he would do such a thing, but couldn't as he realised his orders were to do just that.

"My mission is to bring her to my prince and recover what she stole." Another lie, and another curious look from Leif that he again ignored.

"The sword?" Anais raised her fine pale eyebrows.

Bleu cursed under his breath. She knew much more than she should and she had just given him the best information yet.

The female dragon was in possession of the weapon.

Anais looked towards the back of the cave again, clearly listening to her mate raining unholy hell down on whatever was in the tunnels, growling and snarling, and then back at him.

She whispered, "I don't think Taryn stole the sword."

Bleu's eyes widened and then he frowned at her, not quite able to believe it even when it was exactly what his heart had needed to hear.

He hadn't realised that until a sense of relief had rushed through him in the wake of her words.

He wanted to look at Leif to make sure he was listening, was taking in everything Anais had said and was about to say, but played it cool and kept his focus on the mortal huntress.

"What evidence do you have to suggest otherwise?" He studied her as she glanced at the back of the cave again. Her heart was pounding and he could smell the fear on her. She was afraid her mate would hear her. Bleu moved a step closer to her, regaining her attention. "I witnessed the event, and her markings are unmistakable. It was definitely her."

Even when he was beginning to wish it hadn't been.

Not beginning. Not even close. He had been wishing it for seven centuries.

Anais's blue eyes gained a sorrowful edge as she quietly said, "What if another dragon shared those markings?"

A chill skated down his spine beneath his armour. "Another?"

It wasn't possible. Markings like the ones the female bore were rare. Nigh on unique. In all his centuries of hunting, he had never seen another dragon like her. He had seen white dragons and violet ones, but never a combination of two colours.

Anais glanced at the back of the cave again and her fear grew stronger, and panic lanced him, fear she wouldn't continue when he felt so close to discovering something that might just save the female dragon's life.

"If you have any evidence that might clear her name, you must speak," he said, his throat aching with each word, and realised that only being honest with her would get her to talk to him now. "The elf kingdom is on a mission to retrieve the sword… and I have orders to claim the head of the one who stole it."

She gasped and whipped back to face him.

"No… you can't." Her blue eyes pleaded him, her fear jacking higher as she shook her head. "Loke will kill you… heck, he'll probably kill me for telling you… but from what I've heard, Taryn needs all the help she can get… and if I say nothing… her brother might destroy half of Hell to set himself up as ruler of it all."

Brother.

Bleu could only stare at Anais as that hit him, unable to believe what he was hearing.

The seasoned soldier in him said not to believe it, that the female was lying to protect someone she viewed as a friend.

"Promise to help Taryn… to see for yourself that she took the blame to protect her brother." Anais walked right up to him and grabbed hold of his wrists, squeezing them tightly as she looked up into his eyes, hers darting between his. "Her *twin* brother."

Impossible. He had never heard of dragon twins. She had to be lying, even when the part of him he had kept silent for seven centuries roared that she had to be telling the truth.

He looked down into her blue eyes, and saw the fear and hope mingling in them. He needed the dragon's destination and he knew Anais would give it to him if he agreed to her request, even when he wasn't sure he could uphold any promise he made to her.

No matter how fiercely he wanted to keep it.

"I will do all I can to uncover the one responsible for stealing the sword and see they are brought to justice." Not quite a promise, and not a lie either.

If the female dragon had stolen the sword, he would bring her to justice. It was his duty.

That duty came before his desires and dreams.

He only hoped that Anais was telling the truth and she wasn't responsible.

"The Valley of the Dark Edge."

That took a moment to sink in.

He knew the valley, had saved Iolanthe there once, centuries ago. It was no place for a female.

"Thank you." He bowed his head to Anais and willed his portal, focusing on the stronghold in the elf kingdom when all he really wanted to do was teleport straight to the valley and the female dragon.

Taryn.

He rolled her name around his mind, picturing her at the same time. It was strange to know it after hunting for her for so long.

He appeared in the landing zone a short distance from the pale stone garrison and then called his portal again, teleporting to the gates. He pushed them open and strolled into the courtyard.

Dacian looked up from sharpening his blade, his broad shoulders rolling back as he sat up, revealing his bare honed torso. He uncrossed his black-leather-clad legs, planting his booted feet shoulder-width apart as he ran a glance over Bleu.

He tossed the stone on the bench beside him, pressed his left palm to his knee and leaned his weight on it as his violet eyes settled on Bleu's neck, an unimpressed look entering them. "I should have gone with you. You clearly had a better time than we did."

Bleu gingerly pressed his fingers to the healing bruises on his throat. "If by better you mean angering a dragon and almost dying, then yes, it was tremendous fun."

Leif slammed the wooden gate shut.

Dacian's lips tugged into a smile and he set his broadsword down beside him on the pale stone bench. "Did the dragon work you over too?"

The slender elf noble shot him a black look. "Did you even leave the compound?"

Dacian looked offended. "Are you insinuating I ignored my order?"

"It would hardly be the first time you have done such a thing… today." Leif tensed when Dacian rose to his feet, a barely imperceptible flinch that Bleu would have missed if he hadn't been looking for it. If Leif's armour hadn't already been out, Bleu was sure that it would have chased over his body in that instant as he readied himself for another battle with the larger elf.

He bit back a sigh and stepped between Leif and Dacian before they could start fighting again. As much as he appreciated Leif having someone else to throw his barbs at, he needed them to work as a team, and that meant somehow brokering a peace treaty between them.

"Dacian will not break another rule, will you Dacian?" Bleu straightened to his full six-five height and tipped his chin up, holding the larger male's gaze. He despised veiled threats but he would do whatever it took to ensure that Dacian didn't kill Leif when he left for the valley.

Alone.

Dacian huffed. "No."

Bleu turned to Leif. "And of course, you will not disobey an order."

Leif shook his head, managing to do even that small gesture with a regal air. "Never."

Bleu grinned. "So, I order you both to get along and stop acting like children."

Both males shot him daggers. Poisoned ones. The sort of looks that would have killed if he hadn't found them so amusing.

Fynn strolled out of the squat two storey building, the open sides of his long black jacket bouncing off his trousers with each step, and stopped a few metres from them, his violet eyes leaping from Dacian to Bleu and then to Leif and back again. "I miss something?"

Leif and Dacian grumbled.

"Just issuing orders," Bleu said, dangerously close to smiling properly as his two finest warriors huffed and stomped around the courtyard like adolescent elves who had just been told to eat their leafy vegetables and like them.

Fynn's slight shoulders rolled in an easy shrug and he crossed the courtyard to Bleu. "We got some good intel. It seems offering gold… or what the dragons kept calling treasure with that weird glint in their eyes… was the way to get them talking."

Bleu shifted his focus away from Dacian where he sat sharpening his sword again, a black look on his face as he glared at it, as if he was imagining cutting Leif or possibly him down with it, to the younger elf. "What did they have to say?"

"A few talked. They certainly have no love for the dragon we're hunting and it was definitely her home once." Fynn hooked his thumbs over the waist of his black trousers, pushing them low on his bare hips and revealing a hint of the tattoo on his left one.

A few of the elves under his direct command at the castle had taken to inking their skin with the insignia of their legion. Most soldiers chose a discreet size and location.

Dacian had the intricate design of dragons and stags spanning his broad back, a sign of his devotion to the legion he called his family.

"They called her… ah… Taryn," Fynn said with a frown, as if he didn't quite trust he had her name right, and Bleu resisted the temptation to confirm that he was correct, but also found it interesting that the dragons had sold out one of their own in exchange for gold when they had been so fiercely protective of her before. Fynn stole his attention away from the odd behaviour of their species. "Some mentioned family… a sibling. When we tried to get information on that sibling, the dragons clammed up and wouldn't talk."

A sibling. The twin brother if Anais was correct.

"Not even for more gold?" Bleu looked from Fynn to Dacian.

Both elves shook their heads.

"They got jittery." Dacian set his sword back down.

So the dragons feared the brother more than they feared Taryn.

Bleu nodded. "We have a location where we might find her. I will go ahead and scout the valley, and—"

"What?" All three males spoke in unison, cutting him off.

He knew that he sounded as if he had lost his mind. The sensible course of action was to take everyone with him as backup, and he didn't exactly look as if he was up for the task of a solo mission when his throat was still black and blue from an encounter with another dragon, but he had to go alone.

Bleu held his hand up to silence them before they could unleash the barrage of objections he could see coming from a league away.

"Is this because of what the mortal female told us about the female dragon's brother being the one responsible?" Leif said anyway, obviously intent on ignoring at least one command today to get himself on even footing with Dacian and Fynn, knowing Bleu would have to let it slide.

He nodded. "It is, and as commander of the legions, I have to scout the valley and see if that intel is correct. It won't confirm whether or not the female is innocent, or that the two of them aren't working together, but it is information that requires investigation."

"Then we should go with you. It will be quicker for four to scout the valley." Dacian stood, unfurling his six-seven frame and standing tall, every muscle on his bare chest flexing as he clenched his fists at his sides.

"And more obvious," Bleu countered. "It is easier for one lone male to move around the valley undetected. I will go alone. Do not worry, Dacian. I will not engage the enemy."

Dacian grumbled something under his breath and looked close to either huffing or voicing another objection. Bleu couldn't tell which it would be, but he appreciated the male's concern and knew it had nothing to do with the threat of potentially missing out on a fight and everything to do with how dangerous it was for Bleu to go alone. Dacian wanted to be there to protect him and have his back.

"Leif." He turned to the slighter male. "Report to Prince Loren what we have discovered."

Leif looked as if he wanted to protest but held his tongue and nodded.

Bleu looked at each of them in turn. "Make preparations and continue investigating the dragon realm as a team, in case the dragon has moved on and the valley is a dead end. I will return soon."

He waited for all three males to press their right hands to their chests before focusing on the dragon realm and willing his teleport. The colourful light traced over his body and the darkness welcomed him, a brief rush of cold before it dissipated to reveal a black valley stretching before him.

He settled his gaze on the small village at the centre of it far below him, and then looked beyond the settlement to the mountains that loomed there, rising into the grim grey sky. Wind battered him, warmed by the lands to his right, where the Devil's domain spewed lava that caused an orange haze above the peaks of the cragged mountains.

His eyes remained locked on the range directly in front of him, across the valley from the mountain where he stood. Beyond those sharp peaks was the valley Anais had spoken of, one where he might find the dragon he had been hunting for seven centuries.

Had he been chasing the wrong dragon all this time?

Bleu drew down a deep breath, held it for a second and exhaled slowly. He hated lying to his team, battering the trust they shared, but he hadn't had a choice. They would never have consented to his plan if they had been here with him and had realised what he had in mind.

Not merely scouting the valley.

He meant to speak with the female dragon.

He felt certain that he could talk with her without her attacking him. Insanity, but every instinct he possessed roared that he could, drowning out the doubts that constantly whispered that she had attacked him before.

He'd had her backed into a corner that time.

She had been speaking with him, calm and collected, and then he had advanced on her and she had felt threatened, lashing out to defend herself.

This time, he would let her feel in control, that she had all the power and he wasn't a threat to her. He would keep his distance as he should have three centuries ago.

He would make her feel safe.

He would make her speak with him and tell him the truth.

A truth he needed to know, because he was tired of denying the one he knew deep in his soul.

It was time they both stopped running.

CHAPTER 15

Taryn didn't even have the energy to yawn. She sat on the end of her double bed, hands curled over the edge of the mattress next to her thighs, her eyes fixed on the black wall opposite her. Vision hazy.

It was all she could do to breathe.

Every bone in her body felt heavy, as if someone had poured lead into her marrow. Her mind ached, her heart throbbed, the weariness trickling through her veins like sludge that clogged her up and pulled her down, until she was drowning in it.

Gods.

The dragon she had loved was gone and the one wearing his skin was a stranger to her.

That feeling had been growing inside her for the past few days and it had seized hold of her heart, sinking poisoned talons into the soft vulnerable flesh.

Loke was right.

Her brother was gone. His lust for power had corrupted him, the darkness seducing him with an obsession with possessing all the realms in Hell, clouding his vision and making him view them as the ultimate treasure a dragon could hold.

It was madness.

She tensed as a harrowed scream echoed around the castle, chilling her blood. Her fingers twitched and then she was rubbing her arms before she could stop herself, trying to scrub off the guilt and the fear. Those terrified cries were her fault.

She had caught Tenak chasing a fae male across the valley yesterday morning, toying with him by letting him break a short distance ahead of him before swooping on him, knocking him to the black earth. It had been too cruel and she hadn't been able to stand by and watch the hope reigniting in the poor creature as he found his feet and began running, only to be shattered all over again when Tenak pounced on him.

She was too familiar with such feelings.

How many times had she experienced the same fleeting burst of hope, like a warm light touching her soul and chasing the darkness back for a few short minutes or hours before that darkness crashed back over it and destroyed the light?

Too many times, and each had been more painful than the last, stripping another piece of her soul away.

She had stopped her brother, but he had demanded a reason for her intervention and she had blurted the first thing that had come to her.

She had told him to place the male in the cells instead so they might have some entertainment and she could watch one of his kind suffer as she had.

Gods, she had meant to spare the male more pain, finding a way to allow him to escape, but Tenak had found a startling new way of passing his time, one that had kept her shut in her room, afraid of leaving it, trapped by her memories and fear of what she might see.

It would break her. She knew that much.

Tenak had discovered a lust for torture, now spent most of his time down there in the dungeon inflicting terrible pain on the fae male and the others he had captured.

She shuddered, unable to stop the chill from wracking her tired body when she recalled watching her brother from the window as he had left and when he had returned. He had become so addicted to slowly destroying his captives that he had taken to leaving the valley entirely, flying leagues to find new prey.

So far, the cells contained a siren female, a nymph male, and a shifter male of some sort.

Others had come and gone, killed by Tenak's overzealous attempts to make them suffer.

For her.

Her stomach rebelled and she clutched it.

Dear gods, she couldn't think about it, but it filled her mind, flooding it with the memory of him knocking softly on her door to ask whether she was unwell.

She had made the mistake of opening her door to him, and now she couldn't think about him without seeing him as he had been in that moment, standing proud with blood coating his bare chest and leather trousers, a grin curving his lips as he told her that he made them suffer for her sake.

She retched but nothing came up, her empty stomach churning with acid. She hadn't eaten in a day at least, too heartsick to find her appetite.

Another scream pierced the still air, female this time.

She had to fly.

Taryn pushed onto her feet and her legs wobbled beneath her sudden weight but she locked her knees and remained upright. A second shriek came and she rushed to the door of her room and pushed it open. She marched down the corridor, haunted by the wails of agony coming from far below. They chased her and her steps gained pace, until she was running blind, tears filling her eyes.

She needed to fly.

Tenak expected her in the drawing room in less than an hour but she had time to fly before she had to listen to his sick and twisted plans for the inhabitants of this realm and pretend that they pleased her when all she wanted to do was plunge a dagger into her brother's blackened heart.

Ahead of her, the thick doors of the fortress were closed for once, as if Tenak wanted to make sure none of his prizes escaped, including her.

She hit those doors at a dead run, barging them open and knocking one side off its hinges. Splinters pierced her shoulder and upper arm, but she didn't feel the pain as she shifted, her scales pushing the fragments of wood from her flesh. She beat her wings the second they were free and launched into the air, filled with a frantic need to feel the wind on her face and soar high above the world, so high that she couldn't see the horrors it contained.

The cruelty and madness.

She would fly so high that all she would know was peace at last and Hell would look beautiful again.

Taryn beat her wings and soared upwards, her heart steadying as she gained height and left the castle behind her, no longer feeling as if she was being chased.

She breathed deep and spread her wings, focused on the feel of the wind on their white membranes and the subtle shifts in the air currents. She tipped her head and chest up and caught one thermal, used it to lazily circle higher in the air, until the world below dropped away and silence reigned.

The lands of the dragons and the Devil stretched far below her, the villages only specks on the black ground. In the distance, far from the Devil's realm, at the opposite side of Hell, the elf realm was hazy gold, a beacon that called to her.

Was he there?

Waiting for her?

Searching for her?

She glided across the width of the valley and swooped lower, the sensation of peace growing stronger, flowing through her and calming her. It even restored some of her strength. She let it roll over her and savoured it, embraced and nurtured it, afraid it would go away too soon when she wanted the feeling to stay.

She couldn't remember the last time she had felt so at peace.

So unafraid.

Flying had never made her feel this way before. It had only ever satisfied her urge to feel free, the compulsion to fly and spread her wings, and know that she was no longer shackled and enslaved.

What was different today?

She banked left, swooping towards the black citadel where it rose out of the mountain, and shooting past it, turning at the last second to evade a collision with it. The sense of peace flickered for a heartbeat, wavering like a candle in the wind as she neared the castle and gaining strength again as she flew away from it.

It continued to grow as she beat her wings and headed towards the dragon realm, easing away her fear and imbuing her with strength.

Odd.

She studied the sensation, unable to make sense of it. It ran deep, as deep as her blood or maybe deeper still, and it was strangely familiar, as if she had experienced it before. Maybe she had. Being around her brother had made her feel safe and calm when she had been younger. Was that the sensation she was recalling?

She hadn't felt that way in many centuries though, and for some reason, it didn't seem like the right answer.

She scanned the horizon, convinced and afraid that Loke had foolishly tracked her down. He had always made her feel safe and he knew where she had gone because he had been the one to give her Tenak's location.

Her sharp gaze caught on movement and darted there.

Her breath left her in a dizzying rush and she almost forgot to keep beating her wings.

Her heart plunged as if she had and was falling.

The feeling she had been having suddenly made terrifying sense.

The small black-clad figure on the mountainside slowly lifted their head, revealing a gap in their ornate black helmet, little more than an open strip across their eyes.

Eyes that seemed to pierce her soul and set her blood on fire as they locked on her.

The elf male.

CHAPTER 16

Bleu traversed the rocky black ground, watching his footing as he moved silently and swiftly between boulders, switching his vantage point to get a different view of the valley. It looked quiet. He hunkered down behind an outcrop of rock and scanned the valley basin, picking out enormous bones and gnarled black trees. No sign of life though.

He quickly glanced over the entire valley, from the mountain ranges that reached along it on the left and right, to the far end. Satisfied that no one could see him, he set his gaze on a fissure in a mountain on the right side, one halfway along the length of the valley, and teleported there. He landed silently and immediately crouched behind another boulder, keeping still as he scoured the valley from the new angle.

His gaze caught on a citadel far to his right, at the end of the valley furthest from the dragon realm. Black jagged spires rose from the mountain, as if someone had carved it out of the great peak.

The female had to be there. With the sword?

And the brother?

One dragon was dangerous enough, easily able to kill him. Two didn't bear thinking about.

His pointed ears twitched as a cry echoed from the castle, muffled by the layers of rock but loud enough to reach him. His armoured claws tensed against the boulder and he had to dig them in to keep himself in place and stop himself from teleporting straight to the castle, obeying the primal part of him that roared that it was his mate screaming.

Bleu breathed deep, hoping to settle the powerful urge and stop it from happening again. Impossible. Now that he had admitted that the female dragon was his ki'ara, casting aside the conditioning that had made him forget her, the instincts as her male were awakening.

Gods, he couldn't let them control him. He had to remain objective about everything, including the female. If he allowed his instincts to rule him, he might walk right into a trap or march straight to his death.

Or worse.

He might allow her to use the sword to destroy half of Hell.

He wouldn't be the first male duped into committing atrocious acts by his fated female, blinded by his primal instincts, controlled by them and an overwhelming need to please her at any cost.

He closed his eyes and bent his head, focused on his breathing and recited his mission in his mind, until it cleared and the female was nothing more than an objective again. He would speak with her, somehow, and if she were a threat to the realm and everyone in it, he would eliminate her as ordered.

Bleu leaned his right side against the black boulder, his armour allowing him to blend in to his surroundings in the low light. The slats covering the lower half of his face caused his warm breath to bounce back at him and his horned helmet trapped heat. He ached to remove his helmet but blending in to the landscape to avoid detection was more important than how hot and sweaty it made him.

How stifling it was as he tried to breathe.

He couldn't breathe.

Fuck, what was he doing?

He looked across the dead valley to the castle, felt that question right to the pit of his soul. What had possessed him to come here alone and made him believe that he could speak with the female?

She was his mate, but she was his mission first and foremost. He couldn't allow his instincts as her fated male to corrupt him or sway him from that mission. They were only instincts. He felt nothing for her, not a single drop of emotion. She was a mission.

A shadow loomed out of the gloom, a flash of white and violet, and his breath caught in the back of his bruised throat as he tipped his head back and watched the dragon rush straight overhead.

Enormous wings beat the hot air, sending it thundering down the mountainside and stirring an avalanche of dust that swept past him. He didn't notice it as he watched the dragon, unable to take his eyes off it.

Off her.

Those primal instincts fired, told him that the beast flying away from him, swaying at an angle in the air as she spread her wings wide and skimmed the side of the mountain range, following it back towards the castle, was his mate.

His ki'ara.

And, holy fuck, she stole his breath away.

His gaze followed her as she banked around, her long tail curving to assist her in the turn and white wings lazily beating the air, making it look as if flying was an effortless task. Her white horns almost brushed the violet scales of her neck as she twisted her head, tipped it back at the same time as she flapped her wings, and his heart gave a hard thump as she barely missed the castle's spires.

She turned, swooped lower and then rose higher on a single beat of her wings, heading towards his end of the valley. Her head barely moved as she looked around, large eyes taking everything in. Her talons flexed and she tucked her front legs up as she gained height, pulling them close to her white chest.

He lost himself in watching her. Majestic. Beautiful. He had never seen those two qualities in dragons, not as many in Hell did, but he saw them in her.

Huge violet eyes dropped.

Landed right on him.

The thought that it was impossible she had seen him against the black rock when his armour covered all but his eyes didn't even have time to form in his mind before strange heat flooded him followed by a surge of images, pulled straight from his dreams of her.

A disjointed vision of kissing her, wrapping her up in his arms as he possessed her.

Claimed her.

The mountain shook as she landed hard on the slope below him. She slammed her paws into it, sharp dark violet talons sinking straight into the rock as she clawed her way up the steep incline at speed.

Coming straight at him.

She snapped and snarled, flashing white fangs each as long as his arms.

Bleu held his ground, his years as a soldier combining with his primal instincts to tell him that she didn't mean him any harm.

She meant to drive him away.

It wasn't going to happen.

He had come here to speak with her, and he was going to do just that.

"Return the sword," he said in the dragon tongue and rose onto his feet, moving slowly so he didn't spook her.

She growled and lunged at him, snapped her jaws together just inches from his face, close enough that his portal flickered over his armour, survival instinct bringing it to the fore without him even thinking about using it.

He exhaled slowly, calming himself again.

She snarled, her reptilian jowls rippling with the odd sound, her fangs mere feet from him and filling his vision. She inched closer and the fierce points of her teeth parted enough that she could easily snap them closed over him before he could escape.

But she didn't.

She remained there, growling so loud that it was deafening. Still trying to scare him away. Not serious about fighting him. Why?

In this form, she could easily crush him. She could eat him whole. It didn't make any sense, but he would roll with it. He didn't mind being right and coming away from their meeting with his life.

As casually as he could manage given the proximity of her fangs, he leaned his right hip against the boulder and issued a mental command to his armour. The slats covering his face shifted back, sliding under each other until they had cleared his cheeks and his helmet deconstructed itself, the dragon-like horns shrinking and scales rippling down to join the rest of his armour.

The female edged back, enormous eyes following the transformation. Her elliptical pupils narrowed and she canted her head to one side a fraction of a degree before she jerked it back straight and growled at him again. He had the impression he had just been blamed for something.

Distracting her?

If it would distract her enough to get her to shift into her mortal form, he would strip naked.

His body got the wrong idea about that, blood rushing south. He gritted his teeth and focused on her and his mission. She was just a mission to him. His head didn't seem to be listening to him, because it started throwing flashbacks of his dreams at him, hot and sweaty visions of them tangled together, naked and lost in passion.

Bleu closed his eyes, blew out his breath as he sought some balance again, reciting his mission orders and the reason he was here to purge the images from his rebellious mind.

Or was that his heart?

It would be typical of the damned thing to slip its leash now, when it was imperative that he remained detached and in control.

He opened his eyes, settling them straight on hers, the source of his problem and his damned objective in this mission. She jerked back and flashed fangs at him, snarling low in her throat.

She didn't like it when he pinned blame on her.

Well, it was her fault for distracting him with nothing more than her presence.

Her sweet proximity.

It was playing havoc with him.

He barely resisted the urge to fold his arms across his chest, catching himself at the last second. He was here to speak with her and adopting a threatening pose was a sure-fire way of stopping that from happening. She had to feel in control.

Her eyes followed his right hand as he lifted it and touched the left side of his throat, the scales of his armour cool beneath his fingertips. The scars on it tingled, a reminder of what she could do in her mortal form when she felt cornered. He didn't want to imagine what she might do if she felt cornered when in her dragon one.

Her eyes narrowed and she backed off, even glanced away from him. Guilty? Did she feel bad about what she had done?

He stared at her, letting that sink in, studying her and seeing in her behaviour that she did feel guilty. It strengthened his hope that he had the wrong dragon, because if she had slaughtered thousands of elves as the kingdom believed, she wouldn't have felt a damn thing about clawing one and leaving him scarred.

"If you return the sword and come with me, there is a chance I can convince my prince to be lenient on you," he said in her tongue and wrestled with the urge to say more, to somehow make her come with him and leave this valley of death behind her.

And gods, it had nothing to do with fulfilling his damned mission.

She shifted back right before his eyes, transforming into a female who robbed him of his breath, had stolen it the first time he had set eyes on her and every time after that. Silky hair fell to just below her shoulders, deep violet at its roots but pure snow white where it brushed her chest. He curled his fingers into fists, fighting the desire that surged through him and his need to drop his gaze to her bare body and take in every perfect inch of her.

Sweet gods, she was perfect.

Despite his efforts and keeping his eyes locked on her face, carnal hunger flooded him. His ears flared back against the sides of his head and his vision sharpened, a response to the desire now rushing through him like a tidal wave, obliterating all sensible thought, destroying everything in its path until his entire body came alive with the need to have her. His fangs lengthened and he itched with a need to reach out, grab her slender wrist and pull her into his arms.

He needed to kiss her until she melted against him, moaning his name as he burned her resistance away.

No good could come of that.

Bleu slowly clawed back his sanity and closed his eyes, shutting her out as he tried to piece himself back together and remember his place.

And hers.

Until she had proven that she hadn't stolen the sword, she was his enemy and he had to bring her to justice for her crimes.

It was his mission. His purpose.

He opened his eyes and stared at her, finding her still watching him, her violet-to-white gaze steady. So why couldn't he bring himself to fight her and take her into custody?

Why the hell was he bent on being diplomatic when he had always sucked at diplomacy? He had been born to find peace through battle, not through words. He wasn't Loren.

Her eyes narrowed on him, ran down the length of him and set his body on fire again. Gods damn her. He wanted to growl whenever she looked at him like that, had to fight to restrain himself when all he ached to do was step into her, draw her flush against the body she was checking out, and show her just what his armour concealed, pressing every hard inch of him into her.

He bit out a curse in the elf tongue instead and reeled that hunger in, and cursed every mated male he knew while he was at it. Suddenly, he pitied the poor bastards. When he had watched them fawning over their fated one, acting like pricks, he had thought them ridiculous, lacking strength and self-control.

He had been convinced they had allowed the pull of their mate to overcome them.

He was painfully aware now that it hadn't been the case.

There was no fighting this.

There was only clawing together enough control to keep himself sane and stop himself from acting on every primal instinct that screamed at him to take his female into his arms and bend her to his will.

Clothes moulded over her body, violet leather covering her long legs and a creamy-white corset covering her torso, and matching pale bands closing over her forearms. The hunger he felt abated enough that he could think straight again, and part of him wanted to thank her for having the decency to put him out of his misery by covering herself.

Bleu stared at her, taking her in, recalling all their past meetings and how she had looked then, and comparing it to how she appeared now. At the back of his mind, the sane part of him constantly chanted that she was the enemy of his people, the target of his mission. He should be seizing her now, while he had the chance, and forcing her to return the sword.

But he couldn't.

He couldn't fight her.

He never had been able to do it. Not from the day he had met her. Not even when she had lashed out and clawed him.

He couldn't raise a hand to her in violence.

Not when every fibre of him beat with a need to lift that hand and brush it across her pale cheek as he asked her the question he really desired to voice—was she unwell?

Darkness arced beneath her striking eyes and her skin was deathly pale, ashen almost, and she was thinner than he recalled, ravaged by either a sickness of the body or the mind.

Was his female ill?

The thought that she might be, that she might be taken from him, almost struck him down.

Bleu started to lift his hand. Her eyes dropped to it and she bared her teeth at him. He stilled.

"Will you do as I ask?" he said, denying his burning need to know what had happened to her. He could find that out if he convinced her to bring him the sword and they left the valley together.

"No." Her voice was pure light even though she bit the word out in a harsh tone. It washed over his soul like rays of sunlight chasing over a hillside meadow, bathing it in warmth. Stupid instincts. He shut them down. She scowled at him. "Leave."

Bleu shook his head. "Is it true that your brother is the one responsible for stealing the sword and massacring my kin?"

Her violet-to-white eyes widened.

Her pulse accelerated in his ears.

"Leave," she said, but this time her voice trembled and he could sense the fear running through her.

She wasn't afraid of him.

She feared her brother, just as the dragons in the village did.

"You must leave," she snapped and moved closer, her eyes gaining a desperate and wild edge as they darted between his. "*Leave*."

"No. If you are not the one responsible… you have my word that I will speak with my prince on your behalf if you return the sword. I will see to it that the one who is responsible is brought to justice and your name is cleared." He couldn't stop himself from edging closer, the need to be near her seizing hold of him as he felt her fear increasing.

He needed to soothe her.

She glanced back over her shoulder, her heart pounding in his ears now.

"Leave!" Her eyes were glassy when she looked back at him, her breath coming faster, soft pants that caused her chest to heave against the white leather corset. Her fear rose, swamping her delicate scent with the bitter note of it, and she whispered, "Too late."

Too late?

A roar rolled over the valley, rumbling around the black sky like thunder, and wind beat against him, causing the female to sway forwards, her hair whipping around her face.

A huge violet and white dragon landed hard behind her, shaking the ground, and reared up onto its hind legs.

Bleu leaped into action, launching himself towards the female, muscles burning as he reached for her, filled with a need to pull her out of harm's way and shield her.

A flicker of guilt crossed her incredible eyes, a brief flash of sorrow, and then her right hand came out of nowhere, the back of it catching him across his face. The world flew by in slow motion as he stared at her, mind numbed by one single question.

Was she on her brother's side?

Bleu's spine hit a boulder and he grunted as his arms flew out at his sides and his legs kept going, the impact bending his body like a bow being drawn back.

His head spun, senses swirling together and breaking apart, and he could only breathe as he struggled to piece himself back together.

When his faculties were functioning again, the pain dulling to a fierce throbbing, he looked back at the female.

The dragon loomed behind her.

Not hurting her.

The look in its eyes warned that it wanted to hurt him.

It snarled and lunged at him, and the female stepped into its path without hesitation, whirling so her back was to Bleu, and raised her hand. Bleu opened his mouth to scream at her to run and those words fled his lips as the dragon stopped dead, its beaked snout pressed against her outstretched palm, and its massive teeth bared on a growl.

Words swam in his head, spoken in her soft voice, the ringing in his ears making them impossible to decipher.

The dragon eased back.

Bleu could only stare.

She had just saved his life, which, as Sable would have said, was the biggest mind fuck of them all.

He pulled himself up into a sitting position, his aching back pressed against the rock, and tried to make sense of everything that had just happened. She had saved him. She had risked her life to spare his.

He wasn't sure he should be thanking her when she looked back at him though, her violet-to-white eyes dull and cold, devoid of any light.

He had the sinking feeling he should be praying to his gods to save him from whatever horror awaited him.

CHAPTER 17

Taryn couldn't shake the heat that rippled through her whenever the elf gazed at her. It had always been this way, from the moment she had met him. Whenever his eyes settled on her, she was intensely aware of him. She felt it even now as she faced her brother. A shockwave of fire blasted through her, burning her up inside, making her yearn to look back at the elf male.

Her gaze turned hazy as that feeling flowed through her and she barely noticed her brother shifting back into his mortal form and clothing himself. He was nothing more than a blur of purple and cream against a fuzzy black backdrop. All of her focus was on the elf male, and on controlling the dangerous feelings rising inside her.

She felt possessive of the male and it was becoming impossible to deny the desire to cross the short span of uneven black ground to him, haul him onto his feet and kiss him, staking a claim on him.

She cursed her species and her gender, aware that it was her dragon instincts that were pushing for control over her. Instincts that would not only land her in trouble, but the elf too if she allowed them to seize command. Females of her kind always had trouble denying their desires, feeling them more keenly than the male of her species. Normally those males were all too happy to satisfy any female who came to them, sating their needs with no strings attached.

They couldn't satisfy this hunger for her though.

No one but the male at her back could scratch this itch and she was sure he wouldn't want to help her with it, and she couldn't allow the thought that he might to sway her. She had to remain strong, in control, even when it felt impossible.

Desire ran strong in female dragon blood, but the possessive brand of desire a female dragon felt for her fated one was a powerful force of nature so potent that their history books were filled with accounts of females igniting wars, fighting legions of warriors, just to get to their mate.

Gods help her. She wasn't sure she was strong enough to deny that sort of need.

Tenak moved towards her and she shook as she kept her booted feet pinned to the spot, resisting the sudden urge to step into his path and stop him from reaching her fated male. She turned as her brother passed her and wanted to close her eyes, wasn't sure she was strong enough to watch what he was about to do.

What she had requested he do.

A growl rumbled through her as he stopped before the elf male, and every muscle in her body tensed to a painful degree as Tenak grabbed the elf by his throat and hauled him onto his feet. She silently bared her fangs at her brother's back as he shoved the elf forwards, slamming his back into the boulder, and her male grunted in pain.

Pain that tore through her and had her stepping forwards, her breaths coming faster as she fought the instinct that whispered at her to protect her fated male.

Tenak muttered black things about elves in the dragon tongue as he tightened his grip on the male's throat.

The whispering became a roar in her mind and her heart as the elf's purple eyes slid her way, a flicker of awareness in them. She willed him not to fight her brother, to relax and let the darkness take him gently into its arms. His eyes slowly grew wild. In a sudden burst of movement, he scrabbled against the boulder, wriggling and managing to seize hold of Tenak's bare forearms. Panic flooded the male's handsome face and she had to force herself to keep looking at him, aware that her brother would know if she looked away. She couldn't appear partial to the elf. If her brother thought she had feelings for him, he would kill the male to eliminate any competition for her affection.

It hurt to deny the powerful instinct to protect the elf and watch her brother hurting him though.

The elf's eyes dulled and his struggles slowed, his fingers slipping from her brother's wrists as he tried to grasp them, each futile attempt taking more effort than the last, until his hands fell limp at his sides.

Gods, she couldn't watch anymore.

"Brother," she whispered softly when he showed no sign of releasing the male. "It is done."

Now, she would subtly manipulate her brother's actions so he would incarcerate the elf, and then she would find a way to free him from her brother's claws.

Tenak didn't release the male.

He raised those claws to strike him down and she launched forwards, unable to stop herself from intervening, and caught his wrist, holding him fast even when he growled at her.

"The male might have valuable information for us," she said in a gentle voice, one she had perfected during her time with her brother. He responded best when she was tender with him. It seemed to help him temper the madness that infected him, drawing him back to her. Her grip on his wrist tightened and she eased him back, away from the elf. His other hand remained locked around the male's throat. She placed her hand on that one, covering it, hoping the action would help convince him to loosen his hold, and looked up into his eyes. "I recognise the male. He is a commander from their warrior legions. We have crossed paths before."

Her brother didn't look convinced.

Taryn did the only thing she could to show him that she was telling him the truth.

"Three centuries ago, in the dragon realm, our paths crossed. He questioned me about you and the sword, and I struck the male, wounding him. My claws raked over the left side of his neck," she said and Tenak still looked sceptical. "I will prove it to you."

This time, when she pulled on the hand he had around the elf's throat, he released the male and stepped back. Taryn let go of both of her brother's hands as the elf slumped to the black ground, falling on his right side.

She waited until she was sure her brother was calm, and then turned and crouched beside the unconscious elf. His armour was still out. She wrestled with it, managing to wriggle her fingers beneath the collar after a few minutes' fight, and then growled as she used all of her strength to pull the tiny metal scales down. Damned armour. She hadn't thought it would be so troublesome.

Her brother shifted foot to foot, his agitation flowing over her, mingling with her own as she fought the armour. What was it made from? She had never really bothered to learn much about the elves. She wanted to find whoever had created it and give them as much hell as the armour was giving her.

She panted hard, heart labouring as she wrestled with the armour. It kept snapping back into place the moment she let up on the fight. If she couldn't expose his throat and therefore that she was telling the truth about the elf, then her brother would probably kill him.

Her gaze fell to the male's black clawed fingers.

She dimly recalled hearing once that elf armour was weak against its own material. The male dragon who had said it to another had been laughed out of the tavern. What if it was true though?

She glanced up at her brother, finding him standing close to her, eyes pinned on the male, filled with malice and dark intent.

It was worth a try.

She grabbed the elf's hand, wrapped her fingers around his, and began sawing at the neck of his armour with his own claws, careful to keep them away from his skin.

Her eyes widened as the claws sliced through the scales.

If she ever saw that male dragon again, she would tell him that he had been right. Elf armour was vulnerable to its own material.

Taryn cut a line down from the side of his throat to his shoulder and released his hand, letting it drop to the ground again. She peeled the black metal scales away from his skin and slowed as they revealed not perfect skin but dark bruises, some of which had already changed colour to show they were healing. Her brother hadn't caused these marks. Someone else had tried to strangle the elf recently. Who?

Her eyebrows knitted together and her heart pounded harder as she stared at the deep bruising, her hands shaking as a need to find whoever had hurt the male and make them suffer surged through her. It was little wonder the male had become panicked so quickly when her brother had caught hold of his throat.

Gods, what had she done?

She had asked her brother to render him unconscious but not harm him. She had known he would choose to suffocate the male, a sure fire way of sending him into the waiting arms of darkness without inflicting great injuries.

She looked down at the male where he lay at her side, his face slack and lips parted, strands of his blue-black hair brushing his brow. She wanted to sweep those strands away, ached to flutter her fingers over his sculpted cheek and apologise for what she had done. She hadn't known what he had suffered recently. She had only thought of saving him.

She felt her brother's eyes on her, sensed that she was taking too long and he was growing impatient, and suspicious of her. She forced herself to sit back so her brother could see the three jagged scars that ran over the elf's neck.

She couldn't resist touching them, placing the fingers she had used to create them against the start of each line and stroking down them to his collarbone.

She lifted her eyes away from the marks and up to her brother.

His eyes had turned cold. "Why did you not kill the male then?"

Taryn kneeled beside the elf, her fingers still against his bruised throat. His pulse beat steadily against their tips, reassuring her, and she silently swore to him that she would keep him safe and find a way to set him free.

"He had other elves with him then," she said in a calm, detached tone, revealing none of her turbulent feelings to her brother, afraid Tenak would hurt the elf if she showed even an ounce of remorse or concern about his welfare. "A trio of warriors. There was no way I could have won against them, so I fled. Those elves will be with him again. I am sure of it. They will be hiding somewhere, lying in wait for their commander's return. We must question him and find their locations so we might eradicate the threat completely."

Tenak lowered his eyes to the elf and darkness filled them, infinite ice that warned he was thinking terrible things.

Horrible things.

Her instincts pressed her to bare her fangs at him and warn him away from her male, and it took every shred of her will to stop herself. She couldn't obey that dark territorial urge that compelled her to attack her brother in order to protect what was hers. If she gave in to it, she would sign both hers and the elf's death warrants.

Tenak shifted his gaze back to her and she knew she hadn't won him over yet. He was still unconvinced. She had to do something more to make him do as she wanted, sparing the elf from death, and she knew what that something more was.

Cold crept over her exposed skin and she rubbed at it, running her palms and fingers up and down her arms. It didn't stop the cold. It sank deeper. Grew colder. Became ice in her marrow and penetrated her heart and her soul.

"They might not be alone this time," she whispered and stared off into the distance, falling into the white frigid abyss and unable to do anything but watch walls of sheer ice rise over her. She clawed at them, trying to gain a hold to stop herself, her nails digging in.

Warmth bloomed beneath them, hot against her freezing fingertips.

"Taryn!" Tenak barked and the white walls shook, shattered and tumbled around her, revealing a black valley and her brother where he crouched before her. His hands were warm on her shoulders, his grip fierce. His eyes searched hers, a touch of fear in them, concern that had her following them as they fell to her arms.

Blood.

She stared at it. Blinked. How had it gotten there?

She frowned as she drew her hands away from her arms. Crimson coated her fingertips too. It stained beneath her nails.

"What were you seeing?" Tenak whispered and rubbed his thumbs across her shoulders.

Fingers touching.

Touching.

Caressing.

She jerked free, scooted backwards and bumped into something warm.

Something that soothed the pain that had engulfed her, making her brother's touch feel like that of a terrible fiend bent on destroying her, not someone who loved her.

Taryn looked behind her at the elf male. His thighs pressed against her spine, the touch comforting. So comforting that it stripped her strength away and tears filled her eyes.

"Taryn?" Tenak reached for her and she whipped her head towards him and bared her fangs. He instantly moved back, giving her the space she needed, and she settled as the sense of comfort rolled over her again, sinking harder against the elf's legs, seeking the reassurance of his touch. Tenak settled on his haunches and eyed her. "What were you seeing?"

She shuddered and wrapped her arms around herself. "The arena. The black market. A few lunar cycles ago… the elf was there. He had many more men with him that time."

She swallowed hard, desperate to wet her dry throat and mouth, and rubbed her arms again as a chill went through her.

"There might be more this time. I did not see how many there were back then… the light from the stage… it… it made it…" Her throat closed and she shoved her hands into her hair, tugged it back from her face so hard that her scalp stung. "I cannot."

But she had to.

The pain of her memories, she could handle. She could deal with it. She wasn't sure she would be able to handle the pain of her brother killing the elf. Her fated male. His death would kill her too. She had to keep speaking, telling her brother about what she had seen. She had to convince him to go easy on the male. If she had to hurt herself to make that happen, she would do it.

She would bear any pain to spare her fated male.

Tenak eased forwards, recapturing her attention. Fear and agony collided inside her as she lifted her eyes to meet his, afraid of what she would find.

That fear abated when she found his eyes were soft and tender, and melted away when he spoke.

"We will take the male and question him. Do not think about your past anymore, Sister. I ache when I see you in pain." For a moment, a heartbeat of time, he was the brother she had grown up with back at the village, but then his face darkened and his eyes turned cold. "Think about the future, my precious one, for it will be glorious."

She suppressed the shudder that wracked her. Glorious? Bloodshed and violence wasn't glorious. Slaughtering all who stood in the way of ruling an entire realm wasn't glorious. It was madness.

The sort of insane thinking she had been exposed to and at the mercy of for three centuries.

Her brother shifted into his dragon form. When he reached for the elf male, every instinct she possessed roared at her and she sprang to her feet and launched into the path of his front paw. He halted and his huge eyes moved to her and narrowed.

"I will do it." That didn't seem to be explanation enough for her behaviour, because she could almost feel the suspicions taking root in her brother again. His eyes narrowed further. She rushed out, "You need not sully yourself with the elf. It is beneath you to carry such cargo back to our stronghold. I will do this for you. It is my place."

That seemed to appease him. He pushed back, causing rocks to tumble down the mountainside, and twisted as he beat his wings. She watched him take flight and then looked down at the elf and cursed him, wishing he hadn't been foolish enough to pursue her.

Tenak roared, a command that she felt all the way to her bones.

The shift was quick to come, transforming her swiftly into her dragon form. She skidded down the mountain until her huge paws found some purchase and she was able to claw her way back up to the elf, using a few flaps of her wings to assist her.

He lay where she had left him, the bruises on his throat exposed together with the scars she had given him.

Taryn carefully scooped him up into her right paw, cradled him gently and stared down at him.

Tiny dragon.

He had looked like one when he had been in full armour, his helmet flaring back into two horns and coming down into a point above his nose, and the slats covering the lower half of his face.

He was as fierce as one too. As determined.

Relentless in his pursuit of her.

She canted her head. Did he know why he pursued her so tirelessly?

Why he couldn't let her go?

She wasn't sure that he did. She wasn't sure he knew that she was his mate.

As she stared down at his prone form, his quiet steady breathing loud in her ears, her strongest dragon instincts roared to the forefront, urging her to carry him far away, to a place where he would be safe.

She couldn't.

She could feel Tenak's steady gaze on her. He had stopped a few hundred metres away and was hovering in the air, watching her closely.

She sighed and her breath stirred the elf's dark hair.

He had brought this upon himself, and all she could do was try to subtly control whatever awaited him, lessening the pain her brother would inflict on him and upon her without knowing it.

She curled her paw around her fated male and cradled him close to her. Her heart warmed behind the white plates of armour that spanned her chest as she felt him press against her, and she switched all of her focus to him as she kicked off.

Her wings beat at a slow pace to keep her flight smooth and avoid jostling him too much.

He was cool against her, weighed nothing in her palm, but she knew he was a male whose blood was fire and body was strong. She knew he could survive whatever awaited him, and she wouldn't leave his side. She would protect him as best she could.

She would find a way to set him free.

CHAPTER 18

It stank.

Wherever he was, it reeked of fetid things. Stale water. Putrid blood. Rancid bile.

Bleu groaned and breathed slowly, fighting to get air into his lungs and not only because the foul odour robbed him of breath and made him want to retch. His already bruised and battered throat now felt as if someone had gone at it with a vice, squeezing it until his trachea had been close to breaking.

His wheezing breaths only served to stir the wretched pool of filth beneath him. He mustered all of his strength, planted his palms against the cold stone floor and pushed himself up, opening his eyes at the same time. The dim light from the wooden torch mounted on the stone wall opposite him was a mercy, giving his eyes time to adjust to being used again.

He slowly took in his surroundings. One wall of metal bars in front of him, and two more sets of bars on either side, those ones filling an arch. He looked behind him as much as he could without hurting his throat. That wall was solid black stone.

A cellblock. In the castle he had been scouting by the looks of things. No windows for him to check whether the outside world matched the valley though. Where else would the dragon have taken him?

He was surprised the male had taken him anywhere.

Bleu gingerly touched his throat and winced when even the slightest pressure hurt it. He needed blood to restore the strength his body was already devouring in order to speed his healing process, but he doubted he would get it here. His captor was unlikely to want to keep him strong. With every second that ticked past without him drinking blood, he grew weaker, and something told him that the male wanted that.

Why hadn't the dragon killed him?

A flash of the female shot across his mind and he grimaced and clutched his head as it ached.

Had she stopped him?

He had caught the concern in her eyes, had felt her fear when her brother had been strangling him, and he had the feeling that he owed his life to her. She had somehow gained him a reprieve. He looked around the cell again. Although, he wasn't sure his situation had improved at all.

He pushed his hands against the damp black flagstones and froze.

Bare hands.

Bare arms.

Bare wrists.

Panic lanced him and he looked himself over. Bare *everything*. He growled through his fangs and crawled around the cell, the rough stones biting into his knees as he scoured it for his armour bands. After an exhausting few minutes of searching, he slumped against the solid wall, breathing hard and shivering. Something wasn't right.

It made sense that he would be weak from his body using his blood to speed the healing of his throat, but he shouldn't have been this weak.

Bleu leaned the right side of his head against the cold stones and tried to focus. He dove deep into his body, calling his portal, willing his wristbands to appear.

Nothing.

Perhaps the dragon had them locked somewhere his power couldn't reach. There were many ways of sealing away objects and stopping him from being able to call them.

He focused on his apartments in the castle in the elf kingdom instead and reached for something that held no power and was therefore less taxing. Trousers.

A hazy connection formed, wobbled. He focused harder on it, drawing on his limited strength to reinforce the bond between him and the item of clothing. Sweat beaded on his brow and rolled down his back, cold against his exposed skin. His breath came harder, scraping in his throat.

The link shattered and he slumped against the wall, his limbs like rubber.

Gods damn it.

Bleu looked himself over and his eyes halted on an innocuous red spot on his right forearm. He managed to lift his left hand and rub his thumb over it. The spot didn't go away, no matter how hard he rubbed it, and the area around it was tender.

Drugged.

He twisted and sank with his back against the wall. His breathing evened out but his heart didn't steady. It continued to race, driven by the fear slowly sinking its claws into him.

He drew down a shuddering deep breath.

The scent of blood hit him hard and his fangs itched.

He suppressed his hunger, forced his fangs away, and tried to focus. He could get out of this. Somehow.

He tipped his head back and looked up at the ceiling, and his senses stretched outwards, covering as much ground as he could manage while he was weak. Where was the female dragon?

Taryn.

She had saved him. He knew it. He had lived long enough to recognise when someone had put their life on the line for him, and she had definitely risked her neck for his sake. She had been afraid of her brother but she had somehow stopped that dangerous male from killing him.

He pulled down another deep breath through his nose and closed his eyes, reaching for her.

He could almost feel her moving around above him, and he could definitely smell her. He lifted his fingers to his nose and inhaled, taking the scent of her down into his lungs. She had touched him. Had she been the one to strip him?

Was she in possession of his armour?

He inhaled again, felt light as her scent filled his lungs, dominating the rank odour of the cells with the unique smell of her that was so out of place in this grim citadel that reeked of death.

She smelled like sunshine and blue skies, and he wasn't sure how she could smell of such things when she was restricted to Hell and had probably never seen the mortal world.

Bleu sighed and willed her to come to him, to help him out of this mess he had gotten himself into, or at least let him see her again and drink in her beauty before he died.

He huffed. Idiotic thoughts. He had been in worse situations and had made it through, and this time wasn't going to be any different. He would find a way out of his cell, would escape the castle and lay low until the drugs had left his system, and then he would teleport back to the garrison and admit that he had been a fucking idiot.

Gods, Leif was going to have a field day with this.

He needed to investigate his surroundings before the male dragon came to see him.

The bastard would come, Bleu was sure of that.

Drugging him and putting him in a cell wasn't the end of the male's plans for him. The way the male had looked at him, a sick sadistic edge to his smile, had promised pain and suffering, and it wouldn't be long before he came down to deliver on that.

Someone tossed a dirty rag into his cell through the bars to his right. He frowned at the scrap of black material and crawled over to it, not trusting his legs to bear his weight when his head was still fuzzy and he was growing weaker by the second. He picked up the cloth, looked at it and then peered into the cell beside his.

The female kneeling in the centre of it tensed and shrank back, dirty arms racing to cover herself. She wore similar cloth to that which she had offered him, two strips of it that barely covered her breasts and her hips.

He thanked her with a nod and tied the scrap around his hips, covering himself.

"What is your name?" he said in English, choosing a neutral language. Many in Hell spoke a little of it, but his decision this time was made based on the fact that she was a fae of some sort. Most fae travelled regularly to the mortal world or lived there. "My name is Bleu."

She huddled into herself, her matted brown hair falling down over her face, and shook her head. Her bloodstained fingers jerkily stroked her arms and he grimaced as he spotted that her left little finger was bent at a horrific angle, twisted backwards. The finger beside it appeared broken too.

Those injuries weren't her only ones. There was barely an inch of her that wasn't bruised or cut. What sick things had the dragon male done to her?

"What is your name?" he tried again, this time in the old fae tongue, a language he hadn't spoken in millennia.

She gasped and her bloodshot golden-brown eyes shot to meet his. Tears splashed onto her cheeks and she shuffled away from him, backing into the far corner of her cell. He had seen terrible things in his years, but nothing on this level. He had never seen a female so broken and scarred, withdrawn into herself.

He left her alone, not wanting to scare her when she was already terrified.

The cells beyond her were occupied too. Two males. One alive, and the other not.

The gruesome remains of what had once been a male hung from chains and hooks, suspended from the ceiling, sections of his skin peeled back to reveal muscle and bone, and stomach sliced open, guts streaming from the gaping hole.

Bleu blew out his breath, sucked down another one as his stomach rebelled, acid burning up his throat, and prayed to his gods that they were on his side for once and he didn't end up like that poor bastard.

He pressed a hand to his abdomen and dug his fingertips in. Shuddered.

It wasn't going to happen. He wouldn't let it happen. He was going to find a way out of this mess and he was going to make it back to his team. Leif would berate him. Dacian would give him the old I-told-you-so. Fynn would somehow turn it all into a joke.

He should have brought them with him. Together they could have fought off the dragon male and escaped. Now he was trapped here alone and they had no clue as to his location. Leif didn't know the valley.

It was painful to admit it, but he was a royal idiot for trying to do things solo.

And why?

Because he had wanted to protect the female. He had wanted to keep her to himself.

He scrubbed a hand over his face. Gods help him. He was a bigger idiot than he had previously thought. He was the god of all idiots.

Because he had been blinded by lust again, made to believe something that wasn't there.

She was his fated female, and he wanted to believe she felt something for him, but his current situation was making it hard to believe anything other than that she had stopped her brother from killing him for some nefarious reason.

It smelled of her down here.

She had been in the cellblock, and his gut said it had happened more than once.

For all he knew, she participated in torturing the poor souls trapped in the cages around him.

He couldn't pretend he hadn't noticed the coldness in her eyes, the same ice and darkness that had been in her brother's when the male had been throttling him.

A rumbling growl cut his train of thought short and had his head whipping towards the source of the sound. Footsteps echoed down the spiral stairwell to his left. The female in the cell to his right shrieked and curled into a tight ball, her fear washing over him.

Bleu didn't move.

He knew what was coming and that it was coming for him. All he could do now was prepare himself for the inevitable.

He was going to find out exactly what the dragons did to their captives to turn them into broken messes.

The male dragon loomed out of the darkness, golden light washing over his bare chest as he strode around the perimeter of Bleu's cell and came to a halt in front of it, near the door.

His violet-to-white eyes locked on Bleu and Bleu held them, keeping his breathing slow and his pulse steady. The male's lips quirked into a smile and then stretched into a grin.

"I have the feeling you will be an interesting one." The dragon flicked a glance at the female, sighed and looked back at Bleu. "The others have disappointed me so much… they are weak… they broke easily… but you…"

"Will kick your arse if you give me a few more minutes to purge this damned drug from my system," Bleu growled and rose onto his feet. His legs wobbled but he locked his knees, tensed his thighs and refused to fall. He bared his emerging fangs at the male, his voice a thick snarl as he pushed words out through his battered throat. "You lock your victims in cages and weaken them before you dare set foot in them. You want interesting… I will show you interesting… just a little blood and a few minutes and I will show you how weak you are."

The dragon launched at the bars of his cell, hands slamming into them and rattling them. Bleu held his ground, calmly holding the dragon's gaze as stone dust rained down from the points where the metal bars met the ceiling. The male was strong, but easy to antagonise. Prince Loren's voice rang around Bleu's head, a montage of the million and one times he had told him not to antagonise his opponents.

It never stopped him from doing it.

An angry and frustrated enemy was an enemy who was ruled by their emotions, unable to think clearly. It was an advantage, and Bleu loved to take it.

"You think yourself strong?" The male pulled a set of keys from his pocket, slid one into the lock on his cell door, and twisted it. The door creaked open and the dragon stalked into it, his eyes narrowed and fury rolling off him.

He tilted his head, cracking his neck, and rolled his shoulders, and then slammed the door closed behind him. "I will show *you* how weak you are."

Bleu ducked under the fist that came at his face and tried to evade the one aimed at his stomach, but wasn't quick enough. It struck hard, knocking the wind from him and lifting him off his feet. He grunted and wheezed, and then growled as he tasted blood.

He had said to give him five minutes, hadn't he? The bastard wasn't going to prove anything by fighting him right now, while he was weakened by drugs.

Well, he wasn't going to prove anything other than he was a pathetic male who knew he couldn't win a fair fight so resorted to nefarious means to bring down an opponent.

Bleu spat blood in his face and swung at him. The male dodged backwards and Bleu followed through. The motion sent him off balance and he staggered right, tripped on his own damn feet and hit the black flagstones with jarring force, grunting again as he struck them.

"Pathetic." The dragon grabbed him by the back of his neck and dragged him onto his feet.

"Funny," he rasped, paused when he sounded groggy and shook his head to clear it of the fuzziness that was already encroaching around the edges of his mind, and flashed bloodied teeth at the male in a grin. "My thoughts exactly."

The stone wall greeted Bleu's back with a fierce embrace and he barely stopped himself from crying out as every bone in his body ached from the blow, fire zinging along them and numbing his fingertips. His knees gave out but the dragon grabbed him by the throat before he could hit the floor, hauling him off his feet and pinning him to the wall.

Someone else had done that to him once and it hadn't gone down well then, and it damned well didn't go down well now.

He brought his right leg up and slammed it hard between the dragon's violet-leather-clad thighs. The male grunted, dropped him and staggered back, clutching at his groin. Bleu's feet hit the floor and his legs almost gave out, but he remained standing. Progress.

He flexed his fingers, testing his body's responsiveness. It was improving. Just a few more minutes and he would be strong enough to show this male that he had picked a fight with the wrong elf.

The male lifted his head and slowly released his crotch and rose to his full height. Violet fire flashed in his eyes as he rolled his shoulders back and his honed bare broad torso tensed as he growled.

The fingers of Bleu's left hand twitched and he focused on them and the link between him and his blade, willing it to come to him.

The dragon looked down at his hand and then up into his eyes and hissed at him. He moved faster than Bleu could track, snatching his left arm and twisting it behind his back, shoving his hand up his spine so far that his elbow snapped.

He bit down on his tongue to stop himself from crying out and breathed through the pain as his cheek and chest slammed into the cold stone wall, the dragon's powerful body pinning him against it.

"You will scream for me," the dragon snarled into his ear, breath hot on Bleu's cheek, and pressed him harder against the wall as he twisted his arm at an excruciating angle. "You will scream for her."

Her.

That word pierced his pain-fogged mind.

Taryn.

A part of him reached out to her in response to her name whispered in his skull, seeking her, desperate to feel her.

The dragon sank claws into the back of his neck and yanked him away from the wall, spun him around and slammed a fist into his face. He lashed out with his right hand, trying to shove the male away, to gain enough space and time to stop his head from spinning and find his feet again. The male didn't let up. He grabbed Bleu's throat and punched him harder, pummelling his face.

"Scream," the dragon bit out.

Bleu refused.

He gritted his teeth and didn't make a sound as the male worked him over, not even when he switched to hitting him in the kidney and then his stomach. Not even when he kneed him between the thighs.

Not even when he raked claws down his bare chest and slashed up his back.

He wouldn't give the male the satisfaction of hearing him scream.

Time blurred, the pain stealing focus from him, so his tentative connection with the female slipped away beyond his reach. The world turned red, hazy with blood as it streamed over his face from the cuts where the male had clawed at his skull, holding the top of his head as he had slashed talons over his flesh, cutting through his muscles and scraping over his bones.

Hot liquid dripped down onto his chest, seared the lacerations on it, and everything became streaked with bright colours before it all turned monochrome. Spots of colour came back. Red of blood. Violet. Startlingly vivid against the black and greys.

The male shoved him aside and Bleu skidded on the pool of his own blood that now coated the black stones and landed in a heap in the centre of it.

The dragon towered over him, bloodied chest heaving, eyes burning with violet fire. He held his hand up, a small empty vial held between his thumb and index finger, the source of the flames that had licked across Bleu's wounds and caught his blood alight, and grinned viciously.

"Let us see how you fare now, Warrior." Those words seemed to shimmer in the air before the dragon, twisted and echoed in Bleu's ears as he struggled against the white-hot fire running through his blood, burning it up.

Bleu tried to focus on the male but he wobbled and distorted, blurred one moment and painfully sharp the next.

He sat on his knees, arms limp and useless at his sides, pain and the drug numbing him but setting him on fire at the same time.

His fangs itched, the scent of blood driving him mad with hunger.

Darkness rose in response to that hunger, transforming it into a terrible craving that he couldn't deny. It consumed him, devouring his strength, tearing down his control until he could think of only one thing.

Blood.

He narrowed his eyes on the dragon's carotid.

Launched at him with fangs bared.

The male backhanded him and he shot across the cell and hit the cold metal bars. Lightning sizzled across his mind, jagged tendrils reaching over his skull, and he slid down the bars to the ground, the world around him spinning.

When it finally stopped, the dragon male was gone and the door to his cell was open.

Bleu frowned at it, and then clawed at the ground, slipping the fingers of his right hand into the cracks between the flagstones and growling as he dragged himself towards it.

He had barely moved a few inches before the male was there in the doorway.

He wasn't alone.

The dark-haired female he held by the back of her neck struggled like a wild thing in his grip, screaming and lashing out with her arms and legs.

"You are not allowed to die yet," the dragon snarled and Bleu looked between him and the female, struggling to focus on either of them as his strength ebbed away and the roar for blood grew deafening in his ears. "You die once you have paid for chasing my sister… you die once she has witnessed your punishment and gives you leave to do so. Now… we will make you strong again."

Bleu's eyes slowly widened as the female the dragon held stilled and looked at him, her golden eyes enormous and her skin washing of colour beneath the dried blood and dirt.

He tried to speak, fought to find his voice and tell the dragon not to do it, because the darkness running in his veins was too strong, the hunger too fierce to deny.

She started to shake her head.

The dragon hurled her at Bleu and he pounced on her, taking her down to the ground and sinking his aching fangs into her neck. Blood burst onto his tongue and he moaned low in his parched throat as he gulped it down, a slave to his hunger as it hijacked control of him.

A dim and distant part of him told him to stop but he crushed that voice and sank his fangs deeper into her flesh, relished her cry as she clawed at him, fighting him and causing his teeth to tear ragged holes in her. He frantically lapped at the blood she spilled, desperate for it all, unwilling to waste a single drop.

He needed it.

He snarled as someone moved on the periphery of his senses, dragged the female closer to him so they couldn't take her from him, and bit her again. She jerked in his arms and screamed, her warm sweet blood filling his mouth, feeding the darkness that flowed through him, swirling deeper to wrap black thorny tendrils around his mind and his soul. They tightened their hold as he drank deeper, greedily gulping down her blood.

"Feed," a male voice murmured.

Bleu did so, too hungry to stop now that he had started and part of him silently hoping that if he obeyed the male, he would give him another to drink from.

Once this one was dead.

CHAPTER 19

Taryn rushed from her room and hit the hallway at a sprint. Breath sawed from her lips and burned in her lungs, and her heart beat painfully hard. It leaped into her throat when the agonised bellow came again, joined by a more feminine shriek of terror this time.

The elf.

She bolted down to the next level and pushed herself harder, cursing herself for leaving Tenak's side for even a heartbeat. She should have remained with him at all times, but she had needed a moment to breathe and pull herself together. Her brother had taken advantage of that, venturing down to the cellblock alone when he had sworn he would wait for her.

She cursed him too.

Another chilling high-pitched scream tore through the black castle.

Gods, what was her brother doing to her fated male?

The closer she came to the dungeon entrance, the stronger the sensations running through her became. The clearer they grew. Until she could feel the male's pain and suffering, and the violence that filled him.

The darkness.

She banged her right shoulder on the stone doorframe, winced and pushed on, hurrying down the spiral steps. As she neared the dungeon, she managed to rein back enough control to slow her steps. She slowed her breathing too, fighting the instincts running rampant through her, demanding she reach her male and protect him from whatever wretched thing her brother had in mind for him.

The pain flowing through her grew stronger still, until it beat at her and she trembled. Such suffering. It chilled her blood and she rubbed her arms, desperate to warm herself and shake the images that clouded her mind, tormenting her—a vision of what her beloved brother had done to her fated one.

She had seen the sorts of acts her brother committed in this cellblock and as much as she wanted to push away from the images of her male suffering the same fate, she forced herself to let them wash over her, using them to prepare herself for what awaited her.

Her steps slowed further still, until she was barely moving as she wrestled with her feelings and her instincts, trying to bring them under control. She couldn't fly into the cellblock as she wanted and tear into her brother. She had to keep playing the role she had undertaken and see it through to the end, and that meant ensuring her brother still thought she was on his side, as mad with a hunger for power and vengeance as he was.

It was hard though.

She stopped on the stairs as her legs weakened and wobbled beneath her, the elf's pain so strong that it crashed over her, threatening to send her to her knees. She shot her hands out on both sides, pressing them into the damp walls in the narrow stairwell, and breathed through it.

When her heart had steadied again and her instincts no longer ruled her, she pressed forwards, prepared to face what awaited her and do all she could to stop the elf's suffering.

Taryn took the remaining few steps down to the dungeon and turned her head to her right, fixing her focus straight on the cell beside her.

On the elf male in the middle of it, stripped bare and snarling as he savagely fed from a fae female.

Gods, she had been wrong.

She wasn't prepared at all.

Her breath left her in a rasping rush and she staggered backwards, her bottom hitting the wall.

The elf lifted his head and her knees almost gave out. Blood and gore drenched the lower half of his face and coated his chest, and his fangs were long white daggers between crimson lips as he stared at her, a glassy quality to his violet eyes as they leaped straight to her.

He growled and looked away from her, still for a moment, a heartbeat of time that made her want to reach out to him and tell him to stop, sure that she could get through to him even when he was so far gone, lost to the darkness she could feel in him.

He sank his fangs back into the female another second later, a feral snarl peeling from his lips as he bit her. She cried out, the sound feeble and weak now, and Taryn shifted her focus to her. Her pulse was weak.

The elf was going to kill her if Taryn didn't do something.

She dragged her eyes away from the male and turned towards the bend in the corridor that would lead her around to where her brother stood in front of the elf's cell. The female screamed again, a gurgled sound that sent a cold wave through Taryn. Her vision distorted and she gripped the wall for support, breathing hard and fast again as memories rose up to seize hold of her and drag her down into them.

Her skin crawled, icy fingers dancing across it. Touching. Caressing. Threatening to sink their claws in and tear her sanity away.

Taryn swallowed the bile that rose into her throat and pushed forwards, forcing her feet to move. She couldn't lose her mind now. She had to reach her brother.

She turned the corner and lifted her head, and her eyes caught on his hand. His fingers clutched a small glass vial.

Tenak had given the elf a hallucinogenic drug that dragons used on the eve of battle to stir their strength and hunger for the fight, and destroy any fears they might have. Those dragons took it in powdered form, because it was slower to enter the bloodstream and the effects were drawn out.

In liquid form, the drug was swift to enter the blood, the effect of it hitting the user in a devastating rush that had been known to destroy the mind of even the strongest dragons.

Taryn stared at the vial.

Her brother had given the drug to the elf as a liquid, and she couldn't imagine what it had done to him.

She looked across at the male as she approached her brother. Her breathing came quicker again, flashes of her past overlaying onto the present, flickers of all the cages she had seen and all the poor souls they had contained.

Agony rolled through her, cold and hot at the same time, tearing down her strength and she sank into her memories, unable to claw her way to freedom as she stared at the elf male.

Caged.

Forced to do things against his will.

She wrapped her arms around herself and pressed her nails into her flesh, using the pain to anchor her in the present. It wouldn't last forever. The trick would give her a few minutes at best before the memories regained control and she slipped away again, drowning in them.

A few minutes in which she had to watch her male as he suffered.

Gods, part of her wanted to sink into her memories to escape the terrible sight.

The rest of her demanded she stay lucid and do something.

She looked to her brother. He watched the elf for a few seconds longer and then looked across at her, a satisfied smile on his face. She wanted to claw it off.

"He will scream for you, Sister. He will pay."

She wanted to scream at him that she didn't want that. The elf had done nothing wrong. He didn't deserve what her brother was inflicting on him.

Because of her.

Tenak wanted the male to suffer as payment for hunting her.

She couldn't bear that. She knew her brother couldn't see what he was doing to her, reminding her of the dark things she had survived, keeping them constantly close to the surface of her mind so they tormented her, chipping away at her sanity and leaving her feeling she was close to becoming as mad as he was.

He only thought of pleasing her in his own twisted way.

She looked back at the elf and closed her eyes when he bit down again, snarling as he tore at the female. What terror was he experiencing as he devoured her? Taryn could feel there was a part of him still aware of what he was doing and she knew that when the drug wore off and he realised he had killed the female, the guilt would destroy him.

He was a noble male.

Not a murderer.

She couldn't allow him to kill the female. She couldn't let him suffer more than he had and he would if he took the fae's life when lost to whatever madness gripped him.

The darkness.

She knew enough about elves to know that many lost themselves to the darkness that lurked within them all, a part of them that they needed but feared at the same time, constantly wrestling to keep it under control.

That darkness was slowly sinking its teeth into the male, but her instincts said that it hadn't consumed him yet. There was still time to save him, but she had to act now. If he killed the fae, he would be lost forever in the black abyss.

"Brother," she said, keeping the tremble of nerves from her voice and her eyes on the elf male when Tenak looked down at her. She forced a smile, the most grotesquely twisted one she could manage, and raised her eyes to her brother. "Thank you for making him suffer… but I wish to… I want to make him suffer myself. I want to savour this moment alone. You have had your time with him. Please allow me to have mine."

The fae female's heart stuttered and Taryn's palms began to sweat, her pulse kicking up a notch as she waited for her brother to respond.

He stared at her for long seconds and she almost glanced at the elf male, on the verge of screaming at her fated one to stop what he was doing before he killed the female and damned himself.

"Very well," Tenak said and she had never heard sweeter words.

Relief rolled over her as her brother walked away and she listened to him ascending the stairs, tracked him with her senses to make sure he was moving to a distance where he would be unaware of what she was about to do.

The moment he had moved high into the castle, she tore the cell door open and lunged forwards. The male lifted his head and hissed through bloodied fangs at her as she reached for the fae female. His warning rushed through her, a command to stay away from his prize that she ignored. He wouldn't kill her, but he would kill the fae if she let this go on any longer.

Taryn ripped the fae female away from him, twisted with her and set her down near the door of the cell. Her fingers shook as she groped over the fae's throat, searching for a pulse. It was weak, but it was there, and the relief that went through Taryn almost brought her to tears.

The elf male growled behind her.

It was all the warning she had before the cell spun around her and his fangs were in her throat.

She whimpered as pain seared her, her head spinning from the dizzying rush of him drawing on her blood. He snarled and drew her closer, wrapping his strong arms around her and crushing her against his bloodied bare chest. It heaved against hers, pressing in hard, making it difficult for her to breathe.

Her heart pounded hard and she clutched at his shoulders, tried to push him back. Her fingers slipped in all the blood, sliding off him as she fought him.

He growled a warning this time, a command that she felt to the very depth of her soul. He wanted her to keep still. She couldn't. She shoved against his shoulders, panic at the helm, desperately fighting his hold on her.

"Let me go," she whispered in the dragon tongue.

He bit down harder and she had to clench her teeth to stop herself from crying out. She couldn't make a sound, no matter how much it hurt or how afraid she was. If her brother heard her and realised what she had done, he would kill the elf and she would be next.

"Please." She clawed at his shoulders and wriggled in his arms, and fierce fire licked down her throat as his fangs shifted, slicing through her skin.

He snarled again, released her neck and grappled with her, seizing hold of her arms. She shook her head and fought him, refusing to give in, but she wasn't strong enough. He easily pinned her arms between them, his grip on them bruising as he clutched both of her wrists together in one hand. His other hand grasped her neck and she whimpered as his fangs sank back into her throat.

He moaned.

Tears streamed down her cheeks and she stared at the ceiling of the cell, her strength draining from her as rapidly as her blood as he fed deeply, suckling hard on her neck.

Her vision dulled.

Caged.

In bars made of flesh and blood this time.

She had to break free. That thought pounded through her even as her struggling slowed, her actions becoming weaker as her mind fogged.

She shook in his arms, cold to the bone, no longer strong enough to fight even when she wanted to, desperately needed to break free. She needed to live, but she couldn't move as her life slipped away from her and darkness loomed around her.

A single thought swam around her head, one that chilled her and stole the last of her strength.

Loke had been right.

The elf would be responsible for her death.

CHAPTER 20

Bliss.

Bleu floated in the darkness, lost in his hunger, drowning in it. He embraced it. Caught it in his hands, drew it to his chest and curled around it, tucking it close to his heart.

Blinding light pierced the endless black, a bolt of lightning inside his mind.

No. Not lightning in his mind.

A shaft of sunlight inside his heart.

It warmed him and stirred his hunger, but brought awareness back with it. The taste of blood on his tongue. A warm body pressed against his. He had been hungry before but the smooth, smoky-sweet blood flowing down his throat now had made his thirst unquenchable.

He couldn't get enough, even when a piece of him, a dim part of his mind, warned him to stop.

He was hurting her.

Yet the feel of her hands clutching him, clinging to him, gave him pleasure deeper than any he had ever known, a sensation of being whole for the very first time that left him feeling he had been empty all these years, drifting through his life with part of him missing.

He bit her harder and willed her to tighten her hold on him, to cling to him as fiercely as he clung to her.

Her grip loosened instead.

Her slender body went limp in his arms.

Bleu slowed his drinking, the awareness her blood had awoken in him gaining ground, driving back the darkness. He was endangering them both, but he still couldn't bring himself to stop. He didn't care.

He wanted to drink her down until she was a part of him, fused with him in a way that was unbreakable.

She would belong to him forever.

He would never be alone again.

Something screamed at the back of his mind, a jumbled wave of words that struck terror into his heart, although he didn't know why. He lapped at her blood, moaning at the taste of her. Divine.

His heart faltered.

He frowned and then grimaced as it missed another beat, and then began to slow, and his head felt light, his thoughts tangling together before splintering apart.

The strength that had been flowing through him instantly diminished, fading away until he was trembling, barely clinging to consciousness by the bloodied tips of his claws.

He needed more blood.

He went to sink his fangs back into the female and stopped dead with the very tips of them touching her flesh.

Her pulse beat weakly in his ears.

In *his* chest.

Her fear tainted *his* blood.

The darkness lifted as primal instincts roared to the fore and the words that had been jumbled before fell into order.

He was killing her.

Bleu forced himself back and looked down at the female in his arms. Her face ashen. Throat ravaged.

The dragon.

His mate.

He felt it keenly in his soul as he stared at her where she lay in his arms, her beauty stealing his breath and making him burn even as what he had done hollowed out his chest and left him cold.

"Taryn," he whispered as he carefully shifted her in his arms, cradling her in his left one, not feeling the pain that burned through the still-healing bones. Not caring about his own suffering. It meant nothing. His mate meant everything. He stroked her bloodied left cheek, brushing the backs of his fingers across it. "Taryn."

He willed her to wake and answer him, desperate for her to look at him and let him know that he hadn't killed her.

He couldn't have killed her.

"Taryn," he bit out, harsher now, unable to stop the surge of darker emotions as they swept through him, unleashed by his fear that he was going to lose her.

She didn't respond.

His strength drained from him, hope dying with it, and he curled over her, burying his face in her fall of violet-to-white hair as he clung to her. Fuck, what had he done?

Tears burned the backs of his eyes and he growled into her throat, clutching her closer to him, near mad with a need to feel her warmth against him and hear her tell him that she would be fine. She wasn't going to die.

Her pulse grew weaker, the timid beat echoing in his chest, affecting his own heart.

His eyes widened.

The bond.

Gods, he had triggered it by biting her and taking her blood.

Now it linked them, incomplete but powerful, entwining their bodies.

He pulled back and set his jaw. He wasn't going to let her die. He refused to lose her.

He placed his right hand over her heart, closed his eyes and focused on her blood in his body—on his connection to her. The link shimmered in his blood, began to grow stronger until it burned in his veins. His head turned, the effort draining him, but he refused to stop. He didn't care if he killed himself.

He only cared about saving her.

In his mind, he reached out and caught the ribbon of red that now linked them, curled his fingers around it and clutched it so tightly his knuckles burned.

Warmth flowed through him and he sank deep into the connection, drifting through it into Taryn and using his psychic abilities to forge a stronger link between them. His strength leached away as his powers took their toll on him, but he kept pushing, using all of his will to hold the connection between them open so he could hijack control of her body.

The warmth became a fire, a blaze that burned through him, and flames licked at his throat, white-hot and fierce.

Bleu opened his eyes and stared at the wounds on her throat as they burned on his.

He turned his focus to his body—to his heart—and willed it to beat harder. He drew deep breaths, slowly and steadily filling his lungs, and gradually his pulse grew stronger.

And hers grew stronger with it.

His arms shook where he held her, trembling against her back as his hand quivered against her chest, pressed between her breasts.

Her heartbeat gained strength beneath his palm and in his chest, his own one fuelling hers, keeping it going as he silently urged her to find her will to live again. She was strong. A dragon. Her healing abilities were on a par with his. If he could keep her heart going for long enough, her body would restore enough of her lost blood to keep her alive.

Lost blood.

He sneered at that.

Blood he had stolen from her.

He had almost killed her. What kind of male did that make him? What kind of mate? He was meant to protect her, to keep her safe and never let anything bad happen to her. That was his duty as her mate, and he had failed.

He had failed to protect her, but he wouldn't fail to save her.

He wasn't sure how long he sat with her, the link between them held wide open by sheer force of will alone, his heart beating for hers. Everything faded until there was only Taryn, lying in his arms, teetering on the brink of death.

Until there was only the terrifying thought of losing her and the grim determination to stop that from happening.

His strength faded as he poured all of it into saving her. The world around him dimmed and his hand rested lax against her chest, his body no longer able to power his muscles. All he could do was sit with her resting on his lap and cling to the slender thread of the link between them.

A slender thread of hope.

His vision wobbled and darkness encroached.

Her eyelids fluttered.

Bleu jerked awake and studied her face, a surge of energy blasting through him and driving the darkness back. He stared down at her, willing her to move again, to prove he hadn't been dreaming.

She did one better.

She moaned.

"Gods, I am sorry, Ki'ara," he whispered in the elf tongue, the flood of emotions that crashed over him battering him so fiercely he shook from the onslaught. He managed to lift his hand and stroke her cheek as he stared down at her. "I am so sorry. I never meant to hurt you… I swear it."

Her eyes slowly opened, a frown knitting her eyebrows together. He knew she couldn't understand him, but he wasn't ready to say things in a language she knew, not when she wasn't ready to hear them and he wasn't ready to face everything.

"You tried to help me," he murmured in his own tongue and cupped her cheek in his palm. It was cold. He rubbed it gently, trying to get some warmth back into her. "I repaid you by attacking you… and triggering this bond between us."

A bond that relayed fragments of her emotions, enough that he could feel her confusion and how tired she was.

Bleu's fingers shook as he brushed them through her hair, carefully working the knots out from the violet roots to the bloodstained white tips. She remained relaxed against him, not fighting his hold, not even when he found the strength to curl his left hand around her arm and draw her closer to him. He cradled her and, fuck, she was beautiful as she gazed up at him. Breathtaking.

He didn't deserve such a beautiful female.

He averted his gaze and it settled on the reason he didn't deserve her. Blood pooled in the gouges on the left side of her throat where he had savagely bitten her and steadily dripped onto the dirty damp floor of his cell, mingling with his.

He looked away from her and closed his eyes, shame riding him mercilessly, heart reproaching him. He had hurt her. Damn near killed her.

He swallowed hard, trying to clear the lump in his throat that refused to go away.

Gods damn him.

His fingers tightened against her arm and he gritted his teeth, bit out a string of curses in the elf tongue when all he really wanted to do was scream his rage until his voice gave out. He couldn't. If the dragon male heard him, he might come to see what was happening, and the male would surely kill him then.

What would happen to her?

Her shallow rasping breaths filled the silence, scraping in his ears, tugging all of his fear back to the surface. He was going to lose her. He screwed his eyes shut and focused on her pulse to allay that fear, listening to her heart beating steadily.

A heart he'd had to keep working through their connection.

A heart that he should have cherished enough to recognise it had been his mate he had been drinking dry.

Killing.

His throat burned. Nose stung. Eyes felt as if someone had just poured a shot of Hellfire into them. His lips peeled back off his fangs as he frowned and he ground out another curse.

Trembling cool fingers touched his cheek, icy against his burning skin, and his eyes flew open only to close a second later as realisation blazed through him, self-reproach following swiftly in its wake.

She was trying to comfort him.

The gods knew he didn't deserve it.

He deserved her anger, her hatred.

He didn't deserve this tenderness, this touch that came too close to affection.

Her fingers dropped lower, caressed under his jaw, and he refused to obey that silent command and look at her. He couldn't. He screwed his eyes closed even tighter and his nostrils flared as he drew down a deep breath, trying to find his feet again when the whole world had been tossed off kilter once more.

Taryn refused to give him that moment, her fingers pressing against his jaw, firmer now.

Stronger.

He could almost feel her strength returning, trickling back into her. Any moment now, she was going to give him hell and he wouldn't fight her. He would take whatever punishment she wanted to dish out and wouldn't try to stop her when she walked away from him. He knew the score. He knew that what they shared wasn't meant to be. He wasn't the right male for her and nothing he could do would change that. He had proven it here today.

To her and to himself.

She deserved better.

He shifted his gaze to her and then back down to her throat. Crimson seeped from the wounds he had inflicted, so bright against her pale skin. It covered her chest and stained her cream corset. Drenched the side of her face, drying dark on her skin and in her hair.

Gods damn him.

He didn't want to frighten her, but he couldn't leave her as she was. He couldn't deny the need to take care of her. A ridiculous need. Tending to her wasn't going to give him the result he was looking for. It wouldn't atone for what he had done. It had been an unforgivable act.

Even with those words ringing around his mind, he still couldn't stop himself from carefully lifting her towards him with his left arm and lowering his head to her throat. She tensed in his arms, her heart skipping a beat and causing his to do the same.

"I will not hurt you," he whispered in the dragon tongue and then added in his own language, the one she couldn't understand, "I swear I will never hurt you again, Ki'ara. Never. Let me take care of you… please… for this moment… let me think of you as mine."

Her eyes searched his, implored him to speak in a way she could grasp, but he couldn't. He wasn't ready to acknowledge what was happening or what it meant, that it meant anything at all. He wasn't strong enough to bare that part of himself he had guarded for millennia.

Not when he knew she would crush him in return.

"Let me take care of you," he murmured in the elf tongue.

She seemed to get the message from the gentleness of his voice, or perhaps she was picking up on the feelings running through him, the emotions he wasn't quite able to conceal because he didn't know how to control the connection between them.

If it was possible to control it at all.

She relaxed and he dropped his lips to her throat, coursed them over it and breathed her in, stealing a moment with her before he began licking the wounds to clean them and halt the flow of blood, helping them heal.

A shudder wracked him, pulling a moan up his throat that he managed to swallow back down before it could escape. She tasted divine.

Resist.

He was trying, but, fuck, she was everything sweet and light and warm and he wanted to drown in her as he lapped at her throat, running his tongue over her skin. She trembled in his arms.

Oh, dear gods, resist.

Bleu frowned and stilled, his breath washing back at him from her skin, carrying her intoxicating scent with it.

Sweet gods… even that is too much.

His left eyebrow rose.

His eyes shot wide and he pulled away from her throat and looked over his shoulder at the unconscious female near the open cell door.

Unconscious fae female.

Unconscious *siren.*

He had drunk deeply from her, and by stealing her blood he had temporarily stolen her abilities, a skill all elves possessed and one that was normally useful.

Not torture as it was this time.

Torture because he could hear Taryn's thoughts in his head as if she was speaking them aloud.

He stopped.

Was it wrong that he found it intensely satisfying that she sounded disappointed?

He tried to tell himself to warn her that he could hear her, that he was prying and it was wrong of him, but for some reason the words refused to line up on his lips. Lips that wanted to caress her skin again, because now that he had tapped into her thoughts, her feelings were coming through loud and clear too.

She wanted more.

Desire to satisfy his female had him dropping his mouth back to her throat and tenderly sweeping his tongue over it. He focused on cleaning it and tending to her, and that worked, pushing thoughts of a more wicked nature to the back of his mind.

Until she moaned in his damned head.

Gods, the things this male could do to me with that tongue.

Holy fuck, she had to stop thinking like that. It would be his undoing. She was weak, had suffered heavy blood loss because of him. She should have been foggy and focused on recovering, and mad as hell at him, not thinking the sort of things that were suddenly popping into his head.

Bleu screwed his eyes closed and tried to shut down the telepathic ability.

Nothing he tried worked, and Taryn didn't help him. He couldn't exactly focus on stopping himself from hearing her thoughts when they were all too alluring, painting pictures in his head that had him instantly hard and aching for her despite his healing injuries.

His skin is so warm. Would it feel hot pressed against mine, our bare flesh touching? Gods, it would. I can feel it now, stroking mine as he slides between my thighs, taking me.

A possessive growl rumbled up his throat and he couldn't stop this one from escaping, not when he was imagining everything she was thinking, picturing them tangled together, and their incomplete bond demanded he satisfy his female.

She tensed in his arms.

Is it so wrong that I get flushed with fire whenever he growls?

"Holy fuck, Female," Bleu snapped and pulled back, releasing her and shooting to his feet. His legs wobbled but they didn't collapse. He pressed his palms to his groin, keeping the small scrap of black cloth over it to give himself some dignity, and paced away from her.

He needed to breathe.

No.

What he needed to do was fulfil every damn fantasy running rampant through her mind.

CHAPTER 21

Bleu stalked back towards her and caught himself at the last second, right before he was about to yank her up into his arms and kiss the breath from her, and snarled as he spun on his heel and walked away again.

His blood pounded.

He couldn't do this. Whatever this was. She wasn't his. They weren't meant to be. It didn't matter that she was his fated one. There was no future for them and the quicker he got that message, the better.

He needed more than a biological connection to her to make him belong to her. He needed something that she could never give him. Their history was too dark, too filled with pain and hatred.

She could never love him, and as much as he despised how weak it made him, love was what he needed, what he had always craved from his mate.

He stopped near the back wall of the cell, pressed his forehead against the black stone and exhaled hard.

All of his dreams of his ki'ara had been centred around her loving him.

Taryn had made it clear more than once that what she felt for him was quite the opposite.

Her trying to help him meant nothing. It was probably just her instincts as his fated female making her behave that way. Not her feelings for him.

Gods, his bottom is incredible.

He gritted his teeth and pretended that thought didn't rub his ego the right way. It didn't prove that she felt anything other than hatred or that it wasn't her instincts making her protect him.

But then... every inch of him is incredible.

That sultry low whisper in his mind, almost a purr of approval, rubbed him the right way so hard that he was solid as a rock and tenting the tiny piece of black material around his hips. Holy fuck, he was either weak from everything he had been through and had no control over himself because of it or she had a wicked way with words that worked magic on him. He looked down at his raging erection and huffed when his heart supplied that it was the latter. He was stronger now, his wounds already knitting back together thanks to the siren's and her blood, and very much in control of himself.

Scratch that. *She* was very much in control.

My throat feels better. I am stronger. I should tell him and ease his concern... but I think I would rather remain here admiring the view. Perhaps I could say something to make him look around... then I can take in all that masculine beauty he wears so well.

Bleu whirled to face her, hands dropping to cover his groin as the piece of black cloth threatened to fall off.

"Empty your mind," he snapped, because her thoughts were both a wicked pleasure and sheer torture.

Her eyes gradually widened.

A fierce blaze burned up her pale cheeks.

Dear gods he can hear me!

She scooted backwards, her embarrassment flowing through their link to him, and didn't stop until she was far away from him, her back pressing against the bars of the cell near the door.

As far from him as she could get.

That seemed to be the story of his long life.

The moment whatever was happening between him and a female stopped, they distanced themselves.

He couldn't remember ever spending the night with a woman tucked in his arms. Maybe it had happened. Maybe not.

He felt sure he would have remembered it though, that it would have been special and would have seared itself on his mind forever.

What would Taryn feel like in his arms?

Would she feel as good as she had a moment ago, her body cushioning his, tucked close? Her soft breaths filling his ears and telling him he wasn't alone?

Gods, he could easily imagine passing the long hours of darkness watching her sleep peacefully, safely tucked up in his arms.

He kept his right hand over his groin but shoved the fingers of his left one through his hair, yanking it back. What the hell was wrong with him?

He smiled wryly. Wasn't that the perfect question to sum up his life?

What was so wrong with him that no one could love him?

He wanted to slide down the wall to sit with his back pressed against it but if he gave in to the urge, he was liable to flash his private parts at the female. He wasn't sure whether it would please or shock her.

He wasn't sure of anything anymore.

He just wanted to find his feet again. His place, if he was honest with himself. His purpose.

He stared across the cell at her, a sea of blood-soaked black flagstones separating them. Her violet-to-white eyes locked with his, the rosy hue on her cheeks grew darker, and she dropped her gaze to her knees.

"I'm sorry," he said in her language and she jerked her head back up, her eyes enormous and sweet heart-shaped lips parted. He cast his gaze down at his bare feet. "I'm sorry I hurt you."

"Tenak drugged you," she whispered and it felt so good to hear her voice again that he wanted to moan.

All that came out was a growl as he thought about what her brother had done to him.

She grabbed the bars of the cell and pulled herself onto her feet, held them as she tested her legs, moving a few steps back and forth along the wall. When she looked across at him, she was a different female. Stronger. Darker. Her anger rolled over him, swept through his blood, and he had to wonder.

Could she feel the connection he had forged between them?

Was she aware of what he had done by biting her?

A sound came from above and her head snapped up, eyes scanning the stone ceiling, breath stilling as she searched for the source of the noise. He lifted his eyes to the ceiling too and listened hard, the pointed tips of his ears twitching as he tried to pinpoint where it had come from.

"Tenak will return," she said, her voice stronger now, a commanding edge to it that he found he liked too much.

It stirred wicked thoughts, memories of his dreams of her, and he had to fight to keep his feet planted to the ground, stopping himself from crossing the room and making those dreams come true.

A frown flickered on her brow, her cheeks darkened another shade, and she slid her eyes down to him.

Pierced him with a look that said she didn't need to be telepathic to know his thoughts.

Damn.

Maybe she was aware of the connection between them after all.

"We must go." She shuffled to the unconscious female, crouched and checked her pulse.

Bleu just stared at her, sure he had heard her wrong. The cold that stole over him, pushing all of the softer feelings from his heart and hardening it, said that he had heard her right.

"I cannot leave." He shook his head and shifted his focus back to the ceiling. "I have to retrieve the sword."

There was no way that he could leave it in the hands of her brother. The male was a maniac. Far worse than Vail had ever been. With the sword in his possession, he could fulfil his twisted fantasy of bringing all of Hell to its knees.

"Neither of us are in any fit state to battle my brother," she snapped and rose to her feet, turned and glared at him. "Deny it if you dare."

He couldn't because it was true. While drinking from the fae and from Taryn had restored some of his strength, the drugs her brother had dosed him up with had yet to leave his system. It wasn't the healing wounds his body bore that posed a threat to him either.

It was the darkness.

He could feel it trickling through him still, a deadly undercurrent in his blood that stirred dangerous thoughts that would pierce his mind from time to time, black urges that pushed him to do things he found repulsive whenever the darkness's hold on him faded.

It was only Taryn's blood keeping it at bay right now, restoring the light in his soul whenever the darkness rose to steal control.

The effect she had on him could shatter at any moment and he knew without a doubt that the darkness would seize command again if it did. He needed time to master it again and purge it from his soul. Fighting her brother would do the opposite. He would need to draw on his full strength in order to win against the dragon male, and that meant tapping into the darkness.

He would end up giving it a stronger grip on him, giving it more control over him, and he wasn't sure whether he would be able to come back from that.

Or whether he would end up tainted.

Possibly even *lost*.

Taryn turned towards the open cell door and paused there with her back to him.

"I will have to bide my time," she whispered and her fists clenched at her sides. "When I am stronger, I can return to free the others and deal with my brother."

Bleu stared at her as those words sank in and he realised that she hadn't come to this place to join forces with her brother.

She had come here to destroy him.

He couldn't believe it.

"Was taking down your brother the reason you stole the blade in the first place?" His voice was surprisingly strong in his ears, no longer rough and scratchy. He rubbed his throat, found it no longer hurt to touch it, and then looked down at his body, expecting to find it battered.

The wounds on his torso were healing fast. Thanks to Taryn's blood? He had heard that a mate's blood could swiftly restore an elf's strength, but he hadn't expected it to be this powerful. It was incredible. Far better than the wretched medicine most elves had to take when in this condition, a concoction that could instantly heal but rolled all of the pain the person taking it would have felt during the course of naturally healing into one excruciating blast.

He hazarded a guess that he would be fully healed within less than a day. His body at least. His mind and soul were a different matter. The darkness twisted tendrils tighter around his consciousness, sinking poisoned thorns into him and stirring black desires.

He shoved them from his mind, and pushed away from the wall, and cool air swirled around his bare legs as he walked.

She looked back at him over her shoulder, something glittering in her eyes that he couldn't quite decipher, and then turned away again.

Her voice flickered in his mind, shocking him more than the fact she was on a mission to kill her sibling.

If I told him I did not steal the blade, would he believe me? I have been such a fool. I should not have tried to protect Tenak by taking the sword and the blame with it... no, the elves are to blame too. They should not have turned on me when I tried to give the sword back.

Everything she felt flowed through him too, backing up her words as he experienced her guilt and sorrow, her fear and her anger.

"You were bringing it back," he said in the dragon tongue and she gasped and whirled to face him.

Her legs buckled.

He was across the room in an instant, catching her in his arms and stopping her fall. Her hands pressed against his bare chest as he drew her closer to him, her eyes leaping to meet his, her soft pink lips parted.

"You were bringing it back?" he whispered, transfixed by the electric feel of her touching him and the way she was looking up at him, her beguiling eyes filled with shock but other feelings too, ones he was coming to learn as they filtered through the bond to him. Desire. Hunger. Hope. Fear.

He wasn't the only one afraid of what was happening, convinced that it was impossible.

That gave him strength.

Courage.

Made him brave and a little reckless.

He dropped his gaze to her lips, narrowed it on them. They parted further, a tempting invitation. Gods, he wanted to take it.

He wanted to devour her.

He dragged his eyes away and exhaled hard, purging those desires and restoring balance again. He wanted her but now wasn't the time, and it certainly wasn't the place. He needed to get her away from the castle, get his strength back up and then deal with her brother and reclaim the sword. Once he had done all that, then he could think about asking her whether she might consider falling in love with him.

Like he was falling in love with her.

"Yes," she murmured and he frowned, again convinced for a moment that she could hear his thoughts before he realised she had been answering the question he had posed to her, not the one he had been thinking about.

She had tried to bring the sword back and his men had attacked her.

She had taken the blame for her brother and he knew deep in his heart that wouldn't have changed if he and his men had given her a chance to return the sword. She would have covered for her sibling, pretending she had been the one to take the blade. She would have taken the punishment in his stead.

Brave little female.

Her loyalty and courage only strengthened his growing feelings for her.

Feelings that had started in him centuries ago and he had been denying ever since, but he was too tired and drained of strength to deny them now. With her in his arms, resting gently against him, her eyes settled on his, he couldn't pretend they didn't exist.

She was so beautiful.

A blush crept onto her cheeks again and she dropped her gaze to his chest, the innocent edge to her behaviour only stirring his desire for her, his need to protect her and claim her as his mate.

That blush deepened as she lowered her eyes further.

She slowly pushed out of his arms and fidgeted with the bottom of her corset where it met her violet leathers, her gaze locked on it. Avoiding him. He frowned at her behaviour and was about to ask her why she had pulled away from him again when she murmured.

"M-my magic is weak. My brother received almost all of it… but perhaps I can… um… I-I might be able to…" Her cheeks blazed and she pointed towards him, flicking her finger up and down his body.

He looked down at himself.

He had forgotten that he only wore a ridiculously small cloth around his hips.

Bleu closed his eyes and focused, testing the limit of his abilities. The drug the dragon had given him to unleash his darker nature was different to the one that had been in his system when he had come around in the cell. That one had faded, unlocking more of his gifts.

Including the one that allowed him to teleport a pair of black leather trousers from his apartments in the elf castle onto his legs.

Taryn gasped. "Your magic is strong."

"It isn't magic," he said and pulled the scrap of cloth out of his trousers, tossed it away and then fastened the lacing over his crotch. He looked up at her as he finished tying the string. "I think it is something like telekinesis."

"You are not sure?" She frowned at him and he shrugged, shooting for casual but it came off stiff.

He had never really cared about people questioning his knowledge or his intelligence.

For some damned reason he cared that she was looking at him as if he was an idiot though.

"I don't think anyone is sure how to classify our teleportation abilities," he grumbled and held his hand out to her.

She stared at it as if it was going to bite her.

Or maybe as if he was going to bite her.

"I only intend to teleport you away from this place to somewhere safe." He rolled his fingers, silently ordering her to take his hand.

She didn't move, even though he could sense she wanted to go with him. Something was holding her back.

Her brother.

"I will not allow him to use the sword. As soon as I am strong enough, I will return with my team and we will deal with him." Bleu looked down at his hand and then up into her eyes. "So come with me."

"I changed my mind." She shook her head. "I cannot go. Leave without me. You are strong enough. If my brother discovers I am gone, he will be furious. He will use the sword. I have to stay."

"Stay?" His eyes leaped between hers. "Have you lost your mind?"

Her eyes blackened and he had the feeling he had prodded a very tender nerve.

The last time he had seen her flashed across his eyes, a replay of a dark arena and a black wooden stage, and her fighting on it, attacking her captors like a wild thing. Crazed with a need to hurt them.

His eyes fell to her wrists and she quickly put her arms behind her back, hiding them from him.

She couldn't hide the scars around her neck though.

How many times had she been captured and sold? He wanted to ask her that but her turbulent feelings and her striking eyes pleaded him to keep that question to himself, told him that she wasn't strong enough to answer it right now.

He would give her the time she needed, but she would answer it. He would know the things she had been through, and the faces of those who had done them to her, and he would track them down and butcher them all.

They would pay for hurting his female.

A sharp bang came from above, echoing down the spiral stairwell to them.

"Go," she whispered, a frantic edge to her gaze as it leaped from the stairwell to him. "Now."

"No," he barked and stepped towards her, caught her arm and growled at her. "Not without you. I will not leave without you. I will not leave you here so that madman can hurt you. Never."

She jerked free of his grip and snarled at him. "I cannot go. Tenak will be furious. He will take up the sword and turn his gaze on those he believes are his enemies."

"From what I have heard, that is the whole of Hell. The sword will give him power but he will need an army to back him if he expects to conquer Hell." Bleu grabbed her arm again, his grip tighter this time. Her eyes turned wild, fear lancing her, and he softened his grip, instinct screaming at him that he was terrifying her. He growled low in his throat. By the gods, he would know the things she had been through and he would kill everyone who had harmed her, who had scarred her. "We have time, Taryn. I will not leave you here."

"I will not go with you." Conviction shone in her beautiful eyes.

He felt like a bastard before the words even left his lips.

"Then you give me no choice." He dragged her against him, banded his arm around her waist and pinned her against his chest. "I will kidnap you."

She wriggled and pushed against him, palms hot against his bare flesh, sending a fierce fiery current through him. Her startled gasp said she had felt it too. Her breath hitched, her pupils dilated to devour the white around the centre of her irises, and his heart raced in unison with hers.

"Let me go," she whispered, voice distant, telling him that she was as lost in the sudden rush of emotions and feelings as he was.

Bleu shook his head. "Never."

Her eyes widened.

"You are coming with me whether you like it or not." He growled down at her. "I will not leave you here."

"But my brother will—"

"I don't care," he snapped and she stilled. He softened his tone and searched her eyes. "I don't care… all I care about is getting you out of harm's way. I will deal with the consequences when they happen."

Her throat worked on a hard swallow.

She blinked.

"Take me to the dragon realm then," she said and wrapped her arms around his neck, frazzling his ability to think. He could only feel, and gods, it felt too good to have her this close to him, curling around him, holding on to him. He never wanted her to let go. Her low spoken words reached his ears, shaking him out of his stupor. "Tenak will think I went flying or perhaps pursued you. I will use the time to regain my strength and when I am strong enough, I will return to my brother and tell him that you overpowered me and escaped and I went after you. I will make him believe me."

She would get herself killed.

He tightened his grip on her, willed his portal to open, and focused on his destination.

CHAPTER 22

Darkness swallowed them, cool against his skin, and then separated to reveal the green valley. The grasses swayed in the gentle breeze and sunlight warmed his skin and made the stone of the stronghold look more cream than grey. Beyond the hill where it stood, mountains rose, a range of peaks that were green with trees on the elf side and black as night on the side of the First Realm of the demons.

Taryn looked away from him, incredible eyes scanning the sweeping landscape, and shook her head.

"No," she whispered and snapped back around to face him. Her eyes gained a wild edge again. Panic swept through her and rushed into him. "Not here. It is not safe here."

He opened his mouth to tell her that it was.

Leif, Dacian and Fynn appeared a few metres away from him.

Bleu instantly pinned Taryn to his chest, keeping her face hidden from them so they wouldn't know she was aware of them. She stiffened against him, heart thundering against his chest, causing his own to race.

"Play at being unconscious," he whispered in the dragon tongue, keeping his lips as still as possible so his men wouldn't see he was speaking to her.

Her fingers tensed against his bare chest. He took it as a sign she would do as he asked and raised his head, looked at all three males where they stood opposite him, their eyes on Taryn.

He had hoped they would be away from the garrison, giving him a chance to use it as a safe house for Taryn, a place where they could clean up and rest while he figured out what to do, and came to terms with what she was to him.

Leif drew his blade out of the air and Dacian and Fynn followed suit, arming themselves. All three changed clothing in unison, their uniforms of a long black jacket and black trousers and riding boots disappearing, replaced by their figure-hugging black armour.

Bleu barely bit back the growl that rose up his throat, every primal instinct firing and telling him to protect his female. These males meant to hurt her. They wanted to take her from him.

She trembled against him.

Leif stepped forwards and pointed his sword at Taryn. "Set her away from you. She is dangerous."

Fynn closed in and reached out to grab her arm.

To steal her from him.

A red mist descended and Bleu hissed at the younger elf, his pointed ears flaring back against the sides of his head. He flashed his fangs and narrowed his gaze on the male, warning him to back off and forget any ideas he had about taking his female from him.

She was his.

No other male would touch her.

None would take her from him.

"I will deal with her," he snarled and struggled with the dark urges running rampant through him, the hunger to lash out at these males and kill them all in order to protect his female.

Dacian's eyes narrowed in a way he didn't like. The warrior had remained at a distance, his focused fixed on Bleu, not the female, gaze cool and just a touch too inquisitive. A touch too knowing.

The larger male lowered his broadsword and stabbed the tip of the black blade into the earth.

His eyes didn't leave Bleu.

"The female is dangerous," Dacian said, voice a deep rumble. Testing him. The male pointed, ran a finger up and down in the air. "She certainly worked you over."

Bleu cursed under his breath and realised why two of his men had reacted so strongly to her presence.

He looked like an unholy mess.

He had forgotten that the moment Taryn had been in his arms. He had forgotten all about his wounds and the blood that covered him when she had nestled close to him. Her breath washed across his bare chest, soft pants that tickled his skin. Gods, he was sure he would forget his own damned name if she acted on those desires he had heard running through her mind back in the cell when he had been touching her.

Tasting her.

His cock twitched, hunger rising again, stirred by his thoughts and by the feel of her against him, her warm body pressed close, bare skin caressing his.

Fynn foolishly took another step forwards.

Bleu snarled at him, baring his fangs, and tightened his grip on her.

Dacian's eyes narrowed further.

"The female is not the one who took the sword, and not the one who did this to me." Bleu forced his voice to work, shoved his out of control instincts back in place and faced off against Dacian.

The bastard knew what he was trying to hide.

Bleu shot him a look that he hoped conveyed that the male wasn't the only one who knew a secret someone was trying to keep—another secret related to fated females.

It took a male who had found his fated one to know one.

Dacian's violet eyes slid towards Fynn and then he looked down at his boots.

Bleu hadn't failed to notice the way Dacian had acted around Fynn's younger sister. He felt wretched just thinking about it, but if Dacian dared to mention the reason why Bleu felt so overprotective of Taryn, then he would turn the tables on him and tell Fynn that his little sister was Dacian's fated one.

That would buy him enough time to escape with Taryn at least.

"I must take her to the castle so we can question her." It was the safest course of action now. He could speak with Loren about her and perhaps clear her name.

Bleu slid his hand lower on her back and she tensed against him, a little gasp escaping her.

He tried to tune into her thoughts, hungry to know whether she was thinking wicked things again, was enjoying being in his arms. Her thoughts were hazy and he couldn't make them out. The effect of the siren's blood was wearing off. It was probably a good thing, but he still wanted to curse it.

Those thoughts she'd had back in the cell had given him a clearer picture of her feelings and had made him realise that she didn't hate him, and that whatever she was feeling, it wasn't born of her instincts. She desired him.

Gods, he desired her.

He needed her so badly that he felt sure he might go mad if he didn't catch a glimpse of her face soon, didn't look into her eyes and see them bright with a hint of affection.

He gritted his teeth and resisted the need to look down at her, to catch her under her chin and make her look at him so he could fulfil that desire. He had to keep his head if he was going to get her through this unscathed and without him attacking his own men. If he showed her any tenderness, the two males watching him with their weapons at the ready would question his authority, believing him under her influence and unable to perform his duties.

"We should take her into the stronghold and question her there. It is the safer course of action and will not endanger anyone at the castle. Is that not the reason why we came to this place?" Leif lowered his gaze to the female and flexed his fingers around the leather-bound hilt of his black sword.

"She is not a danger to anyone," Bleu said and all three men looked sceptical. He frowned at them all. "I said she did not harm me. It was her brother. The sibling we heard about from the dragons."

None of them looked as if they believed him and Fynn edged closer again, moving in time with Leif.

"We will take her to the stronghold first and if she offers any valuable information, then we will transfer her to the castle."

Bleu barely bit back the growl that rumbled up his throat as the two elves closed in, their eyes flickering between him and Taryn. Dacian remained at a distance, his eyes fixed on Bleu, never straying to the female in his arms. Wise male. He knew that any attempt to take her from him would incite his rage and he wouldn't be able to stop himself from attacking in order to protect her.

"We should listen to our commander," Dacian said and Leif and Fynn both halted and looked back at him. "He has not steered us wrong in the past. We saw the way those dragons reacted when pressed to speak of her brother… and the female is injured too."

Bleu flexed his fingers around her waist and looked between all three men, sending a prayer to his gods that Leif and Fynn would listen to Dacian and back down. They didn't mean any harm by wanting to take the burden of her from his arms and escort her to the cell, but they were pushing him without knowing it, testing the limit of his ability to control himself.

His eyes leaped from Leif to Fynn and then back to Dacian, a motion he repeated as he monitored all three of them, constantly assessing them as he fought the deep primal urge to lower Taryn to the ground and lash out at them, to drive them back and eliminate them if they didn't relent.

His breathing quickened, heart pumping harder as he prepared himself for a fight.

Taryn shifted against him, a small movement but one he felt to the very marrow of his bones. She brushed her fingers across his chest, a touch that soothed the ragged and dangerous side of himself, the one still dancing with the darkness that the drug and the bloodshed had unleashed in him.

"Commander Bleu?" Dacian said, a note of warning in his deep voice together with an unspoken question.

Was he going to be alright?

Bleu drew down a deep shuddering breath, closed his eyes and exhaled slowly. When he opened his eyes again, all three men were studying him closely.

"The male drugged me." It was a reasonable explanation for his unusual behaviour and one he felt sure they would believe if he added a few details he had intended to keep private. He closed his eyes again and lowered his head, and gods, Taryn smelled wonderful as his breath washed off her hair and her shoulder. His mouth watered, fangs itching for another taste of her. He tamped down that dark hunger and focused on the lighter side of the feelings she stirred in him, the side that drew comfort from her scent. "I was forced to attack someone… a fae female."

Someone gasped.

Bleu lifted his eyes, heaved a sigh and pushed out, "The female dragon stopped me from killing her, and… I attacked her instead. I almost killed her too."

Leif rocked back on his heels as if Bleu had struck him with those words and stared at Taryn, disbelief mingling with fury in his violet eyes.

Bleu had to bite his tongue to stop himself from growling at the male and did the only thing he could do to make them see he was telling the truth about her and the heinous thing he had done as repayment for her kindness.

He gently lowered her in his arms and she did wonderfully well at pretending she was unconscious, her body so limp he was almost convinced himself. Her arms fell away from him as he leaned over her, splaying out at her sides and making her look as if she was falling through the air. He studied her bloodstained face as he kneeled and carefully laid her down on the dewy grass.

His beautiful ki'ara.

He could feel the tremor of her fear in his blood and willed her to feel he was with her and believe that he wouldn't allow anything bad to happen to her. He had gone against her wishes, but the dragon realm wasn't safe for her and he couldn't allow her to commit suicide by returning to her brother without him.

Her violet-to-white hair spilled away from her throat, cascading across the bright green grass, and her head slipped towards her right, revealing the ragged marks on the left side of her throat.

Bleu rose onto his feet and looked down at her.

At what he had done to her.

It was hard to look at her when she was laying on the grass, her knees together and twisted towards her right, hips rotated but shoulders against the earth, and her arms spread at her sides.

Her throat ravaged and blood staining her moon-white skin.

She looked dead.

She might have been if he hadn't stopped when he had. He had come perilously close to killing her.

"I did this to her," Bleu husked. He cleared his throat but it did nothing to remove the rawness from it. "She is not our enemy. Our fight lies with her brother."

Leif and Fynn closed in again.

Leif made the mistake of flexing his clawed fingers around the hilt of his sword.

Readying it.

Bleu couldn't stop the reaction as it swept through him, his defences so battered and heart so bruised that it was impossible to retain control. The male wanted war and he would get it.

No one would touch his female.

He had sworn to keep her safe and he would, no matter what it took.

He fixed cold eyes on Leif and drew his black blade from the air, teleporting it into his left hand.

He swept his right palm up the length of the sword, transforming it into a double-ended spear. His ears grew pointier and flattened against the sides of his head as darkness swept through him, an oily rising tide that obliterated the light that Taryn had brought into his soul and left only black hunger behind.

Bleu snarled through his fangs.

Raised his spear and prepared to attack.

CHAPTER 23

Dacian appeared right in front of Bleu, his right hand shooting out to curl around the shaft of his spear and holding it fast.

"Not wise," the larger male whispered in a low voice, one that told Bleu to listen and consider his actions.

It was hard when Leif was still standing on the other side of Taryn, sword ready to strike her down.

Harder still now that Dacian was standing between him and his female, blocking his path to her, stirring the darker side of his instincts that roared to protect her. The males meant to take her from him. They meant to harm her.

His grip on his spear tightened and he wrestled with Dacian, trying to tug it free of his grip so he could cut the male down and reach his female. A low snarl curled up his throat and Dacian's eyes narrowed, blazing violet as his pointed ears flared back against the shorn sides of his head, a show of aggression that only sent Bleu sinking deeper into the dark hunger for violence rising inside him.

"Listen to reason, Bleu," Dacian growled and Bleu froze, knocked right out of the grip of the darkness and onto his backside by one single word.

He couldn't remember the last time Dacian had used his name without his rank.

"Commander Bleu is still under the influence of the drug and the torture inflicted by the dragon male. I suggest you back down, Leif, as you are inciting his rage and allowing the darkness to gain a firmer hold on our leader." Dacian kept his eyes locked on Bleu's as he raised his voice loud enough that the whole damn valley could probably hear him. There he went again, pulling out the big words. "Unless you would prefer me to send a report to Prince Loren about what happened here and why Commander Bleu reduced your scrawny backside to a pile of blood, skin and broken bones?"

That was the Dacian that Bleu was more comfortable with, the one he could understand. The warrior.

Leif's eyes darkened but he lowered his sword. Evidently threatening to give Leif a bad name with Loren was the best method of keeping him in line. Bleu would have to remember that.

"Your orders?" Leif said, an edge to his expression that told Bleu he knew what they were without asking and he wasn't happy.

"We take her to the castle and I will speak with Prince Loren." Bleu put as much authority into his words as he could muster, making it clear that he wasn't going to accept any objections.

"And get some medical attention," Dacian added, his rugged face sober and unreadable. "You look like hell."

The big warrior cracked a grin.

As if Bleu needed the reminder.

Now that Taryn was no longer in his arms, he could feel every ache in his battered bones, every throb in his muscles as they struggled to hold him upright. Her blood was healing him, quickening the process, but he was still weak. He needed sustenance and something to purge the drugs from his body. Not the damned medicine though. Never the medicine. He hated that shit.

He needed rest.

He doubted that was going to happen.

The moment he told Loren about what had occured and what he had discovered, his prince would send him back out to finish what he had started.

Dacian backed off and joined Fynn and Leif.

Wind blew across the green land, stirring the grass. Bleu looked down at Taryn where she lay at his feet, the breeze playing with the bloodstained threads of her hair. The thought of taking her to the elf castle was both a balm and a poison. She would be safe there, because the castle was heavily guarded, but she would be in danger too. Everyone in the castle still believed she was responsible for stealing the sword.

He would need to make sure she was protected while he spoke with Prince Loren about her and her brother.

He sent his spear back through his portal to his room in the castle, bent and scooped her up into his arms, and she rolled towards him as he adjusted her weight, her head coming to rest against his bare shoulder and skin warming his.

He wished he could teleport her to his apartments as he could his weapon, but while he could send items there directly, he couldn't enter the castle through that route. He had to use the main portal in the courtyard. That meant teleporting her into an area where there were always soldiers around.

Unmated males.

He wanted to stay with her too, to keep her by his side, but it would be impossible. He couldn't take her to meet with Loren. The guards wouldn't allow it, his men wouldn't, and even he wouldn't go through with it, because there was no way in the three realms he was going to place his prince in danger.

He didn't believe Taryn was in on the plan with her brother, but he was hardly thinking clearly right now, his brain addled by the incomplete bond between them.

He had to meet with Loren alone and discuss everything with him.

That meant leaving Taryn in the care of his team.

Leif still looked as if he wanted to hurt her. Fynn no longer looked certain.

Dacian looked as if he would hurt any who lifted a finger to harm her, his powerful arms folded across his chest as he stood guard close to Bleu and his violet eyes challenging Leif to defy his order.

If Bleu had to choose one of the three to stand on his side, he would have chosen Dacian.

The warrior was fiercely protective of those he cared about and loyal to a fault. Not only that, but the thought of Dacian near Taryn didn't stir a black urge to kill the male. Bleu had seen him with his fated one, and the knowledge that he had a female of his own, even one that didn't belong to him yet, tempered the primal instincts that were commanding him to attack any male who so much as looked at Taryn.

He would trust Dacian to take care of her in his stead while he spoke with Loren.

Bleu closed his eyes and willed his portal. He tucked Taryn closer to his chest as the green-purple light flashed over his body and the darkness swallowed him. It felt colder this time, a biting chill that stung his flesh and seared his bones. The darker side that all elves possessed affected everything in their life, including their abilities. The icy air that froze his lungs in the short span of time between disappearing from the land near the stronghold and reappearing in the castle courtyard was a product of that. He had never felt it before, and gods, he never wanted to feel it again.

He would slowly piece himself back together, purge the darkness from his soul, and find his balance again to ensure that happened.

Taryn tensed as they appeared, the leafy green trees and neatly mown grass of the courtyard shimmering into being around them. Warm light reflected off the pale grey stone of the castle but soaked into the darker bands. He lowered his gaze from the towering conical-roof-tipped spires of the castle, down the pale gravel path that led from the arched entrance of the building to the circular portal landing area, and then to her.

Her violet-to-white eyes were huge, speaking of the fear that ran through her blood and through his too.

"You will be safe here," he whispered in her tongue but her expression didn't shift, her dark eyebrows remaining furrowed and eyes fearful.

Gods, he wanted to brush his fingers across her cheek and reassure her.

The feel of so many pairs of eyes on him stopped him though and fear of what might happen should any witness his affection for her, see that he was biased where she was concerned, kept him remaining at a distance.

He set her down on her feet and held her steady when her legs wobbled.

Dacian stepped forwards and Bleu looked over her head at him.

"Take care of the female while I speak with Prince Loren." Fuck, those were some of the most difficult words he had ever had to say. It was hard to remain cold and distant, to act indifferent, when he could feel Taryn's fear and hear her heartbeat kick up a notch as she realised he was going to leave her alone in a castle filled with elves who all thought she had stolen the sword and was their enemy.

It was hard to resist looking at her.

Somehow, he managed it when Dacian pressed his right hand to his chest in a salute.

Bleu pushed off, the ache in his chest growing with each step he took that carried him further from her. Her eyes remained locked on him as he walked the straight pale path that cut through the orchard towards the castle, searing his back with the heat of her gaze, making him itch to turn back around, grab her hand and pull her with him.

Filling him with a terrible black urge to fight any who stood in the way of him taking his female somewhere he deemed safe.

He had lied to her.

She wasn't safe here.

This was the worst possible place he could have taken her but he had to speak with Prince Loren. He needed to speak with him. About the sword. About Taryn.

About everything.

His reason for coming to the castle wasn't solely to report to his prince. It was to speak with Loren about what she was to him. It was to seek his advice.

His palms sweated at the thought of telling Loren everything, confessing that Taryn was his fated female. He rubbed them on his leathers as he approached the entrance of the castle and nodded to the two males guarding it, their black armour a stark contrast against the pale stone of the arch.

Gods, the last time he had felt this nervous about entering the castle had been the first time he had come here over forty-two centuries ago, brought before Loren to tell him about what had happened on the battlefield where Vail had gone mad and slaughtered his own men.

He halted before he reached the entrance, the sound of running water arresting his steps. He turned towards the source of the noise, a fountain off to his left, and diverted course. As he strode towards it, he called a cloth to his hands.

Meeting with Loren while covered in blood would not be a wise move, not if he was going to convince his prince that the female dragon was no threat to them. Loren leaned towards overprotective, a trait that was good for a prince but bad where he was concerned. The male coddled him too much, and seeing him bloodied and battered would trigger an episode of fussing that Bleu didn't want to deal with right now on top of everything else.

He dunked the cloth in the crystal clear water, pulled it free and ran it over his bloodstained skin, scrubbing himself clean. It smelled tinny as he used it to wipe the thick crust of blood off his neck and face. When the cloth was deep red, dripping crimson onto the pale gravel, he sent it away, back to his bathing room in his apartment, and looked himself over. A marginal improvement in his appearance. Deep red gashes still criss-crossed his chest and arms, angry scarlet around their edges, and his skin was still pinker than usual from all the blood, but it would do. He couldn't exactly dunk himself in the fountain as he wanted.

The damned thing was sacred.

He had already gained a multitude of black glares and looks that questioned his sanity by using the water to wash himself off. If he got blood in the water, he would probably find himself strung up in the cells.

He blew out his breath and quickly headed towards the arched entrance of the castle. The guards eyed him as he passed and he swiftly moved through the ground floor of the castle, his bare feet silent on the cool stone flags. The pale stone walls glittered in the warm glow from the lights along the ceiling. White statues towered above him on either side of the grand hallway, standing at intervals between elegantly carved columns that looked like pristine flowers made of ice.

The old kings and queens of the elf kingdom. Loren's bloodline. Bleu had never known any of them, but he had walked this hallway so many times that he knew every detail of their faces and their clothing.

He kept his eyes locked on the wooden door at the far end of the wide corridor, exhaled hard and inhaled again, wrestling with his nerves.

Loren was in the throne room beyond those doors. Bleu could feel him.

He looked back towards the entrance behind him. The brightness of the outside world made the archway a blur of white light, impossible for him to see beyond. His steps slowed and he turned back towards it.

Taryn was out there.

Unmated males surrounding her.

He growled and took a step back towards her, forced himself to stop and spun on his heel to face the closed wooden doors again. As much as he wanted to return to her and protect her from every male in the castle, ensuring none looked at her and that she was his and his alone, he had to keep moving forwards. The only real way of protecting his female was to explain everything to Loren and request he inform everyone in the castle that Taryn wasn't the enemy and was not to be touched.

Or even looked at.

Bleu growled low in his throat, satisfied by the thought of Loren telling everyone that they couldn't so much as look at her.

She was his, and only he could gaze upon her beauty.

He clenched his fists, gritted his teeth and growled again. Thinking like that was only going to get him into trouble—both with others and with her. He had witnessed Loren in the throes of the mating urge, suffering from an incomplete bond to Olivia. He had seen King Thorne of the demons go half-mad with need of Sable.

He had to be stronger than that.

He had to keep control and keep a level head.

He refused to fall victim of his instincts.

Pain shot through him, hot and fierce, tearing his heart asunder and pulling the floor out from under his feet. His knees hit the pale polished flagstones and he bent over, pressing his palms into the cold stone and panting hard. The fire came again, licking at his bones, searing his flesh, and he cried out.

A mighty roar echoed along the corridor at his back.

A chill swept over his skin.

Taryn.

Bleu exploded to his feet and teleported to the main portal of the castle where he had left her.

She was gone.

His heart pounded, her fear colliding with his as he scoured the courtyard for her. Only elves as far as his eyes could see and he wanted to grab every single one of them and rattle them until they confessed her location.

He tried to focus on her blood in his body, but it was hard when every instinct he possessed was screaming at him to find his female. She was afraid. Terrified. In pain.

Suffering.

He snarled when he got a fix on her location and his gaze snapped towards the gate in the inner wall of the castle grounds, settling on the garrison on the other side.

Damn them.

He would kill them all.

He sprinted towards the square three storey stone building, moving in a blur as his bare feet chewed up the distance between him and his female. He issued the mental command to his armour as he ran and growled when it didn't come. Fuck. He had forgotten the bastard dragon had stolen it from him.

He shouldered the main door open, sharp pain splintering across his bones, and ignored the comments some of the soldiers tossed in his direction as he ran towards the steps that led down off to his right. He leaped the first set, landing in the turning, and then leaped down the second, his feet striking the cobbled floor of the cellblock hard enough to get the attention of everyone crowding the corridor between the cells.

A flicker of regret shone in Dacian's eyes, but that wasn't going to stop Bleu from butchering him later.

He had trusted Dacian with his female and the warrior had failed him.

He pinned everyone present with murderous looks, barely holding back the surging tide of darkness, the hunger to do more than glare. He wanted to sink his claws into their flesh and tear them apart for what they had done.

As casually as he could when his blood was thundering with a need to kill and Taryn's fear flowed through him, he walked forwards, chin tipped up and shoulders back. The urge to run to her cell battered him but he somehow managed to reach the group of males without surrendering to it.

They parted for him and he ground his teeth together, his fangs cutting into his gums when he saw Taryn huddled in the corner of the cell.

Bleu turned on his team. "What the hell do you think you are doing?"

"Following protocol." Leif's calm tone only made Bleu bump him to the top of the list. He would be the first Bleu would make acquainted with his claws once he had procured new armour. "She had to be placed somewhere secure while you spoke with Prince Loren."

Bleu curled his fingers into fists and reined in his fury. It instantly slipped its leash again and he had to dig his short nails into his palm to stop himself from lashing out at Leif.

"I cannot argue that it was not the right course of action, but who gave you permission to hurt her?" He flung one hand towards her, pointing at her where she sat curled into a ball, rocking and muttering to herself.

Her pain was crushing, far worse than he had felt in her back in the cell of the dragon castle when he had bitten her. It pressed down on his heart, left him feeling as if it might crush it entirely, until nothing remained and all he knew was agony for eternity.

"No one hurt her," Leif countered. "We brought her down here and she turned crazed."

Liar.

He looked across at his little female as she stared at the opposite corner of her cell, eyes dull and lifeless as she chanted to herself in the dragon tongue.

"He is coming for me… he is coming for us all… he is coming for me… he is coming," she whispered as she rocked, arms wrapped tightly around her leather-clad knees.

Bleu slowly frowned as he realised that the only wounds she bore were the ones he had given her. Leif hadn't lied.

"Unlock the door," Bleu said and no one moved to obey him.

He growled at them, snarling through his fangs as his pointed ears flared back against the sides of his head.

"Need to fly," Taryn muttered in the dragon tongue and her pain worsened, near crippling him as it ripped into his heart.

He had to calm her. He couldn't deny that urge even when he knew that doing so would raise questions in his men and possibly suspicions too. He didn't care. His female was in pain. She was afraid. Suffering. He had to do something to take away her fear and hurt and soothe her.

He snatched the keys from the hands of the male in charge and fumbled with them, his hands shaking as he rushed to find the one that would open her door.

"Need to fly," she whimpered and began clawing at her hair, raking blunt nails over her skin and leaving red marks in their wake.

"Taryn," Bleu said as he found the right key and shoved it into the lock. He growled as his hands shook so violently he almost knocked the damn key back out again and finally managed to turn it.

He shoved the door open.

Her eyes snapped up to him.

Bright and clear.

She launched to her feet with a growl, barrelled into his chest and sent him staggering back into the men behind him, knocking them all down. Her booted foot pressed into his stomach and she kicked off, breaking to her left.

Running for the courtyard.

"Taryn!" Bleu scrambled onto his feet and stumbled over the fallen males who were trying to get up too. He growled at them and broke free, bare feet hitting the cobbles as Taryn reached the first bend in the stone staircase. "Taryn!"

She didn't slow. She didn't even look at him.

Her eyes remained locked ahead of her, up the stairs.

Gods damn it.

The whole courtyard was filled with soldiers and if they saw her fleeing the garrison they would try to stop her, and he wouldn't be able to stop himself from attacking them.

He sprinted up the stairs and rushed out into the daylight, eyes watering at the sudden change in brightness. When his vision recovered, he scanned the outer courtyard for her, and then whipped his head towards the arched entrance to the inner courtyard to his left when shouts came from that direction.

A roar sounded and he growled as her head appeared above the top of the wall, white horns brushing the violet scales of her neck as she reared back, standing over sixty foot tall in her dragon form. Arrows flew at her, bouncing off the white plates across her chest.

He snarled and teleported, landing in the centre of the orchard, facing a small army of archers.

Bleu spun on his heel to face the other direction and Taryn loomed over him, her huge front paws swiping at the arrows zipping towards her. One struck her face and she flinched, enormous right eye closing as she tried to protect her sight.

A thin line of red blossomed along the path the arrow had taken, from her lip up to the top of her snout.

He growled and turned on the archers. "Stand down!"

They all looked at him as if he had gone mad, and maybe he had. Maybe he had been mad from the moment he met her, crazy to deny that she was his fated one.

His ki'ara.

His everything.

Her broad wings beat the air, their white membrane stretched taut as she spread them, easily spanning the breadth of the courtyard from the interior wall on her right to the castle on her left.

She kicked off, shaking the ground and sending a few of the soldiers around him to their knees. Her wings beat harder, sending a gust of wind that drove more men onto their backsides, and she lifted into the air.

"Wait!" Bleu hollered and waved his arms.

She turned wild eyes on him and he knew in that instant that she wouldn't listen. Whatever madness had gripped her, it was too powerful for her to break free of its hold.

He turned as she flew overhead, leaving him as the only male standing, and he could feel her joy as it ran through him, the deep relief she felt as she flew, spreading her wings. Her fear remained though, lingering in his blood, and he couldn't stop thinking about what she had said.

He was coming.

Had it been a vision?

Had she seen her brother coming for her?

For them all?

It had clearly shaken her and he needed to follow her, not only to comfort her. As powerful as that need was, the other that ruled him was equal in strength to it.

He needed to find out what she had seen because he had the feeling that the kingdom was in danger and it was his fault.

He had gone against her wishes and brought her here rather than to the dragon realm, and in doing so, he had turned her brother's focus to this realm and his kin once more. He had given an unbalanced warrior a reason to believe he had kidnapped his sister in order to harm her.

And that warrior had a sword that could cut an entire legion of elves down in one swing.

"Pursue the dragon," Leif shouted, snapping him out of his thoughts.

Soldiers were already forming groups.

Hunting parties.

"Belay that order," Bleu barked and everyone stopped to look at him. "I will go alone."

He teleported before anyone could respond, but in the heartbeat of time between willing his portal and disappearing, he felt the presence of Loren.

Bleu reappeared on the brow of a hill a short distance from the castle and looked back at it, the wind that always raced over the green plains tousling his hair and caressing his bare torso.

Loren had witnessed everything.

He was going to have to answer some tricky, personal, questions when he returned.

He didn't care.

Maybe he would have once, only a few days ago, but now all he cared about was Taryn. Loren could punish him, could question him in front of every soldier in the castle, could strip him of his rank for insubordination and the fact he had endangered everyone in the elf kingdom. He didn't care what happened to him.

He only cared what happened to Taryn.

She was the only thing that mattered now.

CHAPTER 24

Bleu scoured the lands around him. Villages dotted the rolling green hills, marked by the windmills and golden fields of grains that often surrounded them. Taryn would avoid those and any hint of civilisation. He looked over his right shoulder, in the direction of the First Realm of the demons, towards the stronghold. He doubted she would return to the dragon realm and her brother, but he couldn't be sure.

He scanned back around, sweeping his gaze over all the lands to his right and then settling them on the mountain range that separated the elf kingdom from the free realm and the others.

Would she have kept flying straight and true, towards those mountains, or would she have swept around to head back towards Tenak?

He couldn't see her in any direction. Not a single sign of her. He would find her though.

He couldn't let her disappear from his life again, and he wouldn't leave her out there to go through whatever was hurting her alone, not when he knew he could help her.

Bleu closed his eyes and focused on his blood and their incomplete bond.

He turned his thoughts inwards at first, seeking the thread that connected them, and seized hold of it. The slender ribbon of red shimmered in the darkness of his mind and he focused on it, using his psychic abilities to enhance and strengthen it until it glowed. He wavered on his feet, strength draining from him, but he pushed onwards, pouring all of his energy and his power into locating her.

The darkness faded, hazy black rock replacing it, cragged and grim. He frowned and pushed harder, forcing the images to focus so he could discern where she was. Long minutes passed, a tiny span of time in the life of an elf but one that felt like an eternity to him. He needed to find her.

He needed to be with her.

The image came into sharp relief.

A cave.

He clung to that image and teleported, willing himself to go to that location. The darkness swallowed him and when it parted, the cold that had engulfed him didn't go away. Frigid wind battered him, scouring his bare torso with icy fingers, stealing all heat from him. He shivered and wrapped his arms around himself, and scanned his surroundings. The cragged black rock dropped sharply below him, plummeting into a valley before it rose up again into another sharp peak. Similar mountain ranges filled the distance as far as he could see.

The western border of the elf kingdom.

This was no place for his female.

This patch of no man's land between the elf kingdom and the realms beyond was dangerous, the battles between the fallen angels and gods that took place in those lands often spilling over into it. He needed to get Taryn away from this place.

He looked across to his right as wind whistled past him, the wailing noise created by the cave mouth there. Taryn's fear continued to flow through his blood, stronger now that she was close to him again. His little dragon had been afraid and her instincts had driven her to find a cave, a place where she could hide.

He curled his hands into fists at his sides, turned on his heel and strode towards the isolated cave.

He wasn't sure what to expect as he stooped and entered the cave, his eyes adjusting to the near-darkness, but seeing Taryn huddled naked in the corner, holding herself and rocking, hit him square in the chest.

In the heart.

Bleu couldn't stop his feet from carrying him to her or his instincts as her male from teleporting a blanket from his quarters and into his hand, together with a small battery-operated lantern. He twisted the top to turn it on and pale light chased back the darkness.

Taryn looked up at him through the tangled strands of her violet-to-white hair, her eyes bloodshot and wide, tears streaking her cheeks together with a smear of blood that darted upwards from the right side of her mouth, and his heart ached behind his breast.

She tensed when he stopped in front of her.

He slowly crouched before her, set the lantern down and carefully placed the blanket around her shoulders.

"What is wrong?" he whispered in her tongue, his voice as soft as he could manage when part of him was filled with fury, with a dark hunger to seek out whoever had harmed her and make them suffer as she did.

He focused on tending to her instead, using it to keep that hunger under control. She was all that mattered right now.

He drew the blanket closed around her while he waited for her to become accustomed to his presence and find her voice. When she didn't speak, he carefully combed her hair with his fingers, removing the crusted blood.

Blood that was his fault.

He had hurt his mate and he had to live with that, but he didn't have to let her suffer now, when he had the power to help her.

Heal her.

Since the dark moment forty-two centuries ago when Vail and Fuery had shattered his world, he had built a wall around his heart, determined to never allow anyone into it again. He had refused to feel deeply for anyone. He had kept them all at arm's length so he wouldn't be hurt again. He had purged all weakness because he had wanted to be strong.

Invulnerable.

He had done his best to guard himself and his heart, and it had worked for so long.

Or so he had thought.

When he had seen Taryn again and as he looked at her now, he realised that he hadn't been invulnerable.

He had only been in denial.

He had carried pain for four thousand years, letting it fester in his heart, and those open sores had allowed darkness to grow inside him. That darkness made him more vulnerable and weaker than ever, susceptible to it.

He had refused to deal with what had happened to him, had convinced himself that it hadn't hurt him or affected him in any way, and now it might ruin him.

He could feel the darkness inside him, a terrible living thing that Tenak had set free and that he was still struggling to control even now.

Taryn's eyes locked with his, soft and tender despite the hurt he could sense in her, the fear and the despair, and gently cast the shadows from his heart, expelling them and cleansing him.

If anyone in this world could help him come to terms with his emotions and the things that had happened in his past, it was her.

It had always been her.

She had held back the darkness inside him from the moment he had met her. He knew that now as he looked down at her, his fingers tangled in her hair, feeling her warmth on his skin. She had given him purpose, and he had mistaken it for a mission, conditioning himself to view her as nothing more than an enemy because he had been too afraid to risk his heart.

He wasn't afraid anymore.

This feeling inside him wasn't a weakness. It didn't make him vulnerable.

It made him strong.

He was falling in love with her, with his mate, and he would do whatever it took to make her fall in love with him too. He would do whatever it took to make her see that he could be a good male, the right male for her, if she would give him a chance.

That he cared about her above everything else and would never let anything happen to her. He would protect her, cherish her, would love her forever if she let him.

He brought his fingers closer to her cheek and frowned as he felt her trembling. His little dragon was suffering and he would do for her what he knew she could do for him.

He would do his best to take away that pain by helping her come to terms with her emotions and her past.

"He is coming," she murmured and began rocking, eyes darting beyond him to the cave mouth and back again.

Bleu nodded and kneeled in front of her. She caught the edges of the thick black wool blanket and tugged it closed, clutching it so tightly her fingers paled.

"You saw him in a vision?" he said in a low voice, the most soothing one he could manage. At least he hoped it was soothing. He didn't have much experience with this sort of thing. He wasn't sure he had ever taken care of anyone. Not like this. Not even his little sister.

She slowly nodded and her eyes leaped back to him. "They only come when you are near."

He frowned. "Me?"

She nodded again.

His presence triggered her visions. She had mentioned that she had limited magic because Tenak had received most of it. He had thought that meant she couldn't have visions, but she could.

When he was near to her.

As much as he wanted to know more, he had to focus on her and not satiating his curiosity. He would ask about it later, after he had calmed her and eased her fear.

"Are you afraid because your brother is coming?" he said and her eyes darted back up to his.

They dulled.

She rubbed her wrists and began rocking harder, and he turned his frown on them. Her slender fingers unerringly followed the lines of the scarring around her wrists. His eyes dropped to the matching scars around her ankles and then jumped up to the ones around her throat.

He cursed in the elf tongue, the foulest one at his disposal.

It had been being placed in captivity that had terrified her.

Gods, he was going to kill Leif and the others.

He was going to hunt down whoever had placed shackles on his beautiful female and destroy them.

"Taryn," he husked and she blinked, her eyes brightening again but not enough to satisfy him. They were still distant. She was still locked in her thoughts, caged by her memories. He reached out to touch her hand and she flinched away and snarled at him through teeth that were now all sharp points. He withdrew and held his hands up at his sides, showing her that he meant her no harm. "You know me."

He couldn't bring himself to add that he wasn't going to hurt her, because he had hurt her just hours ago, and in her current state she was liable to remind him of that. He wasn't sure he could bear hearing her say what he had done, not when merely thinking about it left him raw inside, hollowed out and sick to his stomach.

"I know you?" she murmured and canted her head, causing her hair to brush her right cheek. She frowned. "If I know you… why do I not know your name?"

Her eyes darkened and her lips flattened, and the sense of power she always emanated grew stronger, rising to a level where his instincts warned she was a danger and was about to attack him.

"You are a liar," she snarled and her eyes shone vivid violet and white, almost glowing in the low light.

He couldn't argue against that. He had lied a hell of a lot in his lifetime. To people he cared about, to her, and to himself.

"I never told you my name," he said and forced himself to remain relaxed even as his instincts roared to prepare for a fight.

Her eyes narrowed.

Silence stretched between them, thickening the air in the cave as he waited to see what she would do. She remained tensed, coiled and prepared to strike. His heart beat harder, pumping blood to his muscles as his body disobeyed him and he readied himself. If she attacked, he wouldn't fight back. He would defend himself and find a way to calm her, because he felt sure that she would feel terrible when the past lost its grip on her and she realised what she had done.

Just as he felt terrible that he had hurt her while lost in the darkness.

She finally eased back, the tension flowing from her and from him at the same time. He let out the breath he had been holding and sank back onto his heels.

"What is your name, Elf?"

"My name is Bleu," he said and sat still while she studied him, raking her eyes over his bare torso and his leather-clad legs, right down to his knees where they pressed into the black ground before she pulled them back up to his face.

He would answer whatever question she posed to him, no matter what it was or whether it made him feel vulnerable, exposed to her. He would do that for her. He would make himself vulnerable so she wouldn't feel alone.

He needed to do it and it had nothing to do with his instincts as her mate and everything to do with his growing feelings for her.

Her dull eyes flitted over his face and a hint of a smile touched her lips. "You are beautiful… but that is your most terrible weapon. I have seen the other side of that beauty."

She caressed the left side of her throat.

Bleu looked away, pinning his eyes on the ground beside her. "And I have apologised for what I did to you… but not well enough."

He sighed, pulled down another breath and lifted his head, locking gazes with her again. She needed to hear it and he had to stop trying to hide his feelings from everyone. From her. It was time he allowed someone into his heart.

"I am sorry, Taryn." He reached out and brushed the blanket aside, revealing the ravaged side of her throat, and stared at it, his heart throbbing madly behind his breast. "I should not have hurt you like that. I should never have hurt you at all… I cannot excuse what I have done and I do not expect you to forgive me for it. Condemn me, do whatever you must to punish me for what I did to you. I deserve only that. I deserve your retribution."

Her face softened, eyes leaping between his, clearer now. "You wish for me to punish you because you did something I did not like… because you disobeyed me?"

He frowned at the words she had chosen and the way the brightness in her eyes faded again. Her breathing came quicker, his heart racing in time with hers, and her pain and fury flowed through him like ice and fire, numbing him and making him burn at the same time.

"I am not like them… do not *ever* think I am like them," she snarled and knocked his hand away, her expression darkening as she flashed sharp teeth at him. "I will not punish you for something you did that displeased me."

Displeased. Disobeyed.

She began rubbing her wrists again, frantically scouring them with her fingers.

"Taryn." He reached for her.

She shot to her feet, the blanket falling away from her to pool at her ankles, and he looked up at her. She towered over him in the dimly-lit cave, naked and beautiful, but terrifying too. Darkness reigned in her eyes, the same madness that he had seen in them back when she had stopped her brother from killing him on the mountainside.

He was losing her to her memories.

"Taryn," he whispered and her eyes narrowed on him. "I take it back. I do not want you to punish me."

I want you to love me.

It beat in his heart with every powerful thump, ran in his veins like a relentless wave, and he couldn't deny that desire as it filled him, opened his eyes and stripped away his strength, tearing down the barriers around his heart and leaving it open to her. Vulnerable.

He had never felt so weak.

So afraid.

It felt as if his very existence depended on the female towering over him.

She started shaking her head, her eyes widening and her fear flooding the link between them. Her hands came up and she shoved her fingers into her hair, dragging it back from her face.

He rose onto his feet and she backed away from him, still shaking her head, her fine eyebrows rising high.

Gods, he had meant to comfort her and he had only made it worse. She had to speak with him, she had to tell him about what haunted her, or he would only keep making mistakes with her.

"I do not want to be punished," she mumbled and looked down at her feet. "I do not want it."

He reached for her and she lashed out at him, catching him across his left pectoral with her claws. He leaped back when she snarled, baring her fangs at him. Blood trickled down his chest.

"Keep away. Do not touch me!" She backed away from him again, until she hit the rear wall of the cave and couldn't move any further. She tossed a panicked look beyond him to the cave mouth.

No. He couldn't let her run away again.

He sidestepped and blocked her path.

She threw a pained glance at him and her face crumpled. "Please do not punish me. I did not mean to escape the cage… but I had to fly."

"I know," he whispered and held his hands up, hoping to calm her. "I will not punish you, Taryn… but someone did. Who punished you?"

Because he wanted a name, something he could go on, someone he could punish for her.

Her eyes turned wild. "The first was a mortal… he was not strong enough to hold me… he was not strong enough to break me."

"The first?" Bleu snarled, darkness curling through him, driving back the light. "How many have tried to hurt you, Taryn?"

"Tried?" she whispered and blinked, and gods he wanted to hold her when she looked at him like that, the truth shining in her striking eyes. The bastards hadn't tried to hurt her. They had hurt her.

He stepped towards her, his bare chest heaving as he struggled to keep control and keep his voice smooth and calm so he didn't frighten her. "Tell me their names."

She blinked again, her eyes darted around, and her fear jacked up, panic and frustration joining it.

She shook her head and looked at him. "I do not know their names."

Gods damn it.

"Then tell me what you do know. Give me something I can use so I can make them pay for the things they did to you." He reached for her again and backed off when she flashed those killer sharp teeth at him, warning him away. He knew she needed her space, but it was hard to hold himself at a distance when he wanted to draw her into his arms and hold her to comfort her.

Her eyes locked with his, clearer again now. "You swear you will make them pay?"

He nodded.

Her pretty face blackened. "You will kill them?"

He didn't hesitate.

"I will *slaughter* them for you."

She took a step towards him. "There are six of them."

"Six is nothing. I can kill six with a mere thought. I will crush them and I will make sure they know they died because they hurt you."

Her violet-to-white eyes leaped between his. "Why would you do this for me?"

Because he loved her.

Gods, he loved her.

He could embrace the darkness inside him if it meant avenging her. He wouldn't hesitate. He would do whatever it took, no matter how bloody or dangerous it was.

"Because…" he started but trailed off, unsure what to tell her. She was in no state to hear about his feelings or anything of that sort.

She smiled. "Because you are my fated one?"

His eyes widened but he nodded. She knew. He had suspected as much but hearing her say it still hit him hard. It unleashed a need to tell her more, to tell her that he had feelings for her and that he wanted to complete this bond between them. He held his tongue instead, because he didn't want to tell her things in the heat of the moment that she might not remember when the madness lost its grip on her.

He needed to know that she was in control and knew what she was saying when he told her and she gave him a response.

He didn't think he could handle her admitting her feelings for him only to forget she had ever said anything about them.

"Tell me," he husked, voice thick with emotion and need to know what had happened to her so he could understand her and help her. He didn't want to hurt her, but he had to know.

She looked down at her wrists and began rubbing them again. "The first caught me three centuries ago. A mortal. He tried to break me but I was too strong… so he sold me."

Her hands trembled and Bleu had to pin his feet to the ground to stop himself from crossing the short span of black rock to her. The need to hold her was overwhelming, battering his control, but he had to keep his distance and let her talk. She needed to tell someone what had happened to her. He could see it in her because he had been in the same situation once, only he hadn't shared his feelings and they had festered inside him, corrupting him.

He didn't want that for her.

"The second was a shifter… a cat… and the third was a witch." A dark smile curled her lips. "Even they were not strong enough. I fought them… I hurt them… and they sold me."

Her shaking worsened.

"The f-fourth…"

She swallowed hard and closed her eyes.

"He was stronger… owned many females. H-he…" Her eyes snapped open, a glassy quality to them. She wasn't with him again. She was lost in her memories, drowning in them. "I wanted to fly. I want to fly."

She looked beyond him.

Bleu inched into her line of sight. "I know. You can fly soon… but you were telling me something."

And it was hurting her.

He wanted to tell her she could stop, but she had to keep talking. She needed to speak about what had happened to her and she hadn't come far enough yet, she hadn't delved deep enough for their conversation to have done her any good. He hated listening to her talking about the things that had happened to her, despised the way her heart would hitch whenever she tried to say that the males had touched her but couldn't bring herself to speak the words, but he would put himself through this torment if it would help her.

"Did they ever?" He couldn't finish that question, wasn't sure he was strong enough to hear her answer without losing his mind and going mad with a need to slaughter every male who had done so much as look at her.

She shook her head. "I fought them… I hurt them."

But they had hurt her too.

It was there in her eyes.

She might have managed to fight the males off to stop them from forcing her into sex, but they had lashed out at her in return, punishing her for disobeying them and not allowing them to paw her and use her against her will.

His strong, brave little female.

Tears lined her eyes and she wrapped her arms around herself.

"The fifth… a fae… an incubus… he kept me in a cage… made me watch… th-things." She shuddered and curled into herself, and he couldn't stop himself from moving closer to her, filled with a need to comfort her. She looked so small like that. Vulnerable. Gods, he needed to hold her. Her eyes squeezed shut and she lowered her head. "H-he liked me watching… he liked it when I tried to make him stop… he hurt females just to see me react… my brother hurts females…"

Her knees gave out and he caught her before she hit the rough ground, wrapping his arms around her and pulling her close to him. He realised his mistake but it was too late. He couldn't undo what had happened. All he could do was brace himself for her wrath.

It didn't come.

Rather than lashing out at him, she buried her face against his neck, her breath hot on his skin as she sobbed.

He straightened with her, closed his eyes and rubbed her back between her shoulders, muttering soothing things to her in the elf tongue. The need to kill that had been surging like a terrible tide within him washed away, running from him as he held her and listened to her ragged breaths and felt the wet of her tears on his shoulder.

"I need to fly," she whispered, lips brushing his skin, and he tried not to draw pleasure from that caress.

"I know," he murmured and stroked her hair, holding her gently and absorbing how good she felt against him, and how good it felt that she let him do this for her despite everything that had happened to her.

She let him hold her even though males had hurt her.

Did that mean she trusted him not to do the same?

He wasn't brave enough to ask, so he voiced another question instead.

"What happened with the fifth?" Because he wanted to kill that male first.

"The sixth murdered him."

Damn.

He would have to settle for the pleasure of killing that male instead.

"Who was he?" He lowered his head and breathed in her scent, using the smell of sunshine and blue skies to calm his furious need to avenge her.

"A demon," she whispered against his flesh. "He grew angry with me when I kept fighting him and managed to destroy half of his home, and took me back to the market to sell me and replace me with someone weaker."

She was lucky that dragons were so rare and valuable in the slave trade, otherwise any one of the males she had fought and denied might have killed her rather than sold her.

"The market where I saw you?"

She nodded and settled her head on his shoulder, and gods, it felt like Heaven. The fingers of her left hand traced patterns on his right pectoral and he could feel her focus was there, on where she touched him.

"Cait helped me escape… a hellcat…" She drew back and looked up at him, her eyes crystal clear and shining. She was back with him, the tide of her memories abating, and deep in the pit of his soul he felt warmed by the knowledge that he had helped her. He would keep helping her. He would do whatever it took, for however long it took, to free her from her past. Her eyes leaped between his. "I knew you were coming."

"Because you saw me in a vision?" He frowned down at her and she nodded again. "They only come when I am near?"

Another nod. A little smile. "Because you are my fated one."

Her fingers paused at their work of driving him mad with a need to caress her in return, to learn her body at the same time as she learned his, taking small steps forwards and closing the gap between them until they finally came together. She pressed her palm against his bare chest, scalding him and branding his flesh with her touch.

"You are my fated one?" Her eyes searched his.

He nodded. "I am… and you are mine."

Mine.

Gods… she was. His mate. Mine.

He wanted to growl that word at her but bit down on his tongue instead, aware that if he uttered it, he would push her back into the past, to times when other males had sought possession of her.

Had tried to rule her.

He wanted nothing of that sort, and the word would simply be an admission on his part, telling her more that he belonged to her now than she belonged to him, but it would frighten her nonetheless.

Gods… he was hers though. He had been hers from the moment he had set eyes on her. He just hadn't known it back then.

He knew it now as he gazed down at her though, her warm body pressing against his, her beautiful eyes tinged with shyness, as if she was aware of his sentimental thoughts, could hear them rattling around his head. Not the thoughts of a warrior, cold and methodical, but the thoughts of a lover, tender and warm. Probably the last thing she expected from him given their history.

Her smile faded and she lowered her gaze to his chest. "I have caused you trouble though."

"You had to fly," he said in a matter of fact tone, one he hoped would make her see that he understood her now and that what she had done mattered little to him because she had needed to do it. Her smile returned and it was hard to hold back and stop himself from caressing her cheek. "My prince will understand when we return to the castle and speak with him."

Taryn stiffened. "I cannot go back."

He sighed and rubbed her shoulders, frowned at how cold they were and teleported the blanket to his hand. He wrapped it around her again, and then encircled her in his arms and drew her against him, using his body to warm hers.

The tension melted from her the instant they made contact and the warmth in the pit of his soul grew hotter, a flicker of flame that she had fanned with her acceptance of his embrace, one that comforted him deeply.

She settled her cheek against his chest again. He rested his chin on top of her head and stared across the cave.

"They will put me back—"

"It will not happen again," he cut her off and held her closer, surprised when she pressed against him, as if she needed to be closer still. As if she needed him. "I will make sure of it. I won't let anything happen to you, Taryn. I will protect you."

She pulled back again and looked up into his eyes, hers wide and filled with warmth and surprise that he could feel flowing through her blood.

He released her and gave up fighting his urges.

He brushed the backs of his fingers across her cheek, and murmured in a husky low voice, "I will protect you… from your brother… from the soldiers… from everyone if I must."

Heat stirred in his veins as she gazed up at him and it ran through their connection too, flowing from her and into him. That connection blossomed, grew stronger as he fell into her eyes, forging an unbreakable link between their hearts.

Her hands pressed against his bare chest, burning him with her touch, turning his control to ashes as her lips parted and she leaned closer.

His gaze fell to her mouth. He tried to look away, but his eyes refused to leave the tempting curves of her lips as she tilted her head back. An invitation. Gods, he wanted to take it, but she was hurting, had just bared the darkest part of her past and was vulnerable. He couldn't take advantage of her like that.

No matter how desperately he wanted to kiss her.

He cursed the part of himself that had suddenly turned all noble. Just days ago he would have had her pinned to the wall and panting his name already, but now he couldn't bring himself to do it.

"Bleu," she husked and gods, his name sounded too good when it fell from her lips like that, breathed on a passion-drenched sigh.

A sigh that stirred the images of his dreams in his mind, the wicked acts they had performed while tangled together, lost for a moment in each other.

Her eyes darkened, pupils gobbling up the white around the inside of her irises, leaving them more purple. She pushed her hands up his chest and looped her arms around his neck, and his breathing deepened as she pulled him down to her, closing the gap between their mouths.

He clutched her hips and felt her trembling beneath his hands. Or was that him? It was difficult to tell. Every inch of him felt as if it was shaking.

He tensed and she stopped with their lips a bare inch apart.

"Tell me you know what you are doing and that you want this… that this means something and you aren't just scratching an itch or trying to make yourself forget things for a while…" He eased back and looked down into her eyes. "Tell me you are here with me, Taryn."

She shifted her hands, caressing them up his neck to cup his cheeks, and held his gaze as she tilted his head down towards her, her gaze earnest and beautiful and her feelings steady.

"I am here with you, Bleu. I want this."

She tiptoed, pressed her lips to his, and whispered.

"I want you."

CHAPTER 25

Bleu seized her lips in a hard kiss, unable to hold back as her sweet taste flooded him and she pressed against him, her words ringing in his mind, stripping away his strength to resist. She wanted him.

Fuck, he wanted her too.

He had wanted her for so long now, had ached for her without ever knowing it, and now she would be his. Every single damned dream he'd had of her was about to become reality. His cock pressed uncomfortably against the lacing of his trousers, instantly hard. Painfully so.

Taryn only made things worse when she loosed a little moan, the wicked sound teasing his ears and sending him spiralling out of control.

His hunger for her took the reins and drove all sense into submission, until there was only a need to touch and taste her, to tease her to climax and hear her cry his name.

His mate.

He would satisfy her.

Her need ran through him, powerful and intense, a force that mastered him until all he could think about was pleasing her and satiating her need.

She needed.

Fuck, she needed and he did too.

He needed to give her everything she ached for, satisfying her until she had no energy left, was limp and spent in his arms.

He growled into her mouth and she stiffened.

Her hands tensed against his cheeks.

Bleu silently cursed himself and drew back, breaking the kiss. Even that was painful for him, took every drop of his will when all he wanted to do was keep kissing her.

He pressed his forehead to hers and breathed hard, struggling to steady himself and claw back some control. Her words rang around his head, ones about her past now, and he found the balance he had been seeking. He couldn't frighten her. He had to be gentle with her, even when that felt impossible.

"Sorry," he uttered and she shook her head.

"Do not be," she whispered, sweet breath washing across his damp lips, teasing them until they tingled with a need to kiss her again. "It startled me… but dear gods, I want to growl too when you kiss me… it's as if my whole body has come alive and I am overloading with sensation."

He chuckled, wrapped his arms around her and pulled her closer. As close as he could get her.

A smile tugged at his lips, one he felt right down in his soul. "You have a way with words that is only going to push me back over the edge, Little Dragon."

She nudged her nose against his. "Little Dragon? You are the little dragon… with your horns."

She pulled back and he didn't like the frown she wore as she looked up at him.

"I am sorry your armour is lost."

He wasn't. Going to find it back in her brother's stronghold would have placed them both in danger, because she would have had to help him, her knowledge of the castle key in locating it.

"Armour is replaceable." He swept the backs of his fingers across her cheek and his eyes darted between hers as she gazed up at him. "You are not."

A blush blazed up her cheeks, heating his fingers, and she looked away from him, but not before he caught the flicker of shyness in her eyes mingling with the desire he could feel in her.

Her palms drifted down to his shoulders and then his chest, and he couldn't keep his eyes open. They slipped shut as the heat of her caress travelled through him, his skin tingling wherever she roamed, anticipation coiling in his gut as he rushed to imagine where she might go next. She skimmed her hands over his pectorals and downwards, her fingertips catching on his pebbled nipples, sending sparks skittering across his flesh.

"Growl," she whispered in a low teasing voice that only heightened everything he was feeling, stirring his desire to painful levels. "I can feel you want to… I like it when you growl, Bleu."

"Why?" Fuck, was that his voice? Strained and low, pulled tight by little more than a light caress? He shivered from head to toe when she traced the ridges of his abdomen with her fingers and he felt the searing heat of her gaze on his body.

Did she like what she saw?

Her thoughts back in the dungeon of her brother's castle flooded his mind, answering that question for him. She had liked seeing his body and hearing him growl. It had turned her on.

"Because I like how little control you have when you are around me," she murmured and dropped her head, pressed wet kisses along his collarbone.

He couldn't contain the growl that rumbled through his chest as she tortured him.

She flicked her tongue across the line of scars on the left side of his throat.

"I like the way it tells me how much you want me."

He grabbed her hips and dropped his mouth to her neck, and growled against it as he kissed her, alternating between nipping her flesh and sucking on it. His mouth watered, fangs punching long from his gums. He screwed his eyes closed further as he savoured her, teetered on the brink of taking things a step further and nicking her skin so he could steal a drop of her blood.

He pushed that thought out of his head and reined himself back in. It was more difficult this time and Taryn didn't help when she moaned and angled her head away from him, giving him better access to her throat. She pressed blunt teeth into his shoulder, her breath hot and moist against his skin.

Bleu clutched her closer and licked her throat, felt the ragged marks under his tongue.

It was enough to ground him and purge the need to bite her.

He drew back and gazed down at the marks. Savage. Vicious. He had treated his mate poorly. She had tried to help him and he had repaid her by attempting to kill her.

He tensed when Taryn's left hand caught his cheek and she drew him around to face her, dragging his eyes away from her neck.

For a moment, he thought she would say something as she had before, offering him forgiveness when he deserved none, but then she did something that unravelled him and tore down what little strength he had left, completely shattering the barriers around his heart.

She kissed him.

Softly.

Tenderly.

There was forgiveness and understanding in the soft brush of her mouth across his, in the tender way she stroked his cheeks with her thumbs and held him.

Heat and light flowed through him, and all he could do was press his fingers into her hips and hold on to her.

He would never let her go.

Bleu wrapped his arms around her and kissed her back, sweeping his tongue across the seam of her mouth. Her lips parted and he delved his tongue inside, loved it when she moaned and pressed closer, her tongue coming to tentatively stroke his. She gained confidence as he kissed her, duelling with him for dominance.

Gods, she had to know how that stoked him, made him burn hotter for her.

She had to feel how close he was to losing control when he was trying to retain it so he didn't frighten her.

His little dragon lost control first.

She wrapped her arms around his neck, dragged him down to her and kissed him harder, loosing a growl into his mouth. The sound of it echoed around the cave, feral and wild, speaking to him of her need as it ran through his blood.

He growled right back at her, earning a moan as his reward, and then growled deeper and longer when she shirked the blanket. Her bare skin was warm and soft beneath his fingers as he ran his hands down her back, curled them over her bottom. It gave beneath his grip and he pressed his fingers in, clutching her against him.

The feel of her breasts against his chest, their bare skin rubbing as she tiptoed to kiss him deeper, was too much.

He groaned and gritted his teeth, breathed hard as a hunger to turn with her and pin her to the wall surged through him. He had to be gentle.

His little dragon was doing everything to drive that word out of his vocabulary.

He tensed when she dipped her head and kissed down the line of his throat, nipped at his collarbone and then continued a path across his chest. Her tongue flicked his right nipple and he growled, tipped his head back and prayed for strength. Gentle. He had to be gentle with her.

Fuck, he was going to lose his mind fighting this internal war.

Every part of him, from his mind to his soul, to his body, screamed at him to surrender to the hunger he had been holding back. It roared at him to give into it. He needed Taryn. She was the air in his lungs and the life in his veins. His very existence depended on her.

It felt as if it depended on this moment.

As if he would die if he didn't surrender to his need.

She caressed his chest and then her hands drifted lower, over his sides before sweeping back in to brush his stomach. He shuddered and moaned with each torturous touch. His fangs lengthened and cock pulsed, both itching with a hunger to sink into her. He tensed and growled when she thumbed his nipples, lips peeling back off his fangs. His ears flared, growing pointier as desire took hold of him, hijacking control again.

Every sweep of her fingers or her lips was excruciatingly wonderful, so intensely pleasurable that it wound him tighter, cranked him higher.

He tried to keep still and let her explore him at her leisure, felt the need that ran through their link, but it was impossible.

She was making it impossible.

Her hands caressed his shoulders, fingers pressing in when she reached his deltoids, a brief flash of her strength that aroused him to the point of pain. The thought of touching her in return tore at the tiny sliver of control he was clinging to, tugging it through his grasp.

But it was the way she feathered her fingers up his throat and then over his earlobes and up to the point of his ears that ripped it from him.

He shuddered, couldn't stop his hips from rocking, rubbing his cock against his trousers as pleasure so intense that it damn near blinded him bolted through him. He breathed hard, fought for control over his body, but she curled her fingers around to behind his ears and rubbed her thumbs up to the tips and his length pulsed so hard he almost came.

He growled, swept her up into his arms and kissed her fiercely, swallowing her gasp as his lips clashed with hers, teeth knocking together. She tensed but he didn't let up, couldn't. He plundered her mouth with his tongue, gathered her closer and bent her to his will. She moaned, the sweet sound driving him on, telling him that she enjoyed this wild side of him.

This side that showed her just how much he wanted her.

Needed her.

Fuck, he would die without her.

He turned and pinned her back to the wall, pressed his body to hers and caged her there. She tensed again but quickly relaxed this time, her short nails pressing into his shoulders as she kissed him back, mouth seeking to master his.

Not a damned chance.

She had pushed too far, shoved him over the edge and there was no coming back for him. Whatever control he'd had, she had shattered it and he couldn't piece it back together. He needed her, couldn't breathe or think, or do anything but feel.

Bleu caught her under her thighs and lifted her legs, made her wrap them around his waist and then cupped her backside.

Fuck.

He couldn't breathe.

The feel of her heat so close to his fingertips would have been devastating enough, but she was wet with the need he could feel flowing through her.

He growled as he shifted his fingers closer to her groin, and she moaned and wriggled, the hunger that constantly ebbed and flowed through their connection turning into desperate need that he couldn't ignore.

She needed him.

He pressed closer, moaned low in his throat when his rigid length met her body and she actually rocked against it.

Holy fuck.

He kissed her harder, broke away from her mouth and devoured the unmarked side of her throat, couldn't stop himself as she rubbed her body against his. He took it back. She could master him still.

She stripped him of his control with little more than a flex of her body against his and he was a slave to her again, lost in sensation and his spiralling need. Fuck, she could do whatever she wanted with him, as long as it felt that good.

He pressed his lips to her shoulder and gave himself over to it, all thought of moving fleeing as she rolled her hips, rubbing herself along him.

It was her dissatisfied mewl that made him move again, pulled him back to the moment and stirred his instincts as her fated male.

Her mate.

He obeyed her when she shoved at his hips, moving back a few inches but keeping a firm grip on her bottom so she didn't fall. She leaned back and he groaned as she fumbled with the lacing on his trousers, her eyes dark with hunger that called to him.

"Bleu," she uttered when the lacing knotted and threw him a desperate look that had him moving in an instant to help her.

He set her down on her feet and teleported his trousers away.

Her eyes darkened further, pupils devouring her irises as she raked her gaze over the taut ridges of his stomach, past his navel to the blunt tip of his cock. Her lips parted and gods, the things he wanted her to do with that mouth.

The thought he had picked up back in the cell when he had been healing her wound flooded him again, aroused him back to the point of pain, and his cock kicked against his stomach, jerking with approval as his mind raced forwards to fulfilling that desire she'd had.

That need to know how good his tongue would feel on her flesh.

She reached a trembling hand towards his shaft and frowned when he dropped to his knees. The rough black ground bit into them but he didn't feel the stab of the pebbles as he gazed at her hips.

At the sweet neat thatch of violet curls at the apex of her thighs.

"Bleu," she whispered, uncertainty lacing her voice, stirring his softer side and the part of him that wanted to be gentle with her.

He looked back up at her.

Fuck, she really was beautiful.

She towered over him, gazing down at him, the shyness back in her eyes as her eyebrows furrowed and she worried her lower lip with her teeth. How could such a powerful female look so innocent? She had been more than wicked in the dreams they had shared, skilled with her mouth and her body, but here in reality she looked ready to bolt.

He lowered his eyes to her hips again and called himself a bastard, because he couldn't let her back down now.

He needed to taste her.

She trembled under his fingers as he ran them up her calves, over her knees and swept them up to her hips. Her throat worked on a hard swallow. He kept his eyes locked with hers and skimmed his palms over her hips and down her inner thighs, brushing the edges of her groin. Her eyes slipped shut and her breath left her in a rush, and the hunger that swept through their incomplete bond damn near had him coming.

Gods, the power she had over him. If only she knew.

He dropped his hungry gaze to her hips and she didn't resist when he carefully applied a little pressure to the back of her left thigh. She let him move her leg, only moaned when he hooked it over his shoulder, exposing her core to the cool air of the cave. Her breath hitched when he leaned in, hands coming down on his head and his shoulder, and a flicker of uncertainty ran through her again.

He blew across her tiny bead and she shuddered and moaned, clutched him tightly with both hands. He swept his up her inner thighs and gently parted her plush lips, revealing her to his greedy eyes. Gods, he wanted to devour her. He would devour her.

Bleu stroked his tongue across her pert nub and she jerked against his face, a bark of pleasure exploding from her lips. He groaned and did it again, drinking down each gasp and moan that left her as she grew accustomed to his caress. When she relaxed against the wall, her grip on him going lax, he delved lower, lapped at her entrance and moaned at the taste of her. Sweet and sublime. He could feast on her forever and never get enough.

He licked back up, flicked his tongue over her nub, took pleasure from her high gasp as she quaked against him. He wanted more. He wanted all of her.

Taryn shuddered again, her hands gripping more tightly when he rubbed his thumbs downwards, teased her slick core with one while he tortured her with his tongue. She moaned and writhed, the hunger that constantly flowed from her into him growing fiercer, mingling with desperation. She wanted release. Needed it. He would give it to her.

He circled her entrance with his finger and slipped it inside, just enough to press against the fleshy part of her that would have her screaming out her climax before long. His tongue flickered over her nub, swirled and pressed as he stroked her with his finger. Her breaths turned ragged and she dug her fingers into his shoulder and tangled her other hand in his hair, twining the lengths between her fingers and pulling on it as she desperately rolled her hips.

Bleu angled his head and suckled her arousal as he added another finger, stretched her and stroked her harder. Moisture ran down his fingers and pooled in his palm, hot against his skin. He groaned and nipped at her bead with his blunt teeth, his cock kicking against his stomach, balls tightening at the thought of being inside her and feeling her juices coating him as they coated his hand.

She moaned and wriggled, breathed sigh after sigh as she sought release. He couldn't stop his imagination from racing ahead, picturing feeding his cock into her core and seeing her face as he seated himself inside her, stretching her and claiming her.

He groaned and licked harder, pressed deeper with his fingers, and she cried out, her entire body jerking towards him and tensing as she quivered around him. Hot liquid streamed down his fingers and he lapped at her nub, listening to her ragged breathing and feeling her heart racing in his chest as her climax swept through her. When she sank against the wall and pushed against his shoulder and head, a giggle escaping her, he drew back, obeying her silent command to give her a moment.

A smile played on her lips as she looked down at him, panting, her eyes twinkling but still dark with desire.

A real smile.

One that hit him so hard in the chest it knocked the wind from him.

He stared up at her and that smile faded as if his serious expression was contagious. She blinked slowly and a thousand things rushed to the tip of his tongue, half of them ridiculous nonsense about how beautiful she was and the other half liable to frighten her away.

He didn't want to drive her away.

He needed her too much.

Her eyes slowly drifted over him and settled on his cock. It kicked in response to the heat of her gaze on it and the way her eyes darkened, hunger reigniting in them.

Bleu withdrew his hand from her and she looked at it as he brought it towards him and then up into his eyes. He held her gaze as he licked her spending from his fingers, relishing every drop as if it was ambrosia. Fuck, it was ambrosia. The greatest drug he had ever known. It sent fire blazing through his blood, stirred his desire to beyond the point of pain, made him desperate for her in a way he had never experienced before.

Taryn looked him over again and then stepped towards him. His breath hitched and he had the feeling that she was about to turn the tables on him and this time he would be the one screaming his lungs out.

Fuck, he wanted that.

She lifted her leg, flashing Heaven at him, and his breath left him in a rush as she pressed her foot to his shoulder and pushed him onto his back. He lay half on the black ground and half on the blanket, unable to move as he stared up at her, anticipation coiling in his stomach again, making his hard length jerk near constantly against his stomach.

Her eyes raked over him again, hungry gaze burning him and stoking the fire, until it was an inferno and he couldn't breathe as he watched her coming to stand over his hips, followed her as she lowered herself and sat astride him.

He hissed as her wet heat encased his cock and tipped his head back into the floor, body straining as bliss rolled through him.

That sense of Heaven only grew as she rose off him again, her eyes on his the whole time, and grasped hold of his cock. She positioned it beneath her and he stilled, dropped his gaze to where she held him, and bit his lower lip as she eased back. The head of his cock pushed against her moist core and he groaned through gritted teeth as her heat scalded him, hotter and wetter than he had imagined. He held back, resisting the need to thrust himself to the hilt inside of her, allowing her to be in control even when he wanted to flip her over and take her hard and fast.

He lifted his hips a little though, impatience tearing at his control, and groaned at how tight she was around him, gloving him and gripping him fiercely. He pushed upwards as she moved downwards, a bit rougher than he had meant to be.

She flinched.

At least he thought it was because he had been rough until his lust fogged mind cleared enough to realise it had been for a different reason.

She was tight and it had nothing to do with his size.

He grasped her hips, tried to stop her but she growled at him, flashing killer sharp teeth. She grabbed his hands, shoved them up to his shoulders and pinned them on the ground there as she inched back onto him. Violet fire flashed in her eyes and the hunger she felt surged through him, more powerful than he had ever felt it, a possessive force that knocked the wind from him.

Not born of violence but born of desire.

Her face screwed up as she sank back onto him, her breath coming in fast pants as she held him pinned beneath her, an echo of her pain trickling through him. It burned brighter but she didn't stop, she pressed down on him, pushed past the point of pain and all of her strength and fight seemed to leave her as the tip of his cock hit the furthest point it could reach. She sank against his chest, breathing hard, heart racing.

Her hands went lax against his and he kept still beneath her, still struggling to take in what had just happened.

She was untouched.

His addled mind banded that around and the more he thought about it, the stronger his feelings grew, until he felt dangerously possessive of her.

Because he was her first.

Her only.

She was purely his. No other male had touched her. No other male had marked her.

She was his alone.

His forever.

The urge to bite her again was overwhelming but he clamped his jaws shut and focused on her instead, on the feel of her wrapped around his hard cock and the way she was resting on him, her cheek pressing against his chest and hands linked with his.

"Why didn't you tell me?" he whispered, voice hoarse and thick, rumbling around the dark cave.

The thought that she was his alone soon gave way to another one, a realisation that hit him hard.

His little dragon must have fought her owners fiercely in order to remain untouched.

When she had been telling him about her past, he hadn't once believed she had managed to stop them from touching her. In the years he had known of her existence, he hadn't once thought she would be intact. He had presumed she would have known males in her past, that she would have taken lovers. He knew of dragons. He knew their females were renowned for their passion and carnal hungers, and that they took lovers whenever their needs arose, using them to sate their desire.

That part of Taryn had been at the helm when she had pinned him to the floor.

"Because I knew you would try to stop me," she said and rose off him, and he groaned as he slid deeper into her heat.

Her eyes darkened again and her hunger mingled with his.

"And I did not want to stop." She wriggled her hips and he moaned again, every inch of him tensing as pleasure blasted through him. "I told you that I wanted you."

She had, but he hadn't realised the meaning behind those words. That she wanted him when she had never wanted another. She had kept herself pure. Now all he could think about was how he was tainting her.

He had known seven centuries ago that she was his fated female, and although he had conditioned himself to forget about her, deep down he had been aware of what she was to him. His instincts as her mate wouldn't have allowed his most primal side to forget her. That knowledge hadn't stopped him from scratching his biological itches with other females though.

There had been no feelings behind his trysts, those moments he had shared with them had been purely a satisfaction of needs, but that didn't stop him from feeling sick to the pit of his stomach as he gazed up at her.

The feeling that he didn't deserve her grew stronger alongside his feelings for her, sinking its claws in deep, shredding his soul and threatening to tear him apart.

Loren had been celibate for millennia waiting for his ki'ara and he hadn't even known who she was and when he would meet her—if he would ever meet her.

Bleu had known of his but he had still slept with many females.

He had told his sister countless times how much he longed for his fated one, and when she had come along, he had turned his back on her and conditioned himself to forget her because he had believed she could never be his.

But now he had hope, he was here with her, and being with her made him see just how hollow the moments he had shared with those females in his past had been, because Taryn filled him up and made him feel whole.

Complete.

Yet he couldn't stop feeling as if he was tainting her.

The gods only knew how long she had been alive. He found it hard to comprehend that she had been around for the seven hundred years he had known her without ever seeking a male's touch. The thought that she had been celibate for longer than that blew his mind.

Stirred his possessiveness.

Fuck, he had to go back to the castle with her at some point and what sort of male was he going to be then, when his little dragon was around so many unmated males?

"Your eyes have gone dark," she whispered, a trace of fear in her voice, and he closed them. Her palms pressed against his cheeks. "You are mad at me?"

"Gods, no," he barked and looked at her, wanting her to see in his eyes that he wasn't. He could never be angry with her. He was angry with himself. He was angry with males he didn't even know, furious at the thought they might look at her. "I just can't stop thinking—"

"So stop thinking," she whispered in a sultry voice and leaned over him, brushed her lips across his chest and licked the scars on his throat.

He wasn't sure he could.

She proved him wrong when she moved, shifting on his cock, rising slowly off it before pressing back down. Fuck, not a single thought remained in his mind as she began riding him, slowly at first, tentative thrusts that had him staring at her through wide eyes as he grew accustomed to how tight she was. How hot.

Her pace gained confidence and speed and he could only growl and tip his head back as he fought for control, tried to let her be the one to master him and take the lead. Hunger pooled in his chest, a dark need to roll her over and take her, to possess her and make her see that her wait had been worth it.

He would make a good mate for her.

She moaned, threw her head back and moved faster, her pert breasts bouncing with each upwards stroke and downwards plunge. Her palms pressed against his chest, fingertips digging into his pectorals. He gritted his teeth, breathed harder as he had to focus to master his own damned body as she clenched him, flexing her wet heat around him. Her slick juices rolled down his shaft, trickled through his curls, dampened his balls.

Holy fuck.

He couldn't do this.

He growled and her eyes flicked open, locking on him, dark and filled with desire.

With a challenge.

One he was quick to take, surrendering to the wild part of himself that roared at him to bend her to his will and bring her to a shattering climax.

He rolled with her, pinned her on the blanket without missing a stroke, and she cried out as he drove into her, deeper than when she had been riding him. Her hands flew to his shoulders and her nails dug into his flesh, tiny points of pain that backed up the flood of feelings rushing through their link. She liked this.

She clung to him as he plunged into her, breathless moans escaping her lips each time the tip of his cock struck deep and he withdrew, pumping her deeply to make sure she felt every inch of him.

To make sure she knew just how hard she made him.

How wild.

Her arms wrapped around him and she craned her neck, capturing his lips with hers as he rocked into her. She pressed the heels of her feet into the earth and pushed her hips up, and he groaned and shuddered as he slid deeper, moaning in time with her. She devoured his mouth as he pumped her and fought for control, to retain a sliver of it when all he wanted to do was let go and allow the untamed part of him that she had unleashed to take the lead.

Taryn didn't seem to have any problem with allowing that. She clawed at his shoulders and hooked one leg around his waist, and rocked against him, countering his thrusts, a wild little thing in his arms. She growled into his mouth and kissed him harder, driving him into surrendering to his need. His control shattered and he couldn't hold himself back.

Bleu drove into her, rolling his hips with each deep thrust of his cock, every plunge that struck her hard and had her quivering against him, whispering wicked things against his lips in the dragon tongue.

She wanted more.

Fuck.

He snarled, grabbed her under her left thigh to hold her backside off the blanket, and curled his other hand around the nape of her neck, clutching it tightly to hold her in place. He thrust harder, deeper, devouring her mouth as he took her and claimed her, stamping his mark on her and ensuring she would want no other male.

She moaned into his mouth and ran sharp nails over his back, scoring his flesh and filling the cave with the scent of blood.

His mouth watered, fangs dropping as he thought about biting her. Her tongue brushed the tip of his left fang, a little gasp escaped her and then the taste of her flooded his mouth. Gods help her. Gods help him.

He snarled and kissed her harder, desperate to taste her again as he took her, drove as deep as she could take him, all thought of being gentle gone. He couldn't stop himself or hold back, and the fear he had of hurting her crushed his soul.

Until she moaned and clawed harder, tugged him closer and kissed him back, as lost to desire as he was.

He clutched her hip and thrust harder, driving every inch of his hard cock into her as his balls drew up, semen rising to the base of his length. He groaned as she stroked his fang again, rubbing her tongue along it, sending sparks skittering down his spine to his balls, twisting them tighter still.

Her hands shifted from his shoulders and she caught the sides of his head, and he couldn't breathe as her palms brushed his ears, teasing their sensitive tips.

The whole universe detonated.

His body shattered into a million pieces, leaving only an explosion of feeling that rocked him to his soul and had him shaking from head to toe.

Taryn moaned hotly into his mouth, quivering beneath him, her ecstasy rolling through him and heightening his own, until they mingled so completely that he was no longer sure who he was and whose feelings they were.

There was only one heart beating rapidly.

One soul on fire.

A perfect union that he would make sure lasted forever.

Now that he had Taryn, the other half of his soul, his heart, he was never letting her go.

She was his forever.

He managed to pull back and look down at her. She smiled, rosy kiss-swollen lips curling in a way that warmed his heart, chased the darkness from his soul and made him feel as if he had come home.

He growled a single word in his mind, one that he felt to the very pit of the soul she had completed.

Mine.

CHAPTER 26

Taryn listened to the heart drumming against her right ear, the sedated rhythm perfectly matching the pace of hers. His steady breathing filled the quiet dimly-lit cave, a sound that she found strangely soothing together with the warmth of him against her and the feel of his arms wrapped around her, keeping her pinned to the side of his body beneath the black blanket.

Bleu.

From time to time in the seven centuries she had known him she had wondered about his name, but she had never caught it. She had never imagined it to be the one he had given to her though, but now she knew it, she felt it suited him somehow.

He warmed her and made her feel free as if she was flying in blue skies.

Blue skies that he no doubt knew.

She lifted her head from his bare chest, wanting to ask him about the mortal world, but the questions fled her lips when she saw his face peaceful in slumber, relaxed and more handsome than ever.

He needed to rest.

She had sensed it in their connection, the one he had forged by drinking from her, triggering the bonding process in an elven way.

She could still sense it in him now, while he was sleeping.

She needed rest too if she was going to be strong enough to face what lay ahead of her, but she couldn't bring herself to close her eyes. It felt as if by doing so she would be squandering this moment of calm with him, this brief time when everything outside the cave didn't exist and there was only the two of them without a care in the world.

She couldn't remember ever feeling like this before.

She hadn't thought it possible.

When lost to her memories, she had told him things she had sworn she would never reveal to anyone, fear of how they would view her forcing her to hold her tongue. In that spell of madness, awareness of what she had been doing had been stripped from her and she had let it all spill from her lips. She had told him everything.

But rather than turning away from her as she had expected, fulfilling her fear that no one would love her if they knew about her past and the things she had done, the terrible centuries she had somehow survived, he had done the opposite.

He had drawn her to him.

Instead of rejecting her, he had forged a stronger connection between them, bringing them closer together.

She still marvelled at that, feeling as if she had dreamed it all. It was going to take time for it to sink in, but even in his sleep he was taking steps to make that happen without even knowing it.

She gazed down at him, the way he held her close to him telling her something that slowly washed away some of the hurt in her past because his embrace was tender, filled with affection that she knew he didn't want to admit to her. She could understand his reservations, because she had them too, was struggling with these new feelings growing inside her just as he was.

He mumbled something in his strange tongue, lyrical words that sounded as magical as many in Hell thought his kind to be. His lips smacked together, his nose twitched, and then he sighed as he relaxed again beneath her.

She lost track of time as she studied him, absorbing everything about him as he slept, unaware of her watching over him. Such a strong male. Fierce. Dangerous.

Possessive.

She had felt that last one in him when they had made love. It had run through her too, awakening her dragon instincts as his female and forcing her to respond to her desire by staking a claim on him and making it clear she wouldn't accept no as an answer.

She had never surrendered to that instinct before, but she had let it overcome her in the moment, had embraced it and had seen the flicker of excitement that had brightened his eyes. He had liked her taking charge, exerting her strength and showing him how fiercely she wanted him.

Just thinking about it fanned the embers of desire in her veins, until she burned for him again.

Taryn tamped them down, aware that she would wake him if she continued to let her desires run rampant and unchecked.

They were bonded now, not in a permanent way but in one strong enough that he could sense things in her.

She could sense things in him too, but some of those things she didn't need a bond to make her see them.

He felt guilty.

She had caught the way his expression shifted whenever he glanced at her throat, the flashes of guilt that crossed his eyes before he dragged them away and the shame and self-reproach that simmered in his veins.

She dimly remembered mentioning it to him when she had been lost in her memories and how wounded he had looked. She remembered it because she had felt bad, guilty about the barb she had thrown at him when he had helped her, had burst into the elven cellblock bare seconds after they had put her in a cage and had freed her from captivity.

Normally when the memories seized her as strongly as they had back then, she couldn't remember anything that she did, relived her past so vividly that she wasn't aware of anything else.

Was it his presence that had helped her retain enough of her consciousness to combat the memories and remain partially aware of the world and the things that were happening around her?

His presence seemed to trigger a lot of things in her, not only a strength to battle her memories or to see a vision of the future.

It triggered a heat in her too, a hunger that was startling in its intensity and felt as if it was impossible to sate.

Even just the feel of his bare skin against hers was enough to have her tingling wherever he touched.

The dark slashes of his eyebrows twitched into a frown.

"I can feel you staring," he rumbled, voice a low drone that soothed her but stirred the heat growing inside her, fanning it hotter.

He lifted his right hand away from her bare back, ran his fingers through his tousled blue-black hair and yawned. No fangs, but his canines were still longer than a mortal's would be, a sign that part of him was still on edge.

Or hungry.

He tucked his right arm behind his head, stifled another yawn and slowly opened his eyes. Pure amethyst. Sometimes she wished her eyes were like his, not strangely two-tone. None would stare at her or think her valuable if she had eyes like that.

"Come back to me, Taryn," he murmured and she frowned at him, was on the verge of saying that she hadn't gone anywhere when it struck her that she had.

She had been sinking into her memories again, thinking of all the horrible things that might not have happened to her if she had been like other dragons, a single and common colour.

Bleu raised his left hand and sifted his fingers through her hair, combing it back from her face, and cupped her cheek.

Her breath hitched as his heat seeped into her, the softness of his caress warming her right down to her soul, and her heart picked up pace in response to the shiver that ran down her spine.

She stared into his eyes, losing herself in them and not wanting to come back to the world, not when it felt so perfect here with him. She felt so safe cocooned in the arms of this male she was falling in love with.

Had perhaps loved for longer than she cared to admit.

He loosed a little moan of pleasure as he stretched beneath her, his delicious body flexing and each muscle announcing itself in a way that had her hungry for another taste of him. She squeezed her thighs together and bit back a moan of her own as she throbbed, still pleasantly sore from their lovemaking.

Bleu shifted position, moving his right arm higher, so it supported his head. His biceps bulged and she cursed them for being such a wonderful distraction.

Together with the rest of him.

The gods had been cruel when they had built her mate so perfect.

She was surprised she had managed to resist him for this long, had been able to tear herself away from him whenever their paths had crossed. The last time, at the slavers market, had been the hardest. She had been so afraid in that moment, tired and battered, on the verge of collapse, and he had been such a temptation. She had wanted to surrender to him, even though she had known that he wouldn't be gentle with her as she had needed, that if she gave up the fight and let him capture her that only death would have awaited her.

Bleu sighed and brushed his fingers through her hair. "I am losing you again."

Taryn blinked herself back to him. "My mind wandered."

"And where did it go?" A half smile played on his lips and she cursed the gods again, because now he looked even more perfect. Roguish. Gorgeous. A little bit wicked.

She pulled her gaze away from him, lifting it up to look over his head towards the mouth of the cave. It was growing lighter, bright enough that she could make out the distant peaks across the valley. He would want to go soon. That made her want to tense and hide, and she had to push herself to remain calm and trust him.

She did trust him.

He had rescued her from the elves who had put her in the cell and he wanted to help her stop her brother. He had promised she would be safe if she returned to the castle with him and met with his prince, and she believed him.

She also believed that he trusted her.

It was there for her to see in what he had said to her.

His prince would understand when they returned to the castle and spoke with him.

He trusted her to meet with the male who ruled the elves. A male she felt Bleu was close to and was more than a master to him.

"And there you go again." Bleu's deep rumbling voice pulled her back to him.

She smiled her apology. "There is much on my mind."

He wriggled beneath her, his naked body rubbing hers in a way that threatened to have her getting lost in her thoughts again, more wicked ones this time.

"So tell me what you are thinking about," he husked and she looked back at him, mildly surprised when he looked deadly serious.

She couldn't remember the last time she had told someone what was on her mind, but she was sure she had only ever shared her private thoughts with Loke. Maybe her brother had been given that privilege too once, before he had grown into a male more interested in fighting in the arena than spending time with her.

"I am not sure where to start," she admitted and his smile almost blew her away.

She really couldn't recall ever seeing him smile and the lack of laughter lines bracketing his mouth said it happened very rarely indeed.

But she kept making him smile.

Her belly fluttered and heated.

Bleu's handsome face turned serious again. "Have I done something wrong?"

She quickly shook her head.

He frowned. "You keep looking at me strangely… as if there is something wrong with me."

Gods, she wanted to tell him that there was absolutely nothing wrong with him since the gods had made him perfect.

She smiled instead. "It is taking me a little time to grow accustomed to you smiling at me."

He chuckled. "Fuck, you sound like my sister."

It was her turn to frown. "You have a sister… and what is this 'fuck'? You say it often."

"I do, a younger one, and it is a mortal expression… ah… an exclamation of sorts to declare disbelief or shock… but taken from the profanity they use for what we… ah… did." He waggled an eyebrow.

Her cheeks burned up.

Well, *fuck*, he certainly knew how to embarrass her.

Bleu tugged her closer, that wicked smile teasing his tempting mouth again. "Tell me about you."

His violet eyes leaped between hers, intent and focused, his curiosity flowing through her in a way that made it difficult to deny him.

"Where do I start?" She leaned over him, resting with her left side on his chest, her breast pressed against his left pectoral.

He groaned when she ran her fingers in little circles around his right one, enjoying the feel of his compact muscles beneath her caress, power and strength that she found alluring. The wounds her brother had placed on him were little more than faint marks now, criss-crossing his smooth skin, and she followed the line of one down towards his pebbled nipple.

"You can start by stopping doing that. I cannot think when you do that." He scowled at her hand and she obeyed, bringing her palm down to rest on his chest. His frown melted away and his eyes met hers again. "Tell me what happened seven centuries ago. I need to know if we are going to clear your name with my prince."

There he went again. Talking about them going together, as if he couldn't bear to part from her. She reminded herself that he had sworn to protect her and that might be the only reason he wanted to bring her with him when he met with his prince. It might have nothing to do with any sort of feelings he harboured for her.

Feelings that were impossible to detect even with the incomplete bond linking them.

He stirred too many emotions in her that his mingled with, blending together, that she couldn't easily pick them apart to discern which belonged to who. She wasn't about to lay her heart on the line after one night of passion by asking him about his feelings though. She had lived long enough to know that wasn't a wise move.

"Seven centuries ago," she started and frowned at his chest, trying to get the story into order to make sure she didn't miss anything vital. She wanted to clear her name too, but not with his prince or the elf kingdom. She only wanted to clear it with him. "I need to go a little further back than that, to where it all began. My brother… we did everything together growing up… but he grew increasingly obsessed with gaining power. It was a poison, one that corrupted his mind and his heart."

"It will corrupt the best of people," Bleu said, his voice a soothing drone in her ear, and brushed her hair behind her right ear.

She nodded. "Tenak began to spend his days planning, searching for a way to achieve the ultimate power and rule Hell. I sometimes think his battles in the arena knocked something loose in his mind. He grew convinced that all would bow before him and that it would be wonderful… and that I would stand at his side and we would have everything we had ever wanted."

She closed her eyes and sighed as sorrow swept through her, a familiar cold and numbing feeling that had been a constant companion when she had been around her brother in the decades leading up to his attack on the elf kingdom and in the centuries that had followed it.

"I only ever wanted Tenak to be at my side and be happy." She opened her eyes and raised them to meet Bleu's beautiful violet ones. The concern and compassion in them warmed her heart and chased away the cold. "I knew that the dark path he had found himself on would tear him away from me and drive him mad."

Bleu looked as if he wanted to say something but she shook her head, not wanting him to speak yet. She had started to talk, to tell him her story, and she had to get it all off her chest because it felt like a weight on her heart, one that was lifting with every word that left her lips.

"Tenak found old writings about an elven sword and grew determined to steal it. It was a treasure. One he could not live without. He had to possess it. It is the bane of our species," she said and his lips twitched at the corners, the sparkle of mischief in his eyes warning her that he wanted to tease her about it.

It was strange being with him like this when she had been running from him for so long. If she had let him catch her, had told him the truth back then, could she have had this bliss for the past seven centuries? She sighed and idly traced patterns on his chest again, not wanting to think about what might have been when her future was hardly secure. Tenak was coming for her, and she would arm her mate with all the information she could in order to help him succeed and survive.

"The sword was the key to gaining the ultimate treasure in his eyes—the position of ruler of Hell. He told me often when I asked him to give up his quest because it was destroying him that the sword was everything. It was power. It would be his." She cast her gaze down at her fingers and heaved another sigh as she recalled how Tenak had looked at her back then, his eyes bright and shining with something that she now knew was madness. He had lost his mind before she had noticed it, too slow to see it to stop its spread. "Each hour we were together, he constantly talked of how the sword would bring all of the realms to their knees before him. It frightened me… but I was too afraid of him to say anything… so I sought the help of a witch."

"A witch?" Bleu frowned at her. "I had not realised you had assistance. All this time I scoured the lands for you, seemingly asked everyone in the realm about you, and not once have I heard you had the help of a witch."

She shrugged. "He was very isolated from everything."

"*He*?" Bleu's handsome face darkened in a way she found she liked, a shadow of envy flitting across it and through his blood too.

She smiled at his behaviour and walked her fingers across his bare chest. "He."

Bleu snarled, flashing sharp fangs. "I will kill him if he touched you."

That pleased her even more, but she concealed it from him, not wanting to encourage his violent behaviour.

"He did not touch me. He wanted a stone in exchange… something about an experiment." She shook her head again, dislodging her lingering curiosity about the witch and his reasons for desiring such a rare gem. "I had one and I offered it to him in exchange for him casting a concealment spell on me. It rendered me invisible to all, undetectable. I followed Tenak and tried to stop him from stealing the sword, but I was too late."

His eyebrows pinched. "But if you were concealed, how did we see you and not Tenak?"

"The spell wore off shortly after I fled the castle. I was shifting to pursue my brother when your team found me."

He sighed. "And attacked you."

She shrugged again. "I am almost identical to my brother when in my dragon form. It was a mistake. Knowing how angry the elves were with my brother, I should have remained in my mortal form and slipped away from the realm before risking shifting. I was in a hurry though."

He twirled a strand of her hair around his fingers and thumbed the tip, flicking it back and forth. "I am glad you escaped."

"Probably not as glad as I am." She managed a smile and then it faded as she thought about what had happened next. "I found my brother and he did not suspect me at all. He was quick to tell me the full extent of his plans and he forced me to go with him to a demon village. I thought he was going into hiding… I did not expect… he used the sword there. When I saw him cutting down hundreds of demon warriors with it, I knew what I had to do. I waited until he was asleep and I stole it, igniting his rage and shattering his trust."

"You tried to return it."

She nodded. "I knew he would stop at nothing to reclaim what he now viewed as his property… his prized possession. The dragon need to protect our treasure is powerful, easily rules us and turns us against even those we love with all of our hearts. I knew that only the elves had the strength to fight my brother, so I tried to bring the sword back."

"We attacked you… again." He closed his eyes, his nostrils flared and he huffed. "I am sorry, Taryn."

He flicked his eyes open and they leaped between hers, a beautiful look of sorrow mixed with an apology in them, a touch of tenderness that soothed her.

"I ordered that assault. If I had given you a chance—"

She pressed her finger to his lips to silence him. Gods, they were warm and firm beneath her fingertip, giving just enough to have her remembering how good they had felt against hers when he had kissed her.

"You were not to know that I was not returning to destroy your kingdom with the sword. I should have done things differently but I had been panicked and in a hurry." Her eyebrows furrowed and she stroked her finger off his lips, traced it along the strong line of his jaw, his dark whiskers tickling the tip of it. "I should have tried to contact your kin or found another way, one that would have made it clear I meant no harm."

Her life was filled with regrets and what might have beens and she couldn't allow them to take hold of her and drag her down. The past was just that. It was unchangeable. She had to deal with everything that had happened, put it to rest and move forwards.

Bleu made the thought of doing such a thing seem easy when he wrapped his arms around her, holding her close to him, a contented edge to his expression that his feelings backed up. He enjoyed holding her like this, laying with her and talking. Spending time with her.

It was such a contrast to how things had always been between them.

No war.

Only peace.

"What did you do after that?" he whispered, his voice too husky and low, telling her he was beginning to think ahead too, to a very short time into the future if the hungry edge to his gaze was anything to go by.

He wanted her again.

Heat pooled in her belly, her blood growing hot at the thought of making love with him again.

She fought the need that rolled through her and focused on their conversation, wanting to finish it now that she had started. She wanted to climb on top of Bleu and satisfy him, but she needed this even more.

"I hid from my brother, constantly on the move, but when I grew tired of running from both him and you, I found the witch again and asked him to cast a concealment spell on the sword. I gave him every drop of gold… every jewel… all of my treasure in exchange for a shot at living."

The soft look that entered Bleu's violet eyes said that he knew how difficult that must have been for her, but he couldn't imagine the half of it. Parting with her treasure had been like cutting off a limb, or tearing out her own heart with her claws. It had left her lost and weak, vulnerable.

"I gave the sword to Loke when I began to fear Tenak was growing close to finding me and after I encountered you in that dragon village."

"That was three hundred years ago."

She nodded. "Loke concealed the sword for me, using his magic to cast a different enchantment on it."

"What happened after that?"

Taryn averted her gaze, unable to look at him. "I was captured by slavers."

"Fuck," he breathed and the force behind that word conveyed everything that ran through their bond from him. Anger. Disbelief. Regret.

His arms tightened around her and he crushed her to his chest. She didn't resist him when he clasped the back of her head and pulled her down to him. She settled her cheek on his chest and closed her eyes, absorbing his warmth and how good it felt to be held like this, wrapped safely in his arms.

She nestled closer and flinched when pain stabbed her.

Bleu tensed, his hand halting halfway through stroking up her shoulder towards his bite mark on her throat. "What is wrong?"

She sighed and appreciated his concern even though it was misplaced. It wasn't her throat that had hurt. He had no reason to feel guilty.

Taryn placed her hand on his chest, breathed in time with him and listened to his heart beating strongly against her ear.

"I am still a little sore."

He was silent for a moment, his fingers twitching against her shoulder, and she could feel his confusion and guilt through their bond. It faded a little as she focused on their link, trying to grow accustomed to it, the confusion disappearing but the guilt lingering. She could almost sense he had realised what she was saying, and that it had nothing to do with him biting her.

"I am sorry. I tried to be gentle." Those soft words curled around her and gave her comfort, but they pained him too, and she couldn't ignore that.

She pushed herself up and gazed down at him, right into his rich purple eyes. "You do not need to apologise. I was not complaining. It is not an unpleasant sort of soreness."

She couldn't quite believe she had just said that, but any foolishness she felt fled when his eyes darkened, his pupils dilating, and heat washed through him and through her too.

Taryn leaned in and kissed him, unable to deny the desire rising within her, the need for an encore and the hunger to learn more about this male.

Her male.

His hands leaped to her backside and he dragged her up his bare body, pinned her to him and kissed her harder.

She sank against him and gave herself over to her passion, stroking the seam of his lips with her tongue and begging entrance. He opened for her and the moment their tongues touched, bright light surrounded her.

It dropped away a heartbeat later, leaving her blinded.

Only sound came to her.

The clash of metal. The agonised bellows of males.

Scent joined it.

The tinny odour of blood.

Her vision returned and she gasped as she saw the battle spread below her, engulfing the rolling plains as far as her eyes could see. Smoke billowed from the broken pale towers of a castle to her left. Fire blazed across the lands in the distance. The once verdant earth was churned with blood beneath the boots of the warriors.

Elves and demons clashed with dragons and demons on the battlefield.

The elf kingdom.

"Taryn… Taryn!" Bleu's voice pierced the screams and roars filling her ears.

She blinked and the vision faded, her world going dark for a few seconds before Bleu's face appeared before her. He was shaking. She frowned. Realised that she was the one trembling all over as she clutched his shoulders, her short claws pressing into his muscles.

His eyes searched hers and he didn't ask her what had happened, or whether she'd had a vision.

He came right out and asked, "What did you see?"

She blinked again, her heart still pounding against her chest, her thoughts jumbled as she tried to gather her wits. Her pulse slowed as Bleu breathed steadily beneath her and she realised he was the one doing it, helping to calm her by using their link to control her. Part of her fought against him, rebelled against the idea of anyone having power over her. The rest melted into him, sought the comfort of his embrace and tried to piece back together the quiet calm that had just shattered.

"Tenak will attack the elf kingdom. I saw the castle in ruin. The battlefield drenched in the blood of demons, elves and dragons."

Bleu snarled. "Never."

She wished she shared his confidence, but all she knew was fear as she recalled the things she had seen. So much death. So much destruction. The thought that Tenak was bringing it to the elf kingdom chilled her blood. It was her fault.

Bleu eased her up into a sitting position and stood. Black leather trousers appeared on his legs and he hastily fastened the laces. She stared blankly at his thighs, ears ringing with screams and roars and the clash of swords.

"Taryn," he snapped, rousing her from her stupor. He held his hand out to her, the steely determination flashing in his eyes giving her a sliver of strength and hope, enough that she found the will to lift her hand and place it into his. He pulled her onto her feet, tugged her against his bare chest and looked down at her. "We have to move. You will be safe. I swear it… but we have to return."

She looked around her at the cave and when she looked back at Bleu, he was gazing at the blanket and lantern, a faraway look in his eyes. It was difficult for him, and gods, it was difficult for her too. She didn't want to return to the world either. She had been happy here, lost in Bleu.

But both of them knew what had to be done.

Neither of them could allow her brother to bring harm to the elves.

She called her violet leather trousers and her white corset, forming them over her body, and then her boots, and nodded.

The resolve in Bleu's eyes was only made more reassuring when a black sword appeared in his left hand and he banded his right arm around her waist.

"I will not allow anyone to hurt you or anything to happen to you. I swear that, Taryn." His fingers flexed around the hilt of his blade.

She knew in her heart that he would protect her, even if it meant fighting his own people. She knew he would do anything for her, because she would do anything for him.

She looked up into his eyes as he tucked her close to his bare chest. Her beautiful, breathtaking mate. Her dark warrior.

The desire in his eyes echoed through her and she didn't resist when he dipped his head and claimed her lips in a searing kiss that was both passionate and comforting, meant to convey something she already knew deep in her heart.

He wouldn't let her go now that he had her.

CHAPTER 27

The darkness evaporated to reveal the courtyard of the castle and Bleu's grip on his sword instantly tightened, his entire body tensing in preparation as he faced off against a line of soldiers with arrows trained on him.

And Taryn.

He growled low in his throat and drew Taryn closer to him, shielding her as best he could.

An urge to teleport away from this place with her bolted through him but he tamped it down, wrestled his instincts as her mate under control and stood firm. He ran a quick assessing gaze over the elves before him.

Around him.

They formed a square, two rows deep crossing the pale gravel paths and beneath the lush green trees on the four sections of grass between them, the front one kneeling while the back row stood. All in all, close to one hundred armoured elves had arrows pointed at his mate.

He narrowed his eyes as he swept them back over the line from his left to his right, searching for any weak spots in their ranks. A few arrowheads wobbled, a sign that elf feared attacking him.

As the seconds ticked by, more began to shake.

They knew their offense was futile.

He could teleport in the blink of an eye and have half of their numbers cut down before they could release a single arrow.

If he wanted to attack them.

He didn't.

Not even to satisfy the dark part of his soul that demanded they pay in blood for threatening his female.

He tugged that female closer, using the feel of her pressed against him to soothe his more dangerous side, keeping it under control.

Gods, he wanted to slaughter them all.

The darkness Taryn had purged from his soul in that isolated cave began to creep back in and he flashed sharp fangs at several of the stronger elves, unable to stop himself from threatening them back as it rose to seize control. He fought it, tried to fill his mind with light, with thoughts of Taryn.

But this time it only made the darkness grow stronger.

She was in danger.

These males meant to harm her.

She trembled against him, their incomplete bond relaying her fear but also the instincts that were starting to rise in her too, birthing a hunger for violence and bloodshed that was as terrible as his own. She wanted to fight these males for daring to threaten him. She needed to protect him.

Now that the drugs had completely left his system, he could feel the bond more clearly, and as he stood in the castle courtyard facing down a hundred soldiers, and watching more pouring into the area, he could feel the strength that flowed through him.

Flowed from Taryn into him.

Under normal circumstances, an incomplete bond would weaken an elf male, because they were usually more powerful than their mate.

His incomplete bond with Taryn only made him stronger, because she was the more powerful one.

It was a little emasculating to say the least, but he was going to roll with it, because right now having that added strength gave him a shot at protecting her.

He scanned the soldiers again and snarled when his eyes settled on one just off to his left. The male's eyes were locked on Taryn, the fingers hooked around the string of the bow pulling back slightly, bringing it into a position where he would release it and send the deadly bolt at Bleu's mate.

Bleu's chest grew tight, the darkness beginning to squeeze the light from his soul as it seized hold of him, swamping everything until all he could feel, all he knew was a terrible urge for bloodshed that chilled his blood even as it made it burn.

Black tendrils snaked around his soul and squeezed, sending jagged thorns deep into it that poisoned his mind, driving all rational thought from it and leaving only a wicked hunger behind, a need to deal justice to the male who dared to threaten his mate.

A red veil began to descend.

"Stand down." A familiar male voice rang through the tense silence, the commanding edge to it brooking no argument.

Bleu refused to heed that order. It wasn't the first time he had ignored such a demand from this male and it wouldn't be the last.

He tightened his grip on his sword and on Taryn, his eyes never leaving the male who was still preparing to fire on her.

"I said, stand down!" the other male barked.

Every soldier in the courtyard immediately turned to face the direction of the castle and dropped to one knee, lowering their weapons and their heads at the same time.

Every soldier except that one male.

His violet gaze remained fixed on Taryn.

Bleu bared his fangs, daring the bastard to try and cut his female down. He would be breathing blood before he could release the fucking arrow, his guts pierced by Bleu's blade.

A black clawed hand materialised out of the air, grabbed the shaft of the arrow as the male finished drawing it back, and snapped it in two.

"It is not wise to disobey me," Loren snarled and whatever dark spell the male had been under shattered.

He dropped to his knees and bent his head.

"I will deal with you later." Loren looked down the line of his straight nose at the soldier, an imperious look that Bleu had been on the receiving end of too many times to count over the four thousand years they had known each other. Loren's clear amethyst eyes slid towards Bleu and narrowed, darkening by degrees. "As for you…"

He tensed, waiting for the reprimand he could feel coming, one that would be followed by an order to return Taryn to the cells. He had disobeyed his prince in front of the entire castle, and Loren couldn't go easy on him. He knew that. This time, Loren would have to punish him for his insubordination.

He could damn well throw him in the cell with Taryn then because he wasn't leaving her side when so many soldiers were lifting their heads to look at her again, the desire to strike her down still shining in their cold eyes.

"Dacian has just finished explaining the situation to me," Loren said and Bleu frowned as he glanced beyond his prince to the large warrior male where he stood near the entrance of the castle with Fynn and Leif flanking him.

Dacian nodded and Bleu returned it. He would have to thank the male later.

Right now, he needed a moment to take in and comprehend the fact that he wasn't about to get his arse handed to him by the elf prince slowly turning to face him, his dark expression softening.

Loren's gaze fell to Taryn and Bleu barely bit back the growl that rumbled around his chest. His prince's violet eyes lifted to him again and Bleu didn't like the knowing edge his smile had gained.

Before Bleu could scowl at him in silent warning not to say a word about his situation, Loren turned around and looked over the soldiers kneeling around him.

Loren tipped his chin up and clasped his hands behind his back, resting them against the tails of his crisp dark purple knee-length jacket. Bleu curled his lip at the silver embroidery on the square tails and across the shoulders. His damned prince had chosen the jacket on purpose, wearing one that depicted dragons and elves. Loren knew she was something to him and this was his way of sneakily teasing him.

Mischievous bastard.

"The female is no threat to us," Loren announced and all thoughts of tackling him to the ground and beating him into a bloody pulp dissipated. "She is a guest and will be treated as such. Understood?"

Every elf in the courtyard made a noise of affirmation.

Every elf except Bleu.

He could only stare at Loren, deeply aware that he owed his prince a huge one for what he had done for him and Taryn.

Loren looked back over his shoulder at him, his eyes relaying a silent command. Bleu nodded, released Taryn and then took hold of her hand. He curled his free hand around the leather hilt of his black sword, refusing to send it away or even sheathe it. He had a promise to keep.

Nerves still flowed through his link to Taryn, fear that was yet to fade as she stood close to him, wary violet-to-white eyes on the soldiers surrounding them. Her grip on his hand was firm, almost painful, relaying her need for comfort. He shifted his hand and slipped his fingers between hers, linking them together in a stronger way, and she glanced up at him.

Gods, it was difficult to resist looking at her, but he couldn't let his guard down and taking his eyes off the males surrounding them would be doing just that, leaving them open to attack.

He followed Loren as the male swept towards the castle, the soldiers in his way parting to allow him through, his long strides quickly covering the pale path that intersected the orchard. A few of the soldiers glanced up as Bleu passed with Taryn and he hissed at all of them, his pointed ears flattening against the sides of his head, a show of aggression that was impossible to deny.

Loren's boots were silent on the polished pale stone floor as they entered the castle.

Bleu's steps were equally as light, but Taryn's footfalls echoed around the glittering stone walls of the broad corridor. Her fear turned to fascination as they left the soldiers behind and ventured deeper into the quiet castle, and her eyes began to dart around to take in her surroundings. He looked at her now, unable to deny the urge any longer, watching her as she studied everything with eyes that sparkled.

As if everything she saw was treasure.

Maybe it was the way the walls glittered, the carved columns at intervals along the corridor shining like stars as they passed and the stone caught the shifting light.

Her eyes drifted over every statue, but lingered on the one near the grand arched wooden doors as two soldiers dressed in full black armour, their helmets in place, opened them for Loren.

Her steps slowed.

Her gaze leaped from the statue to the male who had entered the chamber ahead of them and then to Bleu.

"It is he," she whispered in the dragon tongue.

"My prince." He shrugged casually when she gaped at him.

Blinked. Tossed a look at Loren's back that was part astonishment part wonder.

"He is not what I expected." She looked back at the statue and then at Loren, as if expecting the two not to match all of a sudden.

Had she expected Loren to be a cruel looking male because he ruled a kingdom? A monster?

"He is a good male, Taryn. He will listen to what we have to say." He squeezed her hand and her gaze finally leaped back to him.

Fear rose up in her again as voices rang around the room ahead of them and it trickled through him too. The elders. He hadn't expected them to be present when he spoke with Loren.

He schooled his features when Taryn flicked him a glance, not letting her see that fear. She needed to see him strong right now, confident and courageous, certain that he could clear her name with his prince and the elves across the entire kingdom. He sent his sword back to his apartment above them, hoping it would show her that she had no reason to fear because he wasn't afraid.

The way she squeezed his hand back and a little sigh escaped her reminded him that any attempt to conceal his nerves from her was futile since she could sense them in him.

His gaze dropped to her, and then shifted to the left side of her throat. The marks he had placed on her were still angry red around their edges. His eyes shot down to his boots. Taryn's grip on his hand tightened and he reached for their link, needing to feel her and know that she had forgiven him. He needed it more than anything.

Because she was fast becoming everything to him.

"Bleu." Loren's deep voice echoed with authority through the archway.

Bleu sucked down a breath, held it and exhaled it slowly. He glanced down at Taryn, checking she was ready. She smoothed her hair, concealing the marks on her throat, her little smile relaying that she had sensed his secret desire to keep them hidden from the people who awaited them.

When she nodded, he released her hand and strode forwards with her at his side. She tensed as they entered the grand chamber and this time it had nothing to do with the stunning sight that surrounded them, and everything to do with the three elder elves standing off to the left of the platform on which Loren stood.

Their long black robes reached the floor, a thick embroidered purple sash binding their waists, the only touch of colour and one that did nothing to alleviate the austere edge they shared.

Few elves could boast to have lived as long as these three, and they knew it.

It was there in their violet eyes as they watched him approach with Taryn at his side, an air of smugness that he wanted to wipe off their faces by showing them that age and wisdom that came from books meant little on the battlefield.

The bloody fields of war were an arena for the strong of mind and body, those forged in the fiery crucible and taught tactics, savagery, and skill through the harsh lessons that brought them close to the embrace of death.

He had learned everything he knew in such an arena and it had moulded him into a male who could easily see through their polished appearances and their air of condescension and self-righteousness to the fact that beneath their facades they shared one common feeling.

They were afraid.

They feared that their grip on Loren was weakening and soon their voices would no longer hold sway over him.

Because Bleu wasn't the only male in this grand room who had been shaped by war, taught hard lessons and survived. Loren had been there with him, but his skill as a commander on the battlefield was matched by his skill as a prince of his people, a male of knowledge and understanding, and one who could easily rule without three crones whispering in his ear.

Bleu had fought enough battles to know that their fear of losing power over Loren would make them desperate.

They would make one last fight for power, one last stand to prove themselves still valuable and that they still had control.

That was the reason they were here now.

They meant to use Taryn as their pawn to regain power over Loren.

Over his dead body.

Or theirs.

He would cut them all down if they so much as looked at her wrongly. If they made any attempt to seize her or harm her, he would rip their still-beating hearts from their chests.

"Approach," Loren said and Bleu led Taryn up the aisle between the rows of ornately carved white wooden pews.

Her eyes didn't leave the group that waited ahead of her as she passed each thick towering black column that supported the vaulted ceiling of the chamber.

Bleu's did.

He looked down at her where she walked at his side, steady and strong, bravely striding forwards even when he could sense her fear.

The light that streamed in through the tall arched windows on either side of the long room washed over her as she emerged from the shadow of each elegantly carved column, flickering across her face and making her almost glow.

Fuck, she was beautiful.

Afraid yet fearless.

She walked with her chin tipped up, her head held high, a sharpness to her eyes and a snap to her step that made him want to growl low in his throat in appreciation of his mate. His fierce little dragon. What did she look like to the three old bastards loitering at Loren's side?

Her violet-to-white hair was still stained with blood and black dirt smeared her exposed skin. She looked as if she had been through a war and emerged the only victor, and was ready to slay anyone else who stood in her way.

Damn.

He wanted her.

A touch of colour stained her cheeks, turning her too-pale skin rosy. Her gaze flitted his way, dark hunger growing in it, and then jumped back to the trio of elders, and then locked on Loren.

The blush remained, even grew darker.

She knew his wicked thoughts.

Fuck, that only made him want her more.

He stifled a grimace as his cock twitched, sucked down a deep breath and clawed back control. A meeting with Loren and the elders was no time to get a raging hard-on for his mate, especially when he wanted to keep that little fact from as many as he could until everything was settled.

Until she was his.

Mine.

He couldn't stop himself from thinking it as she walked beside him, marching down the aisle in a room that had recently held the grand ceremony of Loren's marriage to his mate, Olivia.

When they reached the raised stone platform at the end of the aisle, he halted with Taryn and looked up into Loren's eyes.

"You appear to have lost something." Loren gestured towards his wrists.

Bleu pressed his right palm to his bare chest and lowered his head. "My apologies, my prince. The gift you gave to me was taken from me and I could not risk retrieving them. It was too dangerous."

He could almost feel Loren's smile, as warm as the light that washed over him from the windows.

"Then you made the right decision. Such trinkets have no value compared to the worth of your life," Loren said and paused before sighing. "But I do know they meant much to you. I cannot restore them, but I can offer replacements."

Bleu closed his eyes, feeling that warmth seeping into his bones and soothing away the weariness that he hadn't realised was there, lightening the heaviness that had been with him since losing his armour. Loren was too damn wise for his own good sometimes, able to see things that Bleu couldn't, even when they were things about himself that he should have known.

His prince was right and his armour had meant a lot to him.

Loren had bestowed it on him over four thousand years ago, a gift that had been part of the ceremony to celebrate his ascension to the rank of commander.

Losing it had left a piece of him missing, and while he couldn't get that piece back right now, maybe he could in the future, after they had dealt with the dragon who had stolen it from him.

He sensed Loren's gaze leave him and lifted his head, and had to bite his tongue to stop himself from growling at the male when he found him looking at his mate.

Loren flicked him a pointed look, a hint of a smile, and then backed towards his tall-backed white oak throne. He seated himself, crossed his legs and settled his arms on the ornately carved rests.

"I believe you have a report for me?" Loren looked from him to Taryn and back again, before his eyes shot beyond him and shone brighter.

A little smile curled his lips as he watched the person who had entered behind Bleu approach, his pupils dilating and the pointed tips of his ears flaring back against his neat short blue-black hair.

Bleu didn't need to look to know who was on the receiving end of his prince's attention, but he had to wonder whether he wore the same stupid expression whenever he looked at Taryn.

Something between passionate lover and lovesick fool.

Everything in him said to glance at Taryn but he kept his eyes fixed on Loren, charting the subtle shift from sentimental idiot to darkly possessive and hungry male as Olivia swept into view to Bleu's right and ascended the few steps up to the platform where her mate waited.

Impatiently.

Bleu could practically feel Loren's eagerness.

Maybe it was his own damn hunger rising to the fore again, flooding him with a need that echoed the one on Loren's face. That hunger made him want to growl when Loren held a hand out to Olivia, she placed hers into it, and he drew her down to him for a fierce kiss.

Gods damn him.

He did glance at Taryn now, filled with a desperate need to kiss her like that too, laced with jealousy that his prince could openly do such a thing with his mate when he had to stand here with his and resist taking her into his arms as he wanted.

Fuck, did he want that.

He wanted her against him again, her warmth seeping into him, her lips on his as she moaned and writhed, hungry for more of him. More that he would give to her. He wouldn't stop until she was boneless and sated, unable to move from his arms.

Too weak to break free of his hold.

Too in love with him to leave him.

She had to be his.

Mine.

It rang in every fibre of his being, every drop of his blood and ounce of his soul.

He hadn't realised he had growled until Loren cleared his throat and snapped him back to the room. Taryn stared up at him, her cheeks flushed, eyes dark with hunger. He trembled with a need to satisfy that desire, to whisk her away to somewhere they could be alone and could make love for hours.

It was only the feel of the elders' gazes on him that had him turning away from her and facing his prince again. He shut down his feelings, pushing them all back down inside, and focused on the reason he was here.

Clearing her name.

He curled his fingers into fists and cursed the heat of Taryn beside him, radiating from her and warming his skin on his left side, making him too aware of her when he had to concentrate. How much power did she hold over him? It was getting difficult to think straight, to keep his mind on anything other than taking her into his arms, bending her over backwards and kissing the breath from her.

He forced himself to speak, using the dragon tongue. "Taryn, you just need to tell Prince Loren and the council what you told me."

She lifted her striking eyes to him, nodded despite the nerves he could feel flowing through her, and then turned away. She bravely stepped forwards, facing the elders and his prince where he sat on his pale throne, Olivia seated on the smaller one beside him.

As Taryn spoke, Olivia stared not at her but at him, and he glanced across at her, catching the warmth in her dark eyes. She looked well, rested for once. Had she been spending more time at the castle with Loren and less spent travelling between the elf kingdom and her work with Archangel in the mortal realm?

Her chestnut hair tumbled around her shoulders, gold threads highlighting it as the warm light spilled over her from her left, bright on her pale blue dress. She looked down at the silver metal corset constructed of elaborate swirls, raised an eyebrow at it, and then lifted her brown eyes back to meet his and sighed in a way that told him exactly what she thought about elf fashion for females.

He almost smiled as he remembered her tirade about how uncomfortable their corsets and dresses were, and how much she hated them and wanted to wear her mortal clothing of jeans and t-shirts.

And how Loren had desperately fought to convince his stubborn mate that dressing in such a feminine and elven fashion would help her people accept her as their princess.

A deep growl echoed through the room.

From his left.

Olivia's eyes widened and darted there.

Bleu looked down at Taryn.

She had stepped forwards, her hands clenched at her sides, her eyes locked on Olivia and her teeth bared. Every one of them sharp.

Violet scales rippled over her bare skin.

Bleu hastily caught her arm and spun her to face him. She glared up at him, one that froze him with its intensity and the promise of a painful death. What the hell had he done to deserve her looking at him as if she was contemplating bloody murder?

His eyes widened and he quickly glanced at Olivia.

He had been staring at another female.

It shouldn't have warmed him, but it did, heated him right down to his marrow and the pit of his soul. His little female was jealous, and that jealousy was revealing.

She had feelings for him.

Her pretty face darkened and she flashed those killer teeth at him instead. Beneath his hand, her soft skin grew hard, tough scales that were cool to the touch. He rubbed his thumb over an exposed patch of pink skin, hoping that Loren and the others couldn't see the caress.

"She is a wild thing," the tallest of the elders said in the elf tongue and swept his long hair back from his right shoulder. "She should be detained."

Taryn turned to look at the one who had spoken and Bleu growled at the male, baring his fangs in warning. She couldn't understand their language, and while part of him was glad of that because the male had dared to speak of placing her in a cell, the rest of him was pissed as all hell.

"She came here of her own free will and she will not be placed in a cage," Bleu snarled in the elf language and Loren shot him a look that ordered him to back down. He ignored his prince and stepped past Taryn, using his hand on her arm to guide her behind him. "You may try… but I warn you… you *will* fail."

"Enough!" Loren barked and Taryn flinched behind him.

Bleu came dangerously close to turning his growl on his prince.

Only the feel of Taryn pressing closer to him stopped him, calming him enough that he could retain control and tamp down the urge to lash out at Loren for frightening her.

"No one will be placing anyone in a cage or fighting anyone, understood?" Loren stood and glared at the elders and then at Bleu.

Bleu dropped his chin and pressed his right hand back against his chest, thankful his prince had spoken in the elven tongue so Taryn wouldn't hear mention of cages. "Understood."

The elders mumbled their responses.

Loren huffed and spoke in English this time. "Now… I believe the female was telling us important facts before you had the audacity to stare at my mate for so long."

Darkness rolled through the room, power so intense that Bleu's knees shook from the force of it as it battered him.

"Loren," Olivia chided, and Bleu made a mental note to thank her later when Loren wasn't in such a poor mood and liable to kill him for merely looking at his mate.

It seemed he wasn't the only one badly affected by a bond, but Loren's was complete, his mate secure. What hope did Bleu have of restoring some sanity in his life if completing the bond hadn't freed Loren of his need to cut down any male who looked at his female for too long?

Olivia was plain in comparison to Taryn.

Taryn would draw the gazes of males no matter where they went, everything that was beautiful and unique about her making it impossible for her to move through the realms without attracting attention.

The thought of constantly feeling on edge, convinced that one of those males might steal her from him, had him on the verge of growling again.

Her hand settled against his bare back. Feelings flowed through their link, comfort and calm that he knew wasn't something she truly felt but something she was feeling in order to offer it to him in silence.

She stepped out from behind him, her fingers trailing from his back, slipping from his skin and leaving him bereft, and he stared down at her as she continued to talk, telling Loren of her brother and what she had seen in a vision.

Loren's expression turned grave and pensive, and Olivia placed her right hand over his on the arm of his throne, curling her fingers around to brush his palm. Offering Loren comfort just as Taryn had for him.

The longer Loren stared at Taryn, lost deep in thought as he mulled over what she had told him, the stronger the urge to fight him became, until all Bleu could think about was launching forwards, wrapping his hands around his prince's throat and throttling him until he swore to never look at her again.

Gods, he was fucked.

It was rare, damn near unheard of, for an incomplete bond to view even a mated male as a threat, but that was exactly what he felt as he watched Loren staring at his damned mate. He wanted to gouge the bastard's eyes out with his thumbs.

Bleu ground his teeth and pinned his gaze on the floor in front of his boots, breathed through the darkness that clogged his lungs and clawed at his heart. The voices of Taryn and Loren swirled around him, their words twisting in his ears into new ones, whispers of illicit lovers caught deep in a passionate tryst.

He curled his fingers into fists, dug his nails into his palms and wished he had his armour. He wanted his claws. He needed them.

"Bleu?" Taryn's soft voice pierced the dark veil that had descended over his mind, a shaft of light that chased the shadows back.

He exhaled hard, releasing the breath he hadn't realised he was holding, and looked at her, his strength draining from him together with the tension as it left his body and the images of Loren and Taryn locked in a wicked embrace.

He stared blankly at her, feeling empty.

Lost.

He needed to get away from this place. He needed to get far away from everyone. He was too dangerous right now, on edge and unfit to be around any male when Taryn was present.

"I will send men to speak with the Third King, as this dragon Tenak will strike those lands first in order to reach the elf kingdom," Loren announced in English, filling the thick silence, giving Bleu a moment to pull himself back together.

Bleu expected to feel a reaction to the mention of Thorne, but he felt nothing.

It dawned on him that whatever he had felt for Sable, the mortal female now mated to Thorne, it was nothing compared with what he felt for Taryn.

He stared at his little dragon and a blush climbed her cheeks.

When he felt Loren's gaze on him, he dragged his eyes away from her and faced his prince.

"I will relay that order and also issue notice to the First and Second Realms." He needed a moment to breathe, a few minutes to an hour in which he could find his balance again and master his turbulent feelings.

Taryn would be safe under Loren's protection. As soon as she was settled somewhere away from danger, he would leave for the demon realms, returning as quickly as possible to her.

Hopefully as a male able to be around another male without wanting to rip their throat out.

Loren shook his head. "Another will do that task. You are to find quarters for our guest. Perhaps on the second level?"

Bleu frowned at his prince. Loren was meddling. He had known the male for over forty centuries and he was atrocious at hiding it when he was up to mischief. It was right there in his violet eyes. He was placing Taryn on the second level because Bleu's quarters were there and there was a vacant one right next door.

"The third floor would be a better choice," Bleu shot back. "It is quieter and few reside there. The female might like some peace and some space away from us elves."

His prince folded his arms across his chest, firmly shook his head, and barely contained the damned smile Bleu knew wanted out. "No. I am sure the female will feel safest closest to you."

Bleu could almost feel Taryn's blush. Or maybe it was his own damned one.

Loren's lips were finally stronger than his will and they curled at the corners. Beside him, Olivia openly grinned.

Bleu scowled at both of them. "Very well, my prince."

He turned on his heel and stormed down the aisle between the pale wooden pews, barely leashing his desire to grab Taryn's arm to drag her with him. When he reached the arched door, he shoved it open and strode out into the corridor, and couldn't bring himself to move any further.

The distance between him and Taryn already felt too great.

It tugged him back to her, filling him with a sensation that unsettled him.

It felt as if he had left his heart behind.

CHAPTER 28

Bleu paced the corridor, taking swift agitated steps across it, ignoring the two guards watching him as he waited for Taryn.

She appeared in the arched doorway and he immediately looked across at her, his steps slowing as he took her in, her beauty hitting him hard all over again, as if he hadn't seen her in weeks, not seconds.

She flicked a nervous look at the two guards and hurried past them to him.

"You will be safe here," he whispered in the dragon tongue but she didn't look convinced.

He glared at the two guards, gently caught hold of her arm and led her away, back along the wide corridor, towards the entrance of the castle. He turned left before he reached it, leading her up a set of stone steps. Her fingers trailed over the carved balustrade, eyes on the leaves and small animals. Avoiding him.

Nerves still flowed through her, but this time they weren't born of fear of the other elves in the castle.

They were born of fear of being alone with him.

The innocence behind those feelings had him pulling her into the vacant room beside his on the second level, kicking the wooden door closed and drawing her into his arms. He placed one hand against the back of her head and guided it to rest against his bare chest. She was still for a moment but then her arms were around him, palms pressing against his spine, holding him to her.

"I do not like that female."

He smiled at that. Did she know how jealous she sounded?

"Olivia is mated to my prince," he said and she drew back and frowned up at him, her eyes silently asking him whether that was meant to make a difference.

He could hardly say it should when he had threatened Loren for looking at her.

Those knowing eyes leaped between his.

"You are going to leave," she whispered, her soft voice laced with a touch of fear and a hint of hurt.

"Not for long. I will only go to relay orders to my men and make sure the demon kings are warned about your brother." Bleu lifted his hand and stroked his knuckles across her cheek. "You will be safe here."

Taryn cast her gaze around the large room. It mirrored his. With a low line of cabinets against the dark grey stone wall to his right, and wardrobes lining the solid half of the side of the room to his left. Beyond those wardrobes was a huge opening that led into the bathing area.

Her eyes settled on the neat double bed directly opposite the door, against a wall lined with three tall arched windows that allowed light to flood the room, and widened.

Someone had put fresh sheets on the bed.

Fresh purple sheets.

Bleu ground his teeth, rubbed his left hand over his face and cursed Loren's name in his head. This was taking meddling too far. His prince had already prepared the room for Taryn, and had intentionally ordered sheets that matched the beautiful colour of her hair and eyes, a deep shade of violet mixed with cream pillows against the wooden headboard.

He huffed and stomped across the room towards the bathing room.

The huge rectangular pool in the centre of it was empty just as he had expected. It seemed Loren hadn't thought of everything.

He strode past the stone basins that lined the wall to his left, the mirrors above them reflecting him and bouncing light from the bedroom across the room, illuminating it together with a chandelier of glowing crystals that hung above the pool set into the floor.

He felt Taryn's gaze on him as he crouched at the end opposite the entrance to the bedroom, grasped a thick metal ring, twisted it and pulled upwards, opening the sluice gate. Steaming water thundered into the pool.

"It will take time to fill… but be sure to keep an eye on it." He straightened and looked across the pool at her.

Her eyes were on the water.

Light washed over her right side, casting her left into shadow.

She wrapped her arms around herself and he was striding towards her, long legs devouring the distance between them, before she had even lifted her eyes to him. He pulled her back into his arms and closed his eyes as he held her, feeling her trembling.

"I will not be long." He resisted the temptation to press a kiss to her hair and tried to think of something he could say to reassure her. He looked back at the pool. The water was barely an inch deep now. He clutched Taryn's shoulders, gently eased her back and then caught her under her chin with his left hand and tipped her head up, so her eyes met his. "I swear I will be back before the pool is full."

She glanced beyond him to it, something akin to sorrow in her eyes.

He found he never wanted her to look so sad again. He wanted her to always smile. He wanted her life to be happy and filled with joy. She deserved that after everything she had been through.

It was an impossible dream though, a desire he could never fulfil because her brother was coming and he was bringing war in his wake, and Bleu knew that she meant to continue with the mission she had taken on.

She meant to stop her brother.

Doing so was only going to hurt her, but taking her place as her brother's executioner wouldn't lessen the pain she would feel when her twin was taken from her.

He couldn't see any alternative route to stopping the dragon either.

No matter how much he wanted to find one.

He had no love for the bastard, would gladly end him given the chance, but the thought of hurting Taryn tore at him and made him want to seek another path, one where she wouldn't have to suffer the ordeal of losing the brother she so clearly loved.

"The pool is filling fast," she whispered and raised her eyes to meet his. "You will not keep your promise if you do not leave now."

"I know," he husked, captured both of her cheeks in his palms and lowered his head, resting his forehead against hers. "But I cannot leave when you hurt so deeply."

She placed her hands over his and smiled.

"I am tired. My vision weighs on my heart. That is all. I will rest while you do your work." She pulled back and the wicked twinkle in her eyes made it even more difficult to drag himself away from her. "You are filthy too. Perhaps when you return… y-you should bathe?"

He knew what she had meant to say before her nerve had failed her and he nodded, wanting to growl at her that he was going to take her up on that offer she had wanted to extend to him, suggesting they should bathe together.

He backed off and forced himself to turn away, but she caught his wrist and he looked back at her.

"Wait." She released him and he frowned, curious as to what she was doing when she grabbed a square of cloth from near the basin, wetted it and came back to him.

He raised an eyebrow at her as she tiptoed and rubbed the wet cloth over his face and then his hair and down his neck.

She settled back on her heels and preened her fingers through his wet hair in a way that felt too damned good. "There. Now you are more fit to meet with a king."

He smiled. Would she ever stop seeing through him?

He had worded things in a way he had hoped would make her feel he was remaining in the castle as Loren had ordered, but she had seen straight through to the truth—he was going to speak with one of them himself.

He teleported his leathers away, not bothering to cover himself before he called fresh clothes to him, letting her get a quick flash of him naked. Her heartrate quickened, jacking his up with it, and desire flooded the link between them.

"I lied," she rushed out and clenched her hands at her sides, flexed her fingers and curled them again, as if she wanted to grab hold of him and was resisting that desire. "I mean I did not lie as such… but I meant to say… earlier… w-when I talked about the pool…"

His smile widened as tight trousers appeared on his legs, hugging his thighs, followed by riding boots, and then his black knee-length jacket. The one with the pale blue embroidery on the two long rectangular tails on the front and the two on the back, around the cuffs and the stand-up collar. The one that he liked to save for special occasions because it was damned expensive and Loren had given it to him as a gift, but the cut was incredible and he thought it emphasised his physique, and he wanted to look handsome enough that his little dragon would want to eat him whole.

The hunger that filled Taryn's eyes as she raked them over him said that he had been right to think it.

He stepped towards her and husked in a low gravelly voice, "You were talking about bathing with me."

Fierce red coloured her cheeks, but then she straightened, looked him right in the eye and nodded.

"I wish to bathe with you."

He liked that flash of courage in her eyes, that determination in her stance and the challenge in her tone.

He snaked his arm around her waist, hauled her close to him and feathered his lips up her throat to her ear and whispered into it, "You scrub my back and I'll scrub yours."

She trembled, a little squeak escaping her, a deliciously feminine sound that he wanted to hear again and again because it was so at odds with the dangerous side of his powerful little dragon that was all he had ever known. It made him want to stay and learn this new side of her, to learn everything about her, every little thing, leaving nothing hidden.

She tipped her head to one side, moaned as he tongued the lobe of her ear, melted against him before bracing her hands against his chest and pushing him back. He growled at her as she broke free of his grip, stealing herself away from him when he was hungry for more of her, and she planted her hands on her hips and glared at him.

"The pool is filling."

He looked beyond her, cursed when he saw it was almost a quarter full.

"Stay here. Do not leave this room. Lock the door." He pulled her to him for a quick hard kiss that had her gasping into his mouth and then teleported, intent on keeping his promise to her.

He wouldn't break another one.

He appeared in the central courtyard and strode towards the arch in the high wall that led to the outer courtyard. The soldiers who had greeted him in a not so friendly fashion when he had returned with Taryn were gone, returned to their duties, leaving the orchard quiet. He didn't need more than one shot at guessing where he would find his men.

He reached the pale garrison on the other side of the arch and took quick steps down the narrow corridor between the stable block and the main building. A grunt sounded from ahead and Bleu's lips twitched into a smile.

Dacian was in his usual place in the arena, fighting Fynn for a change while Leif leaned against the wall, propped up on his elbows and shouting suggestions to the younger elf as he desperately tried to best the big warrior.

Good luck with that.

Bleu had fought Dacian before and the one time he had won, it had been a hard fought battle that had left him bed bound with strict orders to rest for three days.

He shrugged to himself. Dacian had had it worse though. The medical team had ordered him to rest for three weeks. The warrior male had grown close to losing his mind by the time his term in sick bay had finally ended. Bleu had never seen a male so glad to get back out onto the battlefield.

"Leif," Bleu said and the noble male turned his head and looked over his shoulder at him before straightening and coming to face him. "I need you to relay information to the First Realm of the demons. Fynn and Dacian can hit the Second Realm."

The two males in question broke apart and jogged over to him, both breathing hard and sporting a few new wounds.

"We are to warn them that Tenak will be passing through their lands. He is amassing an army en route. They need to decide how to act… whether that is evacuating any villages along the path the dragon might take or fighting him… but warn them that Taryn, this dragon's sister, has seen a vision of them fighting on the side of the elves in our kingdom in a great battle against her brother."

All three males frowned at that and he could see they had questions, but he didn't have time to answer them.

The damned pool was probably close to a third full now.

Leif's frown stuck. "What of the Third Realm? The dragon lands are closest to that kingdom."

Bleu nodded. "I will take care of informing King Thorne."

He couldn't send anyone else in his place, no matter what Loren had ordered. It was his duty to go to the Third Realm. Nonc of his men had met the demon king who ruled it, but they had met with the First and Second Kings before, during their previous search for the dragon.

He waited for all three males to nod and willed his portal, vowing to thank Dacian later when he had more time and they were alone. Green-purple light chased over the contours of his body and the darkness embraced him, cold against his face and hands, and then dissipated to reveal the courtyard of the squat dark stone castle belonging to King Thorne.

Part of him had expected his clearance to use the portal that exited in the castle to have been revoked and to find himself bounced to the nearest public portal or back to the elf kingdom.

He hadn't exactly been on the best terms with Thorne. He couldn't quite imagine worse ones since they had both been after the same female. Sable.

He took a step towards the nearest demon warrior milling around the courtyard and then stopped when a revelation hit him.

He was testing himself.

Sable would be with her mate and part of him needed to know whether seeing her would affect him as it used to, when she had been unmated and even after she had made her choice.

The demon swung his way, hefted a great broadsword up onto his wide shoulder, and strode towards him, the huge muscles of his bare torso shifting with each heavy step and dark brown leathers reflecting the light from the braziers that burned around the courtyard. The male's dusky horns flared, curling from behind his pointed ears and around on themselves, so they resembled those of a ram.

It was a sign of aggression in demons.

Bleu stood his ground.

The demon was taller than him by a few inches, and broader too, but that didn't mean he was stronger. If the male tried to fight him, he would find that out for himself.

"What you want?" the big male grumbled in broken English.

Bleu snorted. As if he couldn't speak demon.

"I request an audience with King Thorne. I have news for him from the elf kingdom, so if you would be so kind as to stop stomping around acting like you own the place and take me to the male who actually does, I would most appreciate it," he said in the demon tongue, skipping the usual greeting that was often in the form of an insult and earning a deadly glare from the male, one that said he was intelligent enough to recognise he had just been patronised and didn't like it.

The male had started it. Bleu had only given him a taste of his own medicine.

The male's meaty fingers flexed around the hilt of his broadsword.

Bleu's twitched at his side, ready to call his blade to them if the demon attacked.

Another demon strolled over, burgundy leathers creaking as they struggled to remain in one piece over his thick thighs. Bleu recognised this one as a commander, a male he had met during the recent war between the Third and Fifth Realm, one he had fought in on the side of the Third. The demon had put on even more muscle in the few months since he had been here, but apparently hadn't thought to purchase larger trousers.

"King Thorne will see you." The dark-haired male beckoned him and Bleu followed him across the courtyard, keeping one eye on the other demon so he couldn't get the jump on him.

Thorne's castle was nothing like Loren's. It lacked the grandeur of the elf palace, with no conical towers to spear the dark sky. To Bleu's eyes, it resembled a stumpy heavily fortified grey garrison. Stout curved walls enclosed the inner courtyard, with one arched gate off to his left. At intervals along the wall, square three-storey buildings intersected it, the final level at the same height as the battlements. The demons patrolling the walls walked through those levels and appeared out the other side, huge swords and spears resting on their bare shoulders. Another difference from his own home, where no one roamed the walls unless an alarm was sounded. Here, the demons seemed to actively await war, almost as if they were wishing it would come to them.

They probably never had to wait long. A century at most. Often less. The seven demon realms were always at war with each other over something, playing a constant tug-of-war for the lands they shared.

Bleu turned his focus back to the squat three-storey building ahead of him. This one had a huge arched entrance, and arched windows on the second and third levels glowed with amber light. It wasn't square like the others. It curved with the wall, with what looked like an addition to his right, where the windows were smaller. They were the quarters of the officers and the king, a place where he had stayed during the war with the Fifth Realm.

The second level extended on the left too, but only to form a balcony, with an elegant stone balustrade that seemed out of place in such a roughly hewn castle.

Small fire pits burned around the walls of the courtyard with larger ones dotted around the centre, chasing back the darkness that passed as evening light this far from the elf kingdom. Hell would be a black place indeed without the light his kin brought into it. That light bled over into the demon realms and the free realm, giving them a sort of day.

For some damned reason, the demons called it night.

He never had figured out why.

His demon escort led him through the arched entrance of the main building. Torches protruded from the carved columns and illuminated the vaulted hallway and the corridors that extended off from it to his left and his right.

He followed the male through the second archway and into the grand hall of the castle. Two rows of three thick stone columns rose up on either side of the aisle, supporting the vaulted ceiling. The torches slotted into black metal brackets struggled to illuminate the huge space, their warm light catching on the twelve stone columns and casting shadows in all directions around the windowless room.

Another marked difference to the elf castle. This was more of a war room than a ceremonial one. Defensive. Not decorative.

Dull, if you asked him.

He preferred the brightness and beauty of the grand hall in his own castle.

There weren't even any pews in this one. Nowhere for visiting parties to rest. Everyone had to stand to speak with the demon in charge.

The king that lounged on the elaborate black throne at the end of the aisle on a raised platform, two braziers on the back corners of it illuminating the huge tapestry that hung on the rear wall, a depiction of war. Typical of a demon to think war was beautiful enough to hang it on his wall.

Thorne lowered his right leg, removing it from his left knee, and the sound of his boot striking the black stone of the platform rang around the room.

Oaf.

Demons lacked finesse and grace. They stomped around, growled and roared, and lost their temper over the slightest thing.

The Third King sat up, his broad bare chest rippling with muscle and power as he straightened on his black throne and eyed Bleu with dark red eyes that rapidly began to burn crimson.

Case in point.

He had barely been in the demon's presence for three seconds, hadn't even opened his mouth to tell the brute why he was here, and the male was already on the verge of attacking him.

Movement to the king's left drew Bleu's focus there. A slender black-haired mortal female dressed in obsidian leather trousers, knee-high boots and a tight black t-shirt emerged from the shadows and patted Thorne's shoulder in a soothing manner, her amber eyes fixed on her mate.

Sable.

The expected ache in his heart didn't come. It no longer hurt when he looked at her, because it was aching to see Taryn again, and that yearning was far stronger than any he had ever felt for Sable.

The huntress had been right all those months ago.

What he had felt for her hadn't really been love, because although it had hurt him when she had chosen Thorne over him, the pain he had experienced then would be nothing compared with how he would feel if he lost Taryn. If she rejected him, he wouldn't be able to bounce back from it.

He would die.

The demon Sable petted growled low, a rumbling sound of warning that Bleu heeded.

As much as he enjoyed fighting Thorne, he wasn't here to do battle. Nor was he here to fight over Sable. He was here to deliver a message. Two messages, one on behalf of his kingdom and the other on behalf of himself. He would deal with that one first.

And quickly, because that damned pool was probably almost full and he meant to keep his promise to Taryn.

"An angel has been sighted in the dragon realm," he said and Sable's golden eyes widened.

Thorne growled again, eyes blazing like fire as he leaned forwards, his dark claws emerging as he curled his fingers over the ends of the armrests of his throne.

"An angel?" The big male bared his fangs on a snarl. "What business does an angel have in Hell?"

What indeed. Angels never entered Hell. It stripped them of most of their strength and crippled them with pain if the rumours were anything to go by.

"The Echelon," Sable whispered, a frown pinching her fine black eyebrows as she stared at the floor, gaze fixed but distant.

Thorne looked up at her. "The one from Archangel?"

She swallowed hard, glanced at her mate with fear in her eyes and then at Bleu. "He said something to Emelia when he came for me… something about tracking down the dragon who had hurt her and slaying it."

"Well, he is wreaking havoc in the dragon realm, so I would suggest you remain away from that place." Bleu ran his hand over his hair, blew out his breath and held her gaze, not hiding his concern from her.

"Sable will be safe here." Thorne rose onto his feet, towering over Bleu on the raised platform. "But we thank you for the information. You may leave now."

The russet-haired male was a good few inches taller than him without the added height of the platform, and while such a tactic would have worked on him once, intimidating him and making him itch to fight the bastard for thinking he could look down on him, it didn't bother him at all this time.

Sable's golden gaze questioned him. He knew he was acting differently. Before, he would have been curt and would have left straight after delivering his message to spare himself the pain of seeing her with Thorne. Now, he wanted to leave so he could return to Taryn.

"I am not done," he said and Sable spoke over him.

"You seem well."

Bleu frowned, thought about what she had said, and then rolled his shoulders beneath his dark jacket when he realised that he was. "I am well. I am very well indeed."

She smiled slightly. "I'm glad to hear that."

Thorne grumbled something in the demon tongue and looked close to snagging his mate's arm and pulling her nearer to him. Sable tossed her mate a chiding look.

The big demon king folded his meaty arms across his chest, narrowed his red gaze on Bleu, and drew down a deep breath. Stilled. Grinned in a manner Bleu didn't like.

"Does your improved mood have anything to do with the dragon I can smell all over you?" Thorne's grin stretched wider as he preened the dark horns that curled from behind his ears with the air of a male satisfied with himself.

Bleu shot him down with a black glare.

"Thorne," Sable snapped and cuffed him across his left shoulder, earning a glare from her mate. She turned her gaze on Bleu. "I'm sorry. He's been horribly bored and he's taking it out on everyone. Not a day goes by when he doesn't get himself into some sort of trouble."

"You will not be bored soon," Bleu said and the demon's eyes lit up. "The reason I came here was because a dragon has the elven sword and Taryn saw a vision—"

"Taryn?" Sable interjected and smiled again. "Pretty name. Is she pretty, Bleu?"

He ignored her. Taryn wasn't pretty. She was beautiful.

"The dragon will battle us in the elf kingdom," he continued in a gruff tone, blanking the way Sable's smile widened, a knowing edge to her expression. He was growing tired of being teased by everyone. His relationship with Taryn was none of their business.

"Us?" Thorne growled, but Bleu could see he was secretly relishing the thought of going to war again.

He nodded. "The fastest route for the dragon is through your realm, followed by the First or Second. I have sent men to those realms to warn them to evacuate villages in the possible path of the dragon, or shore them up with more warriors… but I recommend the former. The sword this dragon wields is powerful."

"I have heard the legends," Thorne said, his deep voice little more than a rumble as his rough features turned pensive. He rubbed his right thumb across his lower lip and frowned. "I will evacuate the villages along the border with the dragon realm and send a legion of my warriors there."

His red eyes flicked up to meet Bleu's, a touch of warning in his narrowed gaze.

"I must go and see to it." The demon male meant to leave him alone with his mate, but he didn't have to worry. He had no intention of delaying his return to the elf kingdom.

The damned pool was probably close to overflowing now and he couldn't stay away from Taryn any longer. The ache behind his breast had grown too fierce, a mad throb that demanded he return to his female and make sure that she was safe, and then kiss her until she was breathless but panting for more.

Bleu nodded as Thorne passed him, bent his head to Sable, and willed his portal to open and whisk him back to his waiting mate.

Sable stopped him by speaking. "You look happy… and I've never seen you happy before."

He paused, frowned and then realised that it was true.

Bleu smiled at her. "That would be because I have not been happy in a very long time… since I gave up on finding my mate."

Her eyes widened and he teleported before she could say anything.

Eager to return to that mate.

CHAPTER 29

Taryn paced her quarters, bare feet silent on the dark stone floor. It was surprisingly warm beneath them, smooth and silken. She could almost see the appeal of living in such a place over a cave. Almost. She turned when she reached the wall and the low cabinets that ran along it and paced back towards the other end of the large room, her eyes fixed unseeingly on the three dark wardrobes that lined it to the left of the opening to the bathing room.

The sound of water thundering into the pool had grown quieter during the time she had been pacing, a sign that it was getting full.

Where was Bleu?

His scent lingered in the air, but it wasn't enough to soothe her. The castle was quiet around her, but she could sense people moving around below her, and could occasionally hear them outside. She had found the courage to open the twin tall glass doors to the right of the bed early into her wait, and had been pleasantly surprised to find a balcony outside them that ran along the length of the room.

The view from it was stunning.

She had never seen anything so beautiful.

It had held her transfixed for long minutes in which her eyes had delighted in watching the colours of the rolling landscape that stretched into the distance to meet with great cragged black mountains change as the light of the elf kingdom waned. The sky had changed colour, becoming a fiery glow.

Was that what a sunset in the mortal world would look like?

She had heard tales from Loke about the mortal realm, passed down to him from his parents before he had lost them in the dragon wars, but she hadn't been able to imagine anything as beautiful as what she had seen from the balcony of her room.

She could have passed the entire wait for Bleu on that balcony but a combination of fearing the pool would overflow, getting her into trouble with the elves, and the barked orders of a troop of soldiers in the courtyard below had driven her back inside. None of the soldiers marching around the quieter side of the castle grounds her balcony overlooked had noticed her, but she had promised Bleu she would remain safe inside and the thought that they might see her and report to him that she had been outside didn't sit well with her.

She had seen her elf male angry and she didn't want to be on the receiving end of it.

Gods, what had he done to her?

She couldn't believe the effect he had on her, how fiercely she needed him and desired to please him. No other male had affected her this way and she knew deep in her heart that it had nothing to do with the fact that he was her fated one.

It had everything to do with her growing feelings for him.

Taryn tried to push him out of her thoughts but the sound of running water kept him firmly in her mind.

He had promised to return before the pool was full.

She diverted course and checked on it, frowned when she saw that the level of the water was only inches from the brim of the low wall surrounding the deep rectangular pool now.

He wasn't going to make it.

She clenched her fists and then flexed her fingers, splaying them wide open, before curling them back into fists again.

Gods, she needed him back with her.

Thinking about his offer had stirred her hunger, the need of him that seemed impossible to satisfy. She growled, the sound vibrating up her throat, and paced the bathing room instead. She caught her reflection in the mirrors above the basins to her left and frowned. Her eyes glowed brightly, on fire with her hunger.

She needed Bleu.

That need pounded in her blood, drumming in her veins, a fast rhythm that had her breathing accelerating as she studied her reflection. She skimmed her hands down her dirty white corset, over her curves and up to her breasts, cupping them before caressing up her chest to her hair. She tangled her hands in it and lifted it away from her throat, tipped her head to one side. Would Bleu like to see her neck?

Would it drive him mad as he drove her crazy with need?

She wanted to push him to his limit. She wanted him to desire her as fiercely as she desired him.

She searched the room, speeding from the wardrobes to the drawers in the cabinets on the opposite side of the room. There were items in both. She picked a beautiful dress similar to the one the prince's mate had worn, but this one was cream.

Taryn held it up and paused.

What was she doing?

She had never dressed to impress any male before. Dragon males cared little about fashion. If a female wanted them, they were happy to service her needs. Even dragon females rarely wore more than leather trousers.

She had always chosen to cover her top half too.

Perhaps she was more different to the females of her species than she had realised. She had never indulged in the free sex willingly offered by the males of her kind whenever a female was needing, had never even considered approaching a male in such a manner when she had felt an urge to mate. The dragons of her village had always whispered about her, the females wondering whether something was wrong with her because she didn't pursue the males as they did, showed none of the passionate drive to mate that they had. They had started talking about her more when she had matured and had started to wear a corset to cover her breasts.

Now she was standing in an elf castle, staring at a dress, considering wearing it in order to seduce a male.

The females of her species viewed the correct attire for a seduction as nothing. If they desired the attention and cock of a male, they stripped bare and went to them.

They definitely didn't cover themselves up even more, and donning a dress was doing exactly that.

Taryn eyed it, put her left hand behind the layers of sheer fabric, and lifted it, letting the soft material run over her palm.

It was beautiful though.

When Bleu had changed before leaving for the demon realms, he had put on more clothing, and part of her had felt that he had done it to attract her eye. He had been making himself more appealing, more alluring, by dressing in such striking attire. Gods, the way it had hugged his figure.

She had wanted to peel it off him slowly.

Had been thinking about doing such a thing the entire time he had been gone.

The need was so fierce now that she ached just thinking about unbuttoning the tunic and slowly parting it to reveal his powerful honed body.

She bit her lip and squeezed her thighs together when the ache reached there, making her damp with need.

She wanted such power over her male. She wanted to dress in a way that would have him aching for her, mad with a need to have her, to strip her slowly and savour revealing her to his eyes.

Taryn turned, tossed the dress on the bed and stripped off. She kicked her corset and trousers into the corner of the room with her boots, strode to the bed and picked up the dress.

She had never worn one before, but they couldn't be that difficult to master. She sifted through the layers of the skirt, grumbled a few choice curses beneath her breath when she couldn't find the damned centre of them, and huffed. A different approach was needed.

She spotted the lacing on the back of the dress.

Smiled.

If she loosened it, she might be able to step into the dress and pull it up over her hips.

She tugged on the bow at the top of the lacing, worked her fingers down the criss-cross of the ribbons, and opened the dress up. She pooled it on the floor, stepped into it, grabbed the two sides of the corset, and pulled it up. Wriggled when it got stuck on her hips. Sighed when it finally hit her waist and easily came up to her breasts.

Getting the lacing done back up was another fight.

She turned in circles as she reached over her back, snagging the first lace easily but struggling with the second.

Gods!

She growled and stretched harder, grimacing as her shoulder hurt. Stupid dress. She finally caught the second lace, tugged them both up and pulled a face when she reached a point where she could barely breathe. She padded into the bathing room and looked at her reflection.

She did look stunning though.

The cream material hugged her torso, accentuating her waist and her breasts.

She smiled wickedly and tied the bow, and then hurried back to the wardrobes. A flicker of disappointment went through her. There wasn't a corset to go with the dress. She had hoped to find one similar to that which the prince's mate had worn. It had looked uncomfortable, but it had been pretty.

She could almost feel her eyes sparkling. Her fingers itched and she flexed them as she thought about the corset. It had glittered. Silver. Shiny.

She swayed on the spot and then snapped herself back to the room.

Now wasn't the time to get lost in thinking about treasure.

She moved to the drawers in the cabinets across the room and rifled through the one that had contained many different trinkets.

All of them treasure.

Gods, she had to hide them somewhere. They weren't safe where they were.

She growled as she lifted the skirt of her dress and bundled everything into it, every shiny object in every drawer. Her skirt was heavy by the time she had found all of them. She scanned the room, swinging around in a circle, her heart pounding rapidly as she searched for a safe place to stow her prizes.

A pained snarl escaped her.

Nowhere was safe in this damned room.

This was why caves were better.

Caves had secret tunnels, hidden chambers ideal for storing treasure and keeping it safe.

Her eyes leaped to the bed and dropped to the floor beneath it. She would have to sleep on the bed. If she placed her treasure beneath it, it would be safe there. No one would dare try to take it from her if she guarded it so closely.

She scurried to the bed, tossed the covers up onto the mattress on the left side, away from the doors onto the balcony, and began unloading her hoard. She set aside a piece for her hair, a beautiful silver clasp with sparkling amethysts, and pushed the rest under the wooden frame of the double bed. Settling back on her heels, she frowned at the small pile. It was still too obvious.

She scanned the room again and grinned when she spotted her boots.

Taryn sprinted to them, gathering them and her trousers and corset, and hurried back to her treasure. She shovelled the trinkets into her boots, stuffed her trousers and corset into the end of them, and tucked them back under the bed on their sides.

There.

As safe as she could get it for now.

Satisfied at last, she rose onto her feet, drew the dark purple covers down over the side of the bed and smoothed them so none would suspect they hid anything.

She took the clasp from the dark stone floor and went into the bathing room. The pool was close to overflowing now.

Taryn twirled her hair up and pinned it at the back of her head. Strands fell down but she didn't care. She ran her hands over her exposed neck. The marks Bleu had placed on her throat were paler now, healing well. She shivered when her fingertips brushed them, a hit of pleasure rolling down her spine. It was so wrong that it had felt so good when he had been biting her, even when she had been afraid he would kill her.

And the way he had licked her throat afterwards?

The shiver became a burn that had her squeezing her thighs together again.

The sound of water stopped.

She whirled to face the pool, her eyes widening when she saw that the level had reached the spout, and rushed to the sluice that Bleu had opened. She twisted the thick metal ring and shoved down, jamming it shut.

A hot shiver coursed through her, setting her aflame.

She lifted her head and stared across the pool to the other end.

To Bleu where he stood with his eyes on her, his chest heaving with each hard breath he drew. Those striking eyes almost glowed in the low warm light of the chandelier above the pool and the way his pointed ears flared back, the tips growing longer, had all of the heat rushing through her heading south to coil in her belly.

His gaze narrowed as she slowly stood, raked over her and grew heated, dark with the passion and hunger that flowed through their link.

Gods, when she had dressed to seduce him, she hadn't realised just how deeply his reaction would affect her.

She felt beautiful.

Desired.

Needed.

That need was a powerful force, one that rocked her as he strode towards her, a male on the prowl and one who was going to take what he wanted from her. She trembled, all of her strength stripped from her again as she waited for him, eager to feel his hands on her, desperate for another taste of him.

He snarled, looked her over again, and caught her cheeks the moment he was within reach and pulled her up to him for a hard kiss. His tongue delved between her lips as he slanted his head, inhaled hard as if the kiss had sent the same bolt of hot lightning through him as it had through her. She swallowed his throaty moan and clutched his shoulders, digging her fingers into the fine material of his jacket as he possessed her mouth, claimed all of her with only a kiss.

His hands dropped to her backside and he groaned as he palmed it, drew her closer and kissed her fiercely, his desperation sending a thrill through her. She hadn't been prepared for this. It was far more than she had expected. The ferocity of his need startled her, but as she leaned into him, seeking more from his kiss, it dawned on her that his passion and hunger only matched her own.

The thought that she wasn't alone in her feelings gave her courage.

She moved her hands across his chest, found the line of buttons down the centre of his tunic and began slipping them free of their holes.

His kiss slowed, his ragged breathing filling her ears as he eased her back. Their mouths broke apart and he looked down, chest heaving as he watched her unbuttoning his jacket. His need poured through her, swirling together with her own sense of anticipation and eagerness.

When she reached the last button, just below his navel, she lowered her gaze to his chest and slowly parted the two sides of his jacket. Her breath hitched in her throat as she caught her first glimpse of the compact muscles of his torso and then shortened as she revealed more of him, slipping her hands beneath his jacket and brushing it aside by moving her hands over the delicious hard slabs of his pectorals.

Bleu half groaned half growled.

He trembled beneath her and she had never felt so powerful.

She had brought this warrior to his knees with only a touch.

She smoothed her hands up his chest to his shoulders and slowly pushed the jacket off them. He shifted his arms back and it dropped to the floor behind him.

Hungry eyes raked over her, making her shiver again, and he muttered something in his own tongue. She frowned at him, wanting to know what he had said in such a passion-drenched voice, but not expecting him to tell her. He had said much to her in that language, and she knew he did it because he wanted to keep those things secret from her even though he couldn't stop himself from voicing them. What things didn't he want her to know?

The same sort of things she had thought were hidden back in the dungeon of Tenak's castle, when she hadn't realised the fae's blood had given him the ability to hear her thoughts?

"Gods, you are beautiful," he whispered earnestly in the dragon tongue, and her heart warmed, her belly fluttering in response to those low spoken words and the fact he hadn't kept them secret from her.

His violet eyes travelled down the line of her throat, darkening by degrees as his pupils dilated. The tip of his tongue swept across his lips and hunger lit his eyes, a thirst that ran deeper than a need for blood.

He needed her.

She could feel it in him through their link and it called to her dragon instincts, rousing a fierce demand that she satisfy her male.

She stepped closer and leaned in to kiss his chest at the same time as his left hand rose to her hair.

It neared her silver clasp.

Taryn leaped back and snarled at him, flashing sharp teeth.

He tensed, eyes shooting wide, the hunger in them replaced with shock that rippled through her.

"I… I did not…" She wasn't sure what to say. Instinct had stolen control of her, roaring that he meant to steal the clasp and forcing her to warn him away.

She would have lashed out at him if she hadn't retained enough awareness of what she was doing to distance herself from him.

Taryn lifted a hand to the clasp, fingers shaking as she touched it and a strange soothing warmth flowing through her when she felt it was still there.

Still in her possession.

A wicked smile curled Bleu's lips.

"You can keep your *treasure*," he breathed in a sultry whisper and slowly stepped towards her, closing the distance between them, his eyes holding hers the whole time. "But your throat is temptingly bare and I am not sure I am strong enough to resist the need to bite you again… I do not want to hurt you, Taryn."

Her fingers shook for a different reason, the warmth that had been curling through her exploding into a wildfire that blazed in her blood and made her want to moan. Just the thought of him sinking his fangs back into her made her itch with a need to mark him too.

A dangerous desire.

Biting him would seal their bond, completing it and making them mated.

She wasn't sure she was ready for that, and she felt certain that he wasn't. There was still so much to learn about each other, so much to overcome before they could think about forging a permanent bond between them. She wasn't going to rush into this, because the thought of allowing her instincts to mate to blind her, only to realise later that the one she had bound herself to didn't share her feelings, made her heart heavy.

She refused to do anything until she was certain.

Until they were both certain.

So biting was definitely off limits, because as much as she ached to feel his fangs in her flesh again, feel that intense connection between them blossoming once more, she couldn't risk the danger that in the heat of the moment she would bite him in return.

She reached up and pulled the clasp from her hair, letting it tumble back down around her shoulders. The silver trinket was warm in her hand and she stared down at it, mesmerised by how the jewels sparkled at her. Her feet carried her away from Bleu, her instincts sweeping her along unaware of what she was doing.

She crouched beside the bed, raised the covers and carefully tucked her treasure into her boots, safe with the rest of her hoard.

When she straightened and turned back to face the bathing room, Bleu was standing in the grand archway, his right shoulder against the stone frame, his legs casually crossed at the ankle and his arms folded across his bare chest. His left eyebrow quirked.

"What do you have there?" He jerked his chin towards the bed.

She spread her arms out at her sides and growled. "Mine."

He smiled again and she realised what she had done, felt like a fool as he grinned, obviously amused by her behaviour.

"I am not interested in taking anything from you. Whatever you have, you can keep." He advanced on her, his smile slowly fading, an all too serious expression replacing it as his eyes held hers, bewitching her and pulling her under his seductive spell again. "I have the only treasure I need."

She frowned. "You do? I would like to see this treasure."

She would like to make it hers.

He smiled but this time it was wicked, heating her to her core as he held his hand out to her.

"Come with me then."

CHAPTER 30

Bleu held his hand out to her and Taryn eagerly slipped hers into it, excitement bubbling up and tugging at her lips. There was a bounce in her step as he turned away from her but it faded as he led her into the bathroom. She frowned and scanned the room. There were no hidden compartments or anywhere he could hide treasure.

Was he toying with her to make her return to the pool with him?

The thought that he might be made her want to growl at his bare back, only that growl died on her lips as she watched his muscles shift in a sinful symphony with each step he took. Gods. He had called her beautiful, but he was the beautiful one.

She ran her eyes down the line of his spine to the twin dimples above his backside and bit back a moan. She wanted to tongue those dips while he laid on his front on the bed, and she would palm the firm globes of his backside at the same time, finally getting her hands on them.

She was so deep in her wicked thoughts that she hadn't realised they had stopped moving until he spoke.

"Have I lost you again?"

She blinked herself back to him and found herself staring into the mirror above the basin. He stood behind her, his hands on her bare shoulders, his cheek close to the right side of her head and his eyes locked with hers in their reflection.

"Where is your treasure?" she whispered, still eager to see it.

He lowered his lips to her ear. "You are looking at it."

She frowned and all of her excitement deflated, her shoulders sagging beneath his grip as she huffed, "The mirror is nothing special. It is not a treasure."

He smiled, stealing her breath. "It is not the mirror but what it contains."

That made no sense. "It is a mirror. It contains nothing… nothing but a reflection of this room anyway… you and I."

He muttered something in the elf tongue, closed his eyes and sighed. His frustration rolled through her. She pouted and stared at the mirror, trying to see what he called a treasure.

There was nothing special about it, and it only showed him where he stood behind her.

Oh.

Her eyes widened.

Her.

Was he calling her his treasure?

Her heart skipped a beat.

Bleu's eyes slowly opened, fixed on hers in the mirror again and he drew her hair away from the right side of her throat and pressed a tender kiss to it. Her blood heated. She wanted him to tell her that she was the treasure he had spoken of but the frustration that had gone through him had been replaced with nerves and she didn't want to push him, not when his violet eyes gave her the answer to that question as he brushed his lips over her throat, holding her gaze in their reflection.

She was.

She was his treasure and he wanted to possess her.

The heat each sweep of his mouth over her flesh caused slowly spread through her, until she couldn't stop herself from leaning her head to her left and moaning. He lightly bit with blunt teeth, teasing her with a brief flash of pain, a touch of pleasure that only roused a need for more.

Gods, she wanted him to bite her.

She trembled as he slid his hands around her waist, brought them up to cup her breasts, hitching some of the layers of her cream dress up with them. He groaned against her throat and palmed her breasts, his bare torso pressing against her back. She lifted her right hand, skimmed it over his shoulder and curled it around the nape of his neck, sifting her fingers through his silky blue-black hair as she savoured the feel of his lips on her skin and how erotic watching them in the mirror made everything.

"You look too damn good in this dress." He pressed kisses across her shoulder as he looked at her reflection, his eyes dark with the need she sensed in him. He rolled his hips, nudging the hard length in his trousers against her backside. "I do not want to take it off you."

Gods.

She throbbed between her thighs, core clenching at the thought of him being inside her while she stood before the mirror.

He nibbled her shoulder and then her neck, groaning low in his throat, as if he could hear her thoughts and approved of them. His thumbs caught the top of her corset across her breasts and he inched it down, his eyes hot on her as he revealed her nipples. They pebbled the instant the cooler air hit them and a moan left her lips, her eyes slipping shut as a shiver cascaded across her skin.

Bleu mouthed her neck, licked it and pressed his tongue in hard before softening his touch again, gently kissing upwards towards her ear. He sucked the lobe into his mouth and thumbed her nipples, his breath hot on her ear. She moaned as he rocked against her, grinding his cock between her buttocks, finding it hard to focus when every strum of her nipples sent sparks skittering across her skin and his mouth on her and the feel of him behind her was sending fire to her belly.

She arched back against him and he groaned, bit her earlobe and caught her left hip. He held her in place, his fingertips pressing into her flesh through her skirt, and thrust against her, a frown darkening his face. His nostrils flared and he narrowed his gaze on hers in the mirror, ground harder against her backside, until a moan escaped her and she tipped her head back, resting it on his shoulder.

Gods, she needed more.

The hand against her hip travelled lower, hastily pulled her skirts up and found its way inside. She groaned in time with him when he slipped his hand between her thighs, couldn't stop herself from parting for him, spreading her legs as much as she could while still standing.

His guttural growl as he speared her plush lips with his fingers and caressed her nub sent a fierce shiver through her, a hunger to hear him snarl again. There had been need in his growl, approval and male satisfaction, all rolled together into a sound that brought her to life, made her ache to feel him inside her.

"You're so wet," he whispered in her ear and she blushed, suddenly unsure of herself. Was that wrong? He caught her gaze in the mirror and smiled wickedly as he nibbled her earlobe. "I love it… it tells me how much you need me."

Her knees almost buckled.

His right hand caught her hip and steadied her.

He growled into her ear, his face dark with a hungry possessive look that only sent her arousal soaring higher, until she could scarcely breathe.

"My female needs," he snarled in a low deep voice, one that sent a tremor through her and had her on the verge of begging him to do something about it.

She didn't need to ask.

He pulled at her skirts, raising them up to her waist, and she gasped as cold air hit her bare backside and thighs, causing an eruption of gooseflesh. He chased away the chill by planting his hands on her bottom and palming it, his low moans echoing through her as she absorbed the sight of him in the mirror.

She had never seen him looking so hungry. So fierce.

She wriggled as he released her, his eyes dropping from hers, focused on his work, and she heard him unlacing his trousers. Her breathing grew ragged, heart thundering, need swirling with anticipation to crank her tight and make it impossible to keep still.

When his hands claimed her hips again what felt like an eternity later but had probably been no more than a few seconds, she moaned and shivered, raised her backside to meet his touch. He groaned and rubbed her bottom, and then drew her hips back, lifting them until she was tiptoeing and had to clutch the edge of the vanity in front of her to stop herself from falling forwards.

Bleu's dark gaze met hers in the mirror again, locked with it and held it fast. His eyes narrowed, lids dropping to shutter his beautiful irises for a moment as he nudged the head of his cock against her. She lifted her hips higher, desperate to feel him inside her again, his long thick length filling and stretching her.

He tortured her though, rubbing the blunt broad head along her wet cleft to stroke her clit, sending a thousand fiery sparks shooting down her thighs and up her belly. She couldn't bite back the moan as she throbbed, each small contraction making what he was doing feel even more incredible. He groaned and the head of his cock slid back, probed her entrance and stole her breath. She wanted to press back onto it but gripped the vanity instead, resisting the temptation. He slowly fed his erection into her, maddening her with a hunger to make him thrust deep and fast, spearing her to the very depth of her core.

His right hand tightened on her hip, as if he had sensed her need to push back, and held her firm.

She moaned in unison with him as he drove forwards, pushing the head of his cock into her. Satisfaction flowed through her as he sank deeper, bliss following in its wake. She closed her eyes and then opened them again, wanting to stare into his and see the pleasure he felt as he joined them. His violet eyes grew darker but brighter at the same time, and the pointed tips of his ears flattened against his wild blue-black hair. He groaned, a breathless one that thrilled her as he pushed deeper and claimed both of her hips with his hands.

Short nails dug into her flesh and he plunged forwards, until his thighs brushed the backs of hers and his cock was seated to the hilt inside her.

His gaze held hers in the mirror, possessing her soul as fiercely as he now possessed her body. She stared back at him, lost in the hunger and need his showed to her, the wildness that was fast coming to life inside her too, roused by the way he was looking at her and the sight of them in the mirror. Her breasts spilled from her corset, dusky nipples taut with need.

She waited for him to move, to withdraw and thrust back in, beginning their steady climb towards their release.

He didn't.

He swept one hand forwards, delved it between her thighs and fondled her bundle of nerves. She moaned and writhed, flexed around his rock hard length as pleasure spilled through her. His answering groan made another leave her lips, her arousal soaring to the point where control slipped beyond her grasp as he teased her nub, flicking and squeezing it, rubbing it with the flats of his fingers, all the while keeping his cock lodged inside her.

"Gods." He lowered his mouth, brushed it across her shoulder, licked and nipped in a rough way that told her that she wasn't the only one losing control, being overwhelmed by her need and desire. "You feel so fucking good."

"You feel so fucking good too," she whispered back at him and he grinned at her.

She flexed her body around his cock, ripping the smile from his face and tearing a grunt from him that sounded animalistic.

Wild.

He sneered, lips peeling back to flash his fangs at her in a way that sent a wicked thrill through her, and clutched her hip with his other hand, withdrew until his cock almost slipped free of her before driving forwards, sending her rocking towards the mirror. She couldn't contain the moan that left her lips, or stop herself from bracing herself against the slab of dark stone beneath the basin and pushing back against him, goading him into doing it again.

He refused, stopped and gave her pleasure another way, sliding his fingers down to where he entered her and bringing them back up to tease her nub. She moaned and lost herself in the sparks of pleasure that exploded with each expert swirl of his fingers, breathing hard as awareness of everything around her faded until all she knew was the bliss of his touch and the surging wave of release building inside her.

Bleu skimmed his right hand up her side, cupped her breast and teased her right nipple as he kissed her throat. His eyes remained locked on hers the entire time and she quivered as she watched him, felt him kissing and touching her, saw it happening in the mirror too.

She tensed, flexed around him, her face screwing up as the wave inside her built and she reached the crest, on the verge of crashing into her climax.

He chose that moment to withdraw and thrust back into her.

Taryn cried out her climax, a thousand glittering lights exploding across her eyes as her entire body quaked with release, flashed hot and cold at the same time.

Bleu growled and didn't give her a chance to catch her breath. His right hand squeezed her breast, his left one claimed her hip and he plunged into her, hard and fast strokes that had her surging through the haze of one orgasm and barrelling towards her next with him.

He bit down on her shoulder, his fierce need flowing through her, cranking hers higher. She rocked against him, moaned with each deep plunge of his cock into her core as it still trembled with her release. He released her shoulder and kissed up her neck, nibbled her lobe and breathed heavily into her ear as he took her, stroking her with every inch of his long hard length.

His eyes continued to hold hers in the mirror as he raised his left hand from her hip and caught her jaw in it. He tilted her head to her left, held it there as his right hand lowered to clutch her hip to hold her steady as he drove into her with fierce possessive thrusts that left her breathless. She moaned as the pressure built in her belly again, stoked by the long plunges of his cock into her core and the way he held her at his mercy, her throat bared to him.

He lowered his head and kissed her neck, scraped fangs over it and sent a wave of tingles through her, fire that only made her burn hotter for him. Her breasts bounced with each hard stroke of his length, the pressure building higher as she watched them in the mirror, watched him devouring her neck as he watched her.

Dear gods.

He growled against her skin, a low rumbling snarl, and angled his hips, lowering them. She gasped as he sank deeper into her, striking the depth of her core with each long thrust, each wild union of their bodies. His answering moan relayed the pleasure that flooded their link, telling her how close he was, that he balanced on the precipice just as she did.

He nicked her throat with his left fang, wrapped his lips around it and suckled.

Stars detonated across her eyes again, her entire body tensing and jerking as release exploded through her, stealing her breath and making her heart stutter in her chest. Bleu's cock pulsed inside her, the throbbing and the feel of his hot seed jetting into her with each rough thrust of his hips sending aftershocks through her, heightening her pleasure as it mingled with his.

He groaned and shuddered, his mouth still latched onto her neck, breath coming as hard and fast as her own was as she tried to bring herself down again. She had never soared so high, had never felt such a thrill, such intense mind-blowing pleasure.

It was better than flying.

He held her for long minutes, still clutching her tightly. Wetness trickled down her inner thighs as she caught her breath, body numbed from two releases, and she felt sure that if she let go of the vanity she would fall in a boneless heap on the floor.

Her senses slowly pieced back together and she managed a frown when she realised Bleu had slipped free of her and was undoing her dress.

She questioned him silently in the mirror and he smiled, his rich purple eyes hazy with satisfaction that sent a ripple of pride through her. She had done that to him.

"You really need a bath now," he murmured and dropped a kiss on her shoulder.

A sparkle lit his eyes as they met hers in the mirror and he tugged her dress down, revealing her bare body to him.

She supposed he had promised to bathe with her.

She slowly peeled her hands off the vanity, was pleasantly surprised when she didn't collapse, and turned to face him.

Gods, he was naked.

As she ran her eyes down the length of him, the embers of her desire sparked back to life, and the way his soft length twitched back to semi-hard said she wasn't the only one thinking naughty things.

Bleu scooped her up into his arms and she looped hers around his neck, toyed with the longer strands of his hair as he carried her towards the pool.

His wicked smile as he gazed down at her filled her mind with one delicious thought, as if he had projected his into her head.

They were going to do a lot more than washing each other's backs in that pool.

CHAPTER 31

Bleu wasn't sure he knew the meaning of concentrate anymore. He paced the grand war room of the elf castle, the light filtering in through the five tall arched windows to his left flickering over him whenever he emerged from the shadows of the columns that stretched between them to support the vaulted ceiling. Six windows lined the wall off to his right across the room too, and the curved wall at the end of the room ahead of him, allowing so much light in that the pale grey stone looked white. His gaze flicked across to his right as he reached the double doors that led onto a small balcony and turned, settling briefly on Taryn where she stood staring at the huge model of Hell, her beautiful eyes studying the lands near the Devil's realm.

Her thoughts were on her brother again. He could see it in the worry lines between her fine eyebrows and feel it in the link they shared.

Loren stood on the opposite side of the massive table, dressed in the black formal attire of embroidered knee-length tunic, tight trousers, and polished boots suited to the occasion. Bleu glanced down at himself, taking in similar clothing, before marching onwards.

Everyone was late.

They hadn't received word back from the messengers sent to the First, Second or Third demon realms to request the presence of the kings.

What if something had happened in those realms? What if the kings had fallen, torn from their thrones by Tenak?

It worried him, but it wasn't the reason he found concentration an elusive thing, so much so that Loren had ordered him away from the map since he had been more than useless, unable to assist his prince in formulating a plan.

Taryn was doing a better job than he had been.

He flicked another glance at her.

How the hell could she focus when he couldn't string two thoughts together without his mind leaping to ones about her?

"There is a possibility Tenak might have completely skirted the demon realms and travelled up this corridor." She ran a finger up the map, along a ridge of mountains, leaning forwards to reach further.

Gods, he imagined her fingers running over the peaks and valleys of his torso like that, a light maddening touch that would only serve to fuel the fierce craving he had for her.

Her violet-leather-clad thighs pressed against the edge of the map, the front of her white corset touching the mountains of the Devil's realm, and her violet-to-white hair swung away from her shoulders, falling like a veil to hide her face from him.

She brought her right hand up and tucked her hair behind her ear, as if she knew he needed to do such a thing, ached to see her face again.

"It is the easiest route to the elf kingdom, but it would mean travelling through the free realm and would bring him into the kingdom at the furthest point from your castle."

Her soft voice was music in the room, a light and airy sound that soothed him but clawed at his insides.

Fuck, he had missed the sound of her voice.

He had missed the sight of her, the feel of her near him, the scent of her.

Everything about her.

Two whole days caught up in arranging squad movements, planning routes across the elf kingdom, and holding meetings with his senior officers, had pulled him away from her.

But it hadn't pulled his mind away from thoughts about the time he had spent with her after returning from the Third Realm. She had looked so beautiful in the dress that he hadn't been able to keep his hands off her.

Now he couldn't keep his eyes off her.

He needed her and he could feel that she needed him too. It was there in their link and in her eyes whenever she risked a glance at him. Every time their eyes met, the entire room fell away, everyone but her disappearing, and all he could think about was crossing the room to her, pulling her into his arms and kissing her.

How the fuck had he convinced himself that his being away from her, caught up in his work, was a good thing, giving himself some much needed space to think and time to pull himself together to stop his mind from spinning whenever they were near each other?

He found himself staring at her as he paced, unable to drag his eyes away from her.

That time apart hadn't helped him at all. It hadn't allowed him to act more professional, treating her as a guest of the castle and an ally in the coming war. It hadn't dampened his feelings for her or weakened them at all.

It had done the damned opposite.

Their time apart had increased his need of her, strengthened his feelings for her. He had spent two damn days stuck in his offices in the garrison pining for her.

Fucking *pining*.

He had spent every damned night standing in his room, staring at the wall that divided them and aching to tear it down. Only the fact that she had felt still on his senses had kept him from barging into her room. He hadn't wanted to disturb his little dragon. She needed her rest. Still needed it if the dark circles beneath her eyes were anything to go by.

Were thoughts of her brother and what was to come keeping her awake?

Gods, he wanted to cross the room to her, draw her into his arms and tell her that it would all work out in the end. That everything she feared would never come to pass and he would protect her.

It would be a lie though.

Her biggest fear was something that had to happen in order to end the threat to his kingdom, and the other realms of Hell.

Her brother had to die.

Even if they managed to get the sword back.

Tenak would always be a threat and his dragon instincts wouldn't allow him to let go of his treasure. Taryn's behaviour in her room had made Bleu see that. If they took the sword from him, Tenak would keep coming at the elf kingdom until he had razed it to the ground and the blade was his again. Even capturing him and placing shackles on him that could inhibit his ability to shift and stop his magic wouldn't be enough. Eventually, he would gain his freedom and all of Hell would pay for it.

Taryn glanced at him again, sending a hot shiver through him that stirred his need to pull her into his arms, growl 'mine' and then kiss her breathless so she knew it.

Fuck. He scrubbed a hand over his hair, tousling the longer lengths, and ran it around the back of his neck.

He hadn't lied when he had said that she was his treasure, and the way her eyes sparkled whenever she looked at him, that same light that had shone in them when she had protected her 'treasure' she had discovered in her room, said that she felt the same way about him.

He smiled at that and how she had hoarded the knick-knacks she had found. Mere trinkets. Nothing fine among them.

Bleu frowned as he grew aware of another's eyes on him and looked across at Loren, finding his prince watching him with a touch of curiosity mixed with satisfaction in his expression.

He raised an eyebrow at that, and how Loren leaned to his right and pressed a kiss to Olivia's shoulder where she stood beside him, talking to him about something. Olivia lifted her dark eyes away from the map, settled them on Loren and smiled. When she leaned over for a proper kiss, Bleu looked away.

His gaze snagged on Taryn.

She walked away from the map, drifting towards the tall doors on his side of the room beside the windows.

A messenger entered the room.

An unmated male.

Bleu closed the distance between him and his little dragon, but the threat the unmated male posed to his position as her mate wasn't the reason he wanted to be closer to her again. He needed her near him.

He felt empty when she was so far away from him.

It was only a small distance, a few metres at most, but fuck it felt like a league to him.

Loren looked at him again as he spoke with the messenger, and this time his prince looked concerned. His violet gaze shifted from Bleu to Taryn where she stood near the doors onto the balcony and back again before returning to the messenger.

The male saluted and left the room.

"The First Realm will arrive soon, and our other guests are en route. Perhaps we should take a break until they arrive and we can begin our meeting in earnest?" Loren was meddling again. Bleu didn't need to catch his pointed look at Taryn's back to know it, nor the not-so-subtle jerk of his chin in her direction as she stepped out onto the balcony.

Bleu glared at him and followed her. He didn't need his prince telling him to go after her. It wasn't as if he could keep away from her, would follow her to the ends of Hell just to be near her.

How had he managed to stay away from her for so long?

He found Taryn on the balcony, her hands braced on the pale stone balustrade, eyes scanning the vast panorama. The entire elf kingdom stretched before them, green hills rolling into the distance where they met mountains. A glittering blue river snaked between them. Her head tilted downwards and he looked there as he came up beside her, watching the troops moving around the orchard.

Dacian stormed along one of the pale grey paths that led away from the central portal, heading towards the garrison.

Bleu's right eyebrow arched when the portal flared and Fynn's sister strode out of it, looked around, spotted Dacian and went after him. Interesting.

"It is beautiful," Taryn whispered in the dragon tongue and Bleu tore his focus away from Dacian, returning it to her.

He looked out at the view she admired, leaned on his elbows on the railing, and frowned.

"I prefer the one from my balcony at the rear of the castle." He looked to his right, at Taryn. "It is the same as yours since our rooms are adjoining."

"I know… I can feel you there… close to me but so far away." She smiled but there was sorrow in it, hurt that clawed at him, sinking talons deep into his heart.

Bleu cast his gaze down at the courtyard and picked at the lichens on the stone with his right hand. "I'm sorry. I was busy and whenever I finished with my work it was late and I feared I would wake you if I came to you."

Her eyes didn't leave the horizon and her hurt didn't lessen, and he wanted to soothe it away. He just wasn't sure how.

"I wanted you to come to me," she whispered. "I do not like it here."

He frowned and looked across at her. "You are safe here, Taryn."

Her eyes closed. "Am I?"

Bleu pushed up, resting his palms against the balustrade, and growled, "Has anyone made you feel threatened?"

She shook her head.

"Of course not… because…" She opened her eyes, fixing them straight on him, and the coldness in them froze his blood in his veins and chilled his heart. "Because I cannot leave my room without you… I am locked in there… in a gilded c-cage… in a ca—"

Bleu caught her wrist.

Her dull eyes dropped to it, brightened again, and then sharpened and she yanked her arm free of his grip. Wrong move on his part, one he should have known would upset her. She was feeling confined again, a captive, and he had only worsened that feeling by seizing her so tightly. Gods, he needed to learn the right ways to handle his little dragon. It was hard when his instincts said to hold her when she was hurting though, to touch her to bring her back to him and shatter the hold of her memories.

"I need to fly," she whispered and her hands shook, her breath coming fast, causing her chest to heave against the tight confines of her white leather corset. "I need to fly."

Bleu hunkered down, lowered his head to her height, and carefully reached for her. He placed his hands under hers, not taking hold of them, just allowing her palms to rest against his. Her pain flowed through him, rife with fear and desperation.

It wasn't growing weaker. It was growing stronger.

"I'm sorry. I should have considered how you would feel. I should have known and I should have taken you with me… although I am not sure how much you would have enjoyed being shut in my office with me for hours on end." He risked curling his fingers over to press against hers and she looked down at their joined hands, her eyebrows rising high on her forehead, a faraway look shining in her striking eyes. He was losing her. He could almost feel her slipping away. "I'm sorry… it is not a cage, Taryn. I was only trying to protect you."

"I know," she murmured, distant and quiet. "I tried to bear it… but I need air. I need to fly."

"I will take you out when the meeting ends. I will take you somewhere far away where you can feel free." He looked back inside at Loren, found his prince still watching him, and then looked in the other direction, towards the hills and the river.

It was only a short distance from the castle, and Loren would be able to keep an eye on their guest, reassured that they would return and Bleu hadn't gone rogue with her or lost control of her. He caught hold of her hands and willed his portal.

Green-purple light chased down his arms and up hers. She gasped and darkness swirled around them. When it receded, they were standing in the long grass by a bend in the river.

Her violet-to-white eyes widened and she looked around them, drawing back and slipping free of his right hand. He kept his left hand on hers, twisted it to slip his fingers between hers, and watched her as she took it all in. The fingers of her left hand brushed over the tips of the swaying grass that reached past her knees. A smile played on her lips.

"You cannot fly. Promise me that, Taryn. I will take you somewhere to fly soon."

She looked across at him and nodded.

Bleu led her down the slope to the water, where the grass was shorter, and released her. He sat on the bank of the river, leaned back and propped himself up on his elbows. Taryn looked down at him and then slowly turned around, her eyes scanning everything, bright and wide as she took it all in.

"It is even more beautiful from down here." Her smile blew him away.

He had never seen her so happy.

"I agree… the view is even more beautiful from down here." He didn't take his eyes off her and she looked at him, her eyes widened a little further, and a blush climbed her cheeks when she caught the meaning behind his words.

She was more beautiful.

She turned her back on him, crouched and reached out to touch the water. Her hand shot back to her before it hit the surface and she looked over her shoulder at him.

"Will it hurt me?"

Bleu laughed. "No. Of course not. It is only water."

She frowned at him. "There is a substance like it in the dragon realms and some of the demon ones that is poisonous."

"I suppose that is true… but this is only water. Nothing here will hurt you."

She muttered as she turned away from him again, "Nothing but the elves."

He sighed. "I swear they will not touch you. Is my word not enough?"

Her head dipped and she idly ran her fingers through the crystal clear water, her sorrow flowing through him. "It is… I am sorry."

"You do not need to apologise to me, Taryn." He sat up, bent his knees and rested his forearms on them. "I know my kin have not treated you well… I have not treated you well. I have given you no reason to trust me."

He lowered his right hand, plucked a blade of grass and twirled it in his fingers, his eyes on it. Hers roamed to him, heating his skin, but he kept his locked on the grass as it spun, a green blur against the pale blue of the water.

"I do trust you, Bleu," she whispered and he smiled as those words warmed him, chasing away the rising hurt before it could seize hold of him.

She sighed, the sound soft and melodic, and kneeled beside the river. The hurt he had feared would take hold of him gripped her instead and he rose onto his feet, walked over to her and sat opposite her.

"You think of your brother," he said and she nodded. He reached out and caught hold of her right hand, drawing it away from her purple leathers, and brushed his thumb over the back of it. "I know this is hard for you, Taryn."

She lowered her head and let her left hand drift back down to the water, stared at it as the river rushed between her fingers, glittering in the light. "You left me alone and all I could think about was my brother and everything we have shared… how he changed… how it drove us apart… and now I must end it all… I must end—"

Bleu leaned over and pressed the fingers of his free hand to her lips to silence her because he couldn't bear the pain. He couldn't allow her to keep hurting herself. She lifted her eyes to him and the tears that trembled on her lashes tore at his heart.

"I swear," he husked, voice thick, clogged with the emotions she stirred in him—the need, the love, and the desperate desire to make her happy again. "If my presence keeps those dark thoughts at bay then you will not be able to get rid of me. I will stick to you like glue."

"Glue?" Her eyebrows pinched together. "What is glue?"

He swept his thumb over the back of her hand. "It is a product that mortals use to fuse two items together. A sticky substance. I hear it is sometimes made from animal bones."

The pain in her eyes faded, curiosity rising to replace it. "You know the mortal realm well?"

He nodded.

She leaned closer. "Will you tell me about it? I cannot go there but I would like to know it."

Her and all dragons. They were all fixated on learning about it since they had been banished from that realm, cursed to have their powers stripped from them the moment they entered it and to die if they lingered there.

"I will tell you everything about it. Whatever you want to know."

Her smile could have illuminated all of Hell.

Gods, if he had known the mortal realm was the way to her heart, he would have been telling her everything about it since the moment she had driven back the darkness in him in that cell in Tenak's castle.

She opened her mouth to speak.

Someone appeared beside him and she was behind him in an instant, her hands clutching his shoulders and a low snarl escaping her.

Loren arched an eyebrow at her and then flicked Bleu a very emotionless look that he presumed was meant to conceal the myriad of feelings that were shining in his eyes. His prince had always been rather poor at hiding his emotions.

"Our allies have arrived," Loren said, deep voice smooth and calm, but still not hiding his amusement or his twisted sense of satisfaction.

He was gloating.

Bleu scowled at him. So what if he had found his mate and it was obvious he had feelings for her? He was still behaving in a more sane and reasonable manner than Loren had when he had met Olivia, or any of the damned males he knew had acted when they had met their fated females.

Although, using his incomplete bond as an excuse to punch his meddling prince in his perfect face was starting to look appealing.

Loren frowned back at him, his acute senses clearly warning him of the imminent threat.

His prince held his hand out to Taryn. "Would you like me to teleport you back to the war room?"

Bleu shot to his feet and growled at Loren. There was little point in concealing his feelings when Loren knew he felt something for Taryn.

"Hands off." He smacked his left one against the one Loren offered to Taryn, knocking it away. "I will escort Taryn back."

Loren smiled wickedly. "Very well… but I do have one request. You laid a hand on me, and I am required to report such behaviour to the council so you may be punished."

Damn. His prince was up to something. He had provoked him on purpose in order to get something he wanted in exchange for not snitching on him to the council.

Bleu had the sinking feeling he wasn't going to like whatever it was.

Loren clasped his hands together in front of him and cracked a grin that made Bleu reconsider punching him because it couldn't make his punishment any worse than it looked like it was going to be.

"We have a special guest. I will not tell the council about what you did if you are nice to him."

With that, blue-purple light chased over Loren's body and he disappeared, leaving a lingering outline of himself behind that faded as Bleu glared at it. A special guest? More like a living hell to Bleu. A week ago, he would have immediately thought Loren was talking about King Thorne, but now there was only one male who roused Bleu's anger and pain.

There was only one male who Loren would do anything to make sure that Bleu was nice to, even resorting to setting Bleu up so he could blackmail him into it.

"What was that all about?" Taryn whispered from behind him.

Bleu huffed.

"Prince Vail is coming."

CHAPTER 32

Bleu teleported into the main courtyard of the castle and set Taryn away from him, but refused to relinquish her right hand. He clutched it firmly in his left and battled the desire to take her far away from this realm where she felt so unsafe and threatened, to a place where they could be alone.

A place with no other males around to look upon her curves with hunger in their eyes.

He scowled at every unmated male in the courtyard, his glare lingering on those who didn't immediately look away, holding their gazes until they eventually backed down and turned to leave.

Beside him, Taryn was quiet, but he could feel her eyes on him, studying his face, warming his skin, heating his bones.

When every male had finally turned their focus elsewhere and the dark urge to fight had faded to a more manageable level, he shifted his gaze down to her. She smiled, a small one that spoke of knowing and also satisfaction. His little dragon was pleased that he was so fiercely protective of her, had silently challenged every male present and had won against all of them, driving them away.

He flexed his fingers against her hand, locking his more tightly between hers, showing her that his protective behaviour was born of more than a mere promise to keep her safe.

It was born of a deep and dark possessiveness.

It welled from his heart, from his most base and primal instincts as her mate.

She was his, and all who gazed upon her would know it, because he would make them intimately acquainted with pain and suffering, and death.

He tugged her forwards, turning his black glare on the soldiers ahead of them who guarded the grand entrance of the towering castle. The males wisely kept their eyes forwards, focuses locked on a point far beyond him. It didn't stop him from snarling quietly at them as he passed or pulling Taryn closer to him, switching sides with her so he could have his arm around her while still holding her hand, practically pinning her to his side.

He was surprised he didn't send his black formal attire away and replace it with the new armour Loren had given to him, or call his obsidian blade to his hand.

Fuck, being away from her had really messed with his head and his heart, and had apparently driven him deep into his instincts as her fated male, rousing them and bringing them to a point where he felt he was beginning to lose control.

He glanced down at her where she walked beside him, her footsteps faltering as she struggled to walk while held against him, her right arm pulled up by his, locked with his hand where it rested over her shoulder.

It hit him that he was acting exactly as he had vowed he would never behave on finding his mate.

He was behaving like a prick.

But she was his.

Mine.

He felt it in every molecule in his body as he gazed down at her. It drummed in his blood. Beat in his heart. Roared in his mind.

She was his.

Mine.

That word was a low possessive growl that rumbled through him.

It made him want to scrub a hand over his face and groan.

Hadn't he told Loren and Kyter that he would never act like this? Snarling such thoughts, or saying them aloud, felt stupid and cliché to him. He had said he wouldn't act like the other males he knew, but here he was, growling 'mine' over Taryn and getting in every unmated male's face, threatening them whether they had looked at her or not.

Gods help him.

He led her up to the war room, lost in his thoughts, in possessive and dangerous imaginings that had him aching to take her back to her room and stamp his claim on her. She wriggled against him, ramping up his desire as she turned his mind firmly towards thoughts of touching her again, and having her touch him.

He needed her.

The way her fingers toyed with his, thumb caressing and teasing his hand, and the feelings that flowed through their link, said he wasn't the only one indulging in wicked thoughts. Two days apart was far too long. He wasn't sure how he had survived that long without touching her.

He twirled her and had her pinned against the glittering pale grey stone wall of the corridor before she could even react, and had claimed her lips before she could loose a gasp. He swallowed the shocked sound as it turned into a groan, and joined that moan with one of his own as her hands came up to press against his chest, fingertips digging in hard through his black jacket. Her mouth was hot on his, desperate and wild, her kiss so fierce it made his blood catch fire. He gathered her closer, snaking his left arm around her waist, and kissed her harder, as desperate for more as she was.

A sound echoed along the corridor, a dim murmur of voices coming from the closed door far to his left.

The war room.

The sensible part of him said to stop but he couldn't. He needed his female. His beautiful mate.

She had better control than he did though and pushed him back, breaking free of his lips and turning her cheek to him when he tried to kiss her again. He settled for kissing along her jaw and down her neck, his mouth watering as his fangs elongated, a different hunger rising in him as he felt her pulse hammering against his lips.

Beating in his chest.

"Later," she whispered, and he could hear that she didn't want to stop, she wanted to continue what he had started.

But the demon kings and his prince were waiting in the war room.

For them.

Bleu drew down a deep breath to steady himself, closed his eyes and focused to purge the hunger from his mind and his body, slowly clawing back control. When his need had gone from a boil to a fierce simmering in his veins, he reluctantly released Taryn and stepped back.

She looked up at him, her striking violet-to-white eyes dark with the hunger he could still feel in her. His female needed. It was almost enough to have him lunging for her again, dragging her back against him for another kiss. Only her hand claiming his stopped him together with her reassuring smile, one that told him she would keep that promise she had made and as soon as the meeting was done, they would pick things back up where they had left off.

Which only made him want to rush the meeting.

It wasn't important.

So whatever they discussed might affect the future of the elf kingdom as well as the demon realms, and possibly all of Hell.

Big deal.

He closed his eyes and huffed, unimpressed with himself.

His kingdom came first. He had always placed it above his own needs and finding his mate wouldn't change that. He had a mission and he would complete it. Nothing would stand in his way.

No matter how tempting and beautiful she was.

A blush rose onto her cheeks as he stared at her, probably looking like a lovesick idiot. He certainly felt like one.

She tugged on his hand this time and he obediently followed her towards the arched wooden doors of the war room. He steeled himself as they approached it, preparing to see Vail again. The male had been helpful and seeing him with Rosalind had lessened his hatred towards Vail, but it hadn't lessened the pain he had locked deep in his heart. He wasn't sure it was possible to heal that hurt. It would always be there, imprinted on him at a time in his life when he had been most vulnerable, too young to shield himself against it or know better than to idolise someone.

He faltered as she reached for the doorknob and she looked back at him, a curious frown pulling her eyebrows down over her incredible eyes. They searched his, a flicker of concern in them that her feelings backed up.

Bleu sucked down a deep fortifying breath.

"Is it the other prince?" she whispered and turned to face him.

He nodded, because in that moment he realised that he could share anything with the female standing before him. He didn't have to hold anything back in order to protect himself because he knew she would never hurt him. It was right there in her eyes and in the way she squeezed his hand, sympathy and tenderness flowing from her and into him through their link.

"I served in his legion when he turned on his own people. I saw him kill those I called friend, but worse than that… he shattered… a part of me… the part that held him aloft, like a fucking god… idolised and adored him… like a fucking idiot." Bleu looked away from her when her eyebrows furrowed and she reached up to touch his cheek.

Her hand stopped just short, but he could still feel the heat of her skin and the comfort she had meant to offer, and he cursed himself for denying himself both of those things in some ridiculous need to maintain some sort of distance between them. He didn't want there to be any distance between them, not a single drop of air, but it was hard to overcome the instinct to protect himself. He sighed and exhaled hard, and fought to let it go. Taryn had shared her pain with him, and he wanted to share his with her. He wanted her to know him.

"When I joined the army, I worked hard with one goal." He opened his eyes and looked across at her, met her soft and tender gaze, felt it soothe the hurt beginning to brew inside him, tempering it. "I wanted to serve under Prince Vail. When I was placed into his legion, it was a dream come true… but it turned into a nightmare."

"You feel guilty that you survived."

Gods, did he.

"I saw so many die… and I should have died too… I should not have survived… but I did… because…" He sucked down another sharp breath and curled his fingers into fists as he forced the words he had always kept to himself out into the world for her to hear. "Because he spared me."

Her eyes widened.

Bleu broke away from her and shoved his fingers through his hair as he took agitated strides across the wide corridor, his heart pounding hard against his chest. He threw her a glance, caught the pity in her eyes, and growled.

"He looked right at me… covered in the blood of my friends… eyes wild and black… claws raised and poised to strike me down… and then he left… teleported… and I looked at the blood-soaked battlefield around me, a fight only a few had survived, my damn head spinning and ears ringing, and I knew… I knew he had spared me."

"He left because it was you," she whispered and his head spun and ears rang all over again as numbness swept through him on the heels of those words.

A realisation that left him cold.

Holy fuck.

Taryn was right.

Vail hadn't merely spared him. He hadn't been tired from the fight and done with it as Bleu had thought. Vail wasn't that sort of male. He had never backed down from a battle, leaving before his victory was assured.

He had come face to face with Bleu and hadn't been able to kill him, so he had found the strength to leave. He had chosen to end the battle because of him.

All of a sudden, the feeling that had always been with Bleu made a whole lot of sense. Taryn was right, and he felt guilty, but that feeling ran deeper than she knew, and he had ever acknowledged.

He had carried that guilt and shame with him through the centuries, a weight that had pressed down on his heart, not born of the fact he had survived Vail's attack but born of the fact he had subconsciously known he might have been able to spare so many of his friends and comrades if he had only possessed more courage and found the strength to fight to reach Vail earlier in the battle.

Thousands more might have survived.

Hell, he might have been able to stop the assault from ever happening if he had been in the right place at the right time, there near Vail when he had launched the attack.

He wasn't sure how to process that.

He looked at the closed arched wooden doors.

He wasn't sure how to proceed.

Vail was in that room. Waiting. Aware that he was coming. How the hell was he meant to behave around him now? It had been hard enough knowing how to act after discovering that Kordula had been controlling him all those times they had fought. Now he didn't have a damn clue what he was meant to do.

One thing was certain though.

He couldn't bury his head in the sand by turning away and letting the meeting proceed without him. He wasn't that fresh-faced youth anymore, the one who had tried to run away from the battle because he had been too afraid to face the male he had idolised as that male faced his darkest hour.

He had become a male who faced things head on, never backed down from a fight, and certainly never ran from a battle.

This was just another battle, and he would face it head on too, would take it one move at a time and adjust his strategy as he went, adapting to whatever happened. Eventually, he would win this fight and accept the things that had happened, and that there was nothing he could do to change the past, but right now there was a bigger battle that demanded his attention.

A war with a dragon that would decide the fate of Hell.

"You are decided?" Taryn murmured in a soft voice, and he nodded while silently thanking her for giving him time to reach a resolution and choose his course of action.

He took hold of her hand and she squeezed his, her striking eyes silently telling him that she would be there for him when he was ready to talk more about his past. It was an offer he would take her up on sooner rather than later. He needed to do it.

Iolanthe would tease him if she knew, but it was time he shared the burden he had carried for too long with someone else, letting them lift some of the weight from his shoulders. Taryn was that someone. Just as she would come to share her past with him, he would share his with her, and together they would work through everything and deal with it.

He led her to the doors, and shoved them open with his free one.

Almost everyone in the grand war room turned away from the huge map of Hell to look at him. He took them all in with one swift glance. King Thorne of the Third Realm had brought Sable with him, and the slender black-haired huntress stood near the right corner of the table map, her golden eyes fixed on Bleu and her demon mate's left hand on her right shoulder, dark claws pressing into her black t-shirt.

Bleu looked up at Thorne, meeting his red eyes before they leaped to a point beside Bleu. He bared his fangs at the demon, warning him to take his gaze off Taryn. The male obviously sensed the threat, because he pinned his focus back on the map and tunnelled his free hand through his tousled russet-brown hair, pulling it back from the dusky horns that curled from above his pointed ears, following the curve of them down to the lobe.

Beyond him, on the far side of the map, King Tegan of the Second Realm preened his obsidian horns, an act he did often if the smoothness of them was anything to go by. They looked as if they had been polished, the ridges no longer visible, but other markings had been placed on them, intricate tribal carvings that were inlaid with gold. His thoughtful black gaze was the only one to have remained on the map. The impressive seven foot tall warrior had been born for battle, and Bleu had gained the distinct impression the few times their paths had crossed that he resented being born the leader of the Second Realm, one that was peaceful and rarely went to war.

He leaned over the map, planting large hands on the edge of the table, the muscles of his bare chest and shoulders bulging as they supported his weight. A hank of wild black hair fell down and he huffed and preened it back again.

Bleu was glad the male had chosen to keep his attention on the imminent threat and not his female.

The bastard was too good looking for a demon. The gods only knew how many females had fallen victim of him. Bleu had seen him flash a smile at a female once during a gathering and that female had fainted.

Literally fucking fainted.

King Tegan had been all too willing to administer first aid to the poor creature.

She was probably now part of the harem he apparently kept in his black castle.

To King Tegan's right stood a beautiful female with a fall of straight white hair that her milky skin almost matched. It blended into her white corseted dress, and the paleness of her attire, her skin and her hair, made her blue eyes look ethereal and stunningly bright.

Those eyes drifted to rest on Bleu and cold swept through him in the second before he moved his gaze down to the map.

He swore she chuckled right in his head.

The phantom queen of the First Realm.

He suppressed the shiver that tried to run through him. Phantoms were dangerous. Their beauty and grace enchanted males and lured them under their spell, making it easier for the female to turn them incorporeal in order to mate with them and condemning them to an eternity as a spirit. If they didn't feed on their soul anyway.

Somehow, King Valador, Melia's fallen demon mate, had given her flesh and substance, allowing them to live together in the First Realm.

Queen Melia had assumed the role as King of the First Realm after the death of Valador and was set to rule until their son, Tarwyn, came of age.

Bleu lifted his curious gaze to the female beside Melia as the queen spoke to her. They were strikingly similar.

It was only the feel of another's gaze on him that had him looking away from the pair of females.

Off to his left, beyond Loren, Rosalind the witch stood beside her mate, all fairness and light in comparison to him, with her wavy golden hair spilling around her shoulders and almost glowing in the bright light coming in through the tall windows at her back. She smiled softly at Bleu, one that made her blue eyes sparkle.

Vail growled low in his throat and slung an arm around her slender shoulders, his fingers curling over to pull on the black material of her dress. Those pale slender fingers transformed into claws as his armour completed itself. She sighed and looked up at her mate. Bleu looked at him too. Not a single ounce of regret touched Vail's features, ones that were close to Loren's now that his black hair had been trimmed and some of the darkness had left his violet eyes. Vail's pointed ears flared back against the sides of his head and Bleu expected him to bare his fangs on a hiss.

He didn't.

He looked at Taryn instead.

Bleu hissed at Vail, flashing his emerging fangs, warning the male away from her.

Vail frowned at her and then at him, all aggression gone as he raised an eyebrow and his violet eyes filled with curiosity, laced with something that surprised Bleu.

Happiness.

There was no mistaking that glow in his eyes as the corners of his lips curled into a faint smile.

Vail was happy for him.

The world truly had gone mad.

Bleu was heading right there with the rest of it, because while he wasn't sure how Loren had managed to convince the council to agree to Vail's presence in the kingdom, there was a part of him that hoped the elf male could do something in the impending battle that would help his cause. He wanted Vail to give the elders and the people of their kingdom a reason to trust him again.

"Shall we begin?" Loren's deep voice cut through the silence and there was a murmur of agreement.

"The dragon skirted the Second Kingdom, passing along the other side of this mountain range." King Tegan couldn't have sounded more irritated if he had tried as he ran his left hand along the curving spine of mountains to the north of his kingdom, the front of his black leather trousers pressing against the edge of the three dimensional map. "He remained firmly inside the border of the First Realm."

A faint purple-red glow lit his dark eyes, a corona around his pupils that warned the male's mood was already degenerating.

King Tegan was hungry for a battle.

Bleu was surprised he hadn't risked crossing the border into the First Realm in order to engage Tenak.

Still, the male would have his war soon enough.

"He came through my land on this course, decimating all in his path." Thorne charted one that had many in the room falling silent, including Bleu. Tenak had cut right through the heart of the Third Realm. "He has recruited an army along the way. Men from my ranks, traders in the countryside, even some demons from the surrounding realms. We managed to evacuate some of the villages in his path, but others were not so lucky. We have lost many warriors and subjects already."

Thorne sighed and preened his left horn, stroking his fingers along the dusky curve of it. Sable rested her right palm on his shoulder and he looked down at her, pain visible in his crimson eyes. The demon king had lost enough of his men and his people in a war with the Fifth Realm only a few lunar cycles ago. Losing so many more in such a short span of time was taking its toll on the large male.

"We will make him pay for what he has done," Bleu said and Thorne raised his head, looked across at him and nodded.

Queen Melia drifted forwards, coming closer to the map, gliding away from her companion.

"I have had word that the dragon's army has passed through our outlying lands and has banked towards the centre of my kingdom. Scouts have reported he is on a direct course with a point beyond the demon kingdoms, and yours. It seems he is intending to recruit more, possibly from the other realms that lie that way." Her soft voice floated around the room, an eerie quality to it. She ghosted her hand over the map, the motion strangely light and slow. Bleu suppressed another shudder. He had run afoul of a phantom once or twice in his lifetime and the experience had been enough to have his blood freezing whenever he thought about what Melia was. She lifted her bright blue eyes to him, as if she knew his secret fear, sending another shiver through him. "Tenak's army is strong, with many dragons among its ranks. My men are engaged with them now. My advisor Isla came to warn me and she has witnessed the battle, so I brought her with me as she has valuable information."

Bleu had the feeling that Isla was more than an advisor to Melia.

More than another phantom made flesh somehow.

If he had to guess, he would say she was a sibling.

He nodded towards the only realm on the course she had pointed out, wondering why she had chosen to speak of it as if there were more in that direction.

"Do you believe any from the free realm will be joining the battle on either side?" King Tegan said.

Isla stiffened.

Curious.

Melia had avoided naming the free realm during her report, and now Isla had reacted to hearing those words from Tegan's lips.

"No," Bleu said and watched the female closely. "We sent word but none of the sirens, nymphs, incubi and succubi, shifter species or furies offered allegiance and stated they would not side with a dragon either."

Isla didn't react to any of those species. He canted his head as he watched her. She carefully lifted her right hand, tucked a braid that hung from her temple behind her ear, blending it into her long hair. The blue crystals around the end of it stood out against the white of her hair. The braid that hung from her left temple bore crystals at the end too, but these were red. Her pale hand was shaking when she lowered it again, flexed her fingers and then tucked her hands behind her back.

Unlike Melia, Isla wore colourful clothing, tight deep blue leather trousers and a matching corset and knee-high boots that were accented in vivid cerulean where the leather had rubbed.

Bleu almost smiled when he remembered there was another species who called the free realm home.

"Although, we did not come to an agreement with the vampires," he said and she tensed. A vampire then. She feared a vampire. "I am sure the Preux Chevaliers would join us if we turned off the portal and stopped sunlight from entering our realm."

Isla paled, turning as white as her hair.

Loren's steady gaze landed on him, and Bleu glanced at him, fielded a confused look from his prince, but refused to stop when he felt so close to finding out why the female was afraid of a vampire from the free realm, from the Preux Chevaliers no less.

His eyes widened the tiniest amount before he schooled his features, hiding his surprise from the room.

Lord Van der Garde, leader of the Preux Chevaliers, an army of vampires who acted as mercenaries in Hell, had a deep distrust of females and despised liars.

Was it possible?

He couldn't resist finding out.

"Lord Van der Garde even requested we do so as he desired to join the battle." Bleu kept his eyes locked on Isla as the air of confusion around Loren grew and a few others in the room joined him in staring at Bleu. The female glanced at Melia, and Melia drifted closer to her, her ice-cold eyes coming to rest on Bleu, chilling his blood and making his senses warn him of danger. He was angering the First King with his questioning, but he couldn't stop now. "Should we put it to a vote?"

"We do not condone vampires near us," the First King said, her voice as calm and smooth as still water but holding darkness beneath the placid surface, a threat that he knew he would be wise to heed.

He was too fascinated by Isla though.

She looked ready to bolt.

What had happened between her and Lord Van der Garde?

The room whirled upwards and he stumbled backwards, confused for a heartbeat before he noticed Loren's hand on his left arm, dragging him away from the table. Loren shoved him into a corner and Bleu looked at him. His prince did not look impressed.

"Must I remind you that vampires were on the side of the demons from the Devil's domain in the battle a century ago that claimed King Valador's life?" Loren snapped in the elf tongue and the amusement Bleu had been feeling drained from him.

He had forgotten that.

"I am sorry. I will apologise immediately," Bleu said.

Loren shook his head. "It will not be necessary… but why did you lie about the vampires?"

Bleu glanced beyond his prince to the two phantom females. "I have the feeling that the one called Isla is or was somehow involved with Lord Van der Garde."

Loren's right eyebrow shot up and he surprised Bleu by looking back over his shoulder at the female in question. It wasn't like his prince to behave in such a manner. He had expected Loren to resist the desire to look at her and take the more respectful approach of concealing his curiosity by treating her in the same manner as he did everyone else in the room.

"You believe she is the reason?" Loren hissed in a low voice, revealing that his intrigue ran as deep as Bleu's own and that he wasn't the only one who had noticed Lord Van der Garde's behaviour during the time they had worked together on the side of the Third Realm.

Bleu nodded. "I believe she is the reason the vampire doesn't trust females."

"Fascinating." Loren looked back at her again. Tensed. Bleu looked past him and found everyone watching them. His prince released him, cleared his throat and walked back to the table as if nothing had happened and they hadn't been hiding in a corner, acting in an almost conspiratorial manner. "Let us discuss our plan and see what we can come up with. Taryn will lead us by sharing information on a vision she witnessed."

Bleu didn't like the sound of that. The vision had shaken her.

He moved back to her side, standing close to her so she would feel him there, would know that he was there for her if she needed him. He listened to her as she relayed what she had seen in her vision and fielded a few questions from the demon kings, and then tried to focus on everyone else in the room as they began to discuss ideas about what they should do.

Impossible.

Being so close to Taryn had all of his focus drifting back to her the second he tried to pull it away. He took in everything that was being banded around in the room, but couldn't find his voice to speak out against any of it. He felt Loren glance at him several times, and then Sable joined in too, but nothing he did could convince him to take his eyes off his beautiful mate as she stood tall beside him, trying to make her voice heard in the din of chatter.

It was only when she mentioned the garrison where he had taken her when he had teleported them away from Tenak's castle that he felt a stirring need to agree with her. That need only grew when the demon kings and Loren talked over her, ignoring what she had offered and making his little female withdraw into herself.

Bleu frowned at everyone present. "Taryn is right and we should move away from the castle."

Loren arched an eyebrow at him and held his hand up. The room fell silent.

"The stronghold is ideal. It is a defensive position close to the free realm, bordering the First Realm of the demons, and we have supplies in place there." Bleu leaned over and planted his right palm against the edge of the map and pointed to the spot where the garrison was with his left hand, a small area that was close to not only the First Realm but the free one too. "It is away from any villages on both the elf side and the demon side."

Everyone murmured in agreement and he felt Taryn move closer to him, sensed her warmth flow through their link. She was pleased he had made her voice heard in the room. He was glad she had been brave enough to mention it, because it really was ideal.

Her vision had been of the castle in ruins and the battle taking place there. By moving the battle away from the castle, they might stand a chance at changing the future she had witnessed.

He rubbed the pad of his left thumb across his lower lip and frowned at the map. "We will need to infiltrate the enemy ranks to steal the sword back. It is pivotal… whoever possesses it will win. There is no doubt about that."

Rosalind rocked on her heels, almost bouncing on the spot, causing her drab black traditional witch's dress to sway around her legs, and when he looked at her she was grinning, starlight sparkling in her blue eyes. "I have a cunning plan."

Everyone stared at her in silence, stony faces waiting for her to explain it.

Apparently this was the wrong reaction.

She huffed, folded her arms across her chest, and muttered, "You all need to watch more classic British telly."

Everyone continued to stare at her.

"Perhaps you should explain your plan, Little Wild Rose." Vail lowered his head and murmured the words into her ear, and her cheeks darkened, the starlight in her eyes exploded into fire, and she leaned towards him.

Vail's gaze darkened the moment she did, his breathing deepening and eyes dropping to her throat.

Bleu was sorely tempted to tell them to get a room, but he liked his head where it was—attached to his body.

Loren cleared his throat. Vail stilled. Rosalind's blush deepened and she blinked rapidly.

"Um… I was going to address the dragon in the room and say that I will mask Taryn by changing the colour of her scales," Rosalind said, a wobble of uncertainty in her voice now. She glanced at her mate. Dragged her eyes away. Glanced at him again. With each one, her eyes grew darker, pupils expanding to swallow the blue of her irises. She cleared her throat again but couldn't clear the rosiness of desire from her cheeks as easily. "It's a simple spell really, and it should allow her to enter the enemy's camp and get close enough to steal the sword."

"No." Bleu left no room for argument in his rejection, but it didn't stop several people including Taryn from voicing one. He crossed his arms over his chest, scowled at everyone, and made damn sure they realised that he wasn't going to budge on this. "Taryn is not going in there alone. She needs back up."

"Perhaps we could convince Loke to help," Loren said.

"We do not have time," Bleu countered. "Loke is great as a back up plan, but Tenak knows him. Rosalind would have to change the colour of his scales too."

Rosalind shook her head. "I won't have enough strength to cast two spells like that if I'm also expected to shield the garrison and the lands surrounding it as I did for Thorne in the battle in the Third Realm."

There was more to her refusal than a drain on her energy too. It was there in her eyes as she tossed a wary look at her mate. She was nervous about using so much magic around Vail, afraid it would send him off the deep end and drive him back into the madness that seemed to have abated in their time together. Abated but not disappeared. Vail's eyes were already growing black and they were only talking about magic.

Rosalind turned to Vail and Bleu looked away, giving them some privacy as she sought to soothe her mate.

The room grew noisy as a debate broke out about how they could provide Taryn with back up if they couldn't use another dragon.

Bleu held his hand up and came right out with it.

"I will shift into a dragon."

Everyone stared at him, stunned expressions on all their faces.

Loren was the first to find his voice. "How?"

Bleu looked to his left, at his prince. "I will drink Taryn's blood."

He could almost feel the heat of her blush where she stood to his right, and gods, he wanted to look at her. His heart pounded, blood thundering with a need to shift his eyes down to her and take in her beauty as her cheeks blazed crimson. There was hunger in her and it ran through him too, ignited by remembering the last time he had bitten her, a memory that flooded his mind with the wicked thoughts he had heard in hers because of the siren's blood in his veins.

Loren's violet gaze moved to her.

Bleu growled low in his throat, a feral snarl that had a few in the room gasping.

He was halfway to calling his armour and jamming his clawed thumbs into Loren's eyes so his prince couldn't look at his fated female when Loren slid him a black look, but one edged with knowing and a sprinkling of amusement.

He could almost hear Loren's thoughts, and his prince was right. He was acting exactly as Loren had behaved around Olivia, and Kyter around Iolanthe, and even Thorne around Sable.

He had become territorial, extremely possessive and protective, and downright obsessed with his female, and he wasn't going to apologise for it.

Fuck them.

He didn't take his eyes off Loren, but mentally he looked at everyone in the room and said 'fuck you all'. He was a male in the middle of a mating and he didn't give a damn what they thought. The only thing that mattered was Taryn and securing her as his female.

His forever.

"I think we are done here for today. Relay the plan to your people and we will meet again tomorrow to go over the final details." Loren didn't take his eyes off Bleu either, held his gaze even as everyone filed out of the room, leaving them alone in it. When the doors closed, his prince's lips tugged into a wicked smile. "Feeling a little touchy today, are we not? A little territorial perhaps?"

Bleu looked away from him and groaned when he saw that Taryn hadn't left the room. This really wasn't a conversation he wanted happening in front of her. It wasn't a conversation he wanted happening at all.

"You growled at me, Bleu, and looked ready to raise a hand to me again." Loren pressed onwards, mischievous bastard, clearly amused by his plight. "Did I hear and see that wrongly?"

Bleu refused to answer. Maybe if he was silent, Loren would drop it.

Nope.

Loren grinned. "I believe someone is acting like a 'prick'… is that not what you called it when I was territorial about Olivia?"

"I am not," Bleu snapped. "It is nothing. Your imagination is running wild, my prince."

Loren chuckled. "Is that so? Then if I do this…"

He turned his smile on Taryn.

Bleu was on him in an instant, both hands wrapped around his throat as he snarled at him and pushed him down onto the stone flags. He sat astride the male's chest, shoving his arms down with his knees. He tried to pull himself away but he couldn't. His body had other plans, his primal instincts at the helm. Nothing he did made a difference. He kept tightening his hold on Loren's throat, choking him.

Loren managed to wrestle his arms free and his hands snagged Bleu's wrists. He struggled, trying to prise Bleu's hands off him. His prince's lips moved but Bleu couldn't hear anything over the maddening rush of blood through his ears and the dark whispers to kill the male for daring to flirt with his female.

"Bleu."

He snarled and ignored that softer feminine voice as it curled around him. He had to kill the male. No, he had to stop. He didn't want to hurt Loren. Loren had to die.

"Bleu," the female voice said again and this time it caught and held him, and the warmth of his name on her lips broke through the darkness like a shaft of light, driving it back.

He stared at his hands where they held Loren's throat, his eyes widened and he released him and staggered onto his feet.

Taryn touched his shoulder. He jerked away from her and paced across the room, putting himself as far as he could get from Loren. Gods, he had tried to kill him, a male he loved deeply. He hadn't wanted to hurt him, but he hadn't been able to stop himself. That hunger to hurt him still lingered and he feared it would rise up again to overwhelm him.

He shoved his fingers through his unruly blue-black hair, clawed his scalp and drew blood.

Loren picked himself up and rubbed his throat. "I deserved that."

He didn't.

Bleu wrestled with himself and managed to find his voice. "I'm sorry."

"How long have you known?" Loren said.

That question opened a floodgate inside him and Bleu let it all spill out, telling his prince everything, beginning at the moment he had first set eyes on Taryn.

"The bond is triggered?" Loren asked with a concerned glance at Taryn, his eyes only landing on her for a split-second before they wisely moved back to Bleu. He still wasn't totally in control of himself and even that brief glance at Taryn was enough to have him wanting Loren's blood again.

He breathed deep and nodded to answer him.

Loren looked concerned. "Incomplete?"

Bleu nodded again. He knew it was dangerous to leave it in such a state, especially when he was going to be around so many males during the upcoming battle.

Unmated males.

Just the thought of that was enough to have his blood burning again, catching fire. He itched with a need to track down all of the unmated males and kill them before they could look at his mate and try to steal her from him.

She was precious.

His treasure.

Gods, he was thinking like a damned dragon.

He glanced across at Taryn. The way she was looking at him, the possessive heat in her gaze, told him that was her thoughts, her feelings, flowing through him too and bolstering his own ones, making them stronger. She viewed him as precious. Her treasure.

That pleased him way too damn much.

"Do not leave it incomplete, Bleu," Loren said in the elf tongue, concealing their conversation from Taryn.

Bleu sighed and looked back at his prince, all of the fears he had been suppressing rising to the fore as his fight left him. "It isn't that simple. Our history… my history…"

He wasn't a good mate. He wasn't a good male. He hadn't done anything right by Taryn. He had hurt her. Hunted her.

Loren exhaled softly, his expression shifting, revealing tenderness and warmth that was a strange comfort to him, leaving him feeling as if he wasn't alone and Loren was in his corner, a back up he sorely needed.

"I have never seen you like this," Loren said in their tongue. "I know it is not a product of the bond, Bleu… if you love Taryn, then you must fight for her."

Loren was right.

He loved Taryn.

What he felt for her had brought with it a realisation that profoundly affected him, strengthening his feelings for her.

He had never really known love before now.

What he felt for Taryn was powerful. It controlled him, ruled his actions and his heart, and he could think of only her. What he had felt for Sable was nothing but a shadow of what he felt for Taryn, easily pushed out of existence by the strength of the light of Taryn's love for him and his love for her.

It was endless.

Infinite.

Unconditional.

A love that he knew would last forever, even if there was no bond and they weren't mates.

He would love this female with every shred of his heart, drop of his blood, and piece of his soul, whether she was his fated one or not.

He had never felt for anyone the way he felt about Taryn. She was his everything. She was all he needed.

She completed him as no other could. The other half of his soul. But it was frightening after everything he had been through, all the changes that had happened too quickly and had shaken his world.

He wasn't sure he was strong enough to handle her rejecting him.

It would destroy him.

But he had been born to fight, not run from a battle.

And he would fight for her.

CHAPTER 33

Gods, her mate was beautiful.

Even more so now.

He stole her breath, robbing her awareness of the world with it, leaving her feeling dazed and in awe as she gazed upon him. Her incredible male.

Her tiny dragon.

Not so tiny anymore.

She flinched when he crashed into the side of the green hill, scuffing the grass and leaving a long muddy track in his wake as he slowly slid to a halt.

Beautiful but not entirely graceful.

Bleu pushed himself up, huge talons curling into the soft ground that gave beneath his weight, and shook his head, his six long black horns becoming a blur in the bright light.

He snorted, his jowls peeled back off twin rows of razor sharp white teeth, and then his huge violet eyes dropped to her where she stood a short distance away, sharpening as they focused and challenged her.

She didn't dare let the laugh that had been bubbling up her throat slip free. She had made the mistake of laughing at him the first time he had crash landed a few hours ago and that had earned her more than just a growl or a scowl in her direction. He had come running at her, heavy footfalls shaking the ground, tipping her off balance. It had ended with her planted on her backside and her mate towering over her, his beaked snout close to her face.

Her heart had almost pounded right out of her chest.

Not wholly because of fear though.

Bleu's display of dominance, strength and aggression had triggered her dragon instincts, leaving her a quivering mess, aching for her mate to shift back and kiss the breath from her.

She wasn't sure he knew what he had done to her in that moment. How hot he had made her, igniting a wildfire in her veins.

Gods.

Just thinking about it had heat stirring in her blood again, her pulse accelerating and body coming alive, hungry for his touch.

Bleu's huge violet eyes narrowed and he inhaled deeply, stilled and then his eyes widened, his elliptical pupils dilating, and the black spines down his neck and back rippled. He was aware of her need.

He turned towards her and the light reflected off his black scales, sending a blue shimmer across them. She had never seen any dragon like him. It was rare for one of her kind to have six horns, two sprouting from the ridges above his eyes, two from the crown of his head, and a further two from the back behind his ears. He was larger than most male dragons too, packed with sinewy muscle and a wingspan that dwarfed her own.

He lowered his enormous head, his long neck stretching as he stalked closer to her, the underside of his jaw held barely a few feet from the grass. His muscular shoulders worked with each slow step, his wings shifting restlessly and his long tail swishing side to side.

She raised her hand when he was close enough for her to touch him and rested her palm on his hard snout between his nostrils. He exhaled again and then sniffed, and canted his head.

"Shall I show you how it is done?" she said, voice a low murmur as she tried to wrestle her desire back under control and focus on their lesson.

It was hard when her body was still buzzing from the feel of his fangs in her flesh. He had bitten her wrist this time, insisting that he take blood from that spot, and it still throbbed madly, a constant reminder of where he had sunk his fangs into her. She had wanted him to bite her neck again but she hadn't had the heart to push him, not when he had seemed on edge, his feelings relaying his nerves to her and also the lingering trace of guilt. That guilt was there whenever he gazed at her neck, and she wished she could find a way to help him move past what he had done to her. She had forgiven him, but he hadn't forgiven himself.

"Controlling the shift is the easy part," she continued and rubbed between his nostrils, smiling as his eyes fluttered closed. Her mate like that. "Learning to fly is something else, and you will have to learn to fight on the wing too."

She had the feeling it wasn't going to be easy for him. It had taken him a few attempts to shift into a dragon, and he had spent the past few hours lumbering around the valley, barely making it a few metres off the ground before he hit it again. Normally hard.

The valley was filled with the evidence of his failures, long dark scars that criss-crossed the perfect green grass, making it look as if a battle had taken place, not a simple flying lesson.

Bleu snarled and reared back, the suddenness of it startling her and causing her to stagger backwards, placing some distance between them. He threw his head to one side and then the other, a constant growl curling from between his clenched fangs. She gasped and held her hands up to him as immense pain ran through her. Pain that came from him.

"Bleu!" She reached for him but he stumbled away from her, his hind left leg gave out and he slammed onto his side, his head smacking hard off the hillside.

Taryn ran down the gentle slope to him and skidded to a halt as she realised what was happening.

He was shifting back, and by the looks of things, it wasn't a controlled transformation. Something was wrong.

"Bleu," she hollered and raced over to him, reaching him just as his body began to shrink, bones shifting beneath his flesh as it lost all of its scales, turning creamy and smooth.

Another pained growl left his lips and his wild violet eye looked down at her, the agony she could feel flowing through him shining in it.

She couldn't breathe as she kneeled beside his head and petted him, stroking along the line of his muzzle, trying to comfort him and take some of his pain away. His eye closed and he snarled, his jowl peeling back off his fangs, shifting beneath her hand. His body shrank, wings disappearing into it, and his head began to transform. The change was quick from that point, and in little more than a blink of her eyes, he was an elf again.

A very naked elf.

He lay with his head in her lap, curled up on his side and shivering, his pale skin spotted with sweat as he breathed hard.

Taryn ran her fingers through his blue-black hair, smoothing the damp strands back from his forehead and his pointed ear. He groaned when she accidentally brushed the tip of it and his eyes fluttered open. Dark-sounding words in his own tongue left his lips as he looked up at her, violet eyes still swimming with the pain echoing through him. He was cursing. She had noticed he tended to do that in the elf tongue rather than one she could understand, as if she might be offended if she heard him swearing or would think less of him.

"What happened?" she whispered, wanting to know because she didn't understand and she needed to if she was going to find a way to stop it from happening again.

He closed his eyes, slumped against her and blew out his breath. "I ran out."

She averted her gaze when he rolled onto his back, exposing himself for a split second before his armour appeared, black scales rippling over his bare skin in the same way they had when he had transformed into a dragon.

"How did you run out? It has only been a few hours." She frowned down at his face, keeping her gaze locked on his closed eyes.

They opened and met hers. "I did not take enough."

"Oh." Because he had felt guilty about biting her and taking her blood. Her frown intensified. "That was stupid of you."

He frowned right back at her.

She didn't give him a chance to speak.

"I know you think you are being noble by only taking a small amount of blood from me… and that you feel guilty still even though I have forgiven you… but what in the gods' names did you think you were doing?" She almost growled that question at him as her mind filled with all the possibilities, most of them ending with a horrible outcome. One haunted her most of all though, chilled her blood and left her cold and empty, and it was one she knew would make him see sense. "What if this had happened when you had been flying, Bleu?"

"I could have teleported."

She did growl now. "You are weak from the uncontrolled shift… do you think you can teleport?"

He looked away from her and it was all the answer she needed.

"I will not have you kill yourself because you think you are doing me some sort of kindness… sparing me from something. If you will not take enough blood to make your abilities as a dragon last, then I will not give you any at all." She went to stand but his hands shot up over his head and locked tight around her bare upper arms. She looked down at him, right into his eyes, and waited for him to speak. When he didn't, she gave him an ultimatum. "You either take the blood I am offering to you… or I go alone into my brother's camp to steal the sword."

He flashed long white daggers at her, his violet eyes brightening in response to her threat. It was more of a promise.

"Fine," he ground out, eyes darkening by degrees, and dragged her right arm forwards, towards his face. "But remember you asked for this by leaving me no other choice."

She gasped as he twisted her arm towards him and sank his fangs into the tender skin on the underside of her forearm.

The brief sting of pain was followed by a rolling wave of bliss, warmth that heated her right down to her bones, stirring fire in her veins. Her eyes slipped shut and she sank into the flames, let them flutter around her. Dragon fire. He made it burn in her blood, rousing her deepest instincts, the ones that shoved at her control.

A growl curled from her lips as those instincts seized hold of her, forcing her eyes open, making her look at the male drinking from her.

Her fated one.

The hunger to mate with him was strong, near impossible to deny but she fought it anyway, aware that if she gave into it, she might end up with her heart broken.

Bleu's eyes locked with hers, held them firm, cast a spell on her that had her quivering all over, aching and hot with need. She had to mate. The urge crawled over her skin, making it itch and feel too hot. She needed to satisfy this hunger, needed to scratch that itch he had started when he had come at her, all brute force and wicked power. She shuddered as he pulled on her blood, a deeper one that had it all rushing towards him, and gods she wanted him to take more of her into him. She wanted to be bound to him.

She wanted to possess him.

He was hers.

He would be no one else's.

Never.

She bared her sharpening teeth and snarled through them, a deep rumbling growl born of her possessive thoughts. The urge to fight welled up, intoxicating, seeping into her mind and her heart to take control of it. She had to fight whoever might take her mate from her.

A female flickered into her mind.

The one with the black hair and golden eyes.

She had seen the way that female had gazed at Bleu with affection in those beautiful eyes in the war room.

Taryn snarled again. She would claw the female's eyes out, ensuring she could never gaze at her mate again.

Bleu was hers.

No one else's.

She looked over her left shoulder, towards the towering pale castle where the female waited, probably for Bleu.

A roar left her lips and she shoved onto her feet, tearing her wrist away from Bleu's fangs.

She would slay the female and then Bleu would be hers. He would love her.

Forever.

A strong hand clamped down on her right arm just above her elbow and spun her to face the owner. She went to snarl and it ended in a gasp as his mouth descended on hers, fierce and hot, stoking the fire in her blood to a thousand degrees. She moaned and clutched his muscular shoulders, pressed closer to him and lost herself in the kiss, forgetting her desire to kill as it was replaced with a desire to drown in this male and his hunger for her.

His lips broke away from hers, their foreheads pressed together, but his hands still held her, gripping her with the same intensity as she clung to him.

"Better?" he murmured, his husky deep voice making her insides quiver and flip, and she melted against him, unsure how to answer his question because she didn't understand it.

Something had been wrong?

He pulled back and his black eyebrows drew down, his violet eyes searching hers. A sigh left those lips she desperately wanted on hers again and she trembled when he brushed the knuckles of his left hand across her cheek.

"Who did you want to kill?" he whispered and she recalled that she had desired to do such a thing.

She slowly looked back at the castle, felt ridiculous now as she thought about it, but at the time the need had been fierce, gripping her tightly, and it had felt like the right thing to do. The only thing to do.

"The black-haired female," she said in a low voice, little more than a murmur as fear took hold of her, her heart whispering that her male was going to be upset with her and that he was going to defend the female, maybe even confess his desire for the mortal.

Taryn tried to pull away, a sudden need to distance herself gripping her, but Bleu held her too tightly, not allowing her to escape.

He sighed. Husked, “She is nothing to me, Taryn. It is just the bond messing with you. I view all males as a threat, and you view all females.”

That wasn’t true. She didn’t view the phantom females as a threat.

She only viewed the mortal female she knew to be a rival for his affection as one.

“She has feelings for you.” She lifted her eyes to meet his, put force behind those words that she hoped made it clear that he couldn’t fool her into thinking otherwise. She knew what she had seen and she trusted her dragon instincts, and they were the one labelling the mortal as a threat, not the bond.

“As a friend.” There was something in the way he said that and the sorrow that flitted across his feelings that rang alarm bells in her mind and had her on the warpath again.

“But you desired something more?” She broke free of his grip and backed away from him, a dull ache starting up in her chest, one that grew sharper with each beat of her heart.

“Taryn.” Bleu reached for her but she shook her head. She wouldn’t go back to him, not until she knew the truth. He sighed and lowered his hand, his shoulders sagging with it. “I thought I had stronger feelings for her… but I was mistaken. You made me see that.”

Her eyes widened. “Me?”

He nodded. “I was… lonely… and it made me believe that I felt something for Sable… but seeing you again made me realise that I felt nothing for her beyond friendship. I wanted someone to love me, and someone to love, and I settled on the first female I saw who I found attractive.”

Taryn snarled at that.

Bleu held his hand up. “Let me finish before you go on a rampage.”

She had half a mind to refuse, but the tender edge to his violet eyes and the emotions that flowed through their link had her remaining where she was, because she had the feeling that this was a monumental moment for him, that her male rarely spoke of his feelings and this was difficult for him, and important.

For both of them.

“Sable could never have given me what I wanted… because there is only one female in all the realms who could give me that… and that is you, Taryn.” He shook his head when she opened her mouth to speak. “No… not because of fate or a bond… but because of the way you look at me… the way you make me feel when I’m around you. You give me a purpose, and that purpose is to protect you… to always make you happy… to take care of you… because… it is you I love.”

Taryn stared at him, reeling, mind racing and thoughts scrambling.

His look turned uncomfortable and he scrubbed a hand around the back of his neck, and a ripple of hurt went through him. It drove her into action.

Before he could turn away or withdraw or teleport or something equally as annoying, she hurled herself against him, wrapped her arms around his neck and kissed him. He moaned, slipped his arms around her waist, and held her against him so hard that she couldn't breathe, but she didn't care as she sank into the kiss and let his words run around her mind, using them to chase away the ones that had started to haunt her.

Teaching Bleu how to shift into a dragon had brought a moment of brightness into a dark time, but it had also made something else hit home.

Her brother would die if their plan succeeded.

Bleu stopped kissing her and pulled back. "What is wrong?"

She shook her head and kissed him again, trying to make him and herself forget about it. He had just told her that he loved her, and she wanted to say the same to him, but thoughts of her brother stole her voice and darkened what should have been one of the happiest moments of her life. Bleu refused her and his hands caught her shoulders, pushing her away.

"Tell me, Taryn," he whispered, so imploring and tender that tears welled up in her eyes. He frowned at them, lifted his left hand and swept the pad of his thumb beneath her right eye and then her left one, dashing them away. "Why are you sad?"

That question made her truly believe everything he had told her, because the look on his handsome face said he needed to know so he could make her happy again. She wasn't sure that was possible.

"The battle… I might lose a part of myself—will lose a part of myself." She looked away from him and sighed as the thoughts she had been trying to shut out crowded her mind.

"I can imagine how that feels," he murmured and she believed that too. This time, she could feel it in him, a pang that was familiar to her now that she faced losing her brother. He sighed. "I have come close to losing my sister a few times, and I feel I would be empty without her in my life."

Empty.

That hit her hard and tears burned her eyes and stung her nose. She turned away before he could see them this time and stared at the beautiful lands that surrounded her, green and lush, like something out of a fairy-tale. But they seemed to have lost all colour and warmth as she looked at them now, feeling cold to the bone.

Another sigh escaped Bleu. "I can feel you, remember? There is no use trying to hide things from me, not when I feel your pain as if it is my own."

He moved around her and brushed his left knuckles across her cheek, his tender gaze stealing her breath and warming her cold heart. He opened his hand and cupped her cheek, trailed his fingers along her jaw and tipped her head up.

She ached for him to say something, anything that might stop her from thinking about how she was standing on the brink of losing a connection that had filled her from the moment she was born.

She had never been alone.

Never.

She feared it.

He seemed to read that in her mind, because he smiled softly, his violet gaze filled with warmth but also a ribbon of fear, and whispered the most beautiful words she had ever heard. “You are not alone, Taryn. I am yours… if you want me.”

Gods, did she.

She wanted him with all of her heart.

“I am tired of fighting this… are you not tired too? We were made for each other. I honestly feel that… two halves of one soul… two hearts that were always meant to be together… that were created to complete each other.” He swept his thumb up her cheek and she couldn’t deny it, or the fire that burned through her in response to his heated but tender look.

She stood on the brink of losing a connection to someone she had loved, but she was also on the brink of forging a new one with someone she loved.

Someone she loved with all of her heart.

A male who did complete her, who made her feel safe and warm, cherished and protected, but strong too. His love gave her strength and courage, hope and conviction, and she knew that if she accepted the heart he was offering to her and the future he wanted for them, that she would always feel this way—filled with light when she had lived through so much darkness.

She didn’t need to fly. She didn’t need the blue skies of the mortal realm. She didn’t need anything that had once been everything to her.

She only needed Bleu.

He was her infinite sky. He made her soar while her feet never left the ground, made her warm as if sunshine bathed her skin, and made her feel whole.

He was her home. Her everything. Now and forever.

“Say something,” he whispered, a slight tremble in his deep voice that gave away his nerves.

Taryn tiptoed, framed his face with her hands to keep his beautiful eyes locked on hers, and let the words spill from her heart, no longer afraid of voicing them.

“I love you.”

CHAPTER 34

Bleu couldn't believe what he was hearing as Taryn's lips moved, her sweet voice rising above the rushing in his ears, sinking her words deep into his heart.

She loved him.

His breath left him in a whoosh, ears rang and heart thundered as he struggled to take that in and make himself believe it. His eyes darted between hers, her palms warm on his face, the contact keeping the connection between them wide open so he could feel everything that she was—fear, hope, nervousness.

Love.

She *loved* him.

Gods. Holy fuck. Hell.

He blinked hard, fought to convince himself to do something, to form some sort of response.

Loren's words rattled around his head, telling him to complete their bond before the battle began, and everything primal in him responded to that with a ferocious need to finally claim the beautiful female who stood before him.

He growled low in his throat, the raw sound spilling from between his fangs as they emerged, punched long from his gums at the thought of finally having his own mate.

His ki'ara.

Taryn's violet-to-white eyes lit up, hunger burning in them that stoked the fire in his veins and made it flare hotter, until it consumed him and all he could think about was how quickly he could get her to his apartment.

The shift was quick to come, startling him and Taryn both. She gasped and stumbled back as she grew smaller in his vision, the green lands of the elf kingdom falling away as he grew in size, his bones lengthening and distorting as his body transformed into that of a dragon. Her surprise passed, the hunger in her gaze growing as she tipped her head back and looked up at him with eyes that backed up the sudden spike in her desire.

She liked what she saw.

His female approved of his dragon form.

He threw his head back and roared, the sound echoing across the lands, tearing from his throat in a ground-trembling cry of triumph that he couldn't contain.

His female loved him.

Taryn would be his forever.

An answering growl left her lips and he dropped his head and looked down at her, caught the fire that blazed in her eyes as her pupils dilated, gobbling up the white so her irises looked more violet. Like his.

His beautiful female.

He snarled and snatched her up into his paw, and kicked off, huge black leathery wings pounding the air as he lifted into it. Taryn's hot little hands clutched his thumb and index-claw, and he tucked her closer to his chest. His focus fixed on the castle ahead of him and he beat his wings harder, desperate to reach it and claim his female.

The ground came up at him fast and he grunted as his back paws struck it hard and he stumbled across the grass, lumbering as he struggled to remain upright and keep from collapsing onto Taryn.

"You are trying too hard." Her voice seemed so quiet when he was in this form, even when she was shouting.

He staggered to a halt and prepared for another attempt, and growled as Taryn pushed free of his paw and dropped to the grass. He swiped at her but she evaded him, dancing and spinning out of his reach as he tried to reclaim her. What the hell was she doing? He needed to get her to the castle now, damn it, right this instant. He didn't have time for any delay. It was killing him.

He needed to claim her.

He reached for her again and reared back when she shifted, becoming a beautiful slender violet and white dragon. She stood a head shorter than him, her four white horns a contrast against her deep violet scales and bright purple eyes. Her vertical pupils narrowed into thin slits and his instincts as a dragon demanded he satisfy his mate. She desired him.

His jowls peeled back off his fangs as he drew her scent over them, caught the hunger and arousal in it. He stalked towards her, heavy footfalls shaking the ground, driven by a deep need to mate with her.

She blinked, turned away from him and kicked off before he reached her, taking to the air.

Bleu growled and beat his wings, lifting into the air after her. The ground dropped away as she flew higher and he wobbled as the wind hit him and then his stomach fell as the valley suddenly grew tiny. He spread his wings, smoothing out his ascent as the thermal carried him higher, faster, until he was closing in on Taryn where she soared gracefully above him.

She looked down, canted her head, and he swore she was smiling at him.

He didn't want to look down at how high he was now, so he fixed his gaze on her and beat his wings, the rush of fear he had felt on suddenly shooting into the air flowing out of him as his hunger for her swept in to replace it.

When he neared her barbed tail, she let out a cry and dropped, swooping right. He growled and banked, plummeting after her. She beat her wings and circled around, and he mirrored her, giving a single hard beat of his to accelerate into the turn. Cold wind rushed across his face and streamed over his back, but it did nothing to cool his blood as he pursued her.

Whenever he had almost caught up with her, she twisted or turned, evading him. Every time she gained distance, his blood burned hotter, heart pounded harder. He lost himself in the chase, gave himself over to his instincts and embraced them.

Flying had seemed impossible and strange before, but as he pursued her through the cool air, mirroring her every move and slowly closing in on her, it felt as natural as breathing. He was rarely beating his wings when he had been hammering them before, constantly using them with little effect. Relying on them to keep him airborne.

Now, he relied on the thermals and currents, using his wings more as a tool to steer his course, gliding through the air on them and only beating them in order to accelerate.

It was incredible.

Taryn swooped again, rolling in the air as she banked left and downwards, her wings pinned against her back. He furled his and dropped with her, twisting through the sky, and a cry left his lips, startling him, born of the thrill that rushed through him. Taryn unleashed a cry of her own, one that he understood, shocking him again. She was enjoying this too, but her excitement was born of the chase. She liked him hunting her, pursuing her through the sky and slowly gaining ground on her.

She spread her violet and white wings and shot straight past him. His gaze tracked her, head tipping up as he watched her soar into the air until she was a speck. He stretched his wings wide and his stomach somersaulted as he caught the same thermal and rocketed up into the cooler air.

His wing knocked hers as he passed her and she playfully rolled onto her back, their eyes meeting for a heartbeat before she twisted back around the right way and dropped again. Her tail whipped against the air, streaming behind her as she plummeted towards the castle.

Bleu growled and dove after her, his blood rushing and heating as he slowly gained on her. Wind battered his face, chilling his scales, but he didn't feel the pain of it biting into him as he chased her. He felt only heat and hunger, fire that blazed so hot he felt as if he could breathe it if he opened his jaw and roared.

Taryn unfurled her wings a few hundred feet above the castle.

He kept his pinned back, determined to catch his mate. She banked right and he twisted that way, adjusting his course. She lazily flew towards the rear of the castle. Towards his balcony.

Thoughts of claiming her flooded his mind, sending the temperature of his blood soaring, making his heart drum in his ears as he closed in on her.

She turned and looked up at him.

Just as he spread his wings and collided with her back. He grabbed her hips with his rear paws and her shoulders with his front ones, and drove her down. She unleashed a high pitched cry, but it wasn't one of pain.

It was one of joy.

She loved that he had caught her.

They plummeted towards the courtyard and the elves scattered, some yelling obscenities at him as he sent his prize crashing to the ground. Her paws hit the stone flags, cracking a few of them, and he landed on top of her, beating his wings so he didn't crush her with his weight. Instinct drove him, firmly at the helm, and he seized the back of her neck with his fangs.

Pinned her beneath him.

She settled, tucking her wings back, going still.

When he growled against her neck, she answered, her call stoking the flames in his blood when he understood it.

She was submitting to him.

Gods.

He staggered off her and her gaze was shy as she pushed up, but fire still blazed in it, desire that he could feel through their link.

She beat her wings and landed on the shared balcony outside their rooms.

He gave a single hard beat and leaped up to join her. By the time he landed, she had already transformed back, and his mouth watered as she stole his breath again, his mind spinning as he watched her walking into her apartment.

Naked.

She disappeared from view and he growled and willed the shift, eager to follow her. Hungry to gaze upon her delicious curves.

Hungry for her.

He didn't feel the shift when she poked her head back around the tall double doors, her violet-to-white hair falling away from the left side of her throat, exposing the marks he had placed on her. He couldn't feel anything but the fierce heat that burned in him, made him mad with need. He needed her.

The moment he was back in his elf form, he strode towards her, uncaring that he was naked on the balcony and there was a chance someone might see.

The only person he gave a damn about was seeing it and that was all that mattered to him. The fierce edge to her striking eyes as they raked down his body, heating every inch of him, the one that said she wanted to eat him whole, turned his blood to wildfire.

She disappeared into her apartment and he followed her, a slave to his deepest primal instincts, the ones that thundered in his veins and told him to claim her.

She would be his.

He rounded the corner, the sheer light curtains brushing across his bare skin as he pushed through them. They shifted to reveal her room.

It blurred as a hand closed around his throat and his breath left him in a painful rush when his back slammed into the wardrobe. Before he could gather his wits, her lips closed over his, crushing them with a fierce kiss that set his blood on fire. He growled, grabbed her bare hips and dragged her against him as he deepened the kiss, thrusting his tongue past the barrier of her lips. Sharp teeth scraped against his tongue and he moaned in time with her as the taste of his own blood flooded his mouth.

Taryn's hand on his throat slid to his shoulder and her claws bit into his muscles as she writhed against him, sending tiny bolts of hot pain skittering through his body.

His grip on her waist tightened. She moaned deeper, clawed harder, rubbed more fiercely against him. Her heart thundered in his ears and his chest, driving his on until the beat was so quick it was dizzying and stripped him down to his basest instincts, the ones that screamed at him to claim this female.

He obeyed them, running his hands up her sides to her ribs, aiming for her breasts, intent on driving her wilder with need than she had ever been, until she surrendered to him and begged him for more.

She stopped him in his tracks by snarling at him and seizing his other shoulder as her left hand returned to his neck. She shoved him against the wall by it, her grip so tight he had to drag his breaths down into his lungs with effort. Her kiss grew fiercer, a hard demand against his, her tongue stroking his before flickering over his fangs. The pleasure that rolled through him in response had him forgetting the tightness of her grip on his throat for a moment, drove it out of his mind for a few seconds, until he tried to kiss her back and she growled at him again, pressed him harder against the wardrobes.

Prickles chased through his blood, followed by a wicked sort of darkness, an inkiness that swept through him, obliterating the light.

Bleu caught her shoulders and shoved her back, fought her as she tried to keep kissing him, her hisses and growls filling the air.

He evaded her mouth and she went to work on his jaw, searing him with each sweep of her lips and almost making him fall back under her spell as she drifted down to his throat and devoured it with wet kisses and nips of her sharp teeth.

He shook his head to drive sense back into it, because something was wrong.

"Taryn!" he barked and pushed her back, and this time he seemed to reach her because her eyes widened.

But she didn't release him and her body didn't stop shifting, writhing against the air, her face contorting as frustration flooded the link between them. She needed him. He knew that, felt it drumming in his blood, and he wanted to give his female what she desired, wanted to pleasure her until she was boneless on that bed, sated and sleepy in his arms, but something was very wrong. It had been a couple of days since they had touched, but his instincts said that her fervour was born of something more than their time apart.

She tried to reach him again but he locked his elbows, keeping her at a distance. Her eyes flashed fire and she roared at him, and then reared back, shock flittering across her face and through their connection.

She looked down at her hands on him and her eyes widened, horror filling them when she spotted the one wrapped around his throat.

She released him and staggered back, breathing hard against the panic he could feel welling up in her.

"Taryn," he whispered and reached for her, needing to soothe her.

She shook her head. "I need a moment."

Squeezed her eyes shut.

"You need more than a moment… you need me. I can feel it in you, Little Dragon." He advanced on her and she backed away, shaking her head as she opened her eyes and they implored him to keep his distance.

She feared losing control again.

Gods, he feared it a little too, but he was equally as afraid of losing control himself.

He needed her, now more than ever, his every instinct screaming at him to claim his mate at last, to make her belong to him forever.

Love him forever.

She halted and pressed her thighs together, wriggled them and moaned, her cheeks flushed and eyes dark with desire. He could see her control fading again, slowly torn away from her by her instincts. He hadn't realised that the urge to mate would run as fiercely in her as it did in him.

More fiercely in fact.

She was barely in control, writhing on the spot, so hungry for release that she couldn't keep still. It was his blood. She had drawn the smallest amount, not enough to seal their bond, and it was driving her mad with a need for more. He wanted to give that to her, as much as she wanted of him, completing their bond and tangling their fates forever.

Fear flashed in her eyes, fear of losing her weak grip on herself and fear of hurting him. He feared the same things.

"You're not alone, Little Dragon," he husked and her eyes narrowed, lids falling to turn them hooded, and a small moan left her lips, as if he had spoken words of seduction rather than stated simple facts. He held his left hand out to her and her gaze leaped to it, narrowed as she moaned again, wriggled and writhed, so hungry to take it and give in to him. She cast him a pained look and shook her head, tearing a sigh from him. "What is it you fear?"

She swallowed hard.

Sounded breathless, on the verge of release.

"Mating… it is too strong… the urge. I will hurt you… I-I am dangerous." Her breath left her in a rush and she rocked back another step, her violet-to-white eyes glowing with fire. With need. "I am too dangerous like this."

He wasn't about to deny that. She was stronger than he was, and her urge to mate was fierce, too powerful for her to fully control herself. There was a chance she would hurt him in the act, but he wasn't about to let something like that stop him. He stroked the scars on his neck, ones she had given him, and her eyes followed his fingers, pain flashing in them.

"Whatever you deal… I can heal, Little Dragon. There is nothing you can do that will stop me from claiming you."

She moaned. Squeezed her thighs. Nibbled her lower lip in a way that made him growl and take swift steps towards her, unable to hold himself back any longer.

He seized her mouth, sucked that lip into his and nibbled it with his fangs. The sweet taste of her blood filled his mouth and she moaned in unison with him, clamped her hands down on his shoulders and dragged him against her, so her bare front pressed against his. Her breasts were maddeningly soft against his chest, and he couldn't stop himself from rocking against the soft cushion of her belly. Another groan left him as his hard cock throbbed, aching for more.

He needed to be inside her.

Would go insane if he denied himself much longer.

She squeaked against his lips as he swept her up into his arms and then she was kissing him again, little breathless moans constantly escaping her as she drove him mad, pushing him right to the edge with only her mouth.

Bleu kneeled on the violet covers of the double bed and dropped her in the middle of it, covered her body with his and claimed her lips again. She moaned and wrapped her arms around his throat, raked short claws over his back, sending bolts of lightning zinging across his body. He growled against her lips with each one, each zap that had his blood burning hotter, the sparks of pain only heightening the pleasure he took from the feel of her beneath him, as wild for him as he was for her.

"Need you," she moaned in the dragon tongue against his lips and nipped at his lower one, her teeth nicking it and drawing blood. She growled low in her throat, a rumble he felt against his chest, and seized his mouth again, sucking fiercely on the tiny wound. She rocked against him, shoved and fought him, manoeuvred beneath him until she could circle her legs around his hips.

He hissed through clenched teeth as her slick heat scalded his throbbing cock and she ground against it, her moans ripping at his control. He found enough of it to muster the strength to draw back so he could slip his hand between them as he kissed her. She bucked against it as he palmed her, and he groaned as he felt how wet she was. Her nub pulsed against the heel of his hand, the desperate flickering making him want to forget everything and get inside her, because she needed him.

Bleu forced himself to resist that temptation and softened his kiss as he stroked her, teasing her towards a climax he hoped would help weaken the hold her mating instincts had on her. She wriggled beneath him, hot breaths washing across his face as she rode his fingers, moaned into his mouth and sank her claws into his shoulders.

"Bleu," she whispered, and he had never heard a sweeter sound than his name falling from her lips on a passion-drenched sigh.

He slid his hand down, eased two fingers into her, and groaned at how hot, wet and tight she was around them. She shuddered and clawed at him, mewled against his lips as he kissed her and stroked her, slowly withdrawing his fingers before easing back in. He rubbed the pad of his thumb over her clit, swallowed her sweet cries as she constantly undulated beneath him, her need flaring stronger in his veins as his connection to her blasted wide open, Taryn no longer able to hold anything back from him.

Gods, it was beautiful.

He drowned in her emotions as he touched her, teasing her towards release, feeling as if he was journeying there with her, so swept up in her that he shared every flicker of pleasure that danced through her, every sharp breath that left her lungs left his too, and every gasping moan echoed in his throat.

"Bleu."

The desperation in her voice had him stroking her deeper, thumbing her harder, until she was as taut as a bowstring beneath him, quivering on the edge of release. He plunged his fingers deep into her, spearing her liquid core, and her hips jerked up, her hands gripped him so tightly it felt as if his bones would crack beneath the pressure, and her sweet cry filled his ears.

He grunted and rocked his hips, driving against thin air as she trembled around his fingers, throbbing madly. Pleasure flowed through him, bliss that felt as if it was his own release, and he lowered his head and kissed down her neck as he gently stroked her, easing her back down.

She moaned with each little pulse of her body, ones that he loved to hear because she sounded as if she had no control over them, as if they left her of their own volition, born of surprise in the wake of each tremor.

When her trembling subsided, she sank against the bed and her grip on him loosened. Loosened but didn't fall away. Her hands remained against him, short claws still pressing in, and as he lazily kissed her throat, he could feel her desire rising again, stoking the embers in her blood. She turned her face towards him and he claimed her lips again, giving her what she wanted. Her kiss started tender, soft and relaxed, but steadily grew in ferocity until it matched the hunger racing through his blood again, need that demanded he sate it.

He rolled his hips against her, driving his cock against her belly, and she moaned, rocked up against him.

"Bleu…" she whispered against his lips, voice a sweet drone that spoke of satisfaction but also frustration. He had given her release, but he hadn't given her what she needed.

What they both needed.

Her legs clamped around his waist, pulling him into hard contact with her, and he couldn't stop the groan that tumbled from his lips as her soft body trapped his aching length between them. He couldn't stop himself from rubbing against her, shuddering as the sensitive head tingled and sparks of pleasure bolted down his shaft to his balls. Gods, he needed her.

She snarled and kissed him hard, her teeth clashing with his and her claws slicing into his skin. Her body grew hotter, as if the fire in her veins was real and she was burning up, would turn to cinders if he didn't give her what she needed to cool her instincts.

A mating.

Just the thought of it had him rearing back, eager to claim her. He growled down at her, flashing his fangs as his ears grew pointier, flaring against the sides of his head. Her eyes widened and then fell half-shut as a moan trembled on her lips, her hooded gaze only encouraging the part of him that roared to claim her.

To make her submit to him as she had in the courtyard when they had been in their dragon forms.

As if she knew his wicked thoughts, she scratched his shoulders and kicked at him, tried to shove him onto his back. The violet fire flashing in her eyes challenged him, warned that if he didn't drive her into submission, she would be the one to send him to his knees and take control.

Bleu bared his fangs on a snarl, grabbed her wrists and pinned them to the bed above her shoulders.

She moaned, undulated with blatant desire in her eyes, arousal sparked by his dominance.

He didn't know much about dragon mating, had only heard rumours that male dragons were brutal and dangerous when the hunger hit them. He was beginning to get the impression that the females were as dominant and violent as their male counterparts, and that Taryn had good reason to fear she would hurt him.

Her face crumpled and she writhed beneath him, fighting his hold. Her eyes blazed violet fire. Her lips peeled back to flash all-sharp teeth at him.

She wanted to fight him, to drive him into submission and dominate him.

She wanted to be the one to claim him.

It wasn't going to happen.

"I said nothing would stop me, Little Dragon… and I meant that." He tightened his grip on her wrists, shoved them harder against the bed, and felt the flicker of delight and relief that lit her blood as he showed her just how strong he was—strong enough to handle her. "This is a mutual claiming, but you need me to be the one in control. Just focus on that, Ki'ara. Focus on me."

She managed a nod, but whatever control she had gathered was short-lived. It fled her eyes and they burned again, aflame with dragon fire, and he could feel her fragile control slipping from her.

Knew it would continue to leak from her until they had sealed their bond.

He had wanted to do this gently, slowly, with reverence, but his little dragon was too far gone, her instincts too strong to deny, and she needed him to claim her in order to stop her from hurting him by staking a claim on him.

They would do a gentler version of a claiming once her instincts as a dragon were satisfied and they were finally mates.

He gathered her wrists together, clutched them in one hand and growled at her when she fought him. Flashing fangs seemed to be enough to placate her this time, or it might have been the way he moved his hips back. Her eyes fell to his cock, grew hungry and heated, and she licked her lips when he lowered his hand and grasped his shaft.

"Bleu." Her eyes leaped to his, begged him to fill her and claim her, to help her through the madness that had gripped her. She didn't want to hurt him. It beat in his blood, in their joined hearts. She was afraid of losing control.

"Right here, Little Dragon," he murmured and lowered his hips, ran the head of his cock down through her moist folds, and moaned as it found her slick opening. He smiled down at her when she wriggled, mewled and arched against him, desperation written across every beautiful line of her face. "Stay here with me… forever."

She whispered breathlessly, "Forever."

He drove into her and swallowed her low moan in a kiss. Her body quivered around his, white-hot and scalding, as if she really was on fire inside. He groaned and lifted his hand as he slowly thrust into her, brushed his knuckles across her cheek in a tender caress before he ghosted his hand up her arm and took hold of her wrist again. He brought her arms down, pinned them to the bed near her shoulders, and kissed her as he drove into her, as gently as he could manage when it felt as if his blood was rolling towards a fiery boil too.

She wriggled and bucked beneath him, raised her body until her chest was plastered to his and her core clamped down on him. He grunted and thrust deeper, fought to keep a fragile hold on his control. She tore it from his grip when she bit down on his lip, sinking her sharp teeth into it.

Bleu's upper lip peeled off his aching fangs and he growled at her, ripped free of her bite and drove hard into her. She moaned, tipping her head back, her violet-to-white hair spilling around her shoulders, and fuck, she looked beautiful like that.

Wanton. Lost.

He had never seen anything as erotic and intoxicating as the sight of Taryn spread beneath him, her body wrapped around his and her hands restrained by his, every inch of her bared to him. Not just her body, but her emotions. Her soul. Her heart.

Her eyes flicked open and her tongue dabbed at the blood on her lips.

His blood.

It dripped from the tear in his lower lip, splashed onto the pale skin of her chest, stark against it.

Her eyes challenged him again, issued a demand that he was all too happy to satisfy.

He dropped his head and licked the blood from her chest as he thrust into her, and she moaned and lifted her backside, allowing him to slide deeper still. He grunted against her chest, lost himself for a moment, giving the wildness and need spiralling out of control inside him a chance to seize hold of him. Her hips rose higher, he slid deeper. Her hunger shot through him, an urge that he couldn't stop himself from fulfilling.

He bit down on her right breast.

Taryn jerked against him and cried out, her body shuddering against his, her pleasure blasting through him.

He growled when her blood hit his tongue, groaned as it slid down his throat, and made the mistake of letting the bliss of it consume him.

The room whirled past him, the mattress slammed into his back, and strong little hands clamped around his wrists and shoved them down.

She rode him mercilessly as he fed, ravenous for her blood and unable to tear himself away even as a small voice whispered he was in danger. Her grip on his wrists slowly tightened, but he barely paid any notice to the way his fingers numbed, didn't give a damn as he lapped at her blood, let a bead roll down to her nipple and took it into his mouth.

She moaned and writhed, rotated her hips and drove him mad.

If he was going to go insane, she was going there with him. He licked at her breast, sucked her nipple harder, pinched it between his teeth. Hard.

"Bleu!"

She jerked, her body squeezing his cock so hard it felt as if it would burst, and then she snarled.

It was a bit of a blur after that.

Her left hand seized his throat, pushed up to hit his jaw and shoved his head to his right, and then her fangs were in his neck, clamped down hard and made his blood explode into wildfire so hot he was sure it melted his grey matter, because everything went topsy-turvy.

The room spun, twirling into a maelstrom above him, and pleasure so intense it robbed him of his vision blasted through him, a hot endless quivering that numbed him but left him alive with feeling at the same time.

Colours danced across his vision as it slowly returned, but they weren't colours. The red. The violet. The passionate pink. The infinite blue. He could name them all.

Desire. Need. Love. And the feeling of forever stretching before him, and his mate.

He could see her feelings, watched them blend with his as she drank deep of his vein, forging a powerful bond between them.

A bond he needed to be stronger still.

He couldn't hold back, had no control and could only watch as he pulled the hair from her throat and sank his fangs into it, joining their bodies completely. Eternally.

She moaned, trembled, her body quivering around his, and he shuddered and groaned as her release drew another from him. He throbbed inside her, each pulse stealing a little more of his strength, a little more awareness from him, until he was boneless beneath her, unsure where she ended and he began.

It felt as if they were one now, tangled together, never to part.

He had taken her into him, and she had taken him into her, and now he could feel all of her. Every emotion that flowed through her flowed through him, and he knew the reverse was true. She could feel his love for her, just as he could feel hers for him. She knew without question that it was unconditional. Infinite. A love that would never falter, never die.

She was his forever.

And he would be hers.

Nothing would stand between them or stop that from happening. Nothing.

Bleu wrapped his arms around her when she released him, broke away from her neck as the same time as she left his, and kissed her with all of his heart—the heart she now owned.

But as he lost himself in the bliss of this moment with her, the darkness that lurked at the edges of his mind began to close in and in the aftermath of claiming her, he wasn't strong enough to shut it out. It whispered to him.

He had claimed her as his mate, but he hadn't claimed their forever.

He had won the battle for her heart, but there was still one more war to fight if he was going to secure their forever after.

He had to slay a dragon for her.

CHAPTER 35

Taryn had been awkward from the moment she had awoken in his arms after their mating. That had been two days ago. Bleu flicked a glance at her and a blush climbed her cheeks, turning them rosy, and her fingers absently hovered above her breast, over the white leather that concealed the marks he had placed on her.

He wasn't sure he would ever tire of the way she blushed like that, how she couldn't seem to stop herself from reaching for her mating marks, and couldn't stop her striking eyes from drifting to his neck, to the marks she had placed on him.

Bleu fingered them and her blush only deepened, and she cast her gaze down at her boots, the shy edge to her expression pushing him into action. He crossed the busy courtyard to her, navigating his way through the small army of demons who had gathered in preparation for the coming battle, his eyes never leaving her.

When he was within a few metres, she slowly raised her gaze to him again, looking at him through her dark lashes, and though the shy edge remained, fire began to burn in her violet-to-white eyes.

Her pupils dilated.

Her teeth toyed with her lower lip.

Bleu growled, his pointed ears flattening against the sides of his head as the hunger he could feel in her raced through him too, demanding he whisk her away to some quiet corner of the garrison and satisfy them both.

A demon stepped into his path and Bleu snarled at him.

The snarl died on his lips when he met the black gaze of the male who towered before him.

King Tegan of the Second Realm.

The big black-haired demon king raised an eyebrow at his threat, but thankfully didn't seek to put him in his place. He merely looked over his wide shoulder at Taryn. When his eyes returned to Bleu, they were darker than before, his pupils ringed by purple-red fire, and menace rolled off him, sparking Bleu's instincts. He spread his feet shoulder-width apart, adopting a fighting stance, ready for whatever King Tegan was about to throw at him. The male wanted a fight, and for some reason seeing Bleu heading for his mate had put him in the firing line.

A large hand clamped down on the demon's shoulder, short dark claws emerging slightly as fingers closed over and pressed into sinewy muscle.

"Perhaps it is best we leave the little elf to his business, King Tegan? I am sure Prince Loren would be more than happy to answer whatever question you desired to ask the commander." Thorne's rough deep voice rumbled around Bleu and he flicked a glance at the Third King.

Thorne's chiselled features softened into a smile as Tegan looked across at him, and the breath Bleu hadn't realised he had been holding rushed from his lungs as the bigger demon gave a curt nod and allowed Thorne to lead him away.

Question Bleu's arse. Tegan hadn't had something to ask him, he'd had something to tell him. With fist, fang and claw for some reason.

Bleu looked at his beautiful mate, and then over his shoulder at Tegan's bare back as Thorne led him through the crowd towards Loren. Now that he was thinking about it, there had been a marked change in Tegan's behaviour since leaving the castle. The demon king had been genial during the meeting prior to Bleu's mating with Taryn, but since then, he had given Bleu the cold shoulder and whenever Bleu had approached him about preparing his part of the army, the male had looked ready to kill him. Bleu had put it down to the stress of leading his men coupled with a dash of excitement about finally getting his claws bloody again.

Now, Bleu suspected the change in attitude had little to do with the impending war and a lot to do with Bleu's newly mated status.

It seemed Grave wasn't the only male with a chip on his shoulder about a female.

Bleu looked back at Taryn and caught her glaring in Tegan's direction, her eyes bright violet and shimmering like fire. His fierce little dragon. The sight of her warmed his heart. She had noticed the hostility between him and the demon king, and she wanted to put the bigger male in his place.

He stared at her as he strode towards her and her glare slowly faded, her eyes drifting back to him and that pretty blush rising onto her cheeks again.

"How are prepara—"

Bleu cut her off, sweeping her into his arms and claiming her mouth. She stiffened, moaned and wrapped her arms around his neck. The tension melted from her as she kissed him, and his faded too, purged by the feel of her in his arms, her body pressed against his and their mouths fused. Gods, she felt perfect against him.

She kissed him deeper, stroked her tongue along his, teased his emerging fangs, and then broke away, breathless. Her wicked smile sent heat shooting straight to his cock and the way she seized his hand had him forgetting his duties and all too eager to go along with whatever his mate wanted.

Because it looked as if she wanted him.

She tugged him towards the far side of the courtyard.

Towards where it was quiet.

Bleu growled low in his throat, pulled her back into his arms and went to sweep her up into them so he could teleport them both there.

A horn sounded.

He cursed in the elf tongue.

Taryn muttered, "*Fuck.*"

He almost grinned at that. She was certainly embracing the one mortal swearword she knew. He was tempted to teach her others once the battle was over and their forever began, because there was something charming about the words when she said them, so out of place in amidst her formal way of speaking that it tickled him.

Bleu set her down and away from him, and forced himself to turn back, towards the gathering army that filled the courtyard of the garrison. A wall of bare muscular backs stood between him and the point where Loren stood on the broad stone stairs that led up to the walls, a mixture of demons from three separate kingdoms.

He sighed, cursed the gods for their timing, and her brother for interrupting them. If he had needed a reason to kill Tenak, the male had just given him one.

Taryn's fingers slipped between his and he looked down at their joined hands, and then up into her eyes. They told him everything—how much she loved him, how fiercely she needed him, but also every fear that filled her heart.

It was time.

Bleu didn't want his mate to hurt, but he also knew nothing he could do would end her pain. All he could do was remain close to her during the battle, offering her his support and his love as she fought her own flesh and blood with the intent of killing him.

Tenak's death would spare all of Hell from suffering at his hands, but it wouldn't spare Taryn. It would deal a blow to her that would be every ounce of pain everyone would have experienced at her brother's hands rolled into one consuming agony that he feared would tear her apart. It was going to take her time to overcome the grief and guilt she would feel, but he would be there for her, would do everything in his power to ease her pain and hold her together. He wouldn't let her slip away from him. He wouldn't lose her.

Her hand trembled in his and he tightened his grip on her, silently telling her that he was there for her, and vowing that he was going to do whatever he could to make this easier on her.

Heat shimmered across his skin beneath his armour as her gaze landed on him, the fire she always stirred in his blood rushing back to the fore, making him burn all over again for her. He slowly lowered his eyes to meet hers, held them as he lifted his free hand and brushed his knuckles across her soft cheek. Her eyes slipped shut and he inhaled hard as she leaned into his touch. He opened his palm and cupped her face, sighed as she shook against it, and swept his thumb across her cheek.

"I am here with you, Little Dragon," he whispered in her tongue and her violet eyebrows furrowed. A second later, they drew down and her jaw tensed, her lips flattening. He could feel the internal war she waged, the ferocious battle between fear and pain, and her natural strength and courage and the thought that she was doing the right thing. "I will always be with you."

Her eyes opened and leaped up to his, and his heart went out to her as they searched his, an edge of desperation about them, backing up her feelings that flowed into him through their bond. She needed more reassurance, needed him to soothe her and hand victory to her courage and the strength that was pushing her to spare Hell her brother's wrath by taking his life.

"I love you, Taryn," he murmured and her eyebrows furrowed again, and then she was in his arms, hers snaking around his neck to draw him down to her. Bleu slid his arms around her waist, pulled her close to him and kissed her. She sank against him and he held her up, giving her his strength, hoping she would feel that he would give her every last drop of it if she needed it from him. He would be her pillar. She could lean on him. Now and forever. He broke the kiss and pressed his forehead against hers, raised his hands and framed her face with them. "I will be there with you. I will not leave your side. Never."

"Bleu." His name was a breathless whisper on her lips and it told him everything she couldn't say. It conveyed how much his being with her meant to her, that she was going to hold him to his words. He hadn't broken a promise to her yet and he wasn't about to start now.

Loren's voice rose in the silent morning air, but Bleu paid him no heed as he held his mate, opened his heart to her and let her feel everything through their deep bond, holding nothing back. She drew down a deep breath and he felt the change in her, the shift as her heart grew stronger and she slayed her fears and doubts, and rose to the challenge ahead of her. His strong little female.

Taryn's hands closed over his and drew them away from her face. She smiled as she pressed soft kisses to his knuckles and then opened her eyes and lifted them to his. The fear that had coloured them was gone now, leaving behind the formidable female he had encountered more than once on the battlefield.

She nodded, a small action but one that said she had made her mind up and she was ready.

He lowered their joined hands, released her left but kept hold of her right. He slipped his fingers between hers, squeezed her hand tight and led her through the crowd. They skirted the edges, picking a path through the demons of the Third Realm, heading towards Loren where he stood on the steps with King Thorne, King Tegan and Queen Melia of the demons, and Prince Vail, Rosalind, Sable and Olivia.

When his steady gaze landed on Sable as she busied herself with checking her throwing knives and crossbow, Taryn loosed a low growl.

Bleu dropped his eyes to his mate. She blushed hard but her gaze didn't leave his, it held firm, challenging him to say something about her jealous outburst.

He couldn't, not when he wanted to growl whenever she looked at another male.

Gods, he was as bad as Vail. He had thought the urge to strike down any male who looked at her, mated or unmated, would pass when he had claimed her as his forever, but it hadn't abated at all.

Bleu paused in the middle of the throng of warriors, turned to her and caught her other hand. He sent his armour away from his chest and neck, a ripple of cold following the scales as they rushed over his flesh, leaving it bare. He raised her hand and placed it on the marks on his neck, a series of puncture wounds that were still healing and perfectly matched her sharp little fangs.

"Yours, remember?" he husked and the heat on her cheeks had nothing to do with embarrassment as she lowered her eyes to his throat and her marks.

"Always?" she murmured and stroked the marks, and fuck he wanted to do the same to hers. Her soft caress sent a fiery shiver through him and he bit back a groan.

He nodded. "Forever."

Her smile blew him away.

She fingered the scabs, following the curve of them, and her eyes began to blaze, a slow steady burn that had him thinking about heading back in the direction they had come.

Loren's deep voice shattered the silence again and the spell Taryn had cast on him with it. He sighed at the same time as her, made a silent promise that they would finish this after the battle was done, and called his armour back. The black scales rushed over his bare skin, warm against it, and Taryn snatched her hand back, as if they were going to bite her.

He smiled when she muttered under her breath about preferring him as he had been—half naked.

"Sure you don't prefer me completely naked, Little Dragon?" he husked as he continued to lead her through the crowd.

The sudden spark of desire that lit her blood bolted through his too, courtesy of their bond, and fuck, he had to stop teasing her now that they were mated. It was torture. His primal instinct to please his female had been strong enough before, a force that had him panting to pleasure her whenever she needed, but now it was a divine sort of torture, one that hijacked control and had him rock hard in an instant, ready for her.

He felt her gaze on his backside as he walked, could almost hear her low purr of approval and the wicked thoughts running rampant through her pretty head.

Holy fuck.

He glared over his shoulder at her but she didn't repent. She just smiled at him and had the audacity to give him a saucy wink.

Minx.

She was determined to keep his eyes on her and off other females, and she was doing a damned good job of it. He didn't mind her scrambling his mind with lust, but he needed to focus. He hadn't heard any of what Loren was droning on about, and while he was sure it was just a standard speech to rouse the troops, it wouldn't reflect well on him if his prince questioned him and discovered he hadn't been listening.

Gods, he could well imagine how Loren would tease him.

He doubted Loren wouldn't be alone too. Olivia would be his co-conspirator, and he was ninety-nine percent certain that Thorne and Sable would join in. Hell, Vail and Rosalind would probably take a poke or two at him too.

He didn't even want to imagine how Leif would berate him if he knew. He flicked a glance off to the right of Loren where the elves had gathered, split into divisions led by Leif, Fynn and Dacian. His three warriors stood at the head of each legion, arms folded across their armoured chests, all of them paying attention to their prince as he spoke. They were doing a better job of being a perfect soldier than he was right now, but finding his mate had been a long time coming and he was still searching for balance, trying to grow accustomed to the new instincts and feelings flowing through him. That was his excuse and he was going to stick with it, because he knew Loren would forgive him if he blamed it all on his beautiful new mate.

Bleu reached the bottom of the stone steps just as Loren finished and turned to the small group who would command sections of the army.

"Rosalind, are you ready?" Loren said and the petite blonde witch nodded.

Vail shifted foot to foot beside her, his violet irises already black around their edges. He fiddled with the black and silver bands around his wrists, his serrated claws scratching at them. When Rosalind placed her hand on his forearm, he hissed at her, flashing huge fangs as his pointed ears flared back against his blue-black hair. His face crumpled a moment later as he realised what he had done and he shoved his fingers through his hair, held his head and dug the points of his claws into his scalp.

Bleu wished he could revive the dark witch Kordula, the female responsible for Vail's pathological hatred of magic, and kill her all over again.

Rosalind turned towards her mate, skimmed her hands up his forearms, gently took hold of his wrists and carefully drew his hands away from his head. The points of his black claws glistened with his own blood in the bright light. She sighed, brought them to her mouth and kissed each one, staining her lips crimson.

Vail growled, pulled her into his arms and kissed her hard.

Complicated wasn't a strong enough word to describe his prince. He balanced on the brink of insanity whenever he felt magic, but he couldn't get enough of his mate. Bleu had thought fate had been cruel to him by making his mate a witch when one had tortured him so vilely, but he was beginning to see that Rosalind was the balm Vail's heart and head needed in order to heal.

It was there in the way she cradled him gently in her arms even though he was being rough with her, his claws digging into her hips as he kissed her hard, dominating her. She stroked the back of his head, returned the kiss, and Vail slowly calmed, until he was being gentle with his mate, kissing her softly.

Making Bleu want to take Taryn into his arms and kiss her like that.

Loren cleared his throat.

Vail lifted his head, a distant look in his clear violet eyes as they shifted to his older brother.

Leif, Dacian and Fynn joined the party, and Bleu nodded as he looked beyond Loren to them. They would lead the elves in his stead and command a legion each, close to one thousand elves apiece, was a huge step up for them, but he was sure they would each excel. Even Fynn.

The wise-cracking male was unusually sober today.

Bleu could understand why. The fate of their kingdom and Hell rested in their hands—a kingdom that included Fynn's sister and family. Bleu was glad that Iolanthe was in the mortal realm, far away from the battle about to take place.

"Rosalind. Vail." Loren turned from one to the other, nodding as they did the same.

Vail closed his eyes and steeled himself.

Rosalind placed her hands on her mate's face, cupping his cheeks, and shut her blue eyes. She swayed on the spot as she muttered soft words in the old fae tongue. Colourful sparks of light drifted from her fingers and danced in the still air, illuminating Vail's face as it twisted and he snarled.

"Focus, Vail. I am here," Loren whispered and settled his hand on his brother's left shoulder.

Vail relaxed again.

"I feel it," he murmured, a frown pinching his black eyebrows. "The sword… is close. Beyond the mountains."

Loren looked down at Vail's hands as they curled into tight fists. The scent of blood filled the air and Bleu frowned as it seeped from the cracks between Vail's fingers and dropped to the grey stone steps.

"Enough," Loren snapped but Vail shook his head.

"It is near the border. A small settlement." Vail gritted his teeth and his face contorted, and the sense of danger that he always emitted rose sharply.

"Stop," Loren barked.

Rosalind opened her eyes and looked between Loren and her mate, her blue eyes swirling with silver stars. "A little more. He can take it."

"He cannot," Loren countered and reached for her hands.

Vail bared his fangs on a snarl. "More. I can take more."

Loren looked as if he wanted to argue that he couldn't and snatch Rosalind's hands away from his brother, freeing him of her spell, but he lowered his hand instead and huffed. Olivia sidled closer to her mate and Loren glanced down at her, a wealth of hurt in his eyes. She smiled softly, her dark eyes sparkling with it, and reached for his hand.

Bleu's senses blared a warning.

He shoved Taryn down the steps and lunged for Loren just as Vail turned on him, his lips peeling back off his enormous fangs. He pulled Loren out of the path of Vail's attack and Vail's claws raked down his chest, breaking through his armour in places. Fire burned in their wake and Bleu grunted as he staggered backwards into Loren, knocking him off the steps. Olivia shrieked his name and rushed after him. Rosalind bit out something harsh in the old fae tongue and launched at her mate.

Bleu snapped his hand around Vail's throat before she could reach him and kicked off, slamming the male into the stone wall. Vail's breath left him in a sharp puff but the shock that rippled across his face quickly morphed into darkness, anger so black that Bleu shuddered as he felt it wrap around him.

Tainted.

But not lost.

Not yet.

He shoved Vail hard against the wall and the male lashed out with his left hand, claws aimed at his throat. Bleu caught it and pinned it above his head.

"You do not want to fight me, Prince Vail," Bleu snarled in the elf tongue.

Vail stilled, the fury draining from his face as he stared at Bleu, a flicker of confusion in his black eyes. Violet seeped back into them, driving the black back, and he looked down at Bleu's arm in front of him and then back up into his eyes and blinked.

"Bleu?" Vail's face crumpled and Bleu's heart bled for him as he looked around him, an edge of despair in his eyes. They came back to Bleu and he shook his head. "I never wanted to fight you."

"I know," Bleu whispered and slowly loosened his hold on his prince, allowing him to find his feet again. Vail sagged against the wall and Rosalind rushed in to fuss over him. Bleu backed away, holding Vail's violet gaze, reading what he couldn't bring himself to voice. He was sorry. Not for what had just happened, but for what had transpired millennia ago, and in the centuries that had followed. Bleu nodded, accepting the silent apology. "I know."

"Vail." Loren leaped back up onto the steps and joined Rosalind in checking Vail over, ignoring everyone as they advised him to be more careful.

Bleu didn't join them. Vail wasn't a threat to Loren. He loved his brother and it killed him whenever he lashed out at Loren. He had only lashed out at Loren because he had been the one closest to Vail when the flow of magic around him had made him snap.

He took the few steps down towards Taryn and she came to meet him, fussed over him in her own way by planting her hands on her hips and glaring at him.

"I thought we tackled things together now?" she said in the dragon tongue.

Bleu shook his head. "Not this. Never this. Vail is volatile and I won't let him near you. It is safer that I deal with him alone when he is like this."

She smiled and he frowned at her, confused as to why she was looking at him as if he was wonderful.

"You knew he would not hurt you," she said and his frown deepened as he supposed that he did. He had placed himself between Vail and Loren on instinct, but that instinct had said that Vail wouldn't hurt him, that out of everyone present he was the one who could reach his prince, just as he had that day on the battlefield forty-two centuries ago. "You have forgiven him."

Bleu considered that and slowly nodded as it dawned on him that he had forgiven Vail in a way. He hadn't absolved Vail of his sins, because that was something only Vail could do by making amends for his actions, but he had forgiven him for the pain he had caused him and the years they had come to blows.

"I want you to remain in the garrison with Rosalind," Loren said and a low growl erupted behind Bleu.

He stepped to one side, allowing Taryn to claim her place beside him again, and looked across at Vail where he still rested against the wall with Rosalind clutching his arm.

"No," Vail snapped, flashing fangs. "I will not leave your side, Brother. Not again."

The look in Loren's eyes said that he wanted that more than anything. It wasn't possible. Loren had fought hard to convince the elf council that they needed Rosalind's assistance in this battle, and that meant allowing Vail to enter the kingdom. The elders had agreed to Vail's presence in their realm, but Bleu had the feeling that welcome had a time limit attached to it. As soon as the battle was done, they would want Vail gone.

Bleu found himself hoping again that Vail could do something that would help his cause, at least enough that he could visit Loren without the castle going on red alert and hunting him down.

Loren placed his hand on Vail's shoulder, sighed and nodded. "Remain close to me."

Vail nodded.

In the silence that fell, the elf prince dropped a bombshell that Bleu was going to make damn sure reached the elders on his behalf, because it was perfect for gaining him a reprieve.

"I know the exact location of the sword."

CHAPTER 36

Fucking Valestrum.

Bleu shuddered as he fought his way through the enemy horde, cutting down demons and fae with his double-ended spear.

Of all the places Tenak could have chosen as his base of operations, he had chosen the ghostly settlement near the border of the free realm.

A town that had been abandoned since Vail had slaughtered hundreds of elves in his own legion here four thousand years ago. No wonder Vail had lost himself to the darkness when he had pinpointed the location of the sword through Rosalind's spell.

Valestrum had been a bustling settlement then, a place where people of the free realm and elves had traded goods, acting as a market that had drawn hundreds to it each day.

The stone buildings lay in ruin now, the clock tower still rising above the roofless squat houses that lined the main crossroad and circled the market square at its centre.

Bleu flicked a glance back at Vail, checking on him as they fought close to each other, in the rear half of the attack. Loren's gaze lit on him and then his brother, and Bleu could almost feel his relief as he saw that Vail was still holding it together, somehow retaining control.

He had tried to convince Vail to take Loren's advice and remain at the garrison with Rosalind, but Vail had insisted on coming with them, stating over and over that he was strong enough to fight the darkness and the memories that would provoke it. He had told them the same thing so many times that he had sounded as if he had been trying to convince himself more than everyone else.

The only thing Bleu was convinced of was that it was only a matter of time before the memories of this place, the horror Vail had inflicted here at the start of Kordula's reign over him, took over and the darkness seized hold of him.

He knew it because the memories of that terrible night were pushing at him too, goading his darkness, and it was growing difficult to hold it back as he tried to harness the strength of it at the same time in order to fight to the best of his abilities.

The tip of his black spear sliced upwards across the bare chest of a demon from the Seventh Realm and the huge male staggered back, snarled as he looked down at his chest and touched the crimson gash, and then kicked off, launching himself at Bleu. Bleu teleported as the male reached him, reappearing behind the demon in time to see him stumbling through the shimmering ghostly form he had left behind. He slashed again, cutting deeply up the demon's back.

The male grunted and staggered a few steps before he collapsed to his knees and then kissed the churned earth. Blood pooled swiftly in his lower back and ran to the ground, staining the crushed blades of grass red.

Before this battle was done, the whole of the valley would be crimson.

The snarls and cries of the warriors around him as they clashed filled his ears, but he paid them no heed as he checked on Vail again.

His gaze caught on a large elf male sprinting across the uneven terrain, a black blade held point down in his fist.

Running in the opposite direction to the battle.

Bleu slowly turned his head, following the male's trajectory, and his eyes widened and tracked back.

Loren fought two demon males, his twin blades a blur as he ducked and dodged, lashed out to deal blows that would weaken his opponents.

Bleu's violet gaze leaped back to the elf male charging towards him.

His eyes were black.

A cold judder wracked Bleu, realisation that hit him so hard he rocked back on his heels before he kicked off, sprinting hard towards his prince.

The male wasn't running to help Loren.

Darkness embraced Bleu as he leaped over a fallen fae female and cold swirled around him, and he willed the fates to listen to him as he jumped into his portal and get him to his destination before the male reached Loren.

He dropped out of the air just as the elf launched his blade at Loren and thrust his spear forwards, ramming it deep into the male's side. The sudden jerk to the right the male made as Bleu drove him to the ground wasn't enough to throw his aim off and Bleu could only shout as the black knife flew at Loren's back.

He pulled his spear free as the blade connected, striking Loren in the right shoulder and slicing straight through his black armour. Loren toppled forwards as he bellowed in agony and hastily swept his obsidian sword out to block the silver blade the nearest demon aimed at his neck.

Bleu raced across the battlefield and snarled as he reached Loren just as the demon struck again, more force behind the blow of his broadsword this time. Bleu swept his spear up, grimaced and grunted through clenched teeth as it clashed hard with the male's blade and vibrations rang along its length, numbing his hands. He shoved upwards with his double-ended spear, knocking the demon back, and spun on his heel, bringing the second blade of his spear around in a deadly arc. It sliced through the demon's exposed stomach and Bleu didn't bother to watch him fall as he gargled, the scent of his blood flooding the air around him.

He rushed to Loren and caught him as he dropped to his knees.

"Loren," Bleu barked and growled at the blade protruding from his back, his fangs lengthening as rage threatened to consume him.

"Tenak… he must have…" Loren breathed hard and snarled through his own fangs, his face contorting as he tried to sit back, with more than pain this time. He was angry. Bleu could feel it and he wanted to tell Loren not to beat himself up about the fact this had happened. It wasn't his fault. Loren hunched forwards again, clutched his shoulder with his left hand and grunted.

An unholy roar shook the battlefield and the air swirled around them, darkness rushing over Bleu like an oily tide, pulling his even closer to the surface. Bleu fought it back and looked up at Vail where he towered over Loren, his near-black eyes wild with fury that rolled off him.

Bleu bit out, "Tenak has turned the tainted in our ranks against us."

Tainted were weak, vulnerable to control by witches. The way Vail's gaze narrowed, his irises turning completely black, and he lifted his head to scent the air said that he knew what Bleu had been trying to say without mentioning the W word or bringing up magic.

Vail spared Loren a glance, and the moment Loren looked up at his younger brother with fury mingled with regret written in every line of his face, Vail nodded and teleported, leaving an icy chill in his wake.

Screams erupted on the battlefield around them and Bleu looked over his shoulder, barely able to keep up with Vail as he went to town on their own ranks, hunting out any tainted like a bloodhound, as if he could recognise the disease in other elves because he was so dangerously acquainted with it.

"Gods," Loren muttered and lowered his head, his eyes falling shut. The muscle in his jaw popped and he ground out, "It will be too much for him."

Bleu felt Loren's fear because it beat in his heart too. Vail had undertaken an unsavoury task, one most elves would have refused. Not every tainted on the battlefield had been turned against them. For all they knew, only that one male had been corrupted by magic. The effect hunting his own kind would have on most elves was nothing compared with the effect it would have on Vail, a male who was still coming to terms with the sheer number of elves he had murdered under Kordula's control.

If this nightmare Vail had thrown himself into didn't gain him favour with the elders, Bleu was going to see that their heads rolled. Vail deserved a damned medal for leaping into action as he had.

"Rosalind needs to be here," Loren muttered and tried to stand. His knees gave out and Bleu steadied him as he breathed hard, fighting the pain.

"I have to remove this." Bleu eyed the dagger protruding from Loren's shoulder and his prince nodded. "It will hurt."

Loren shot him a black look, one that said he damned well knew that, and gritted his teeth before nodding stiffly.

Bleu gripped the handle of the blade and yanked it hard, pulling it free as quickly as he could manage. Loren's bellow drowned out the din of the battle around them as he lurched forwards in Bleu's arms. When he had run out of air, his cry fading as he exhausted it, he sank against Bleu and breathed hard. The strong scent of Loren's blood filled Bleu's senses and he frowned as he eased Loren away enough to check the wound. It was deep. He wouldn't be able to fight with both hands, and that made him vulnerable.

"Gods damn it!" Loren growled and then flashed his fangs on a snarl as he threw his left hand forwards.

Two demon males and a fae who had been fighting their way towards them flew through the air as the blast of telekinesis hit them.

Bleu kept his mouth shut, aware that he didn't need to tell his prince what he was about to do. Loren was royally pissed, angry enough that Bleu could see he already knew what was about to go down.

He closed his eyes, held Loren against him and willed his portal.

Green-purple light chased over both him and Loren, and then darkness swallowed them. When it parted, they were on the hill outside the garrison, more than two leagues from the battle.

"Damn it," Loren bit out again and tried to shove onto his feet.

Bleu rose onto his and helped Loren stand. Blood pumped down his back, turning the black scales of his armour shiny.

Making Bleu feel sick to the pit of his stomach.

Gods. What if he hadn't reached Loren? What if he had been too distant from his friend to notice the elf male?

Loren could have been killed.

His blood chilled, but then warmed as Loren's left arm wrapped around him and tugged him hard against him, causing his chin to hit his prince's shoulder.

His friend's shoulder.

He had been wrong.

Olivia hadn't replaced him. It echoed around his numb mind as Loren held him and he felt how close he had been to losing him.

"Thank you," Loren said.

Bleu's eyes slipped shut, warmth curling through him at the familiarity of that voice, at the reassurance that his friend was safe and would be healed soon.

He pulled back and cleared his throat, rolled his shoulders in a shrug that felt anything but casual. "It was nothing. I was just doing my job."

Loren's eyes searched his. "As my second in command?"

Gods, Bleu was about to sound like a sappy prick, but he couldn't stop himself from saying, "As a friend."

Loren dragged him back into an embrace that only made him feel more awkward. He patted his prince's back. Clumsily.

"We're not that close," Bleu muttered and Loren chuckled and released him.

The smile on Loren's lips died as his violet gaze drifted away from Bleu, settling on a point in the distance behind him. Bleu looked there, aware of the battle taking place just a few miles from them, feeling an urgent need to return to it and ensure that Vail was safe too, and the others. Three demon kings, a mortal huntress and three idiotic elf warriors fought there, battling an army of demons, fae, witches and other species.

The dragons were yet to make an appearance, but it was only a matter of time before they joined the war.

"Tenak might anticipate our attack if he is using the same tactics." Loren's voice was a low whisper, concern thickening it.

Bleu nodded. "It's still the best plan we have… and we must give it a shot. The time is drawing near. According to Taryn, her brother prefers to have his army weaken the enemy before he enters the battlefield to claim victory. I haven't scented a dragon there yet, and our numbers are falling. Our time to act is coming."

He looked towards the squat garrison below him, his senses reaching out to his mate. She had been annoyed when he had ordered her to remain with the others in the safety of the stone bastion, until he had explained that he would return when it was time for them to head out and put their plan into action.

Every instinct he possessed as a warrior said that time was now.

Bleu helped Loren down the hill, his arm slung around his prince's waist to support him. Loren muttered dark things in the elf tongue beneath his breath, his rage still simmering in his violet eyes. He had no doubt that as soon as he was patched up and healing, he would be back on the battlefield. He wanted to tell him to remain in the garrison, but he couldn't bring himself to say those words when he thought about Vail alone out there. If it was Iolanthe in his place, and Bleu the one forced to retreat, he would be just as anxious to return to the fight and to her.

The elves milling around outside the garrison, assigned to protecting those within it should the enemy reach them, all jerked their heads in his direction as he approached. Several pairs of eyes widened as they landed on Loren, and then they were rushing towards them. Loren waved them away as they all tried to help him.

Bleu led his friend through the main arched doors of the garrison and into the courtyard.

"Shit!" A female voice rang through the silence and feet pounded the stone flags.

Loren lifted his head, his expression softened and he straightened, tipped his chin up and stood tall despite the pain Bleu could feel in him.

Olivia's hands fluttered as she reached them and she checked her mate over, her dark eyes wide and brimming with tears. "What the fuck happened?"

It wasn't like Loren's princess to swear, and it caused half of the elves in the courtyard to stop and stare. Loren growled at them all, flashing his fangs, and they hurried away, leaving the courtyard quiet and empty save him, Bleu and Olivia.

And Taryn.

She rushed out of the building in the centre of it and raced over to him, her striking eyes filled with the fear that he could feel flowing through their link. He smiled, hoping to show her that the blood all over him wasn't his and that he was fine.

Olivia took Loren from him, and Loren threw him a pained and pleading look as she led him away, chastising him and talking about administering elf medicine. Loren had little love for the medicine she spoke of, just like Bleu, but he knew his prince would stomach it this once so he could quickly return to the battle.

If Olivia would let him go.

Bleu had the feeling he was going to have to break Loren out of the infirmary in order to get him back to the battlefield. Olivia was already talking about days' worth of bedrest, despite her mate's protest that it was just a knife in the back and he would be fine with a little fluids, his hungry gaze hovering on her neck.

Taryn collided with him, knocking the air from Bleu's lungs, and he didn't have a chance to speak. Her lips clashed with his, arms holding him so tightly that it bordered on painful. He wrapped his around her, pulled her close and kissed her back, letting her know that he had missed her too and soaking up the comforting feel of her in his arms.

"Gods, I was worried about you," she whispered against his lips in the dragon tongue and pressed her forehead to his. "I can hear the battle… I have been watching from the walls but cannot see what is happening. The reports coming back with the wounded say that we have heavy losses… I need to be out there. I have to stop this madness."

Bleu gathered her closer and pressed a kiss to the tip of her nose, and then claimed her mouth again, savouring the kiss as she instantly responded, a sweet desperate edge to her kiss. She really had been worried.

"It is time," he murmured and drew back, his eyes leaping between hers as he reached for their bond, strengthening it so he could feel whether she was ready, truly prepared for what they were about to do.

Her resolve came through loud and clear, but there was pain and fear there with it.

He lifted his hands and framed her face, kept her eyes locked on his as he brushed his thumbs across her cheeks, absorbing her beauty. His mate.

His ki'ara.

"Are you sure about this?" he whispered, unable to stop himself from posing that question, needing to give her a chance to go back on their plan. He would go alone if she did, would fight her brother for her.

The resolve in her eyes grew stronger, shone so brightly it was dazzling.

His strong, brave, beautiful little dragon.

She nodded.

Snarled.

"I will end this."

CHAPTER 37

Taryn surveyed the battle stretching below her from her perch on the side of the nearest mountain, struggling to focus on the clash of the two armies as her neck throbbed close to her shoulder, Bleu's recent bite demanding she give him and the hunger he had roused in her all of her attention. He stood beside her, his violet gaze on the warriors far below them, looking for all the three realms as if his focus was there.

She knew it was really on her, on the need that had sparked inside him the moment her blood had hit his tongue.

Desire that had been a low simmer in her blood over the past day or so, steadily climbing towards a boil at times. Every time fate would intervene and ruin their plans. She needed her mate and he needed her, it was there in his eyes whenever he looked at her, in their bond if she focused just a little on it, strengthening it.

Gods, she needed him.

Her eyes scanned the warriors as they fought, swords clashing, bodies slamming, fists smashing and claws slashing. It was brutal, but she needed to see it. She had witnessed demon wars before, but they had never been on this scale and the males involved had never been so vicious, violent beyond compare.

Her brother had caused this.

Bleu had informed her that his madness had even reached a terrible peak, his disease infecting elves and turning them against their own kind.

Her gaze picked out Prince Vail where he fought, his brother Loren close beside him. They were near the back of the battle, forming a line with a mixture of demons and elves meant to cut down any enemy forces who had made it that far and were close to breaking through to reach the garrison.

She shifted her eyes right, to the middle of the mad throng, where King Thorne of the Third Realm of the demons fought hard beside his mate, the two working in a majestic symphony as they twisted and turned, backs pressed together one moment and breaking apart the next. They seemed to always know where the other was without looking. Their bond was strong. Beautiful.

A bond similar to the one she shared with Bleu. She had been able to feel him on the battlefield when she had been back at the garrison with Loren's mate Olivia, trying to help the mortal doctor as she patched up the wounded teleported away from the front lines. Olivia's worry about her mate had been infectious, sinking deep claws into Taryn, making her tense and cranking her fear higher with each dull echo of pain on her body that had come from Bleu and her connection to him. She had been so relieved when he had returned.

She lifted her hands to her chest and pressed them to her heart, a heart that beat for him now.

Bleu's warm hand settled on her bare shoulder and she glanced at him, reassured him with a smile when he looked concerned. He returned it, his lips curling at the corners, his violet eyes sparkling with love. She absorbed the warmth of his caress when he brought his hand away from her shoulder and brushed his knuckles across her cheek.

Her eyes began to slip shut.

A mighty roar rose above the din of the battle and her heart leaped, her gaze seeking the source of the sound.

Her brother?

The pounding of her heart eased when she found the male and saw that it was Tegan who had unleashed such a vicious and feral noise.

The Second King of the demons.

The burly black-haired male fought right at the front and centre of their side, leading the charge, an impressive sight with his black horns flared and his huge obsidian wings on display. He hacked down any who dared to attack him, his broadsword a silver blur and his bare chest stained crimson with the blood of his foes.

She had never seen anything like him.

He was brutal as he swept through his adversaries like a wraith, his black wings assisting him as he dodged blows meant to cleave him in two from swords as huge as his own wielded by demons from many different realms. He towered over them all, a formidable and deadly male, his eyes fixed straight ahead as he ploughed a course through his enemy.

Demons from the second realm followed on his heels, dispatching any he had injured and left in his wake, tackling the fae and demons who tried to reach their king from the sides as he constantly cut a straight line through their brethren.

Her gaze tracked their leader. He held nothing back, led the charge and never hesitated. He roared again and the enemy forces seemed to still for a second as it rolled across the land, all eyes drawn in his direction. They feared him. She could understand why. It was as if one of the Devil's demons had come to war with them, not a male from a peaceful kingdom.

She tore her gaze away from him and looked towards where he was heading, charting the path he would take if he remained on his current course. Her blood chilled as she saw the large black tent near the edge of a ruined settlement, surrounded by smaller red ones.

As she saw the male emerging from it, his eyes on the battle playing out in front of him.

Tenak.

"Damn," Bleu bit out beside her and her eyes darted to him. His were fixed on the battle below.

Taryn looked there and wanted to echo him as she spotted the Second King on his knees, a blade sticking out of his chest and a demon towering over him.

The male pulled his broadsword free and spun on his heel, and Taryn didn't want to watch as he aimed it at King Tegan's throat, but she couldn't take her eyes off him. Chills raced over her skin and she swiftly prayed to the gods that his men would reach him in time, even when she knew they wouldn't.

The blade reached the Second King's throat.

Taryn's breath caught.

A female appeared between the two males, shoved her arm against the enemy demon's one and caught it in her hand, stopping him just as his blade was about to slice through King Tegan's neck.

The small female leaped at the enemy male, and Taryn's breath left her in a painful rush and Bleu's muttered curse swam around her head as the female didn't attack the male as both of them had expected.

She kissed him.

Was the female involved with that demon?

Taryn shook that thought away. No female would throw herself at a lover during a battle, especially when he had been about to claim a victory the size of the one the demon warrior had been close to seizing.

But nothing else made sense.

Until the demon male fell to his knees, the female nimbly leaped away at the perfect moment to land on her feet beside him, and watched as he crumpled onto his side. She levelled a hard kick at his head, turned and stilled.

The female rushed to the Second King, kneeled and gathered him into her arms.

Disappeared with him.

Taryn's eyebrows shot up.

Beside her, Bleu let out a low whistle. "I wasn't expecting that."

She silently seconded that thought as she watched demons from the second realm turning in circles, confused looks on their faces. A fae had just abducted their king.

Part of her expected them to all flee the battle in search of him, but a male stepped forwards, barked something in the demon tongue and they set off again, charging forwards as if nothing had happened.

Taryn looked back towards where they were heading.

Her brother still stood outside the black tent.

Waiting.

She could feel it as she stood on the side of the mountain, the gentle wind flowing over her exposed skin and the light from the portal warming it.

Tenak moved forwards, stopped, took another step towards the battle. He was itching to join in. It was only a matter of time before he took the sword from the black tent and wreaked havoc with it on the remaining warriors of her side.

Time that she wouldn't squander.

Every second he spent watching the battle unfold was a chance for her to sneak into his camp and steal his sword. Now that he had left his tent, the time had come for her to act.

She turned away from the battle and Bleu followed her, caught her hand and darkness embraced them, cold against her skin. When it evaporated, they were on the other side of the mountain range, within the border of the First Realm of demons.

"Ready?" Bleu said beside her as he released her arm.

Taryn nodded. "Ready."

She stepped fowards to give herself more room to shift. Bleu grabbed her arm, pulled her into his and kissed her, a brief firm press of his lips that soothed her fear and her nerves, and spoke volumes about the feelings that flowed from him and into her through their bond. He was worried, and he loved her.

"Be careful," he breathed against her lips.

She clutched his upper arms, nuzzled his nose with hers, and savoured this brief moment of calm, putting it to memory.

"You be careful, too," she whispered back at him.

He kissed her again and she claimed his lips, couldn't stop herself from deepening it, desperate to take more from him, afraid that this would be the last time they kissed.

She drew up her courage from her feet, sucked down a deep breath and found the strength to step back from him. She had to do this. Her brother was a threat to everyone in Hell, and potentially everyone in the mortal realm too. If he won this war, the power he would wield in Hell would only satisfy him at first. It wouldn't be long before his hunger grew and he turned his mad gaze on the mortal plane, finding a way to enter it and bring it to its knees before him.

And then what?

Would her brother attempt to covet the greatest treasure and claim Heaven for himself?

She fisted her hands at her sides, clenched her jaw and silently vowed that would never happen.

It ended here.

This day.

She willed the shift, and the ground dropped away as her body transformed. Her black paws seemed foreign to her, as if she was looking through another's eyes. Bleu's dazzling eyes. She looked across at him as he towered beside her, a huge black dragon with six horns and enormous obsidian wings. His scales shimmered blue in the dying light of day as he turned his head towards her, his violet eyes locking on her. The softness in them spoke to her, told her of his love for her and that he intended to remain close to her for as long as he could.

Taryn looked back down at her own black scales. Strange. She had always longed to be a different colour, to be a normal shade for a dragon rather than a two-tone one that drew attention to her, but now she missed seeing her violet scales and white chest. The black made her feel like someone else. Someone not her.

Bleu had told her back at the castle after mating with her that he thought her hair and eyes beautiful, and she had blushed but hadn't quite believed him. Now as he gazed at her, raking his violet eyes over her, and she mourned the loss of her colours, she knew he had been telling the truth. He honestly thought her unusual colouring added to her beauty and he didn't want her any other way.

She no longer wanted herself any other way either.

Bleu had made her feel comfortable in her skin and now she could see how much that unique colouring was a part of her. She stood out but she no longer cared who stared at her, or if she drew the attention of others. She only cared about the way her mate looked at her, the desire and love that shone in his violet eyes whenever they rested on her, and how her appearance drew his attention to her.

She beat her wings and he kicked off, taking to the air with grace that had her lingering a moment on the mountainside to watch him. He flapped his huge black wings, a lazy beat compared to the flustered ones he had used during his training, one that said he was comfortable with being a dragon now.

A striking one at that.

The sunlight caught his scales again, sending blue shimmering over the ridges of his snout and brow, and down the long lean line of his neck, and up his muscular wings. He flicked his tail, the heavy barbed tip cutting through the air, and tucked his back legs up against his stomach, streamlining his body.

He let out a short cry, one she understood.

Taryn launched into the air, obeying his order to follow her. She beat her wings, lifting herself to the same altitude as him, and fell into place beside him. He banked right and soared downwards, towards the valley floor, and she followed, mirroring him. The wind buffeted her face, cool against her scales, and joy swept through her despite her crushing fear of what lay ahead.

Bleu gave a single hard beat of his wings as he reached the side of the curving mountain range and shot upwards only a few metres from the cragged black rocks. She could feel his joy as it flowed through their link, his excitement as he mastered flying and experienced the thrill that she felt whenever she flew. He gave another keening cry as he launched into the sky above the ridge, caught a thermal and twisted in the air, so his body pointed downwards again. He dropped fast, spinning through the air with his wings pinned back, and disappeared beyond the ridge.

She followed him, somersaulting as she reached a crescendo on the thermal coming up off the mountain range, and diving towards him as he soared down into the valley on the other side.

Her senses sparked and she sharply looked right.

Three dragons.

A red male, a gold male and an emerald female.

They were heading towards the camp. Coming to join Tenak for the final stage of the battle.

The bigger red male called and Bleu answered, and Taryn thanked the gods for being on their side as her mate fell into line with the three dragons, joining their ranks. She hadn't expected to have cover like this, but she wasn't going to complain. It would be easier to slip into the camp if they looked as though they were part of incoming reinforcements.

Taryn joined Bleu, flying beside him, as close as she could get as her nerves began to get the better of her again.

The tents came into view as they rounded a corner, sending her heart pounding as those nerves suddenly shot up. Bleu looked across at her and made a low coughing noise through his fangs that was meant to reassure her. A sound reserved for mates. The red male turned his head her way, his amber eyes narrowing, and Bleu's enormous head swivelled towards him.

Bleu growled, flashing his fangs, and darted left, slamming his big body against the male and knocking him into the gold dragon. The red male called, a sound of submission, and flew upwards, breaking away from them and dropping to the back to the emerald female.

Taryn's blood burned hot.

Her mate was powerful and his display of dominance stirred the fire in her veins until she was aching for him again, unsatisfied need rolling back to a boil.

Bleu lifted his head, his six horns catching the golden light of evening coming from the elf kingdom, and roared, robbing her of breath as a shiver chased through her.

Her senses sparked, warning her of eyes on them, and she diverted her gaze away from Bleu, settling it back on the camp.

Tenak.

He watched their approach with a broad smile, folded his muscular arms across his bare chest, and she could feel his satisfaction as it ran through him. Her heart thundered now, beating so fast she felt dizzy. Bleu brushed his wing across her belly, the swift caress causing a thousand warm tingles to spread over her scales, his way of telling her that he was still there with her.

They would be victorious. Rosalind's spell would hold, masking her scent and her colour. They would find the sword. They would be victorious.

Taryn told herself that on repeat, a mantra she used to settle her fears as they neared the camp. Tenak looked away from them as the emerald female came into land, turning his focus back to the battle.

He would want to join it soon.

Time was running out.

Several big demon males closed in around Tenak, speaking to him while he remained focused on the fight down in the valley.

The gold dragon set down and shifted back, the emerald female joining him. Taryn looked at the black tent. How was she meant to reach it and shift back to enter it without her brother noticing her?

Bleu provided the answer to that question.

He landed hard, crushing one of the smaller tents and sending everyone in the area scattering as he turned with a roar and lashed out at the red dragon male. His front right paw snagged on the dragon's wing as he went to pass him, coming in to land with the others, and sent him crashing to the ground. The male reacted in an instant, shoving onto his paws and turning on Bleu, snapping at him with his fangs.

Bleu reared back and pummelled the male with his front paws, long black talons raking over the male's scales as he tried to evade Bleu.

Tenak shouted something and stormed towards them.

Taryn saw her chance and took it, silently thanking her mate for his diversion and sending a prayer to the gods that he wouldn't be found out, or seriously hurt.

She drifted overhead, unnoticed by her brother, and the moment he had his back to her, striding away from her with his demon entourage in tow, she pirouetted in the air and dove towards the ground. She shifted before hitting it, landing naked in a squat behind the black tent.

Threw a glance to her right, towards Bleu where he still clashed with the red dragon, their wings beating the air and paws smashing against each other.

She didn't bother to use her limited magic to clothe herself, fearing it would mess with Rosalind's enchantment. She tugged the black material of the back of the tent up and scrambled underneath it, her heart leaping around in her chest. The grunts and snarls of the fight grew dimmer and she shoved to her feet, her gaze flying around the tent.

The sword had to be here somewhere.

She checked every wooden trunk that lined the circular wall, threw the piles of cushions that formed a bed aside, scattering them in all directions, and huffed as she didn't find it. She closed her eyes, drew down a breath to steady herself and then pulled the air in through her nose. The sword was here somewhere. She could smell it.

Taryn opened her eyes and the sound from the fight between Bleu and the red dragon grew louder, Tenak's barked orders rising above the thuds of flesh meeting flesh.

She scoured the room again and then shut her eyes, focused on her dragon instincts and tapped into them.

The sword was here.

The sword was treasure.

The most beautiful treasure.

The ultimate treasure.

Her senses tingled, her feet drawn towards something in the far corner, near the open flap at the front of the tent. She opened her eyes, everything around her shimmering as her desire for treasure took hold.

Treasure.

She obeyed her feet, allowing them to carry her towards it, lost in the desire running through her, the excitement and need. She was close. The treasure would be hers.

She squatted in front of a low long black box. Her hands shook as she reached for the gold clasp on the polished stone lid. She flicked it open with her thumb, held her breath as she raised the lid. That breath shot from her as her hungry gaze fell on the black sword. She ran trembling fingers down the blade, feeling the engraving on it, the power that flowed through it.

Intoxicating.

A roar sounded, closer now.

The ultimate treasure.

Not the sword, but the male who had birthed such a feral powerful call.

Her mate.

She closed her fingers around the hilt of the blade, pulled it from the box and rose to her feet.

She raced to the back of the tent, tugged the black material up and rolled under it, coming to her bare feet on the other side.

Her entire body froze.

Gaze slowly edged to her right.

To the male there.

Tenak's lips peeled back off his fangs as he snarled at her, his violet-to-white eyes flashing dangerously. He went from a walk to a sprint, long violet-leather-clad legs eating up the distance between them. Her heart shot into overdrive.

Bleu reared up behind him and swept his left paw down, caught her brother in his side just as he closed in on her and sent him flying across the camp and slamming face-first into the stone wall of one of the abandoned buildings.

Before she could say or do anything, that same paw closed around her and lifted her off the ground. Bleu tucked her against his chest, cradling her as his heavy footfalls shook the earth and Tenak roared in the distance. The hairs on the back of her neck rose on end and she didn't need to see to know her brother had shifted.

Bleu snarled and launched into the air, his huge black wings beating it hard as he tried to gain some distance between them and her brother.

Taryn clutched the sword, pulse pounding as she called her violet leathers and white corset, and her boots. As Bleu banked, she looked back in the direction they had come, and her eyes widened as she saw not only Tenak after them but the three other dragons too.

The red male and emerald female broke away from Tenak, coming around to flank Bleu.

Bleu snarled, jowls peeling back off his razor sharp teeth, and dove, twisting in the air at the same time to drop beneath them. He straightened at the last second, spread his wings and glided over the heads of the warriors clashing on the battlefield.

In the distance, the garrison came into view.

It stuttered, darkness flickering over it, before the world came back. Bleu snarled and she felt his frustration, knew the cause of it. He had tried to teleport with her but he wasn't strong enough to use his portal when he was in such a large form.

He jerked forwards, a pained cry tearing from between his teeth, and dropped hard. He pulled his paw up, pressing her against his neck, and she shrieked when she came face to face with her brother. His enormous violet eyes narrowed on her as he sank his fangs into Bleu's left flank and dug the talons of his front paws into his wing membranes.

Pain exploded across her back as they crashed together, hitting the ground hard, and rolled. Bleu lost his grip on her and the world twisted around her as she flew through the air, tumbling and turning. He snarled and flashed across her vision, a broken image of him shifting back. The pain. Her brother had bitten him to drive him back into his weaker form.

Taryn grunted and cried out as she slammed into the ground and tumbled across it. The sword she clutched stabbed into her right thigh, sending white-hot fire blistering across her flesh from that point. The scent of blood filled her nostrils. She growled as she came to a halt face down on the grass, the tip of the black blade still sticking into her thigh, the angle of it pulling at the wound.

She rolled onto her back and bellowed as she pulled it free of her flesh, breathed hard as she let it fall to her side together with her arms and fought the pain back.

The sound of the battle was dim in her ears, her senses telling her they had landed a good distance from it, in a clearing in the valley.

A roar curled around her.

Her mate.

Taryn rolled onto her front, pressed her hands into the grass and pushed herself up. Blood pumped from the wound on her thigh. She gritted her teeth, grasped the sword and shoved onto her feet, wobbling as her entire leg burned beneath her weight. She had to fight.

Her hazy vision cleared as she blinked, revealing the brutal fight between Bleu and her brother. The three dragons on her brother's side circled lazily overhead, watching the two warriors as they clashed, both in their mortal forms.

A mighty war cry off to her right and the sound of thundering footsteps said they wouldn't be alone for long. The battle was coming to them.

Taryn's grip on the sword tightened and she kicked off, heart filled with resolve and every instinct she possessed screaming at her to protect her mate.

Bleu clashed hard with Tenak, sending her brother staggering backwards, and lashed out with the serrated claws of his black armour. Tenak leaped back, barely evading the tips of them, and kicked off the moment he landed, throwing himself at Bleu while he was still following through with the strike. Her brother slammed into his side, driving him down, and landed on top of him on the ground.

Her mate threw his head to his right, dodging the punch coming at his face. Tenak's fist smashed into the earth and her brother snarled as he drew his arm back and struck again. Bleu growled and bucked up, sending her brother off balance. Tenak fell to his left, tried to right himself but it was too late. Her mate was already breaking free from beneath him.

Bleu tackled Tenak, landing on top of him now and gaining the upper hand.

Until the red dragon swooped and forced him to roll off Tenak to evade his massive paw as it swiped at him. Bleu's head shot up and he snarled through his fangs at the male. The dragon turned in the air, dove right back at him. Bleu disappeared, leaving a shimmering ghost of him behind that the talons of the dragon disturbed as they raked through it.

A hot shiver coursed through her when Bleu appeared behind her.

She ran at Tenak, raising the sword as she roared a battle cry of her own. Strength flowed through her, determination that made her blood run hot and her courage rise. She would end this now.

Tenak's head lifted, his violet-to-white eyes wild with a hunger for violence, thick ribbons of blood painting the right side of his face and dripping down his bare chest to soak into the waist of his purple leathers.

He shoved to his feet and his gaze swung her way.

Landed right on hers.

Familiar eyes that gained an edge of sorrow as they locked with hers.

All of her strength left her and she stumbled to a halt just metres from him, her hands shaking, rattling the black blade that suddenly felt too heavy in her grip. It dropped to her side, her shoulders slumping as she stared into her brother's eyes.

Her brother.

Tears filled her eyes as she stared at him, fighting to convince herself to move, to do what was right and end him and spare all of Hell his wrath.

Bleu's steady gaze on her heated her back as the sound of battle fell away, silence stretching around her, and she felt only her mate and her brother on her senses.

Her future was behind her, not in front of her. Her past stood there, a male she had loved once, but no longer.

It was hard to force herself to accept that as she stared at him, caught in his gaze. Such a familiar gaze.

Such familiar eyes.

Those eyes had laughed at her, had shown her the deepest love and greatest affection, had comforted her when she had hurt and lifted her heart again, restoring her faith in the world whenever it had faltered.

The tears filling hers blurred her vision and she blinked to clear it, drew down a breath to steady her heart, pushed against the tide of the memories that felt as if it was going to carry her away, sweeping her back to her past rather than forwards to the future she wanted with all of her heart.

That future stood behind her, waiting for her to claim it.

With the stroke of a sword.

It would be hers.

She tried to move her hand, to raise the blade that felt so heavy in it and claim that future she wanted with her mate, putting her past to rest, but it refused to respond as Tenak turned to face her.

Her brother.

Taryn looked down at the sword and then up into Tenak's eyes.

She wavered, torn between dropping the blade and using it against him, her heart on fire as she battled the pain ripping her apart.

A roar sounded behind her.

Darkness rushed past her on black wings.

CHAPTER 38

Tenak shifted in an instant, becoming a dragon and rearing onto his hind legs just as Bleu hit him hard in the chest, sending them both to the ground in a tangle of wings. Bleu didn't give him a chance to lash out at him. He struck hard, sinking his fangs into the white line down the front of Tenak's long neck, puncturing his scales and tearing a pained roar from him.

Taryn's hurt pounded in Bleu's veins and beat in his heart, driving him on.

He hadn't been able to stand there and watch her suffering, to sit back while she wrestled with herself, torn and hurting. When the pain in her heart had grown so fierce it had brought tears to his own eyes, he had known exactly what he had to do.

He had to deal with her brother for her.

He couldn't allow her to fight Tenak, because he knew it would destroy her. At the risk of her despising him forever, he would fight her brother and would end him.

Tenak rolled with him, pinning him to the ground. The male beat his wings, driving his full weight into Bleu's stomach and pushing the air from his lungs. Bleu snarled and lashed out at him with his tail. The barbed tip sank deep into Tenak's hindquarters and he yanked it back, slicing through Tenak's violet scales and ripping a pained cry from him.

The second Tenak threw his head back on that cry, Bleu struck again, snapping at his chest and scratching long grooves in his thicker white scales with his fangs. Tenak shoved off him, beating his broad wings to lift him into the air.

He called to his three dragons and they dove towards him, coming to his aid.

No damned way Bleu was going to let the bastard escape.

He lumbered onto his feet and kicked off, reached out with his left paw and just missed Tenak's front right one. Tenak spotted him and snarled, and the barbed tip of his tail smashed into Bleu's wings, slashing the black membrane. He dropped hard, beat his wings to try to decelerate but it was difficult when his left wing had taken heavy damage.

His hind paws hit the ground hard just as Tenak's army of demons and fae reached them, and Bleu growled as they hacked at his paws and tail. He turned on them and lashed out with his tail, sending males flying in a wave through the air as it ploughed through their ranks. Terrified screams rang out from them and he turned his head and snapped at them, caught one between his jaws and bit down hard. The male's garbled cry cut short as one of Bleu's fangs punched a hole right through him and the two parts of his body dropped from his jaw, spiralling towards the demons at his feet, spraying blood over them.

Bleu kicked off again, weathering the storm of swords and spears that pierced his scales, gaining enough height to evade them. Some of the fae hurled spears at him.

He went to turn on them.

An invisible wave cut through the horde, sending them shooting into the air, coming down hard on their own ranks. Bleu cast a glance towards the source of the blast.

Vail stood just in front of Taryn, his clawed hand outstretched before him, his violet eyes narrowed on the enemies he had just sent flying. Those eyes lifted to Bleu, and Bleu nodded his thanks and twisted away, beating his wings as he went after Tenak and the three dragons.

The blood sliding over his black scales cooled as the wind rushed over him, stealing more of his strength as it made him aware of his injuries. His wounded wing ached as he flew, but he gritted his teeth and pushed onwards through the pain.

Behind him, the battle grew distant, becoming a murmur in his ears.

Ahead of him, Tenak turned.

Bleu snarled through his fangs and pinned his gaze on the bastard.

Big mistake.

He cried out as pain splintered across his right side like lightning, searing his bones. The red dragon snapped at him and he threw his head left, barely evading the blow aimed for his throat. Talons raked over his shoulder and his right wing, tearing through the membrane. The male dragon growled as he beat his wings, sending Bleu spiralling into a free fall with him. Bleu fought him, lashing out with his fangs, trying to seize the male's throat to pull him away.

He snarled as he managed to get hold of the male.

Too late.

White-hot fire blazed over his left side as he hit the ground, the weight of the red dragon landing on top of him emptying his lungs on impact. His vision darkened and then slowly returned in time for him to see Tenak diving towards him, talons poised to strike. The red dragon kicked off, claws tearing free of Bleu's flesh, and Tenak hit Bleu hard, sending darkness shooting across his vision and his mind.

Numbness swept in, a strange sort of emptiness that rang alarm bells in Bleu's head.

He fought the encroaching unconsciousness and twisted beneath Tenak as the male rolled him onto his back, an agonised bellow tearing from between his clenched teeth as his wings bent awkwardly beneath him, bone snapping.

Bleu mustered all of his strength, pushed beyond the limit and reached for more. One last stand. One last shot.

He scrabbled at Tenak's chest, clawed the bastard and tried to get his talons between the plates of white armour protecting his heart.

He was going to tear it out.

The tip of his right talons caught on a crack in Tenak's scales, and his paw hung there limply no matter how fiercely he tried to convince his talons to press between the scales and plunge into his chest.

Gods damn it.

Weakness infested every inch of his body, throbbing among the pain, mocking him.

Tenak loomed above him, violet scales dark in the low light of evening, but his purple eyes shining like fire.

Thoughts of his mate filled Bleu's mind and his aching heart, thoughts of the future he had wanted to claim for them on this battlefield, a future that was slipping through his weakening grasp, replaced with only darkness—the death that shone in Tenak's eyes.

Gods damn it all to Hell.

It couldn't end here, with him so close to securing the future he had dreamed of since he had been a boy, one where he would live forever with his ki'ara, could it? Would fate be so cruel?

"Get your fucking paws off him!"

Bleu didn't have a chance to pull his wits together enough to recognise the feminine voice that had snarled those words in the dragon tongue before a blast of white-blue light blinded him, seared his scales and felt as if it was setting him on fire as it rushed past him.

A pained roar shattered his eardrums.

His own?

He felt as if he was burning to ashes in the fiery light.

The weight that had been pressing down on him lifted and the light faded, the world going dim for a few seconds before his vision adjusted and came back.

Revealing he still had all four paws when he was sure he must have lost some in order to make him cry like that.

The scent of singed flesh accompanied by low whimpers drew his hazy focus towards a point a short distance from him.

To the violet-and-white dragon who was limping backwards, a paw-less right arm tucked against his white chest and left wing grotesquely bent and dragging across the grass. Where the right wing should have been, there was only a smoking stump. Pale wisps curled from the shorn white horns on the right side of the dragon's head too, wafting in the breeze that gently swept across the land.

Everything slowly fell into place as a female came into view, her violet-to-white hair billowing in the breeze, fluttering around her slender bare shoulders as she advanced on the wounded dragon, fire raging in her striking eyes.

She held a black sword point down at her side, and swirls of white-blue light rose off the blade, curling from it and catching the breeze. They brushed across the violet leathers that tightly encased her long slender legs, drifting up towards the small strip of toned stomach exposed between her trousers and her white leather corset.

Recognition sparked inside him, drove the haziness from his mind as his heart beat quicker and his instincts roared to the fore.

His mate.

His ki'ara.

His forever.

She didn't take her eyes off Tenak as she advanced on him, no trace of sympathy in her eyes now or fear in her blood as she held her head high.

Tenak shifted back, snarling and growling in agony as his body shrank and distorted. He grunted as the transformation finished and clutched his right arm, pain written in every strained line of his bloodstained face. Crimson ran down the right side of it, darkening his short hair, the smell of it strong in the still evening air.

Silence reigned around them as he faced off against Taryn, both Bleu's enemies and his allies collectively holding their breath as they waited to see what would happen.

"Sister," Tenak said in a throaty murmur, edged with pain, and reached his left hand towards her, his gaze imploring.

Her face blackened, but a spark of agony lit her eyes and called to Bleu.

He shifted back, wanting to fulfil the desire to go to her, to stand at her side where she needed him in this, her darkest and most challenging hour. The shift was quick to come, but the pain that tore through him as he transformed, his flesh splitting open where his scales had been wounded, stripped what little strength he had gathered and all he could do was lay on the ground and watch, breathing through the agony as Taryn faced off against her brother.

Her grip on the sword tightened.

"I stopped being your sister the day you stopped being my brother," she bit out and flashed sharp teeth at Tenak. "But you made yourself my sworn enemy when you chose to attack my mate."

Tenak's eyes leaped to Bleu and then back to her.

Taryn snarled, "You brought this fate upon yourself."

Her brother's eyes shot wide.

Taryn swept the blade to her other side and then slashed upwards, and a brilliant arc of pure white-blue light erupted from it, flying through the air towards her brother. Tenak didn't have a chance to loose a cry, didn't have a chance to even open his mouth or move a muscle. The beam reached him in the space of a heartbeat and engulfed him. His shadow hovered in the light for a second before it disintegrated and the arc streaked across the land beyond him, leaving a deep scar in the earth.

Leaving nothing behind.

Taryn stood motionless, her eyes locked on the point where her brother had been, her pain ricocheting around inside Bleu together with his own, hers burning so fiercely that it eclipsed his.

Long seconds passed, and slowly her face morphed from darkness through to anguish and onwards towards relief.

The sword dropped from her hand, struck the earth point first and wavered there as she turned away from it and from the dark scar across the valley.

The relief that he had felt in her disappeared when her violet-to-white eyes landed on him, and tears filled them as she ran towards him, her beautiful expression relaying all of her love for him together with the link that would tie them together forever.

She sank to her knees beside him, her heart thundering in his ears, her lips moving soundlessly as she checked him over. Her dark eyebrows furrowed as her gaze flickered between his and his body. He mustered enough strength to send a mental command to his armour, and the small black scales rippled over his body. Pain shot through him in their wake and he grunted and clenched his teeth against it.

The tears on Taryn's lashes spilled over, slipping down her cheeks and cutting through the dirt and blood.

She frowned at him, and he knew that later when they were alone, she was going to give him Hell for what he had done, but all that mattered right now was how good it felt to have her fussing over him, her hands on his body and her heart calling out to him through their bond, telling him everything she felt.

All the love that filled her heart.

"Why?" she croaked.

Bleu slowly raised his right hand, tensed his muscles to stop it from shaking, and brushed her hair behind her ear, curling his fingers around it and savouring how she leaned into his touch, seeking more from him.

"Because you were hurting," he whispered. "I had to do something. I couldn't let you hurt like that."

She closed her eyes, turned her face towards his hand and brushed her lips across his palm.

"And now I am still hurting… the sight of you fighting… you falling… the thought that you might get yourself killed just to protect me…" She sighed and looked back at him, caressed his brow and admonished him with her eyes. "I am stronger than you think, Bleu. You do not have to fight my battles."

He closed his eyes and relaxed against the cool grass, using the connection their touch formed to ease his pain with the knowledge that she was safe and it was over. When he opened his eyes again, hers were no longer chastising him. They shone with affection, mixed with worry, drifting over his body and pinpointing all of his injuries even though his armour concealed them from her eyes. She could feel them echoing on her body just as he could feel hers.

He never had been able to hide anything from her.

Never wanted to if he was honest.

"I'm your mate, Little Dragon. I will always want to protect you." He sighed and cupped her cheek, and she looked back into his eyes, hers soft with understanding. It ran both ways. He wanted to protect her, and she wanted to protect him. An endless circle. As infinite as their love for each other. "I will always do whatever I have to in order to take away your pain and stop you from hurting."

He sensed the lands around them emptying, Tenak's side quick to teleport or fly away as it became clear they had lost this battle. His side had emerged the victors.

Because of Taryn.

Her courage had done more than won the war.

It had saved all of Hell.

His brave, strong and beautiful little dragon.

"And I will always do whatever I have to in order to protect you, and to take away your pain and stop you from hurting," she said in the dragon tongue and raised her hand towards her face.

He growled low in his throat as she caught her hair and swept it over her shoulder, pinning it to the back of her head, revealing the smooth column of her neck.

Taryn placed her other arm beneath him, raised him up and cradled him to her. He swiped his tongue over her throat, shuddered at the same time as she did, and closed his eyes as he sank his fangs into her. She moaned low in his ear, one that trembled and sent another shiver through him, had his body shooting hard in an instant despite his injuries. He gave a soft pull on her blood and shuddered all over again as her blood hit his tongue and he swallowed a mouthful.

It slid down his throat like warm ambrosia and spread fiery tendrils through him, ones that seemed to dull the pain wherever they touched.

He had seen the effects of a mate's blood when Loren had been injured and had fed from Olivia, but he hadn't realised how strongly it would affect him. Bleu sank against her, taking sips of her blood, his strength slowly returning until he had enough to wrap his arms around her and hold her to him.

She smoothed her hands over his back, her touch comforting.

Beneath his armour, he felt the shallower wounds knitting together and the deeper ones beginning to heal as Taryn's blood flowed through him, restoring his strength and sending his healing abilities into overdrive.

She moaned against his ear, a strained one that she had tried to keep quiet but had slipped free, and tensed. Her embarrassment flowed through him and he wanted to tell her that she didn't have to be ashamed that she enjoyed the feel of his fangs in her throat.

Only his senses came back online at that very moment and it struck him that it wasn't shame that had made her tense and stifle her little groan of pleasure.

It was the audience they had gained.

He could feel Loren and Vail nearby, King Thorne and Sable with them, and at more of a distance was Queen Melia and Isla, and the entire army.

Most of them watching him feeding from Taryn.

He reluctantly withdrew his fangs and lifted his head, shot Loren a black look that he hoped conveyed how annoyed he was that his prince had chosen to hold court to the rest of the army just feet from him when he had been sharing a private moment with his mate.

Vail's lips curled into a wicked smile but at least he had the decency to turn his back. Loren just kept staring.

Waiting, Bleu realised, for Taryn to emerge so he could thank her.

His prince had damned awful timing.

His presence was only made more annoying when Loren held up a small teardrop glass vial with a leaf-shaped lid and raised his eyebrows as he waggled it. Medicine. Bleu curled his lip in disgust, wanted to refuse his prince's silent order and tell him he would be fine with just Taryn's blood, but in the end heaved a sigh instead and accepted his fate and the imminent blast of pain he was about to experience.

Because he knew Taryn would feel better, brighter, if he was healed. So he would bear the pain.

Just this once.

For her.

Bleu eased her back and gave her a look that he hoped told her to go along with Loren's plan to thank her. They would be alone again soon. Just the two of them. The way it should be.

The way he needed it to be.

He pulled his legs up to his chest as she stood, concealing the evidence of his desire, and caught the small vial Loren tossed to him. He popped the lid off with his thumb, steeled himself and then knocked the liquid back. Fire blazed through him and he gritted his teeth against the white-hot pain that felt as if it was ripping him apart in order to put him back together, refusing to let everyone around him hear him scream in agony.

Taryn touched his knee, her caress comforting and soothing him as the pain began to ebb away, leaving him struggling to catch his breath. Her hand slipped from his knee and he looked up at her as she awkwardly received a handshake from Loren, and the cheers of the entire army gathered before her. Embarrassment blasted through their bond as she stood beside Loren, all eyes on her, but hurt began to creep back in, pain that had Bleu finding his feet and going to her.

He caught her arm and pulled her away from the spotlight, looked over his shoulder at his princes as he walked with her across the valley. Vail nodded, tugged the black blade from the earth and presented it to Loren. Loren took it and nodded at Bleu, the look in his violet eyes telling him to take all the time they needed, and then he disappeared, leaving only a pulsing shimmering outline of him behind.

The entire battlefield emptied, everyone teleporting back to the garrison.

There would be a celebration, but Bleu didn't feel like rejoicing, not when the price of this victory had been high.

He turned to Taryn and pulled her into his arms, enfolding her in them and holding her against his chest. He sent a mental command to his armour, clearing it from his chest and arms but leaving it covering his legs, wanting her to be comfortable as she rested against him. She trembled, her pain rising again, fiercely burning in her heart. The salty tang of tears filled the air as that pain got the better of her and he sighed as he held her to him in silence, uncaring of time as it trickled past. He stroked her back, wishing there was something he could do to ease her pain as she sobbed in his arms, grieving for her brother. The sky was black by the time she emerged and swiped her palms across her cheeks to rub away her tears.

He had hoped to spare her this pain, but in the end he had probably only added to it by getting himself wounded in the process.

Bleu eased back and sighed as he brushed his thumbs across her cheeks beneath her eyes, capturing the last of her tears. She drew in a deep shuddering breath, exhaled it hard and raised her eyes to his.

This wouldn't be the last time she cried over her brother and what she had done, but he would be there to hold her whenever she grieved, to tell her how much he loved her and that in time her pain would fade until she had forgotten it and her brother was only a memory.

He would always be there for her.

She fingered his chest, brushing their tips across a pink round fang mark on his right pectoral that one of the dragons had left on him.

"Damn you for being so noble and throwing yourself into my fight," she said but there was no trace of anger in her words, only love and fear. He had frightened her. It hadn't been his intention, but he had. He never wanted to frighten her again, not when it clearly hurt her.

"I just wanted to protect you," he whispered, his eyes holding hers, drinking in all the love they showed. Her love for him. It was deep and endless, and gods, it was beautiful. Everything he had ever dreamed and so much more. "I didn't want you to suffer and I can feel that you are."

She lowered her eyes to his chest.

"I cannot deny that. Killing Tenak… I feel as if I am bleeding inside… but I do not feel empty as I had expected." She raised her gaze back to meet his and carefully laid her palms on his chest, warming him. "Because my connection with you is there within me, filling me with warmth and light… flooding me with your love."

Bleu lowered his head and caught her lips in a soft kiss, one designed to tell her just how deeply that love ran and that it was endless, a torrent that would never stop flowing.

He sighed as he broke away from her lips, held her face in his palms and breathed her in, still struggling to believe that she was finally his even when he could feel and smell her, could see her and hear her words of love ringing in his mind, and still taste her blood on his tongue.

Blood that she had given him to heal, despite her own wounds.

He closed his eyes and focused on their link, delved into it and flowed into her, sought the deepest of her wounds and seized them. He gritted his teeth and grunted as pain erupted on his body where those wounds were on hers, strongest on his thigh, and she gasped.

Broke free of his hold, severing his connection and halting the process.

She huffed. "I did not give you my blood so you could take my wounds… they are mine to heal."

Bleu opened his eyes and rolled his right shoulder in a shrug, refusing to apologise for what he had tried to do. She had eased his pain by giving her blood to him, and he had only wanted to ease hers. Besides, the medicine had healed him and he was strong enough to take on some of her wounds for her. It was either that or make her take the medicine herself, and he had caught the look in her eyes when he had been fighting the pain after taking it, the one that had said there was no way in Hell she was going to subject herself to it.

Maybe if he gave her blood, it would help her heal. He wasn't sure how dragons worked in that respect.

His gaze drifted down to the puncture marks on her neck. Crimson welled in them, beads that trembled on the brink of falling, and he groaned as he realised that he had been so concerned with everyone watching them that he had forgotten to seal them.

He lifted his eyes to hers, held his hand out to her and waited.

Taryn touched her neck, her fingers came away bloodstained, and her eyes darkened as she stared at it.

Not with anger or pain.

With desire.

She placed her hand into his, allowed him to pull her flush against him and tipped her head back as he wrapped his lips around the wound on her throat. She moaned as he gave a shallow pull, her hands jumping up to clutch his shoulders and her fingers digging into his muscles.

Bleu groaned against her neck, the need he had been fighting for what felt like forever now spiralling back out of control as her sweet taste flooded his mouth and the connection between them grew even stronger.

"You need to rest and heal," she said in a voice thick with desire that told him resting and healing wasn't the only thing on her mind involving a bed.

"I'm healed, I swear… but I will rest later if it will alleviate your worry… right now I just need you," he whispered against her flesh and licked the wounds, shuddered as heat shot through him. "You need me too."

She didn't deny that. Just moaned in his ear and melted against him, her pain fading into nothingness as desire roared to the foreground, need they had denied too long.

"I do… but…" She sounded breathless already, panting softly as he tongued her neck and lowered his hands to her backside. "You must rest."

He knew that he should, that he was hardly in any position to be considering the things running through his mind, images of him and Taryn naked and tangled together. His body was healed but he was still weak. He tried to rein them in.

Taryn didn't help matters.

"Perhaps we could rest together."

Dear gods.

He wouldn't be doing any resting if she shared a sickbed with him, that was for sure. He growled and kissed her throat, following the line of it up to her ear, and she moaned when he sucked the lobe between his lips.

"Or we could rest later," she cried and clutched him, claws pressing into his shoulders. "Do not stop doing that."

"I don't intend to," he husked into her ear and she shivered against him, a little moan escaping her. "I intend to keep doing this forever."

She stilled in his arms, leaned back and searched his face in the low light.

"Forever?"

He nodded and righted her, and smoothed his hand across her cheek as he sensed the trickle of fear that went through her, the need for reassurance and to hear him say it all over again. Although desire reigned, pain still lingered in her heart, born of losing someone she loved, and that hurt clawed at her whether she felt it or not, placed doubt in her head that he would do all in his power to extinguish.

"I told you, Taryn. I love you and I'm yours, and I will always be yours. Nothing will ever change that."

"Always," she echoed, a distant edge to her soft voice. "I like the sound of that."

Not as much as he did.

She leaned in close, tiptoed and brushed her lips across his. "I will love you forever… for always… for all eternity, Bleu… and I will always be yours… and nothing will ever change that."

Nothing.

He liked that word almost as much as the words 'always' and 'forever'.

Nothing would stand between them. Nothing would keep them apart. Nothing would change their feelings.

They would always be together. They would always love each other.

They would always look forwards.

He dropped his head and kissed his mate, losing himself in her as he always would, losing track of time as they stood together on the battlefield where they had slayed their pasts to set free their future.

A future that began as his lips danced with hers and she held him tight, and their love flowed through their bond, completing each other.

The clock in Valestrum struck the hour, bells ringing twelve times in the distance, and filled him with warmth as he held Taryn closer, his heart close to bursting as something dawned on him.

Yesterday had been the end of their past, a time that would fade into memory, put to rest for eternity.

Today was the start of their forever.

The End

ABOUT THE AUTHOR

Felicity Heaton is a New York Times and USA Today best-selling author who writes passionate paranormal romance books. In her books she creates detailed worlds, twisting plots, mind-blowing action, intense emotion and heart-stopping romances with leading men that vary from dark deadly vampires to sexy shape-shifters and wicked werewolves, to sinful angels and hot demons!

If you're a fan of paranormal romance authors Lara Adrian, J R Ward, Sherrilyn Kenyon, Gena Showalter, Larissa Ione and Christine Feehan then you will enjoy her books too.

If you love your angels a little dark and wicked, the best-selling Her Angel series is for you. If you like strong, powerful, and dark vampires then try the Vampires Realm series or any of her stand-alone vampire romance books. If you're looking for vampire romances that are sinful, passionate and erotic then try the best-selling Vampire Erotic Theatre series. Or if you prefer huge detailed worlds filled with hot-blooded alpha males in every species, from elves to demons to dragons to shifters and angels, then take a look at the new Eternal Mates series.

If you have enjoyed this story, please take a moment to contact the author at **author@felicityheaton.co.uk** or to post a review of the book online

Connect with Felicity:
Website – http://www.felicityheaton.co.uk
Blog – http://www.felicityheaton.co.uk/blog/
Twitter – http://twitter.com/felicityheaton
Facebook – http://www.facebook.com/felicityheaton
Goodreads – http://www.goodreads.com/felicityheaton
Mailing List – http://www.felicityheaton.co.uk/newsletter.php

FIND OUT MORE ABOUT HER BOOKS AT:
http://www.felicityheaton.co.uk